THE FOUR SEASONS

The

FOUR
SEASONS

A NOVEL OF VIVALDI'S VENICE

Laurel Corona

V
VOICE

Hyperion • New York

Library of Congress Cataloging-in-Publication Data

Corona, Laurel
    The four seasons : a novel of Vivaldi's Venice / Laurel Corona.
        p. cm.
    ISBN: 978-1-4013-0926-8
    1. Vivaldi, Antonio, 1678–1741—Fiction.   2. Women—Italy—Fiction.
3. Venice (Italy)—History—18th century—Fiction.   I. Title.
    PS3603.O7687F66 2008
    813'.6—dc22

                                                                2008024597

Hyperion books are available for special promotions, premiums, or corporate training. For details contact Michael Rentas, Proprietary Markets, Hyperion, 77 West 66th Street, 12th floor, New York, New York 10023, or call 212-456-0133.

Designed by Jessica Shatan Heslin/Studio Shatan, Inc.

FIRST EDITION

10 9 8 7 6 5 4 3 2 1

To Lynn, without whom I wouldn't know
what it means to have a sister

And to Jim, for just about everything else

THE FOUR SEASONS

PROLOGUE: 1695

For the hour it took the baby's wails to run their course through misery to fury to exhaustion, no one thought of anything but how God had favored Venice above all other cities. The radiance of the Blessed Virgin and all the saints emanated from one spot, the balcony over the altar of the chapel of the Pietà. From there, benediction flowed over the black-cloaked nobles seated on the scarred wooden benches to the ragged workers crammed in at the rear. It filtered out the door to the people spilling onto the walkway of the Riva degli Schiavoni, and to those straining to hear on small boats bobbing in the Venetian Lagoon.

For that hour, heaven opened and God spoke. Two dozen women in red and white dresses were his messengers. No counterpoint, however frantic or interlocked, was beyond the skill of the musicians of the Pietà, hidden behind an iron grille draped in black gauze. No subtlety of harmony was overlooked, no languid musical line ever rushed. If music were fabric, that of the figlie di coro would be brocade, lace, gossamer.

And the singer was the golden thread. *"Qui habitat,"* Michielina sang, *"in adjutorio altissimi."* Each note floated over the listeners like a feather held aloft by the breath of angels. While many of those listening could not have understood the words, those whose ermine-trimmed cloaks spoke to their high position in life would have understood the Latin and perhaps noted the aptness of the psalm. If indeed there were a place on earth to glimpse the dwelling place of the Most High, it was surely the balcony of the Pietà.

When the last notes vanished, the figlie di coro disappeared into the secret places of the Pietà through a door in the rear of the balcony. The heavens closed, and the people began to spill out into the October twilight.

"Michielina is better than Paola at the Mendicanti, don't you think?" A young nobleman opened a side door of the chapel. "After you," he said, gesturing to his identically dressed companion.

"I prefer the Mendicanti," his friend said. "But Michielina . . ." He inhaled sharply to show his appreciation. "She is very good. Perhaps a bit breathy at times but—"

"Ugly as a toad and walks with a limp, I've heard."

"Ahh," the first man said with a sigh, "such a tragedy. Perhaps we should be grateful we can't see them."

Before the second man could reply, what might have been mistaken for a sack of rags draped over a small packing crate in a doorway caught his attention. From within the box a loud intake of air was followed by a choking cough and a hoarse, exhausted wail.

As one of them moved forward to take a closer look, his boot touched the edge of the sack. It moved, and he saw a small arm appear from under one of its folds.

He bent over and jostled the shoulder of the child. "Little one," he said. "Are you all right?" When he turned her over, she did not startle or wake but fell as limp as the dead. The upturned face was that of a three-year-old girl. Her eyes rolled toward her drooping lids, and her mouth fell open to reveal a row of perfect white teeth above a lolling tongue.

"Laudanum," he said. "I think she's had a dose." He tried to pick her up in his arms but found she had been fastened to the crate by a thick silk cord from a dressing gown. "Someone didn't want her to wander off and drown."

There was also a baby, drenched with sweat from its prolonged screams but now snuffling and falling back asleep. Wedged under its head was an envelope on which the word "Pietà" had been written in a meticulous hand.

"Vying with Michielina for attention?" the second man said. "No wonder no one heard you." He stood up and began banging on the door.

IN THE CORNER OF THE SMALL EXAMINATION ROOM OFF THE infirmary ward of the Ospedale della Pietà, the little girl had been stripped down to her underclothing and was seated on top of the overturned crate while a wet nurse for the baby had been fetched from one of the surrounding homes. After the baby had fallen contented from the woman's breast, she was laid on a long wooden table, bathed, and left to fall asleep.

Even in the dim light of the oil lamps, for by now night had fallen, the baby's wrappings told the story that was undoubtedly contained within the unopened letter. The shawl in which she had been nestled was soft, honey-colored wool, with a sunburst pattern emblazoned in crimson and gold silk.

"Expensive," one of the nurses said, holding it up to get a better look. She folded the shawl and placed it on the end of the table. "Get the book," she said to a girl of about twelve standing beside her.

The girl went to a cabinet, brought out a large leather-bound register, and put it down next to the shawl, returning to the cabinet to bring the pen and ink.

"And put the iron in the fire," the nurse ordered. She opened the envelope, and as she pulled out the letter, three gold coins fell from its folds. She moved closer to the lamp to examine them before putting them back in the envelope.

She turned to look at the girl. "I told you to put the iron in the fire."

The girl's eyes darted toward the small child seated on the crate before she turned away and fetched a metal object from a hook on the wall. As the nurse read to herself, the girl poked at the fire with the rod before leaving its tip at the edge of the coals.

"Just as I thought," the nurse said, breaking the silence. She began to read aloud.

"God help me, I am abandoned by my patron, who says the baby is not his," the letter read.

My delivery left me damaged in ways it is not seemly to speak of, and I dare not even show myself to those who once wished for nothing more than a chance to supplant him in my affections. For three years I have been able to keep my daughter out of sight and under the care of my servants, to maintain that appearance of a carefree youth so important to those in my trade. I had intended to do the same with the infant, who was born three months ago, but I no longer know where I will live, or even if I will live much longer, having little money and no appeal to any but the coarsest of men.

I am plunged into the pit of grief by the decision I must make, and I pray you to understand that it is only because I cannot protect my children that I give them to you. I have named the older one Maddalena, in honor of the saint to whom I have prayed to intercede for my forgiveness and thus preserve my soul. She has already been baptized with that name. The baby has a way about her that brings brightness into my heart, and almost from the moment of her birth her eyes were the color of a clear sky. I have taken that as a portent of happiness for her in her life, and I pray you for that reason to baptize her with the name of the Virgin and call her Chiaretta.

The nurse picked up the pen and wrote the date in the left column of the register. "Maddalena," she spoke aloud as she wrote. "And Maria Chiaretta."

She continued to read.

I have enclosed all the money I can part with, to help with the burden of finding a wet nurse who will also take in Maddalena, so they can remain together. I put my trust in the infinite mercy of God, who makes all things possible and hears the prayers of the fallen, and though I do not deserve or even dare hope to see my children again, I have also included a token, divided into three, so that if it pleases God that I may ever return for them I may know them, and they may have a means to know each other if circumstances pull them apart.

"Bring me the tokens," the nurse said to the girl. "I need to describe them in the book." She took the two pieces of ivory into her hand and strained to see the details in the lamplight. "An ivory hair comb," she said, "broken into three pieces. Each girl has one end, with a carved flower. The mother's piece will fit between, which is how she will prove who she is if she ever comes back for them."

"Will she?" the girl asked.

"No," the nurse said. "But some of them need to hope." She put the letter back in its envelope, wrote the description of the shawl and the broken comb into the book, and gave the pen to the girl to clean. "If you don't want to help, go find a box to store these things. And while you're at it, go to the refectory and bring her back some bread and a little cheese." She looked over at Maddalena. "Are you hungry?"

By now the small dose of laudanum had begun to wear off. Maddalena had pulled herself back up to a sitting position on the crate and was rubbing her eyes, too dazed to reply.

As soon as the young girl hurried from the room, the nurse got up and pulled the iron rod from the fire. The tip glowed red as she blew ash from it. She picked up one of Maddalena's feet with a jerk, and the little girl fell onto her back on the crate. Pulling her lips into a thin line, the nurse brought the end of the red-hot poker down onto the bottom of Maddalena's heel and held it there for a moment.

The nurse had dropped her foot and was returning the iron to the fire before shock turned to screams of pain and betrayal. "There, there," she said as she came back with a drop of salve on her finger. "It will heal."

As she grabbed Maddalena's foot again, the little girl squirmed and struggled to get out of her grasp, but the nurse held her ankle in a grip so firm it left white halos around her fingers. She looked for a moment at the blackened rectangle enclosing the letter P before dabbing the ointment on the wound and going to find a bandage. By the time she found one, Maddalena's screams had quieted to a few gulping sobs, and the girl watched in stunned confusion as the nurse wrapped a clean cloth strip around her foot.

"We don't take in anyone but babies," the nurse said, in a tone neither harsh nor tender but matter-of-fact, as if she were explaining it to the walls as much as to the little girl. "They don't remember it for more than a minute. It wasn't as simple for you, I'm afraid, but it couldn't be helped."

She rubbed her hands on her coarse apron as if to wipe away her involvement in the act. "You'll be gone in a few days, and it's how we'll keep track of you." She removed the branding iron from the fire. "It's how we'll get you back."

"I don't want to come back!" Though the pain had undone the last effects of the laudanum, Maddalena's words were muffled and slurred, as if she were crying out in her sleep. "I want to go home."

"You'll forget." As the nurse examined the glowing tip of the iron for a second time, Maddalena panted, too frightened to scream, but this time the nurse walked toward the table where Chiaretta had begun to stir. She picked the baby up by the ankle and dangled her upside down next to the table.

"Don't!" Maddalena screamed as she tried to scramble down from the crate. The nurse pressed the branding iron onto the baby's heel, and the room filled again with the shrieks of the two girls and the smell of charred flesh.

Part One

THE MARK OF
THE PIETÀ

1701–1703

ONE

THE BLACK-AND-SILVER BOW OF THE GONDOLA DISAP-
peared into a fog so thick it hissed as it parted around the hull.
Around each stroke of the oar, a vague, uncapturable melody
swirled and trailed away in the water.

The gondolier had been moving so slowly he wasn't quite sure
he had reached the mouth of the Grand Canal. The air seemed
hemmed in by the facades of the grand homes where the noble
families of Venice were finishing their suppers, but in front of him
it opened up like a yawn as he entered the broad lagoon.

He leaned forward and squinted, cocking his head to pick up
the calls of other boatmen. A song was traveling across the water
from near the basilica of Santa Maria della Salute, and as he listened he could hear it getting louder. Finally he could pick out the
words the boatman was singing.

A group of gentlewomen I did see
On All Saints' Day, 'twas just a year ago;

The fog swallowed up the gondolier's reply.

The one in front moved with a special grace,
And Love at her right side did seem to be.

The other boat had drawn so close the gondolier could hear a change in the sound of the water before they slid past each other in opposite directions.

Such a pure light did from her visage flee,
'Twas sure a spirit radiant and aglow;

The words faded as the boats pulled away. But in Venice, song was in the breath. The two gondoliers sang out together through the mist until they were too far apart to continue.

Grown bold to look, I saw then in her face
The spirit of an angel, truthfully . . .

As the gondolier's voice died away, the curtain of the felce parted, and a stout middle-aged woman wearing a loose, dark cloak and veil peered out from the cabin. "I can barely see you," she said. "Where are we?"

"The Broglio. I'm tying up there."

"The Broglio?" Her voice turned up with disapproval. "You were supposed to take us to the dock at the Pietà."

"Hell of a night," the gondolier said by way of explanation, clearing his throat and spitting a mouthful of thick phlegm into the lagoon. The boat bumped against the dock, and he muttered a low curse as he jumped off. The bucking motion made the woman lose her balance, and she sat down with a grunt.

"Look," the gondolier said, coming back onboard to help her up. "You can walk the five minutes to the Pietà faster than I can take you on the water. I'm finished with this night."

The woman growled, as if to say that he would hear more about this in due time, before turning back toward the cabin. In a few minutes she emerged to put a satchel and a covered straw basket on the floor of the gondola.

She turned her head. "Don't dawdle now," she called back into the felce.

A small, bare hand pulled back the curtain, and a face peered out. A girl who looked to be no older than six stood motionless until she was prodded from behind.

"Go!" the voice behind her said. Within a few minutes two little girls, the other about nine, were standing on the dock.

The woman picked up the satchel and basket. "Come along," she said without looking to see if they were following. She crossed the small piazza so quickly the girls almost lost her in the fog, before stopping at the point where the spiky, red- and cream-brick facade of the Doge's Palace began to emerge from the mist. Having oriented herself, she turned to the right and resumed her pace. The girls struggled to stay no more than a step or two behind as they passed one column after another of stone so close to the color of the fog they could sense more than see them.

The woman muttered as she stumbled over a crate left behind by one of the merchants whose stalls spilled out onto the Riva degli Schiavoni during the festival period just before Christmas. Faint odors of wet straw and the contents of baskets in which dried flowers and herbs, clams, sausages made from wild game, and pungent salves and tonics had been laid out for sale wafted up from the detritus of the day.

A stone bridge loomed in front of them and then another, before the woman turned abruptly in to an alley. She banged the large bronze knocker on one of the doors, and the grate over a peephole slid open.

"Who's there?" a woman's voice asked.

"Annina. With the two girls."

They heard a bolt being thrown and the groan of hinges as the door creaked open. A woman in a white cap, dressed in a cloak just like Annina's, motioned them in.

"Hurry. It's cold," she said, her voice echoing along the walkway of the courtyard in which the girls found themselves. "You will sleep down here tonight. Annina will stay with you. No point in disturbing the others so late."

The room she left them in was bare except for a small wooden prie-dieu and a bed, on which the girls sat stiff and motionless. Outside, the two women lingered, talking in low voices.

"Chiaretta—the younger one—can sing," Annina said. "And she's quite pretty."

"And the older one?"

"Maddalena. Hardly speaks. They told me she's good with her hands, and more obedient than the other one, but I can't see that there's much to her."

They nodded good night, and Annina turned to go into the room while the other woman disappeared into the mist without another word.

CHIARETTA CRIED HERSELF TO SLEEP. HER BLOND HAIR WAS matted and tousled on a lumpy makeshift pillow, and her dress and coat served as a coverlet for her bare arms and legs. Next to her on the pallet Annina had arranged for them on the floor, her sister Maddalena lay, startled back from the edge of sleep by every unfamiliar sound.

Maddalena could hear the rattle in Annina's breath and make out her form on her cot. She had glimpsed Annina without her heavy cloak and hood for only a moment, and she lay in the dark unable to remember what the woman looked like. Annina was so intimidating that Maddalena had spent most of the last two days looking at her own feet.

A few days before Annina arrived in the village where they lived, the family's routine had been so disrupted it seemed as if the doge himself would be paying a visit. The chicken pen had to be raked clean of droppings and feathers, and even the dog was washed and groomed. Their foster father did not escape either, getting a haircut that left him looking as forlorn as a shearling lamb.

Maddalena and Chiaretta had no time to chase the chickens around the yard after collecting their eggs, or talk to the goat as he nuzzled in their apron pockets for food. They were forbidden to leave home in search of butterflies willing to alight on their fingers, or to find ant holes to pour water into and watch the ants scurry out carrying their glistening white sacs of eggs. Instead, they scrubbed the stone floor of the cottage and wiped the cobwebs from the low ceiling with a long pole and a cloth, while an older girl, the daughter of Chiaretta and Maddalena's foster parents, pounded and scrubbed the spots out of all the girls' dresses and mended holes in her two brothers' pants.

Their foster father and the boys chopped a huge pile of firewood, while the mother kept the fire going for nearly a whole day, preparing not just the usual polenta and beans but honey cakes and roasted meat from a lamb her husband slaughtered out of view of the two little girls.

Chiaretta and Maddalena had seen nothing like these preparations before, except one or two times a year when everyone in the village was readying for a festival, or when someone was getting married. Chiaretta was beside herself with excitement, thinking the guest must be someone terribly important. Maddalena was almost paralyzed with anxiety. Of the children in the house, only she and Chiaretta had marks on their heels. Only they were not family, did not belong, would not be staying. Someday, she had been told, someone would come for them.

On the day the guest was to arrive, their foster mother gave Maddalena and Chiaretta a bath, washed their hair, and helped them put on their best clothes. For several hours they sat with their shoes off until the visitor arrived.

"Are these the girls?" Annina did not wait for an answer. "Have them take off their stockings so I can see."

"Show me your heel," she said to each in turn. Then, satisfied that they were indeed the wards she sought, she had nothing more to say to them.

The visitor's attention to them was enough for Chiaretta to decide that all the work had been for a party in her honor. She spent the whole evening pulling the boys to their feet to dance with her while she sang, even though no one else was in a festive mood.

"It's not a party," one of the girls said. "Why don't you quiet down?"

"It is too a party." Chiaretta pouted, dropping her head and drawing an arc on the floor with her foot. "We haven't had meat in a long time."

Her foster mother got up at that and marched over to Chiaretta. "Sit down and be quiet. We eat like this once a week."

Chiaretta's look of astonishment at the lie was enough to earn her a strong twist on her ear and a place on the floor in the corner, where she cried until she saw everyone intended to ignore her, at which point she promptly fell asleep.

Maddalena had known what Annina's interest in their heels really meant and had barely been able to swallow a bite. Even after hearing stories about someday going to live in a place where many little girls lived, a place where people were so happy they sang all the time, she wanted to stay where everything was familiar. In the village, she had her own secret name for everyone, from the boys to the geese that waddled along the path leading to the riverbank. She could tell Chiaretta's blanket from her own by the smell of the wool, and in the orchard she knew each foothold to reach the apples that swung from the upper branches. But the choice of where to live wasn't hers, and she knew nothing would sway the family to keep the two extra mouths they would no longer be paid to feed.

AND NOW TONIGHT SHE WAS IN THAT PLACE OF GIRLS AND singing she had been promised. Chiaretta stirred and rolled over, pulling Maddalena's coat along with her own. Maddalena shivered, and when she couldn't pull the coat back, she nestled in closer to her sister to keep the cold from seeping in. Burying her face in her sister's shoulder, she felt her head fill from the inside with the pressure of tears she had held in all day. She shut her eyes, and though her swollen eyelids didn't fit very comfortably, this time she let them stay closed.

Maddalena had barely slept when she felt Annina shaking her. "Get up," the woman said. "Don't you hear the bell?"

Annina prodded Chiaretta in the back. She wriggled away, saying "Don't!" in a tone somewhere between a snarl and a sigh, before she bolted upright. She looked around the small room, trying to remember where she was. Maddalena was sitting up also, rubbing her eyes.

"Get dressed!" Annina said. She went to the prie-dieu, knelt, and crossed herself, speaking under her breath with her eyes closed. *"Aperi, Domine, os meum,"* they heard her say, her voice dropping lower until only her lips moved.

The girls watched as Annina continued. Then she crossed herself again and stood up.

"Don't you pray?" she asked, and when Maddalena nodded her head, she added, "Well, do it then! *Pater noster . . .*"

Maddalena crossed herself, and Chiaretta followed suit. *"Qui es in caelis,"* they continued, *"sanctificetur nomen tuum."* They murmured their way through the rest of the Lord's Prayer and a Hail Mary before Annina told them to get to their feet.

"You'll have to learn how we do things here," she said.

"Didn't we do it right?" Chiaretta asked. She and Maddalena had been rattling their way through those prayers for as long as she could remember.

"You didn't do it fast enough to be in the chapel on time for Lauds," Annina said. "Leave your dress unlaced and put on your cloak."

When they had finished pulling on their shoes, still damp from the night before, Annina looked the two girls over. Maddalena was much taller than Chiaretta, more than the three years' difference in their age could account for. Her hair was brown, with undertones of red and gold, like autumn leaves. Her solemn hazel eyes were round, and her chin was pointed, making her face resemble a heart. It was a face free from noticeable defects, but one that did not quite coalesce.

Chiaretta's hair was the light straw color of the white wines of the Veneto. Her curls formed a halo around cheeks still chapped from the cold of the journey the day before. Even in the candlelight her eyes, fringed with thick lashes, were the sparkling blue of lapis lazuli. But at the moment, the overall impression was of total dishevelment. Her hair was a tangle that could not be dealt with in time for chapel by any other means than anchoring it behind her ears, and her dress had gotten soiled by something she had spilled on it at mealtime the day before.

"Stand still," Maddalena said as she reached up to pick the sleep crumbs from the corners of Chiaretta's eyes. Her little sister froze her face and pushed her chin forward in obedience, revealing a row of small teeth as perfect as a string of pearls framed between the petals of her lips.

When Annina opened the door and motioned them into the corridor, they found themselves in the midst of girls and women passing through in one great wave, several hundred in all, wearing dresses that looked like the color of mud in the dim light as they moved without speaking through the courtyard.

Light had just begun to filter through the milky white glass over the main entrance to the chapel, but on the sides obstructed by other buildings, the windows were still dark. The dresses of the women lighting candles to illuminate the altar had taken on a rich crimson hue, under aprons and hoods the color of fresh cream.

When Maddalena and Chiaretta got inside the chapel, Annina guided them toward a marble pillar. "Stand up against this," she said. Holding hands, the two girls watched as the church filled. By the time the last people were inside, their backs were pressed against the pillar and they could see nothing except the dresses of the women crowded around them.

"*Domine, labia mea aperies,*" a woman called out in plainsong, exhorting the Lord to open her lips for prayer.

Around the two girls, the congregation sang their response. "*Et os meum annuntiabit laudem tuam.*" Chiaretta tried to lift her back up against the pillar to see who was singing in such a clear and radiant voice a few feet away, and Annina elbowed her to be still.

"Who is that?" Chiaretta whispered.

Annina scowled and put a finger to her lips. "A figlia di coro."

A daughter of the choir? Chiaretta could not ask what she meant—not then at least—so she turned her head away from Annina, feeling the cool of the marble against her face while the air around her grew warm and thick from the press of bodies. When people began singing again, instead of trying to see the woman, Chiaretta looked at the air in front of the voice, trying to understand how something invisible could be so beautiful.

SEVERAL LARGE POTS OF WATER WERE SIMMERING ON A GRATE in a huge fireplace, next to a metal washtub. A young woman tied on a wide work apron and began pouring the warm water into the tub.

She told the two girls to undress and sit down, and when Maddalena complied, another woman lifted up her hair in one handful and, without warning, cut it off at the neck with two savage clips of her shears.

Chiaretta shrieked as if her sister's throat had been cut. She ran toward the door, and when she could not pull it open, she pressed her back against it, taking in great sobbing gulps of air. The first woman left the tub and crouched down in front of Chiaretta.

"Come, cara, it doesn't hurt." Her voice was soft and her hand gentle as she guided Chiaretta's chin in Maddalena's direction. "See?"

Maddalena held the rough ends of her hair in one hand, staring in shock while her foot toyed with the auburn strands on the floor.

Chiaretta kept her back pressed against the door, but the lady kneeling in front of her seemed nice, and Maddalena, though a little dazed, did not appear to be hurt. Eventually Chiaretta allowed herself to be coaxed to the chair.

After her haircut, each of them was handed a smaller version of the red dress the women wore. When the dresses had been tugged and smoothed into place, small white aprons were tied around the girls' waists. After a few minutes in front of the fire, tousling what remained of their hair, Maddalena and Chiaretta covered their heads with lace-trimmed hoods that draped over their shoulders. The women placed a white cap on each of their heads, and the transformation of the two girls into wards of the Pietà was complete.

A FEW ANEMIC FINGERS OF GRAY WINTER SUNLIGHT FILTERED through the grimy windows of the children's ward. The coal in the fireplaces at each end of the room had been damped down until evening, and the lamps were unlit as the girls made their way between the rows of neat cots.

"Where are the children?" Chiaretta asked.

"They're at work." Anzoleta, one of the ward matrons, signaled toward two of the cots. "These will be yours," she said.

Maddalena sat down, feeling the hard frame through the thin mattress. She looked at Chiaretta, who had sat down on the other bed, rubbing the coarse wool blanket as if trying to make friends.

A bell rang from somewhere inside the walls of the Pietà. "It's time for Sext," Anzoleta said. She knelt and crossed herself. *"Aperi, Domine, os meum,"* she began, but before Chiaretta and Maddalena had time to get to their knees, she stood up again, continuing a string of Latin words.

"You'll learn the daily office soon enough," she stopped long enough to say. "For now, pray the Our Father and the Hail Mary until I've finished, and then we'll go to dinner." Chiaretta and Maddalena hurried to make the sign of the cross as she went back to her prayers.

THE REFECTORY WAS FILLED WITH THE SOUND OF RUSTLING robes and the scrape of the benches pulled across the stone floor to make room to sit down. From the kitchen, girls carried tureens to each table, while those closest to where they left them got up and began to ladle a thick soup of rice and peas into bowls. Others carried baskets of bread, placing a torn piece at each place. Prayers were said, and the meal began.

Maddalena and Chiaretta finished their meal in seconds, picking the last flakes of bread crust off the table with wet fingers. As the remaining soup was doled out, an older woman in a velvet dress left the head table and went to a lectern. She crossed herself before opening a book.

"Cease to be anxious for yourselves, for He bears your anxiety, and will bear it always," she read. Maddalena looked around and noticed that some of the older women at other tables had stopped eating and were listening with their eyes downcast, while others, mostly the young, were fishing the last bits of rice and peas from their bowls and looking to see if any more bread remained in the baskets.

Within a minute or two she felt Chiaretta's body jerk, and Maddalena flung out her arm to keep her sister from pitching forward into her soup bowl. Chiaretta's eyes were red with exhaustion, and she was on the verge of tears. Maddalena put her arm around her, and Chiaretta rested her head on her shoulder.

Within a few seconds Maddalena heard knuckles rapping on the table. "No!" the woman at the head of the table mouthed, and Maddalena shook Chiaretta awake.

The woman at the lectern closed the book. Everyone rose at this signal, offering in unison a prayer of thanksgiving before falling silent again as they filed out of the refectory and up the stairs to the wards.

BY THE TIME MADDALENA AND CHIARETTA REACHED THE DOR-mitory, dozens of girls in red dresses were taking off their aprons and head coverings and unlacing their shoes. Chiaretta sat on her bed, watching as one by one the girls knelt and crossed themselves, said a short prayer, then lay down on their beds. *I guess I'm supposed to pray too,* she thought. *But I already did today.*

Never in her life had she seen so much praying. Except perhaps, she thought, when a boy in the village had fallen on his head and didn't wake up for two days, or when someone died having a baby, or when her foster father was caught in a sudden flood and didn't come home for so long they thought he had drowned. At those times the women of the village crossed themselves so often it seemed they would wear the tips right off their fingers.

Why are they always praying here? she wondered. *Do they think something awful is going to happen?* She rolled over to ask Maddalena but saw that her sister had fallen asleep.

AFTERNOON SHADOWS WERE CASTING DARK TRIANGLES IN THE corners of the dormitory when the girls put their shoes and hoods back on and marched through the halls to their assigned rooms for two hours of work or lessons. Chiaretta was led off to a classroom and Maddalena to a room where several dozen women and girls sat on stools making lace.

Within an hour, Maddalena was practicing a simple row of knots and twists that the lace mistress, Zenobia, had taught her. The grimy threads were spotted in places with blood from needle pricks, and Maddalena's eyes had begun to sting in the dim light. *Is it always going to be like this?* she wondered. *How can they stay inside all day? Don't they ever get to see the sky?*

Finally, Maddalena's and Chiaretta's first day was over. They greeted each other only with their eyes as they came back to their beds, too intimidated and exhausted to offer even a touch of the hand for reassurance. Laying their outer clothing on a wooden cassone at the foot of Maddalena's bed, they stood by their cots among the pale and narrow-shouldered girls who were bowing their heads and commending their souls to God before they slept.

TWO

IN THE HANDS OF ZENOBIA AND A FEW OTHERS, LACE making was like alchemy to Maddalena. They could turn simple thread into scenes where angels or mythical beasts stood among Greek columns and vases, linked by elaborate scrolls, fans, and arabesques. And then, with no more than a passing glance, they unpinned a finished work, placed it in a basket, and started another.

For the first few months Maddalena was at the Pietà, one after another of her gray and bloodied scraps was thrown into the fire, worth only the tiny pop of light it gave before disappearing, but eventually she produced her first piece of work that ended up as white as the thread it had started with. A simple border meant to be sewn to the bottom of a girl's petticoat, it was whisked away in the basket with the other finished work at the end of the day.

"What happens to it now?" she asked Zenobia.

"What do you mean? Tomorrow you'll start something else. Now that you've earned a little money, they'll start an account for you with the bank." She shrugged as if something so obvious and inconsequential was not worth more of an answer.

"I just wondered who will get my lace."

"It was only a little piece. Maybe some tourist will buy it."

Maddalena felt her mind slowing, like cream turning to butter in a churn, as she struggled to understand. "I don't know what a bank is," she said, "or a tourist either."

"A visitor. Someone who comes to our city to listen to the coro."

Lying on her cot that night, Maddalena realized she had been too distracted to ask Zenobia about the other thing she had said. *Why am I being paid?* she wondered. *And if we're paid, where is the money?* She knew that a few of the others came down to the lace room before the work bell to talk among themselves when no one was there to tell them to be quiet. Maddalena fell asleep having made a plan to go early herself the next day to get her answer.

"YOU HAVE TO HAVE A JOB, DON'T YOU?" A LACE MAKER NAMED Francesca said. "Better here than changing bandages in the hospital or washing dishes." The other figlie murmured their agreement.

"And if we have to sit here for hours we might as well make as much money as we can, so the fancier the lace the better," another figlia named Alegreza added.

"But why does that matter when there's nothing to buy?"

"Of course there is," Francesca said. "Maybe not now, except for little things like a rosary with pretty beads, or maybe a better pair of shoes. Or even a prayer book with pictures and a pretty cover. You've seen Zenobia's, haven't you?"

"But what you make is so beautiful. Don't you care?"

"Not anymore, not really," Francesca said. "Or maybe just for a second. And besides, they'll make you do penance if you act too prideful about it."

"But you'll have to do a lot more than that little border you did to have enough money to buy anything," a figlia named Veronica added. "It's when you can do the placket of a nightgown for a bride, or the bodice of a dress . . . " The others murmured in agreement. "That's when the money starts adding up."

"And later it's part of your dowry," Alegreza said, "and if you don't get married, you can buy a nicer cell in a convent with your savings."

Alegreza's tone was so matter-of-fact it seemed to Maddalena that she saw both of these as excellent and practical goals to work toward, but Maddalena did not see how thinking about becoming a nun or a wife could make anyone's fingers fly any faster or better.

"Well," Francesca said. "I'm not planning on any of that. I want to stay here and be priora someday." She mimicked the way the priora squinted as she read after meals in the refectory, and the others joined her in laughter. "Then I could boss everyone around. I'd wear whatever I wanted and live in my own place."

"She lives here, doesn't she?" Maddalena asked.

"Silly girl! Not on the ward. And the others who sit at her table don't live there either. If you're still here when you're forty, you retire, and then you get your own room. If you ever go into the priora's study, you can see how nice it is. And her clothes aren't coarse at all, like ours."

"So they can buy what they want when they're old?"

"Well, not everything, I suppose."

"They couldn't buy a pet monkey from the organ grinder on the Riva," Alegreza said. "With his hairy little . . . thing." The figlie all giggled behind their hands, and Maddalena felt the heat rising in her face, as if a joke was being told at her expense.

"Oh, come now," Alegreza said. "We weren't laughing at you."

"After a while they can spend their money on anything they want," Veronica added. "At least what's left after you've paid room and board for all these years."

Several of the figlie sighed and got up to look in a cabinet for their lace cushions. Seeing Maddalena's blank face, Francesca went on. "The Congregazione take most of what all the figlie earn and keep it as payment for the cost of feeding you and giving you a bed, but they leave you with a little for yourself."

"What about people who don't make money?"

Francesca looked puzzled, as if she had never considered this. "I don't know. I guess they don't pay."

"They say we're learning about money because we might need to know." Alegreza had come back with her cushion and sat down. "Zenobia told me it's part of being a good wife. This is almost as good as being in the coro, if you want to get married."

"But not if you want to make money," Veronica said. "The figlie di coro get paid every time they perform." She rolled her eyes and then stood up and put her hand over her heart. Taking a dramatic breath, in a voice not loud enough to be heard in the hall, she began to sing harshly and off-key. Then, bowing to the applause, she adjusted her skirt and sat down to begin her work.

"As well they should," Francesca added in a tone icy with sarcasm. "The figlie di coro are better than the rest of us, you know. Even God knows that. Especially God knows that."

MADDALENA'S DISCOMFORT WITH THE CONVERSATION HAD come on as suddenly as a headache, but it trailed off after Zenobia's arrival and had been forgotten by the end of the afternoon. Hearing her own soft breathing as she bent over her work, Maddalena lost track of the cold penetrating through the windows and up through the threadbare carpet on the stone floor. Then Zenobia began to hum, and as the other figlie joined in her soft song, something deep inside Maddalena responded.

Whatever else was happening at the Pietà—or in the city out-side, or even in the village that now lay so far away—did not matter at all. The tiny beginning of a new work that would grow in her hands, and Zenobia's voice so warm it cut through the draft of the dying fire—this was the center of everything. The other girls could joke if they wished, but from then on, she would come to the lace room when Zenobia did, and not a minute before.

❧❧❧

BY THE TIME MADDALENA WAS ELEVEN AND CHIARETTA WAS eight, their lives had a pattern as secure and predictable as each knot in one of Maddalena's lace collars. They rose at or before dawn, prayed as they dressed and walked to chapel, heard Lauds, studied or worked for several hours in the morning, stopped to pray at Prime, Terce, and Sext, before their midday meal. In the afternoon they rested until None, then worked or studied until Vespers. Supper was around sunset, followed by Compline and bed.

As much as the activities, the sounds gave each day its shape. Bells pealed, and the smaller girls giggled and sang as they played games with hoops and balls in the courtyard during the daily rec-reation time. Idle chatter was what the long hours of enforced quiet were meant to keep at bay, and duty and piety were the main reasons for breaking the silence. Maddalena had come to love the soft tones of the women who read from St. Augustine, or Cathe-rine of Siena, or Francis of Assisi in the refectory, and the singsong of the girls reciting their lessons in the schoolroom. All these sounds, more than the rehearsed perfection of the coro, soothed the needle pricks, the hollow stomach, and the chattering teeth of winter dawns.

For Chiaretta, no sounds mattered but those made by the coro. Trying to get attention by singing with great enthusiasm in the chapel hadn't gained her anything except nods of approval for her religious fervor, which were canceled out by the scowls and scolding she got for fidgeting during the rest of the service. Chiaretta's dreams danced in the breath between her parted lips as she listened to the choir each Sunday afternoon and feast day from the recess of the chapel reserved for the figlie di commun. Every day she tiptoed past the closed door leading up to the choir loft as if she were being careful not to break something. *Don't touch,* it seemed to say. *Don't dare.*

And then, one day, the door was open. The recreation period was beginning, and the figlie di coro were spilling down the stairs and into the corridor as Chiaretta was passing. She stepped out of their way and waited for a chance just to look up the stairs.

And then, she heard it, a rich alto voice like a pomegranate burst on the ground of an orchard, redolent of blood and jewels. *"Filiae maestae Jerusalem,"* the voice sang, calling on the mournful daughters of Jerusalem to behold their crucified Lord.

Hypnotized by the sound, Chiaretta made first one, then another step upward. Without even being able to say how it happened, she found herself standing at the entrance to the choir loft. The room was the color of dark amber from the reflected hues of the paintings in the chapel. Grainy ribbons of silver light traveled the distance from the small clerestory windows to the keyboard of a small organ. Looking past several music stands on which sheet music lay open, Chiaretta saw the wrought-iron balcony grille through which she often stared up from the chapel below. Against it she saw the silhouette of a woman holding her arms around herself and swaying as she sang.

Chiaretta moved closer and stumbled over a small pile of books that had been left on the floor. The woman stopped singing and wheeled around.

"Who are you?" she asked.

"I—I'm sorry. Please don't be angry. I heard you from downstairs and—"

"You're not supposed to be here," the woman said, and though

Chiaretta could not see her well, she could discern from her tone that she was more surprised than angry.

"What's your name?" the woman asked.

"Maria Chiaretta," she stammered. "But no one calls me that. Just Chiaretta."

"Do you know who I am?"

Chiaretta nodded. Michielina was one of the maestre, and though she was in her late thirties and had been singing for nearly two decades, she was still one of the most renowned soloists of the Pietà. Whenever she passed by her in the refectory, Chiaretta kept her eyes on the ground, to avoid looking into the eyes of someone with a hidden place big enough to contain that voice.

Michielina moved toward Chiaretta with the limp of one born with a deformed hip. "Come into the light so I can see if I recognize you," she said. In the lamplight, Michielina examined what of Chiaretta's face was visible under her cap and hood. "I've seen you in the refectory," she said, smiling. "A very pretty girl with blue eyes and a good appetite."

Michielina's face looked flattened, like a clay head stepped upon before it had completely dried. Still, her eyes were kind, and her smile wide enough to reveal a missing tooth on one side. "Do you sing?" she asked.

"No—I mean yes. I mean"—Chiaretta took in a breath—"I don't know. Not like you."

Michielina limped back toward the railing. "Would you like to hear what it sounds like to sing from here?"

Chiaretta nodded, and Michielina gestured to her to join her at the rail. "Go on," she said. *"Agnus Dei,"* she sang. *"Qui tollis peccata mundi."* Even though her song seemed like a whisper, it filled the chapel, but Chiaretta's voice died before it reached the balcony railing.

"Take a deeper breath, from here," Michielina said, circumscribing Chiaretta's waist with her hands. She took her hands away and stepped back, motioning to Chiaretta to sing. "Lamb of God, who taketh away the sins of the world," she repeated.

Chiaretta pulled herself up from the hips to gulp in air, feeling her lungs deflate as she sang out the notes. "Have mercy on us." Her voice grew larger, and she went through each phrase with increasing confidence until she heard it feeding back to her from the walls of the chapel.

"Brava," Michielina clapped. "And the next time anyone asks you if you can sing, say yes."

The strange breathing had made her dizzy. "Yes, Maestra," she murmured.

"And now you can help me carry this music back to the practice room. If anyone wonders where you've been, I'll say I asked you to help me. But"—she turned toward Chiaretta—"now I must scold you. You must not take it on yourself to go wandering around, going up staircases and whatever else pleases you. Difficult girls can find themselves very unhappy here. Do you understand what I'm saying?"

"Yes, Maestra," Chiaretta said, wondering how what Michielina said could be true. *I'm happier than I've been since I came here,* she thought as she hurried down the stairs to find her sister.

THREE

CHIARETTA'S WAS THE FIRST VOICE TO BE HEARD WHEN chatter and laughter was allowed, and she was the one most often ordered to settle down when the time for frivolity was over. If she and Maddalena were not known to be sisters, the matrons sometimes commented, they would be the most unlikely candidates on the ward.

If not for Chiaretta's urging, Maddalena could go for days without speaking to anyone. She daydreamed and made up stories in her head, and the cloister and solitude of the Pietà suited her. She loved how the dust floated in the golden light of the lace room, how a spider wove a perfect web in a corner of the children's ward, how the candles in the chapel bobbed before releasing long tendrils of smoke into the air when the celebrant of the mass walked near them. She knew where every bird nest was in the eaves of the courtyard and knew without looking up when the nestlings had flown.

Even if she had wanted to join in at the Pietà, the enforced silences meant that most of the time the figlie's lives pointed inward. Much better, Maddalena decided, to make a satisfying world of her own. At the Pietà, needing others too much was unwise, especially when, without a good voice or an instrument to play, she was unlikely to get much attention.

Maddalena did, in fact, have an instrument to play. As with the other figlie, a small part of her week was taken up with music lessons. At nine, she had come back to the Pietà later than most, but within a month or two she had already had a somewhat belated assessment of her musical ability. Annina had been right, the maestra concluded. She was nothing special. Maddalena's hands were deft from her hours as a lace maker, and she learned the fingerings of the lute without too much difficulty, but she practiced as if it were just another form of work.

Maddalena, the older women agreed, was turning out very well. A good wife for someone someday. Pretty enough and healthy, but not flighty like her sister, who was too willful for her own good. Altogether too willful for her own good.

FOR THE PAST FEW MONTHS CHIARETTA HAD BEEN ASSIGNED TO the embroidery workshop. The task had appealed to her briefly, when she saw the swirling patterns in gold set off against the luminescent crimson, or emerald, or aquamarine silk that would one day adorn bodices and waistcoats. But when she discovered that she could not manage to finish more than an inch or two in an afternoon, and her work was not crisp and clean enough to win her any praise, the room had come to feel like a prison.

Several days after her visit with Michielina, Chiaretta got a reprieve. Michielina's assistants kept track of the music and organized the rehearsals, but she had requested a girl who could make sure keyboards were covered to keep out the dust, music was in neat stacks for filing, and stands were kept clean. The Pietà was full of young girls to keep occupied, but Michielina had one particular figlia in mind—one who was not shaping up to be much of an embroiderer anyway.

From then on, Chiaretta was permitted to leave the embroidery room early to assist in the practice room and choir loft. Michielina was approaching retirement and was losing her vision after copying scores year after year in dim light. Whether her eyesight had taken a turn for the worse or whether, as some thought, she just enjoyed Chiaretta's company, within a few months Chiaretta had been excused altogether from embroidery and was at the maestra's side much of the day. Within a few months she could follow sheet music well enough to turn the pages at rehearsals, singing along under her breath while Michielina nodded her approval.

"The maestra's little lapdog," a few of the girls whispered under their breath. But Michielina was loved, and everyone knew she was not well. The figlie di coro, at any rate, knew how to keep their most unbecoming thoughts to themselves.

❦❦❦

WHEN A GROWTH SPURT HERALDED MADDALENA'S INCIPIENT puberty, she was ordered to collect her belongings for a move to another ward.

"If I don't see you here, I'll never see you at all," Chiaretta cried. Though she had meant to whisper, her words had come out in hoarse sobs loud enough for the matron to threaten her with solitary confinement if she didn't immediately quiet down.

Maddalena's face crumpled in despair as she picked up her belongings in a single armful and carried them to the ward for adolescent girls. Awakening after her first rest period on her new cot, she saw that the girl with the cot next to hers was already sitting up and staring at her.

"I wanted to see if I could get you to wake up just by looking at you," she whispered. "What's your name?"

"Maddalena. Who are you?"

"Anna Maria. What do you do?"

"I make lace."

"I'm in the coro, and I'm a prodigy."

Maddalena didn't know what a prodigy was, but she had no trouble figuring it out. Jiggling her heels up and down, Anna Maria ticked off on her fingers all the instruments she could already play, and the ones she was planning to learn.

"What do you play?" she asked.

"I'm learning the lute."

"Oh, please ask if I can be your teacher! I'm going to get a new pupil soon, they told me." The jiggles had now moved upward as Anna Maria put her hands beside her hips on the cot and began to bounce up and down.

She has even more energy than Chiaretta, Maddalena thought. Thoughts of her sister invaded her mind with such intensity that for a moment she could not breathe. A bell sounded, and the ward fell silent except for the rustle of girls bending over to tie their shoes and standing up to straighten their dresses. Putting on her hood, Maddalena pulled it down by the hem and held it there with her eyes shut, but whether she was trying to keep something safe inside or something else out, she did not know. She let out her breath, opened her eyes, and put on her cap. Anna Maria fell into step beside her as they left the ward.

HIDDEN BEHIND THEIR HOODS AND CAPS, MOST OF THE GIRLS of the Pietà would be difficult to identify by name. Anna Maria was an exception, not because of remarkable beauty or ugliness but because of the intensity of her eyes, which were always so wide open she seemed perpetually amazed or startled. When she blinked, which she did energetically and often, it added to the impression that Anna Maria burned as if she were powered by some hidden star.

Anna Maria did not appear to have even a single friend. When Maddalena had lived alongside Chiaretta on the children's ward, she had watched with no more than casual interest how the other girls allied themselves. Her sister was the one friend she needed, and the Pietà afforded little time to seek out others. Now, seeing how desperately Anna Maria wanted to be her friend, how she positioned herself on her cot so she could see her the second she came through the doorway, Maddalena pitied the girl. She pitied herself as well, now that she no longer had Chiaretta to wake up next to. Within a few months, however, Maddalena's imaginary conversations with Chiaretta as she lay in her bed had dwindled in favor of real ones with her new friend.

Anna Maria had two favorite subjects—her music and her future—and to her they were one and the same. "I'm going to be"—she grasped for a word—"indispensable."

"Indispensable?" Maddalena chided. "That's not a job. You're supposed to say I'm going to be a nun, or something like that."

"Well, I'm just going to be indispensable. They'll say, 'We need a theorbo and a harpsichord,' and I'll be there. I can play violin and viola already, and I'll learn cello and bass when I am a little taller. And the organ, but I can't quite reach the pedals now."

The two girls started another circuit of the courtyard where they took their recreation, and Anna Maria chattered on. "I'll become a sotto maestra and maybe even the maestra di coro. Hopefully before I start to smell as bad as she does." Anna Maria tried to contain her laughter behind her hands, but as usual it escalated to loud snorts that echoed off the ceiling and walls of the open corridor, earning them both a scowl from the matron.

Anna Maria had been assigned to give Maddalena her first lessons on the lute, but within a few months they had both concluded that Anna Maria's dream of Maddalena joining the coro was not going to happen. She could accompany someone if the piece was not too complicated, but Maddalena's lute playing did not appear headed for any more than that.

"They'll probably give you a recorder teacher pretty soon," Anna Maria said one afternoon. "You're supposed to learn two instruments before—" Her face grew somber and she did not finish the thought. The girls fell silent and looked away from each other until Maddalena heard Anna Maria sniffling.

"What's wrong?" she asked.

"First I won't get to be with you as much when you stop learning the lute." Anna Maria's voice caught in her throat. "And then I won't see you anymore at all when you go away."

"Who says I'm going away?"

"Well, they'll make you leave someday, tell you to go be a nun or something. I don't know!" Anna Maria buried her face in her hands.

The prospect unnerved both of them enough that they began disappearing during the recreation periods to practice in the empty sala.

It still wasn't enough. "I don't know what the problem is," Anna Maria said. "You're not like Annetina, who makes me want to die before the end of our lesson." Anna Maria took the lute from Maddalena and played in a way that sounded like a donkey plodding under its load, throwing in a few misfingered chords to complete the effect.

"I don't know why I'm not better," Maddalena said. "I try hard enough. Maybe it's just too far between my fingers and my head." She pulled the lute up, and bending her head so her cheek grazed the edge of the instrument, she strummed. "I wish I could hear it."

Anna Maria screwed up her face. "What do you mean you can't hear it? Are you deaf?"

Maddalena didn't know how to explain. "I mean hear it better. Maybe it's just not the right kind of loud." She thought for a moment, not sure what she had meant.

Anna Maria shrugged and handed her back the lute. "Play the part with the arpeggios again. As loud as you want. No one else is here."

"You know what I would like more?" Maddalena asked, and before waiting for a reply, she went on. "To hear you play. But not the lute."

Anna Maria got up. "What then? The mandolin? The violin?"

Maddalena had heard the mandolin only once or twice and wasn't quite sure she liked its sound, but the violins always sounded nice in the chapel. "The violin," she said.

"I'm tired of the stupid old lute anyway. Let's go."

Anna Maria took Maddalena into another practice area, where she picked up a violin case and carried it into a small room paneled in wood. "This is where the most senior violinists get their private lessons," Anna Maria said. "I've never played here, but they've never actually said we can't." She shut the door behind them. "Maybe we'll get in trouble, but I don't think anyone will hear, and I want to know how it sounds."

From the moment Anna Maria started to play, something inside Maddalena began to surrender. She settled into an old chair, and even when it could give no more under her weight, she felt as if she were still sinking, so deep that she could fold up on herself until she was a small package of perfect contentment. The room filled with sounds that gleamed like polished brass, melted like caramel in the mouth, and raised the hairs on Maddalena's arms.

Anna Maria stopped. "You'd better close your mouth or you'll drool."

Maddalena startled and pulled herself up in her chair. "Play more," she said in a voice so low it was almost a whisper.

Anna Maria began again. Maddalena thought she could hear every hair on the bow as it caught the strings. The music whirled and flirted with the air, spinning like snowflakes in an alley.

"Do you like that one?" Anna Maria asked. "I'm just making it up." She looked at Maddalena. "Your mouth's open again."

Maddalena stared at Anna Maria for a moment before hearing her and then closed her mouth, biting her lip to keep it shut. Finally she spoke. "I don't want to play the lute anymore."

Anna Maria shrugged. "I like all the instruments pretty much the same." She handed the violin to her. "Put it under your chin," she said. "No, not like that—pull your cheek back a little." She curled Maddalena's fingers around the neck of the instrument and placed them in specific spots. "Keep them there," she said, "and just run the bow over the strings."

Maddalena winced at the harshness of the sound.

"Don't hold the bow so tight, and keep your wrist straight."

Maddalena loosened her grip and tried to pull the bow with the same delicacy with which she finished the last stitches of a collar. The result was a far cry from the tones Anna Maria could make, rich notes redolent of the glint of light on the water, apple blossoms, laughter. In Maddalena's hands, the violin sounded like the creak of rusty door hinges, but she didn't care.

She opened her eyes and saw Anna Maria staring at her.

"You really like this," Anna Maria said. "I think you like it more than I do."

Maddalena didn't know what to say. She didn't want to look at Anna Maria for fear of giving something away before she even understood what it was. She looked down at her hands. The nails were ragged and tipped with calluses, but in the last year her fingers had grown long and slender. *Maybe they were made for this.* She shut her eyes, her head full of music yearning to be played.

❦❦❦

"*SICUT ERAT IN PRINCIPIO, ET NUNC, ET SEMPER, ET IN SAEC-ula saeculorum.*" The priest's voice echoed off the walls of the church of San Sebastiano, but Maddalena and Chiaretta were barely listening. On the edge of a group of figlie who had been brought to mass there, the two had tipped their heads back so far that when they tried to join in saying amen, the muscles of their necks tugged and left their mouths gaping.

"Look there!" Chiaretta whispered to Maddalena, pointing to the ceiling. "I can almost see up under that man's shirt."

"Move along." The chaperone pushed the girls lightly on their backs. For once her tone was not harsh, for after all, Veronese's ceiling frescoes of the story of Esther were what the figlie had been allowed to leave the Pietà to see.

"Mea culpa, mea culpa, mea maxima culpa." Maddalena and Chiaretta joined the other figlie pounding their chests in repentance for their sins as they walked toward the altar.

Chiaretta looked up at the ceiling again and let out an inadvertent whimper. Maddalena reached out for her hand as they stared upward at two horses, one black and one white, which from where they were standing appeared to be galloping toward them through the roof. The women in the fresco watched with fearful eyes from a palace balcony, and three male figures strained to hold the wild-eyed beasts back to avoid trampling everyone in the church when the animals burst free from the plaster and thundered to the floor. The scene overhead swirled and threatened, and Maddalena looked down. Chiaretta continued to stare so hard she had to grab on to Maddalena to steady herself. They giggled as Chiaretta staggered, mimicking her loss of balance until the chaperone's hisses made them stop. Squeezing each other's hands, they forced themselves to pay attention to the mass.

Afterward, the figlie gathered in the piazza in front of the church. "We're walking now to the convent at Santa Maria dei Carmini," one of the chaperones said. "The nuns are going to feed us a special dinner, and then we'll head back to the Pietà."

The girls walked single file along a narrow fondamento until they turned onto a broader walkway along a bigger canal. The brick walls of Santa Maria dei Carmini rose up on their right, while in the water to their left a few ducks paddled, and a seagull sat on a post. To the cloistered girls of the Pietà, the ducks' feathers were as rare as jewels, and the chaperones stopped to let the girls watch them for a moment.

Eventually, Geltruda, the older of the two chaperones, clapped her hands. "Come along," she said. "The sisters are waiting for us."

Ahead, the bridge leading to the Campo dei Carmini came into view. The girls had been almost alone on the fondamento, but the bridge was crowded with small groups, most of them young men, talking in excited voices loud enough to be heard from a distance as they hurried across.

One of the chaperones, walking at the head of the group, stiffened and slowed down. Geltruda came from the rear to talk with her.

"Do you see that?" Maddalena overheard her say. "Do you think . . ." Her voice trailed off as Geltruda appeared to complete the thought with her eyes.

The two of them cast worried looks in the direction of the bridge. "I told the priora it was a bad idea, taking them out this time of year," Geltruda said, "and now look . . ."

"Shall we go back? We can ask the cooks to give the girls something to eat at the Pietà."

"In what? The gondola won't be here until afternoon to pick us up."

The chaperones watched, holding back the girls as people continued to rush over the bridge onto the Campo dei Carmini.

"We'll stay in the convent and wait for the gondola," Maddalena heard Geltruda say. "It's not possible to go back to the Pietà on foot. We don't know the way except by water. I don't see what other choice we have."

She made a hurried sign of the cross before turning to the group. "Walk quickly and stay together," she said, motioning with her hand for them to follow.

The crowd paid no attention to the girls. Chiaretta watched them cross in front of the church and disappear down a side street. "Where are you going so fast?" she called out, but no one stopped to answer.

Next to her, a man stripped to the waist passed by, surrounded by teenage boys chanting his name. One of the boys was carrying a breastplate of laminated cardboard decorated with colorful designs. "Nicolotti! Nicolotti!" he chanted.

"Hey, watch what you're doing!" someone yelled, as two children, each carrying a long loaf of bread, pushed their way through. When they reached the edge of the Campo dei Carmini, they began to run, waving the loaves like victory banners. Behind them Chiaretta could hear a man's voice calling out, "Stop them! Thieves!"

Watching the commotion, Chiaretta had not noticed she was falling behind the group. Geltruda grabbed her hard by the shoulder and shoved her forward. "Little fool!" she said. "Show some sense. Get inside!"

Even in the dim light of the chapel where the figlie were gathered in the pews, the worry on the faces of the chaperones was clear. "Let us pray to the Blessed Mother of God for our safe deliverance from peril," one of the nuns who had greeted them said. Chiaretta and Maddalena crossed themselves and bowed their heads.

The nun repeated the Hail Mary before she addressed the girls. "Sometimes the world can be very frightening," she said, gesturing with her head toward the door and the commotion outside. "But aren't you fortunate to have someone who loves you and protects you? Just think, to the Blessed Virgin you are her children as much as her Son is! What greater honor could there be than that?" She knit her brow and rubbed her forehead, as if she were trying to dredge up more to say.

Maddalena turned her head and felt it bump against the carvings on the stall where she was seated. Looking up in the dim candlelight, she saw strange creatures carved into the dark wood, so close they seemed ready to whisper in her ear. A bare-chested mermaid stared at her with blank eyes, and a lizardlike beast looked as if it had just jumped off the armrest and begun twisting its way up the back of the stall. Maddalena sat without moving, as if paying closer attention to the nun, who had by now moved on to the subject of sin, could put the monsters in retreat. Out of the corner of her eye, she saw the Mother Superior, who had arrived moments before, huddled in conversation with the chaperones.

The Mother Superior came to stand in front of the figlie. Her face was a study in calm except for two fleeting creases between her brows that she seemed to be trying to will away. "Girls," she said. "There was an unfortunate disturbance outside, and I am sorry you had to witness it."

She took a breath as if she intended to say more, then closed her mouth and looked down. "That is all," she said. "We will adjourn to the refectory, where dinner has been laid out for you." Then she turned and swept out of the chapel.

Young novices were laying out platters of roasted meat and vegetables and bowls of polenta when the figlie came into the room. The Mother Superior led the group in a prayer of thanksgiving for the meal, but just as she sat down another nun entered the refectory, walking so quickly her habit tangled around her knees. She bent over the Mother Superior and said something that caused the older woman to get up, motioning to Geltruda and the other chaperone to come with her. Within a few minutes they both had returned.

"The gondolier is here," Geltruda said to the figlie, "and he has made it clear it is best to leave without delay. You will need to leave your meal behind, but you may take a piece of bread with you."

Across from Maddalena and Chiaretta, a girl reached over to grab a large piece of meat with her hands, but something about the grim faces of the chaperones made Maddalena's stomach harden, and she pushed away from the table.

Chiaretta, watching the girl chewing on the meat, reached toward the platter herself, but Maddalena grabbed her arm. "Get some bread and come!"

In the courtyard, Maddalena could see the gondolier pacing and taking an occasional look through a peephole in an outer door. "Listen," Chiaretta said, her grip tightening on Maddalena's hand. The high walls and covered walkways of the courtyard could not entirely buffer the cheers and boos, hisses and shouts, oaths and hoarse catcalls coming from outside.

The chaperones hurried the girls over to the gondolier. Oblivious to whether the girls could overhear, he began speaking to the chaperones.

"They were fighting at the Ponte dei Pugni, but the police came to break it up, and they decided to come over here. They're fighting where I was supposed to pick you up."

"The gondola is outside?" the chaperone asked with such alarm in her voice that one of the girls near Maddalena began to whimper.

"No. I left it back at San Sebastiano. I think if we go out this way we can get there." He looked through the peephole. "The crowd isn't that big yet, and there's no one outside over here. But we need to go now!" Without waiting for the chaperones to reply, he threw open the outer door and told the figlie to come with him.

Maddalena and Chiaretta were in the back of the crowd of girls who rushed along the side streets toward San Sebastiano. Chiaretta tripped over a loose stone and fell hard to the pavement, bruising her knees and twisting her ankle. Maddalena grabbed her by the arm and held her up as she took small and painful steps.

Geltruda took Chiaretta's other arm. "Hurry up," she said. "The others are so far ahead I can barely see them."

Just then a pack of several dozen men came running at full speed along the canal. Geltruda lost her balance and held tight to the girls to keep them all from being forced into the water. Before they could recover their footing, another wave of people came rushing by, this time a mix of men and women of all ages shoving and calling one another names.

Chiaretta shrieked as she felt hands around her waist, lifting her down onto a small, flat-bottomed boat. Another set of hands grabbed Maddalena, and within moments Geltruda and the two girls were seated in the peota, alongside a man and a woman and their two children, a boy and a girl roughly the girls' ages.

Geltruda sucked in huge gulps of air as she called to the sky for the protection of the saints. The man swore a string of oaths as he maneuvered down the canal, which was by now clogged with boats. Chiaretta and Maddalena hid their faces in each other's neck, peering out from time to time at the scene around them.

"Are you all right?" the woman asked the girls.

They nodded without speaking.

"Are you Nicolotti or Castellani?" the boy asked.

Maddalena stared. "Nicolotti or Castellani?" he repeated.

"I don't know what you mean."

"Which side are you on?" the girl asked, annoyed at Maddalena's ignorance.

"I'm not on any side."

"Oh, leave them alone," the father said. "They don't belong here."

"We just couldn't leave you there," the woman said to Geltruda. "We'll put you off someplace safe, when we can."

Geltruda nodded. She clung to a rosary she had taken from her pocket, her lips moving as she stared at the bottom of the boat.

On the pavement, fights were breaking out, and people watching from upper windows of the buildings along the canal began hurling garbage and broken pottery down on the crowds below. Maddalena saw someone crawl across the roof of one building and pry loose a roof tile. He hurled it into the canal, missing a boat in front of them by no more than a few inches.

"Why are they doing this?" Chiaretta screamed.

"What, this?" the woman said. "You haven't heard of the pugni? The wars of the fists?"

"No," Chiaretta sobbed. "And I hate it! Make them stop!"

The children laughed. "Stop? It's just starting!"

Their mother reached across and cuffed them. "Little ruffians!"

"But I want a real brawl!" the boy said, shouting *"Frotta! Frotta!"* at the top of his lungs.

"Me too!" said the girl. She stuck out her tongue at Maddalena and giggled.

The man had been nudging the boat farther down the canal, trying to get a better view. To their right, two young men jumped off the fondamento and began crawling over the boats to get to the other side of the canal.

"Nicolotti! Nicolotti!" the family cried out, grinning and waving their fists in the air as the two jumped into their boat just long enough to cross it. One of their knees knocked down the girl, and though her face crumpled, she recovered without crying and stood up yelling alongside her brother.

Within minutes the bridge next to the convent was filled with men pushing toward the capstone at the top, the Nicolotti faction on one side and the Castellani on the other. Blows from fists knocked some of them back toward the fondamento as sticks pounded down on the shoulders of others. Near the top of the bridge, men grabbed each other and wrestled until one or both tumbled into the canal. One man floated motionless where he fell, blood creeping in ribbons through the water from a gash in his head. He was pulled into a boat, where several people bent over him.

"Is he dead?" the woman called out from Maddalena and Chiaretta's boat.

"Knocked out," they replied, "but breathing." The two children groaned with disappointment.

THEN, JUST AS SUDDENLY, IT ENDED. ONE GROUP PUSHED THEIR way across the capstone, and the best efforts of the other could not force them back. Wild cheers burst from the far side of the bank, while the losers clustered, shaking their heads. The crowd began to disperse, and soon the canal had emptied enough for Chiaretta and Maddalena's boat to begin to move.

When the danger had passed, Geltruda came to life, crossing herself again and again.

"You ones in red," the man asked her. "You're from the Pietà, right?" When Geltruda nodded, the man broke into a grin. "Ah! Your singers are the best in Venice!" He broke into a melody the coro had sung the previous week.

Chiaretta and Maddalena stared in surprise. "You go to our church?" Chiaretta asked.

"Whenever I can." He continued the song, but Mary had been replaced in his version by a beautiful maiden with lips like rubies, and the language was no longer Latin but the Venetian dialect. His wife joined in to harmonize, and soon from the bank of the canal another voice joined in the song, and then another from a window.

They rowed down the Rio di Santa Margherita, singing one song after another, joined by gondoliers and people on the bank. Chiaretta sang along in Latin whenever she could remember it, ignoring Geltruda's scowls.

Maddalena watched as around them in the canal bobbed lost caps, pieces of cardboard armor, and a lone shoe. Garbage flung from windows collected along the bank, outlined in an oily shimmer that caught the light and looked like rainbows. The ducks returned, and Chiaretta trailed her hand in the water, calling to them to come closer.

As they approached the Grand Canal and turned in the direction of the Pietà, the setting sun turned the fronts of the mansions into radiant squares of ocher, russet, and rose. Gondoliers' voices mixed with the cries of gulls making their last flights of the day, a choir of the hopeful and contented, calling out to the world to forget everything except the sublime.

BY THE TIME THE BOATMAN HAD ROWED THEM BACK TO THE Pietà, the rest of the figlie had been given something to eat and sent to their wards to recover. Geltruda and the two girls were met at the outer door by an ashen-faced woman who made the sign of the cross when she saw them.

"We heard that six people were killed," she said as a sob of relief broke from deep within her. She crossed herself again. *"Ave, Maria, gratia plena, Dominus tecum,"* she began to recite under her breath as she led them in the direction of the priora's study.

The priora rushed toward them, her rosary beads dropping to the floor. "What happened?" she asked Geltruda.

Neither Maddalena nor Chiaretta remembered Geltruda being as brave as she was in the story she told. Perhaps, they both thought, they just hadn't noticed how forcefully she had defended them.

"And you," the priora said, looking at Maddalena, "were you afraid?"

Images swirled in Maddalena's mind. The horses on the ceiling of the church thundered above her, while on all sides people pushed and shoved with their twisted faces, and blood ran in the canal. She shuddered, and when the priora put her arm around her, she began to cry.

Chiaretta had been looking around the room, taking in the large rug with its patterns of crimson, blue, and gold; and the green velvet curtains at the window, pulled back with golden cords that had thick tassels on the ends. A fire burned in the fireplace, casting a glow that lit up the rich leather of the chairs in front of it.

"And you?" the priora asked her for the second time. "Were you scared too?"

Chiaretta was puzzled by the question. "I was scared sometimes," she answered. "But not always."

The priora smiled. "God was watching over you."

She had meant something else. *I was outside,* Chiaretta thought. *I saw ducks, and people painted on ceilings, and I rode across the Grand Canal, not in a felce but out in the open. And I got to sing with the people in the boat. Most of the time I wasn't scared, I was happy.* She took in a breath as if she wanted to explain, but when she saw the grim faces of Geltruda and the priora, she decided they wouldn't understand. "Yes," she said. "God and the Blessed Virgin too."

A BOW FOR

MADDALENA

ROSSA

_____*1703–1709*

FOUR

A CHILDHOOD SPENT BITING HER LOWER LIP HAD pushed Silvia the Rat's front teeth forward so they now rested comfortably only outside her mouth. That, together with her round, monochromatic brown eyes and indistinct brown hair, gave Maddalena's violin teacher a rodentlike appearance that long before had led to her unflattering nickname.

Silvia scurried around the violin practice room, simpering as she did little tasks to court the approval of Luciana, the maestra dal violino. When Luciana made loud, offhand remarks about the other students, Silvia would smirk until the other figlie turned away in disgust.

Luciana's favor had nothing to do with Silvia's talent, which even a new initiate like Maddalena could see was mediocre. Still, in the cloistered world of the Pietà, being able to get along was essential, although to Luciana this was synonymous with getting along with her.

Anna Maria practiced with Maddalena for several months before asking Luciana to listen to her play. Even Luciana had to admit that Maddalena was already better than some of the other recent iniziate, but she was annoyed that Anna Maria had usurped her prerogative by beginning Maddalena's training on her own. Whereas with any other figlia Luciana showed her irritation by a barrage of criticism that didn't stop until the girl was in tears, Anna Maria seemed insulated from such treatment.

"I heard her say I was getting too famous for my own good," Anna Maria whispered to Maddalena one morning. "Isn't that wonderful?"

The only regular chastisement Anna Maria got from Luciana was for her pride. "Do you think the Virgin Mother would be pleased with such a boastful girl?" Luciana had once demanded, to which Anna Maria had replied, "No, but I think she might be pleased to hear me play."

Luciana's face had reddened at what seemed to be the boldest of insolence, and Maddalena had trembled for her friend. But when Luciana saw Anna Maria's solemn and matter-of-fact expression, she had in the end only grumbled and given her the mild punishment of sitting in the corner and playing the scales in each key, note by distinct note, for an hour. After all, everyone in the room, including Luciana, suspected that what Anna Maria had said was true.

Instead Luciana took out her irritation on Anna Maria's protégée, by ignoring Maddalena altogether and assigning her to Silvia. Silvia taught Maddalena exactly the way she herself was taught, but when the best of the violinists played, Maddalena saw how body, instrument, and music fused into something intimate and complete that lessons could not account for. By now, when she drew the bow across the strings, the tone was so sweet and rich that she sometimes forgot to breathe. Long after her lessons, she remembered how her fingers had flown and fluttered on the strings, part of something mysterious and sacred.

Her pleasure at becoming an iniziata in the coro shortly after she turned eleven had been muted over the past year, however, by having Silvia as a teacher. But even so, she yearned for every opportunity to pull her violin from its satin-lined case, slide rosin across the bow, and enter a world where nothing existed except its sound.

That world was once again being violated. "No, no, no! It's like this!" Silvia grabbed Maddalena's wrist and rotated it sharply outward.

Glaring at Silvia, Maddalena put the bow to the strings and played the series of arpeggios again. Her eyes closed as she slid into a languid melody, and forgetting Silvia altogether, her back began to sway to the contours of the music and her scowl melted.

Silvia clapped her hands twice. "Why do you do that?"

"Do what?"

"Shut your eyes like that and start moving around."

Maddalena stared at her for a moment, unsure of what she meant. "Do I do that?"

"Yes, and stop it. You need to pay attention and stop doing whatever you feel like. This is a lesson."

Maddalena shut her eyes. "I know."

"And besides, you make me nervous when you do that. You're supposed to play the music, not get all—all dreamy about it."

The bell to assemble for the midday meal had not yet rung, and their lesson would not be over until then, but Maddalena loosened her bow.

"I have a headache," she said. "I'll practice today during our free time, if Maestra Luciana permits."

Silvia's upper lip curled with scorn, revealing even more of her front teeth than usual as she shook her head. "You'll never get better if you don't listen." *Fifteen years old and you already sound like an old goat,* Maddalena thought. *My only headache is you.*

Maddalena walked among the pairs of figlie bent over their violins and violas to where she saw Luciana sitting with one of the older girls. Maddalena and the other figlie knew that, despite her present appearance and demeanor, Luciana had once been the most famous violinist in all four of the ospedali, and the figlie were often admonished to be grateful they had her to teach them. By now, gout had attacked her feet to the point that she could wear nothing but slippers. Any softness or kindness that might once have been part of her personality had vanished in years of pain.

Like Michielina, Luciana would soon be allowed to retire and remain at the Pietà until she died, in a special group of retired musicians known as the giubilate, but because no one else knew as much as she did about how to coax sound from a violin, she was required to serve on, despite her infirmity. She continued to show up in the sala every day, often in so foul a mood it seemed to Maddalena as if the temperature dropped and what little sunlight made it through the grimy windows vanished the second Luciana walked through the door.

When Maddalena came toward her, Luciana motioned to the girl to stop playing for a moment. "Yes?" She arched her eyebrows. "What do you want?"

"I am not well today, Maestra. I have a headache and would like to stop my lesson."

Luciana's loud exhalation made her annoyance clear. "The Congregazione has hired a violin teacher to take over some of my duties. He's here today, meeting with Maestro Gasparini, and they are planning to look in on us. He needs to see how many we are and how hard we work." Her thin lips turned down at the corners. "Self-indulgence is always unbecoming, Maddalena. You see how I suffer and you are thinking of a small ache in your head? Find a corner to sit in and practice until he comes."

THE DAY WAS CLOUDY, AND THOUGH THE LIGHT WAS BRIGHTER near the window, the draft from an unseasonably chilly September day had kept the corner unoccupied. Maddalena shivered as she tuned the strings and tightened the bow. She already felt better, having needed nothing more than to escape from Silvia, to play alone the way she wanted to, out of the reach of Luciana's glare, beyond the sala, somewhere even beyond the Pietà, where perfect music teased and beckoned.

The cold had already stiffened her fingers, but she soon forgot her discomfort as she made her way through her favorite piece, a gentle lullaby that reminded her of the trees swaying outside the cottage where she had been raised. Her eyes drooped as she played, without the interruptions of Silvia's clapping hands. Toward the end she reached a section where the fingering was still too complex for her to get through without intense concentration, and with her eyes shut, she tried it again and again.

"Signorina?" She looked up, startled at the sound of a voice that, though high and nasal, definitely belonged to a man. The first thing she noticed was his hair. Backlit by the sunlight filtering through the window, it was bright as sunset, lapping like flames over the shoulders of his black priest's cassock.

The violin teacher. Maddalena jumped to her feet. Luciana was standing nearby with a member of the Congregazione, dressed in the black robe of a Venetian nobleman.

The red-haired priest took the violin from Maddalena. "May I?" he said, putting his hand out for the bow. He put the violin to his chin and improvised a lead-in to the part she had been struggling with. He thought for a minute, tried it again, and then handed the violin back to her.

"It's not as hard as it seems," he said. "Try it like this." He took her fingers and moved them a different way.

She played until her fingers fell easily in place, then repeated it twice more for the pleasure of it.

"Good for you," the priest said. "Can you play the rest of the piece for me?"

Maddalena felt her face go hot. "Now?"

"Certainly, if you wish."

Maddalena's heart leapt. Though she wanted to play her best for Luciana to hear, she hit one false note after another. Somehow she managed to crawl back into control by the end, but as she looked up, all she could remember were the mistakes. Luciana's face flickered with disapproval before going back to a practiced lack of expression.

The priest was staring at her, puzzled. His young face was round, and his chin thrust forward as if it were in league with his long, thin nose to succeed someday in closing a circle between them. His fiery hair and small stature reminded Maddalena of the stories she had heard of gnomes who came out of the woods to make mischief in the villages. Unlike them, he was neither ugly nor repellent but instead exuded a wiry energy that seemed to draw the whole room in toward him.

Before she could apologize for the way she had played, he spoke. "You are not afraid of the difficult," he said. "And the music"—he tapped his forehead—"it's enough to keep all of us humble. What's your name?"

"Maddalena." Her voice came out almost in a whisper.

"Maddalena. Maddalena Rossa," he said, pulling on his hair. "Red. Like mine." A quick nod of his head, and he was off to rejoin Luciana and the others across the room.

Maddalena sat down to wait for the men to leave so she could get the scolding from Luciana over with. When the visitors were gone, the maestra walked back toward her. She touched her shoulder, and the unexpected tenderness weakened Maddalena's resolve not to cry.

"I was horrible," she said, burying her face in her hands. "I so wanted to impress you, and now . . ." She didn't finish. *Now I will be stuck with Silvia forever.*

"Your playing was quite awful," Luciana concurred, "but he saw something in you and wishes you to have special attention. Starting tomorrow you will be studying with me. Not promoted, mind you, but by special arrangement, an hour a week."

Maddalena looked up, astonished. "With you?"

"Who else? Do you expect private lessons from Don Antonio Vivaldi himself? He's the best violinist in Venice."

"No, Maestra," Maddalena mumbled. All she had hoped for was someone a little better than Silvia, and embarrassed to have her meaning misconstrued, she looked away from Luciana. All the figlie in the sala, instruments in hand, were watching. Maddalena looked at the floor, frightened by the inscrutability of their stares.

IF MADDALENA THOUGHT HER MOMENT WITH DON VIVALDI would work miracles with Luciana, she soon came to know otherwise. Before Maddalena could have her first lesson, Luciana had an attack of gout and had to be treated in the Pietà's hospital. She came back in early November in a fouler mood than usual and called Maddalena for her first lesson. Wincing, she lifted the hem of her robe up over her knees. Veins sketched purple lines in her sallow flesh. Her big toes, disappearing inside her slippers, were huge with swelling and the colors of a setting sun.

"You'll have to put up with me being so indiscreet," she said. "Even feeling the touch of my hem is like being set on fire."

Maddalena was horrified not just by the sight of Luciana's feet but by the intimacy of her revealing her bare legs up to her knees.

"Stop staring," Luciana said. "If you want to be a nurse, go to the hospital. If you want to be a violinist, play!" She motioned to Maddalena to pick up her instrument.

"I don't know what Don Vivaldi sees in you," she said, ending the lesson early. She told Maddalena to go practice by herself and waved away an offer of assistance after Maddalena helped her to her feet. Then, leaning heavily on a cane and wincing, she hobbled from the room.

The maestra is horrible enough even without those feet, Maddalena thought. She went back to the ward wondering how much of an improvement on lessons with Silvia this arrangement was going to turn out to be.

❦❦❦

ONCE A YEAR, ON THE FESTIVAL OF THE PRESENTATION OF THE Virgin, burchielli and peote, shallow boats of varying sizes and shapes, lined up side by side across the canal, forming pontoons on which a temporary bridge was laid down. A procession led by the doge went from his palace across the bridge to offer prayers of thanksgiving at the basilica of Santa Maria della Salute. All day and well into the evening, thousands of Venetians also walked across the bridge to light candles in the church for the health of their loved ones, and gondoliers brought their oars to be blessed by a priest on the church steps.

Maddalena and Chiaretta were among the figlie making the trip from the Pietà. The hazy morning brought with it a faint odor of post-harvest burning on the mainland, and the air was so crisp and cold they blew their breath into their fists to warm them.

The girls sang religious songs as they marched along the main thoroughfare between the Piazza San Marco and the church of Santa Maria del Giglio. Ahead of them, the bridge bobbed and lurched in water disturbed by dozens of boats hovering nearby. Some were filled with people cheering and waving to those crossing the bridge, while others waited their turn to pass under an arched segment in the middle, barely high and wide enough to accommodate even a small boat. As each boatman threw his body down flat and slipped under, the voices of the crowd fell and rose again in mimicry of his motions.

Several of the girls had to be taken by the hand and coaxed across the moving bridge. Maddalena had gone ahead of Chiaretta, putting one foot in front of the other with such deliberation that she never looked up until she reached the far side. When she did, she was surprised to see her sister was not behind her.

"Come along now, don't be afraid," one of the chaperones said to Chiaretta, who was standing motionless on the quay. In one of the boats, a woman dressed in the pale yellow of sunshine sat amid a collection of richly textured pillows. Her hair was almost as blond as Chiaretta's and her skin as fair. The man next to her was throwing a black cloak over her shoulders, and she was leaning back against him, laughing.

Chiaretta did not hear the chaperone call to her. *That's me in the boat,* she thought. *That's me being held. That's me laughing.*

"What is wrong with you?" the chaperone said. "Stop grinning like a monkey." She took Chiaretta's hand and pulled her across the bridge. On the other side, Chiaretta turned to look back, but the chaperone yanked on her arm to move her along.

In the church, the chaperones handed each of the girls a candle and motioned her to the prayer rail in a side chapel, where dozens of candles were already burning. "Light it," one of them said, "for the health of the doge and everyone at the Pietà."

As Maddalena lit her candle, she shut her eyes and whispered, "Please, Blessed Mother of God, help me to play the violin much, much better." She opened her eyes and began to go back to the chaperones. Remembering their orders, she turned around and crossed herself again. "And bless the doge and the Pietà." She thought for a moment, watching a wisp of black smoke from her candle snake up toward the ceiling of the chapel. "And please bless Chiaretta and keep her well." She crossed herself again and went to join the others.

Chiaretta knelt at the railing. "Please, God," she said, "make me the lady in the boat."

FIVE

CHIARETTA WINCED AS MADDALENA STRUGGLED TO PULL the comb through her hair. It had last been cut short when she was nine, almost a year earlier, and because it was rarely visible, Chiaretta did little more than push the loose strands back under her hood each morning.

"If I cry I won't be pretty," she wailed.

"If I don't get your hair combed, you'll be the only one wearing a hood and cap." Maddalena stopped and looked at her sister. "Is that what you'd prefer?"

Chiaretta said nothing but hunched down on a chair in the dressing room off the balcony of the chapel, stiffened her shoulders, and endured her sister's ministrations until her hair glowed like pale honey poured down her back.

"There," Maddalena said. "Sit down and hand me the pins." As her sister leaned over her, Chiaretta listened to her soft breath and felt its warmth on her cheek. She looked up into Maddalena's eyes and felt a flood of love at seeing her sister so close but unaware she was being observed.

Satisfied with her work, Maddalena tucked her own hair inside her hood in preparation for her day. Unlike Chiaretta's, it was going to be ordinary. "Let's get your dress on," she said, "and then I have to go back downstairs." Running her fingers over the silk skirt, she straightened its soft gathers and then held it out for Chiaretta to put on.

The older figlie di coro, their heads uncovered and their hair coiffed in demure rolls at their necks, filed into the dressing room wearing their concert uniforms, modest black or dark red dresses that some of them fancied up with a V-shaped collar of white lace. Chiaretta's dress was a mismatch, hastily located from a secondhand dealer in the Jewish ghetto when yet another of the singers had fallen ill with influenza, and several of the iniziate were told they would have to fill in for Sunday mass. Chiaretta was delighted with the dress, meant for a rich little girl and fit for a party. The ivory-colored bodice revealed her collarbones over several rows of dainty lace ruffles. The skirt was a matching ivory that rustled as she twirled around in her stocking feet.

Then her face darkened. "I'm sorry you won't be there," she said to Maddalena. "I thought you would be first."

THE LAST YEAR HAD BEEN A DIFFICULT ONE FOR MADDALENA. After playing the violin for several years, she had been told by Luciana that her time with it would be reduced so she could study other instruments. The encounter with Vivaldi might as well never have happened.

"Your violin playing is good enough, if a bit undisciplined, but we have plenty of figlie to play the stringed instruments." Luciana's eyes had darted when she told Maddalena her decision, as if to evade the unfairness of her evaluation. "You can come down to the sala, if you wish, in your spare time to play. That would help you keep up your skills, in case we should need you for a ripieno, but you won't be chosen as an attiva."

"But I just have a few free minutes a day—" Maddalena broke in.

Luciana held up her hand to stop her from finishing. "I made a generous offer with a valuable instrument, and I hear a complaint? Perhaps I should reconsider."

"I'm sorry, Maestra."

"And you should be trying harder to make yourself useful. Like your friend Anna Maria. It isn't about what you want, you realize. The coro is the backbone of the Pietà. Any girl who receives a musical education will be used as Maestro Gasparini deems necessary."

"I see that, Maestra," Maddalena said, casting her eyes down.

"And who knows?" Luciana's tone softened so unexpectedly that Maddalena looked up at her. Her brow was knit with feigned concern as she patted her arm with a motherly gesture so false it made Maddalena flinch. "Perhaps all those skills will bring you a marriage proposal someday."

It had taken all Maddalena's strength of will not to run from the room at Luciana's words. She would choose the violin over marriage any day, choose it over food, choose it over a cloak to wear in winter. *I would choose it over God,* she said to herself, then banished the thought out of fear of the consequences. *I didn't mean it,* she whispered the following morning as she made her daily devotion before a statue of Mary. *But please don't abandon me. If you do hear prayers, hear mine.*

Luciana had turned her over to one of the girls who played the recorder, and Maddalena found herself back to where she had been with Silvia. Now it felt even worse, because at least then she'd had the violin to lose herself in while Silvia pecked at her.

Perhaps Silvia had dreams too and got so mean and bitter because they slipped away, Maddalena thought as she fingered the recorder. Playing the notes wasn't the same as playing the music. Silvia did not understand that, Maddalena thought, or perhaps she had just given up caring about the distinction. No matter. She would have to try to play the recorder as best she could. But all the while, Maddalena imagined a violin, and a bow smelling of rosin, lying in a case in the dark, waiting for the music.

The one advantage was that Luciana was maestra of the stringed instruments alone, so Maddalena would now see her only in passing. Maddalena knew Luciana had resented giving over lesson time to a figlia in the first stage of training just because the Red Priest, as many called him, had swept through the room one day and happened to take a passing interest in her. Maddalena watched how the other girls were with Luciana, praising her, flattering her, and she couldn't see how she could manage to get such words out of her mouth. Maddalena had never caused any trouble, was never disobedient, and rarely took a minute of Luciana's time. All she had wanted was to win the maestra over by good behavior, but instead she had become invisible. A dull girl, she had once overheard Luciana call her. Not like Anna Maria. Not like her at all.

THANKS TO MICHIELINA'S LESSONS, CHIARETTA'S VOICE NOW carried so well that anyone who heard her sing could not believe a tiny girl could produce such sound. Before Michielina retired, she had seen to Chiaretta's initiation into the coro, but short of her tenth birthday, she had not yet had the spurt of growth that would bring her to her full size. Though her face had yet to take on its adult appearance, the figlie still talked as if it were already decided that Chiaretta would catch some rich man's eye and go off from the Pietà as a wife. But for now, there was no speeding the time until she grew up. She took singing lessons and rehearsed with the choir, but until that day she had never performed.

On a table near the door to the balcony, a bowl was filled with pomegranate blossoms. One soloist had a few of the delicate flowers tucked in front of her ear, and the other figlie di coro were finding spots for them in the bodices of their dresses.

Agata, a figlia with a voice low enough to sing baritone, picked up a sprig and tucked it into Chiaretta's hair. "Are you scared?"

"No," Chiaretta said, her voice coming out in a croak. A few of the figlie smirked.

"Cough a few times and try again," Agata said. Chiaretta had to force her voice out as if she were coming down with a cold, but other than that it sounded almost normal.

"It happens a lot when you're new." Agata put Chiaretta through one of their daily solfeggio exercises, running up and down the scales two octaves below Chiaretta, changing keys and adding flourishes with each new run.

The maestra clapped, and Chiaretta followed Agata and the other figlie through a small door and onto the narrow balcony where two years before she had first sung with Michielina. She leaned forward to peer through the gauze covering the iron grate. The church was crowded, and an anticipatory hush filtered up to the balcony at the sound of the coro taking their places.

"In nomine Patris, et Filii, et Spiritus Sancti," the celebrant called out as he approached the altar. *"Ad Deum qui laetificat juventutem meam,"* "To God, the joy of my youth," the choir replied. Chiaretta had sung her first notes. She looked over at Agata, who nodded.

After the confession, it was time for the Kyrie, the first real music for the coro. Two violins and a cello led in, and Chiaretta took a breath, joining the chorus in an explosive *"Kyrie!"* They repeated the word, stretching out each syllable as long as they could manage on one breath before moving on to the next word. *"Eleison,"* they sang in staccato syllables before their voices fell away.

A soloist stood on one end of the balcony. She took a small step forward as the accompaniment died down to a violin and cello continuo. Her voice pierced the air with a single note she held out like a precious jewel before continuing the melody.

As the orchestra reentered, Chiaretta gazed across the chapel to a painting of Mary and tried to imagine what it would be like to have that soft, full body envelop her. Then the chorus picked up again and she entered the clean, pure wash of sound. *"Kyrie eleison,"* "Lord have mercy," they repeated, as Chiaretta willed her voice to take wing and soar across the chapel to the Blessed Virgin, who heard the prayers of the faithful even when they were hidden inside the singing of a choir.

WITHOUT HER VIOLIN, MADDALENA'S THOUGHTS DARKENED. All she wanted was to crawl into bed and do nothing. The following Sunday, when the regular figlie di coro had recovered enough to resume their duties, Chiaretta's mood was equally glum as they walked around the courtyard at recreation time.

"I hate it here," Chiaretta said.

"You don't really. You're just bored," Maddalena retorted. "And anyway, tell me where you'd rather be."

Chiaretta went in seconds from being slumped with dejection to making a twirling circle in front of her sister. "I would be on-stage! An opera singer!"

Maddalena burst out laughing. "How do you know about that? And what part is there for a girl who isn't even ten?"

"I don't mean now," Chiaretta said. "When I am a grown lady. There's a girl, Antonia Morosini, who comes for lessons, then goes home. Do you know her?"

Maddalena shook her head.

"Her father's part of the Congregazione, and she lives on the Grand Canal. She says there are lots of women in Venice who have dozens of beautiful dresses. Some of them sing in the opera, and some of them— Well, I guess their job is just to be beautiful so men will want to take care of them. I'm not sure how it works."

"Just be beautiful? That's not a job."

"Operas have people dressed like gods who get dropped down from the ceiling on clouds," Chiaretta went on, ignoring Maddalena's comment. "Antonia goes all the time. She says it's wonderful!" She twirled again as she sang the last word.

"Chiaretta, calm down if you want more than bread and water for dinner."

"All right," she groaned. "But if I can't sing in the opera, then I'll marry a rich man."

"Marry the doge—I don't care—but please don't get us in trouble!"

Chiaretta sighed and resumed their stroll. "Maddalena?" she said a few seconds later. "Do you think it will happen? I don't want to stay here forever."

Maddalena looked away but said nothing. *If I can't play the violin, I have no idea what I want,* she thought, shutting her eyes to try to empty her mind. Chiaretta stared, waiting for an answer to her question, but none came.

SOON CHIARETTA MOVED ON TO THE ADOLESCENT WARD AND again slept next to her sister. She had earned a small amount of money for her performance with the choir—enough, when added to the pittance her limited skills in the silk workshop had yielded in her time there, to buy a small sketchbook and pencils similar to ones Maddalena had bought a few months before. However small, each of Maddalena's possessions seemed like a way she had carved out a life separate from her sister. The sketchbook, already half full of drawings of angels with beautiful wings and the flowers that grew in the cracks between the stones in the courtyard, was her most prized possession.

"How will we tell them apart?" Chiaretta asked when she unwrapped her package and saw that, having been bought from the same shop, her notebook was indistinguishable from her sister's.

Maddalena put a lace bookmark in hers to know it at a glance, but the next day she still pulled out the wrong one from the cassone they shared. Sitting on the edge of her cot, she drew a sketch of Chiaretta's sleeping face in her own book, then wrote underneath it, "I have an idea," forming each letter with the slow deliberation that came from having few opportunities to practice writing.

Chiaretta was enchanted with the sketch. Forgetting the rules, she opened her mouth, but Maddalena put her finger to her lips. She reached for her sister's sketchbook, feigning a scribble with a quizzical look, to ask her permission to write. Chiaretta nodded.

"I see girls passing books when we can't talk. We can do that too."

Maddalena handed the book to her sister.

With the tip of her tongue showing between her teeth, Chiaretta wrote back. "You are the most"—she crossed out a word and tried to spell it again—"maganifacint sister. Now I wont explod before I can tell you my sicrets."

CHIARETTA HAD BEEN IN THE PRIORA'S OFFICE ONLY ONCE before, on the day of the fight at the bridge. This time, she was brought by a figlia di commun who had summoned her from her lessons. There, a middle-aged man sat chatting with the priora and the maestra of the vocalists of the coro.

"Enchanting," he said when Chiaretta entered. "Even prettier than I had been told. A fine Venetian face, broad across the forehead, with a mind behind it to match and eyes to break men's hearts." He paused. "Do you know who I am?"

The priora rushed to answer for her. "He's one of the Nobili Uomini Deputati," she said. "Part of the Congregazione. The ones we pray for at dinner." She arched her eyebrows to convey she expected Chiaretta would know what to say.

"We are very grateful to you," Chiaretta said, bowing her head. What had he said? Something about a mind and breaking men's hearts? *I'm only ten,* she thought. *I must have misunderstood.*

"I heard you sing in the chapel and I asked myself, Who is that tiny girl I can barely see—the one in the white dress making all that noise?"

Figlie were punished for making noise. Chiaretta's eyes darted in alarm toward the priora.

"Beautiful noise, I should say," he added, seeing her distress.

The maestra did not approve of having young girls' heads turned in this fashion. "He has come to hear you sing," she said with a frown. "Sing the Amen we rehearsed this week."

Chiaretta glowered. Like other figlie at her stage of training, she was to shadow the attive, gaining experience by learning the music they learned and rehearsing with them. When the maestra told Chiaretta that even though she had done a good job filling in she would not be performing again soon, Chiaretta had become sullen and restless in rehearsals and had not bothered to learn any of the music very well. The threat of having her hair chopped off and spending several days in solitary confinement had brought her into line, but the maestra's expression showed that she had a good memory of where they had left things.

"Brava!" The man clapped when she finished. He pulled some sheet music from his jacket. "Can you sight-read?"

The maestra bristled. "All our girls can. Surely you know it is one of their regular lessons."

"Of course, but she is so young, I thought perhaps . . ." He handed several sheets to Chiaretta. "Would you try this?"

The maestra snatched it away and read the title. "This is an aria from an opera," she said. "Excellency, it is quite inappropriate. And besides, this is in Italian." She looked over to the priora for support. "The figlie di coro sing only in Latin."

"Maestra, she does not need to sing the words anyway. I would be happy just to hear her vocalize the notes."

"But still, the source . . ."

"Indulge me."

The maestra tightened her lips and handed the music to Chiaretta.

"Do it again," the man said when she finished. "And I'd like to hear it with a lute." The priora clapped, and the young girl who came in was told to fetch one from the sala.

Chiaretta knew when the maestra was angry, because the skin on her neck grew blotchy. Now the color was spreading upward to her cheeks. When the lute arrived, she picked it up and, without saying anything, began to play a simple accompaniment while Chiaretta vocalized.

"Delightful," the man said, applauding, when they finished. "And now, Maestra, tell me what you need, to compensate for the trouble I've put you to."

"Coal for the fire," she responded almost before he had finished asking, as if she had a mental list at the ready for any such occasion. "There is never enough to keep the girls' throats open. And more lamp oil for the music copyists. We always ask for the same things, but we are never given enough."

If he heard her subtle rebuke of the Congregazione's parsimony, he did not acknowledge it. "I'll make the request myself," he said.

He nodded toward Chiaretta. "It's good to see the Pietà's future so well assured."

BY DINNERTIME THE MAESTRA HAD NOTIFIED CHIARETTA SHE would be going with the figlie di coro to a picnic on the lagoon island of Torcello in two weeks' time. It would be better if the honor went to a more deserving girl, a properly behaved girl who learned her music, the maestra told her, but the Congregazione obviously did not understand her position. Chiaretta would be putting on her ivory silk dress again sooner than she had thought.

SIX

O THE FIGLIE DI COMMUN, THE CONGREGAZIONE WERE a shadowy group they could not name and whose faces they would not recognize. Men did not come inside the cloister except under the rarest of circumstances. Nevertheless, the Congregazione were just one step below the saints in importance.

Only the figlie di coro knew them at all. Gondolas picked up small groups at the dock in front of the Pietà a few times a month, to take them to sing and play at parties in the homes of the noble families of Venice. Chiaretta had watched with jealousy and longing as the older figlie di coro came back with stories about the beauty of the homes and the charm of the hosts, and complaining of stomachaches from all the food.

The best stories they brought back involved flirtations with the guests. Chiaretta had already heard about several marriages of figlie to men who first heard them in the chapel and later found that their beauty and charm were a match for their voices. For every such story, however, others found their chances dashed by crooked teeth, or pocked skin, or a limp. Many of them were never invited to parties at all.

At first Chiaretta had assumed the figlie would be punished for flirting, but she saw instead that the ones who could please in this fashion received more invitations than the rest. Why this would be so she wasn't certain, except that the older girls talked from time to time about how an event at which one or another of them made a big impression had led to a pledge of a large sum of money to the coro.

At her age, what most interested Chiaretta was the food. Sometimes, when no one was looking, she clutched her belly as she had seen Caterina do, whispering, "I never ate so much in my life," and trying to imagine what such a feeling might be like. And now, much sooner than she had expected, she had gotten her first invitation to put her fantasy to the test.

In the sala where the singers took their lessons, Chiaretta had made friends with Antonia Morosini, a Venetian girl her own age. Her father was one of the three most important men to the coro, a member of the Nobili Uomini Deputati charged with overseeing the music program at the Pietà.

"My father talked about you all week!" Antonia said when she next saw Chiaretta. Noticing her friend's puzzled look, she went on. "You know—the man who listened to you sing."

"That was your father?"

"Silly! Of course it was! The way he talked about you, I think if he didn't already have two daughters he would bring you home. Or maybe just throw us in the canal and take you instead."

Antonia giggled, but Chiaretta could not see the humor. More than anything she wanted to be Antonia, wanted her silk dresses, the silver filigreed band holding back her hair, her confident laughter, her freedom to move about in the world.

"It's because of him you get to come with us to Torcello next week," Antonia went on.

"You're coming?" Chiaretta had assumed the picnic would be a small event attended by only a few members of the Congregazione, the figlie di coro, and their chaperones.

"Of course!" Antonia began to prattle on about tables of meats, fruits, cakes, and sweet wine; musicians and games; and chances to walk along the canal path to chase butterflies and listen to birds.

What Antonia described was so far beyond Chiaretta's experience that she almost couldn't take in her friend's words. In the five years she had lived at the Pietà, Chiaretta had been outside perhaps ten times. She loved riding in the gondolas, peeking through the curtains and watching the boats carrying fish, vegetables, or even furniture up and down the canals. One time she had seen a wedding gondola festooned with flowers, and another time a special one for funerals, with its felce draped in black and a casket visible inside. The Grand Canal was a world of constant activity and openness, whereas life at the Pietà was more like the scenes on the carved altar in the chapel, in which dozens of figures were crammed for all eternity into one frozen space.

The most recent time she had been out was to the church of the Frari to see Titian's painting of the Assumption of the Virgin. On the way, she had paused to stare at the colors in a greengrocer's stall. The artichokes were purple as bruised skin, and the peapods were fuzzy as caterpillars. The chaperone had dragged her away before the man inside could meet Chiaretta's gaze.

"If you look at them, they look back at you," she had said. "It isn't proper." She'd shaken her finger. "You behave, Chiaretta," she'd said, "or you won't be coming out again."

That trip had been several months before. As the figlie neared puberty, they went out less, and after they reached it, unless they were in the coro, they rarely went out at all. Dull and getting duller was Chiaretta's assessment of her life after her fleeting taste of singing with the choir, and the last week had been even worse because Anna Maria was in the infirmary with a stomach ailment and she had missed seeing her in the practice rooms.

Chiaretta came into the ward for the rest period and saw that Maddalena's back was turned away, and she appeared to be asleep. She lay down but got up as soon as she was allowed and began to write a note to her sister.

I saw Antonia today and she is comming to the party. She says there will be games and more food than I have ever sen. She is bringing a nett for us to catch buterflies. If I can, I'll bring you one.

Maddalena stirred and turned over. Her face was blotchy, and her hair was pasted to her cheeks as if it had been wet. "What's wrong?" Chiaretta whispered, looking around to see if she had been overheard.

Maddalena shook her head, tears welling up in her eyes. Chiaretta handed her sister her sketchbook and pencil, agonizing while Maddalena wrote with violent strokes.

Susana cracked her bow, and Luciana gave the one I use to her. She told her to leave it in the cabinet so I could use it too, but she didn't look like she cared if she did or not.

"Luciana is a devvil from hell," Chiaretta wrote, showing her words to Maddalena before crossing them out so vigorously the marks dented the next two pages.

MADDALENA PASTED ON A SMILE AS CHIARETTA SLIPPED ON the ivory dress the morning of the picnic. An otherwise unnoticed growth spurt had left the waist already an inch too high and the hem too short. Maddalena had to tug hard on the laces to close the dress in the back, but Chiaretta was too distracted to care.

In the stillness that followed her sister's departure, Maddalena wrapped her arms around her chest to keep from dissolving with emptiness. The small amount of extra free time on Saturdays stretched before her less like a blessing than like an ordeal. Until then it had felt as if her life and Chiaretta's were entwined into one existence, but now she could not deny that Chiaretta's was taking its own path, one that wasn't always going to include her.

And her path? Best not to think too much about that. The sun had not risen quite high enough to brighten the sala dal violino, so Maddalena tapped her fingers around the inside of the cabinet where the maestra had told Susana to leave the bow. She tapped again. Maddalena felt heat pouring up through her chest into her neck and face. *What am I supposed to do? Play pizzicato?* She pictured Luciana's spiteful face and remembered Chiaretta's crossed-out words. *Luciana* is *a devil from hell,* she thought. And despite all her prayers, the devil was winning.

A door creaked open on the other end of the room, and Maddalena moved into a shadow in the corner to avoid being seen. Perhaps if it were Luciana, she could tell her what had happened and implore her to get the bow back. Instead she heard a man's voice. *"Domine, ad adjuvandum!"* he muttered. "Only thirty zecchini for paper? And five for rosin for the bows? What do they know about any of it? *Deus in adjutorium!"*

She heard the sound of a heavy shoe kicking a chair, sending it across the stone floor. Maddalena held her breath, not sure whether she should reveal her presence or hope he left before he knew she had overheard. She recognized the high nasal tone, and even though he was a priest, he was still a man, and they should not be in a room together alone.

The muttering continued as she heard him opening a violin case, and then the sound of a bow passing over strings. He stopped to tune for a second, then began playing. His bow streaked over the strings, like a sea hawk rising and falling in the air currents over the lagoon. His pace mounted until he was assailing the violin with the frenzy of a trapped and wounded animal. The notes lifted like the flight of the seeds of thistles floating in the summer air before his bow bit the strings hard, like a dog snapping at a stranger. Sometimes he was at war with the strings, and other times he kissed them with his bow in the way she sometimes thought she remembered her mother kissing her, delicately, barely touching her skin, then burying her face in her small body, pecking her belly and shoulders until she screamed with laughter.

The sun had risen enough for the room to brighten. As the first beams began to glow through the window, Maddalena could see his back turned to her, his red hair catching the light. Then she heard him moan and saw him clutch his chest with his bow hand. He bent over, making an odd, croaking noise as if he were being strangled. He staggered to a chair and put the violin and bow down, hanging on to the back of the chair and gasping for breath.

She ran across the room and helped him sit down. His eyes were glazed. "I'll go for help," she said.

"No." He waved her off. "I'll be all right in a few minutes."

Her heart raced as she watched Vivaldi struggle, but soon his pain began to ease, and he was sitting up, pale and sweating, but recovered.

"I know you," he said when he was breathing more normally again. "You're the girl with the violin. Maddalena. Maddalena Rossa." He tugged on his hair. "What are you doing here?"

"I—I came to practice, sir."

"To practice?" A smile played at the corners of his eyes. "Doesn't the maestra work you hard enough?"

Maddalena looked down, trying to think of what she could say.

"Well then," he said, filling the silence. "Let me hear how you have progressed."

"I—I can't, sir." She had meant to say nothing more, but before she knew it she had spilled out the whole story of Susana and the bow.

"This will not do." Vivaldi's brow furrowed as he listened. "Here," he said. "Play on mine."

"Oh no, sir," Maddalena said. "I couldn't. It's too valuable. And I really shouldn't be here."

"Nonsense." He winked. "I'm a priest." He handed her the violin. "Play."

HE WAS STARING AT HER WHEN SHE FINISHED. "YOU HEAR IT in your heart first," he said. "That's important. Most people just play with their hands. Or worse, sometimes only with their heads." He paused. "Why are you crying?"

Maddalena realized for the first time that her cheeks were wet.

"I'm crying because your violin is so wonderful," she said, and though his instrument was warm and resonant far beyond her own, that was not the only reason. "I rarely get to play anymore. They don't need more violinists as much as they need someone for the recorder."

"It's a nice instrument too," he said, with no real enthusiasm. "They have you playing that instead?"

She nodded.

"Do you like it?"

Maddalena knew that the answer should be yes, but she couldn't get the word out.

His face began to flush, and Maddalena thought for a moment he might be having another attack. "It's just a business for them," he muttered, looking out the window. "No ear. No soul." Then he turned back to her, changing the subject. "Best for both of us if we leave now without having to explain."

Maddalena nodded, handing back his violin. "Are you well enough, sir?"

"Oh that? It happens from time to time. Keeps me from having to say mass." He winked again, and Maddalena covered her mouth to hide her smile.

CHIARETTA CAME BACK FROM TORCELLO JUST BEFORE BED-time, but the stern looks of the matron signaled that the stories of today would have to wait until tomorrow. Chiaretta got out of her dress and sat down on the bed next to her sister. Maddalena kissed her on the forehead. Her hair smelled of dust, and her skin tasted salty with dried perspiration and sea air. She touched Chiaretta's shoulder and motioned with her eyes for her to turn around so Maddalena could untie her hair.

All Chiaretta wanted to do the next day was draw flowers and dragonflies to show her sister what she had seen. "I walked farther than I ever have in my life," she said as they sat in the courtyard, sketchbooks in hand. "I must have seen a thousand birds."

She looked up at her sister. "Why is it that you never see little birds? They're always scrawny little babies in the nest, but every one you see flying around is always grown."

"I don't know." Maddalena had been half listening while trying to recall how Vivaldi's violin had sounded and remembering his wink. "Were Antonia's brothers and sister there?"

"Her brother Claudio," Chiaretta said. "Her sister's in a convent already. There's enough for one dowry, and the parents chose Antonia to be the one who marries. They think she's the smartest and the healthiest, that's why."

"What did her sister think?"

"I don't know. Antonia didn't say. Her parents decided for her."

Maddalena felt a chill at her core as Chiaretta shrugged off the destiny of another person. *What will happen to us?* she wondered. *Do nuns play the violin?*

"Are you cold?" Chiaretta asked.

"No."

"I thought I saw you tremble. Anyway, most families can't afford to marry off all their sons either, so they stay in their own apartments in their parents' homes. That's what Claudio does. Antonia has another brother who's already married and lives far away from here in a city with a funny name I can't remember."

"Well, if no one gets married, how are there ever any children?"

"I don't know!" Chiaretta, annoyed with her sister's questions, had raised her voice, and Maddalena quickly put her fingers over her lips. A bell sounded, and her gesture became unnecessary as the Pietà fell silent once again.

RAIN FELL ALMOST WITHOUT CEASING THE WEEK AFTER THE picnic, flooding the courtyard and driving the girls inside. The pages of Chiaretta's sketchbook began to fill up with drawings of tents and tables laden with fruit and wine, meats and candies, and fields with grazing sheep and chestnut trees, as she struggled not to forget even the slightest detail. "I didn't know what some of the foods were," she wrote under one drawing. Under others she had written, "I walked on a path in this fild," and "I walked along this cannal and saw kinfishers."

Chiaretta had secreted in the cassone a small object wrapped in a napkin that she brought back from Torcello. The next day she brought it out. "Antonia said I should save this for you as a surprise on a gloomy day," she said to Maddalena. "It's called a blood orange." Chiaretta pulled out the round, puckered fruit and held it to her nose, breathing in the fragrance, before handing it to her sister. "Smell!"

Maddalena rolled the strange reddish orange ball around in her hand, feeling the fruit's hardened skin with her fingertips before holding it to her nose. When the warden's back was turned, at Chiaretta's insistence Maddalena bit hard into the fruit to tear off a small piece of rind.

Inside, the fruit glistened with the hues of sunset, of harvest, of the halos around the heads of stained-glass saints. Trickles of juice ran onto her fingers, thin and red. She put each finger in turn into her mouth, savoring the sweetness.

LUCIANA'S BROW WAS KNIT AND HER MOUTH TURNED DOWN AS she waited for Maddalena to arrive for her recorder lesson. "There is a package for you from Don Vivaldi," she said. She handed her a long, thin cylinder wrapped in plain paper. "I took the liberty of looking inside already. How was it that he was under the impression you needed a violin bow?"

Maddalena felt the blood rush to her cheeks. "I—I came in last Saturday to practice and I couldn't find it."

"You should have come to me. But still, Maddalena, it hardly explains why he knew about it."

Maddalena stood looking at the floor. She could never describe how she came to be having a private conversation with the violin teacher without sounding as if every rule of propriety had been violated. But she would have to say something.

"It was the day the coro went to Torcello."

Luciana waved her off. "I know. Don Vivaldi explained when he brought this that he had fallen ill, and you heard his cries for help as you passed by in the corridor."

He changed the story, she thought, amazed. "He asked me to play, and I couldn't, because I had no bow. He let me play his violin for a few minutes. That's all."

"So you did not take the opportunity to complain about your treatment?"

"No, Maestra. I know I am very fortunate to be here, and I am well treated," she said. "I am sorry if I have caused any embarrassment."

Luciana reddened. "Embarrassment? That's hardly the point. Really, how can the Pietà function if girls are going over the heads of their teachers?"

"Maestra, I said nothing to him."

Luciana kept her eyes riveted on Maddalena, as if deciding whether to believe her. Maddalena did not flinch, and eventually Luciana looked away. "Well," she said, "I didn't think you would be so foolish."

"Maestra, it's the truth. He was so sick, I thought he was going to die, and then he asked me to play when he felt better . . ." Maddalena's face clouded. "Do you know what's wrong with him?"

Luciana harrumphed. "Don Vivaldi has a reputation as a shirker. Your beloved Red Priest celebrated mass a few times after he was ordained, then claimed he couldn't do it anymore because he had so much trouble breathing." She sniffed. "If you ask me, it was an excuse to spend all his time playing music. He seems to be well enough for that!"

Keeps me from having to say mass, he had said. And winked. But still, the attack was real. Maddalena couldn't imagine how anyone would want to get out of one thing by suffering something else that awful.

"Are you listening to me?" Luciana was scowling.

"I'm sorry, Maestra. He was clutching his heart and gasping, and I didn't know what to do. I'm sorry if I did something wrong."

Luciana ignored her. "Apparently—according to him at least—I have made an error in putting your violin training aside."

Maddalena's heart jumped. *If I could just play again, I would work so hard all the saints in heaven would fight for me.*

"He wishes to give you lessons himself," Luciana said. "You will start tomorrow, once a week for an hour. I am to supervise your daily practice and discuss any progress with him."

The maestra dismissed her with a wave of her hand and began sorting through sheets of music. She looked up again. "Close your mouth. It is most unattractive to gape like that."

Maddalena pursed her lips. She held out the long, thin package. "Where shall I keep this?"

"What, do you think it's yours to sleep with? Put it in the case and keep it with the others." Luciana looked up and saw Maddalena's hesitation. "No one will take it, if that's what you're thinking." She snorted. "Not when it's been bought specifically for you by the man himself."

Maddalena went to the music cabinet and pulled out the familiar case of the violin she used. She unwound the paper in which the bow was wrapped and ran her fingers along the shiny wood, crooking her thumb underneath to stroke the loosened hairs. She lifted the bow to her lips and kissed it, looking around to make sure she had not been observed. She tiptoed from the room, and when she had reached the corridor she broke into a grin and took a single skipping step before recomposing herself as she turned in the direction of the lace room.

SEVEN

THE POSTER ANNOUNCING THE CONCERT WAS TATTERED and blurry from the sleet that had covered Venice for two days. It had been taken down and tossed aside in the sala di coro until the weather cleared and a replacement could be put up.

"Did you see the tavoletta?" one of the figlie asked, handing it to Chiaretta.

Chiaretta stared at it, reading down through the names of the soloists until she reached the last one.

"Chiaretta—Soprano." Chiaretta's heart pounded as she ran her fingers over the two words, caressing the wrinkles out of the paper.

"Congratulations. It's your first, isn't it?"

"What?" Chiaretta hadn't heard the question.

"Your first tavoletta. Never mind. I can see it must be."

CHIARETTA HAD HANDLED A FEW SMALL SOLO PARTS ALREADY, but none important enough to deserve mention on a tavoletta. Just the week before, when Maddalena filled in for an ailing recorder player, she had heard Chiaretta's voice floating out over the church as she sang the Sanctus during Sunday mass. Though she had heard her sister's voice many times before and knew she could not be objective about whether it was more beautiful than the others, from the way her skin prickled Maddalena knew that she had experienced something magical.

More than just Chiaretta's voice had undergone a transformation. She had grown inches, her hair hung in long waves, and the almost unnoticed first changes of puberty had focused her in her singing. As a result, she had been promoted several years ahead of schedule to the second stage of training, becoming at age twelve an attiva with the coro. Even her spelling had gotten better, as she attacked her lessons with the fervor of someone anxious to improve herself as much, and as quickly, as possible.

Warming up her voice, she stretched her palate upward until the bones of her skull vibrated and mucus shook loose from her sinuses. It ran out her nose, and whole mouthfuls clogged the back of her throat and had to be spit into her handkerchief. She forced air up from her diaphragm with such ferocity she would sometimes gag and have to wrestle down the urge to vomit. Other times belches or gas as loud as thunderclaps would escape without warning in the middle of a lesson.

Her voice no longer jumped out of her throat but emanated from deep within her. She was still a year or two away from her full size, which would always remain rather small, but her solos could already fill the chapel. No longer was she recognizable from the floor by her ivory dress, which had been replaced by the adult uniform of the coro, but by her tone, as clear and supple as the song of a meadowlark, as gentle and clean as mist on the cheek after a rainstorm.

THOUGH IT HAPPENED TOO GRADUALLY TO NOTICE, AT SOME point Chiaretta stopped being Maddalena's little sister and became simply her sister. Their experiences were similar enough to make the three years' difference in their ages unimportant. Their personalities, however, were another matter. Sometimes Maddalena thought that if strangers were to observe their threesome, they would think Chiaretta and Anna Maria were the two who were related, so alike were they in their enthusiasm for chatter. There never was much time for Maddalena's thoughts, most of which were in any case too private to share.

In the practice room with Don Vivaldi, Maddalena was a different person. She played with a fearlessness she couldn't summon otherwise, and when she talked, words tumbled from her lips.

"Do it again," he would say in the heat of their lessons. "Again! Play it like you mean it!" At other times he would throw out a word. "Rain," he would say, or "hawk," or "embers," or "dawn," and she would try to make the image come alive as she played.

Sending his bow skittering across the highest strings, he once asked, "What does that remind you of?"

"Birds singing in a tree."

He nodded. "And this?" He played a darker, excited scramble of notes.

"Something has scared the birds and they're flying away."

Over time, she began playing musical images of her own for him. "Snow falling on my face," she would say, or "Alone in the dark."

Back in the village she used to run until she doubled over, panting and dizzy, then stand up straight and watch the horizon right itself. Finishing a piece with Vivaldi was like that. In those moments, the silence was perfect, so different from the enforced quiet of the Pietà, which announced what was forbidden rather than suggesting what might be possible.

"We are kindred souls, Maddalena Rossa," he told her one afternoon, using the name that he alone called her. "We both see that music is poetry." Maddalena felt her cheeks growing warm.

"But . . ." He leaned back in his chair, shutting his eyes as he pondered. When he opened them again, his expression was puzzled.

He picked up his violin. "I can't say what I want to in words."

Standing up, he began to play a jig, tapping his foot and bouncing his head in time. Then still playing, he took off across the room, dancing in little patterns, bending his knees and shifting his hips, twisting his waist, rotating his shoulders, with a wild grin.

"Try it," he said after he stopped.

Maddalena had been too surprised to do anything but watch. *Try it?* She felt nailed to her chair. "I don't want to," she said. "I mean, I can't."

"Can't? Why not?"

"I—I don't know." *Because I don't know how to use my body. Because frivolity isn't allowed. Because I don't like things I'm not used to. Because you frighten me.*

Vivaldi came over and sat across from her. He was wheezing, but his cheeks were rosy and his eyes glistened.

"Maddalena, do you know how to feel happy?" he asked. "Where you want to stand up and shout? Where you want to pick up your skirt and twirl in circles just because it feels good?"

"I—"

"I didn't think so. Happiness like that is not condoned by the Pietà." He took her hand. "Listen to me now. Your playing is beautiful. I hear the best musicians in Venice—in all Italy—and some of them don't make the music mean half what you do, even though their technique is better. And it should be. After all, most of them have been playing longer than you've been alive."

He noticed he was still holding her hand, but instead of pulling away, he squeezed it. "But I have never heard a happy note from you. The poetry in your head is— What is it? Sad? Lonely?"

He pulled away his hand, and Maddalena clasped hers together, wringing them. "I don't know how to talk this way."

"Well, try! Find a word for what your images mean. One bird in the sky? A leaf falling? A flickering candle? What do these things say about you?"

It was like grasping a handful of ashes. Her thoughts slipped away, refusing to form. Then she whispered something.

"I couldn't hear you," he said.

"Small," Maddalena said. "I just feel small."

"That's better. Now we will start work on making you feel bigger." He stood up. "May I have this dance?"

Maddalena's stomach felt like a pan of water reaching a boil. "I don't know how."

"Neither do I. I've discovered it's much better that way." He pulled her to her feet and placed her hands in his. Then he began to hum, and she found her feet moving, a bit clumsily but in step with his. The third time through the melody, she lifted onto her toes and joined him in humming. He was so close she could see the prickles of sweat turning his red hair brownish at the temples, the flecks of green in his gray eyes—eyes that were probing hers, daring her, demanding something she did not quite understand. Then he pulled away.

"Oh my," he said, sitting down and mopping his brow.

Panting, she dropped in a chair and shut her eyes. *All my life I have waited for something like this to happen. All my life I wanted someone to look across a room of girls in their red dresses and white caps and see me. You—no, you over there in the corner. The one with the auburn hair. Come here. I know who you are. I know what you need.*

When the blood stopped pounding in her ears, Maddalena

heard whispering in the hallway, and the sound of giggles suppressed behind hands as the rustle of skirts receded into the distance.

"Did you hear that?" she asked Vivaldi.

"Next time we should ask them to join us." He was still smiling.

The moment was gone. *I am in trouble,* she thought, wildly hoping she was mistaken.

"YOU DANCED WITH HIM?" ANNA MARIA SCOWLED. "WHAT does that have to do with music?"

Maddalena stared at her, dumbfounded. "People dance to music."

"Not the people who are supposed to be playing it."

Chiaretta wasn't listening. "I wish he would dance with me," she said. "Well, maybe not him, but someone. A handsome man." She turned sideways and took a few tiny, skipping steps as they walked toward the practice rooms the morning after Maddalena's lesson. "Was it like this?"

"Chiaretta, I can't show you. Everybody's watching me."

Maddalena dreaded each step toward the sala dal violino, where she knew Luciana would be waiting, furious but exultant. She had to have heard, because gossip carried in no time up and down staircases and along corridors from one workroom to the next, until it had reached every wing of the Pietà. A few hours after her lesson with Vivaldi, the figlie in the lace room had grown quiet when she came in, and she had seen them giving each other smirking looks all afternoon. Anna Maria and Chiaretta had both heard the story of the dancing violinists before Maddalena had a chance to tell them that evening. To Maddalena's relief, what they heard had not been much embellished in the telling, but the truth was embarrassing enough.

Luciana pretended not to see her when she came in, and Maddalena opened her violin case inch by inch, her front teeth locked in a grimace, as if the slightest squeak might betray her. As she took out her bow, she heard the maestra tapping on the table.

"Before we start today," she said, "there is a matter to take care of."

"Oh, no," Anna Maria whispered.

Luciana was staring at Maddalena so intently that the other figlie turned to look at her. "It's clear," she said, addressing all the figlie, "that some of you fail to understand your work here."

Maddalena felt her temples pulse. Anna Maria moved close enough to brush against her as Luciana went on. "This is not a room full of soloists. You are members of an orchestra. Your job is to play the music that is put in front of you, to rehearse the music you have been assigned to play."

Luciana was looking at Maddalena again. "The sotto maestre are aware of how best to help you improve, and they know our ways. That is why I have always thought we should employ as few outside teachers as possible. You have all been here long enough to recognize anything out of the ordinary, yet some of you obviously cannot, and where judgment in these matters is lacking in both instructor and pupil . . ."—her voice lowered to a growl as she addressed the group again—"you hurt the coro. You hurt the Pietà. And who knows what can come of that?"

She said no more, leaving all possibilities open to the imagination, as she shuffled to her chair and sat down. She motioned for her pupil to come take her seat, turning her back to where Maddalena was standing. The other figlie went to their appointed places as quickly as they could, too intimidated even to look at one another.

"You'd better go talk to her," Anna Maria whispered.

"I know," Maddalena said without moving.

"Now, before she gets started." She gave her a push in the small of her back, and Maddalena crept across the room to the maestra.

"Yes?" Luciana looked up.

"I just wanted to say I'm sorry. He was trying to teach me—" *He was trying to teach me not to feel small.*

"I don't care. You know I have never approved of this special little arrangement." Luciana's snort echoed through the room, loud as a horse. "Apparently, I'm sure you'll be glad to hear, Maestro Vivaldi has been successful at explaining himself to the priora and the Congregazione. They have, in their superior judgment, not found it necessary to fire him, or to stop his current lessons. And they have decided you are not to blame, and that two days of bread and water are an appropriate punishment."

Maddalena felt a shudder of relief travel through her body.

"But he has been admonished most severely," Luciana went on, "and you, Maddalena, should consider that you have been also." She shook her head, curling her lip. "Dancing!" She turned away in disgust. "And now, leave me, please."

The figlie had been listening to Luciana's every word, just as she intended. When Maddalena turned to go back to her seat, they huddled over their music, giving her furtive looks as she passed. She scarcely noticed. Bread and water were nothing. Her life was not over after all.

A SUBDUED VIVALDI GREETED MADDALENA THE FOLLOWING week. "I must have caused you a great deal of embarrassment," he said.

Maddalena averted her eyes, running her finger over her bow strings.

"The Congregazione were not amused by my—peculiar, I think they called it—teaching style," he said. "I assured them it wasn't my style, just a thought I had at the moment."

"Are you sorry you had it?" Maddalena's voice was barely audible as she continued playing with the bow.

"I said over and over again how sorry I was. But I didn't mean a word of it." He stifled what sounded like the beginning of a laugh.

"They told me not to take any more liberties where you"—he corrected himself—"where the figlie di coro are concerned."

Were you sorry you danced with me? Maddalena was too afraid of the answer to ask. Vivaldi had already taken his violin out of its case, and his head was bent over the strings as he tested one of them. He sighed and, resting the violin in its case, walked over to the stove, turning his back to her.

"The coro is—so competent. But where is that flash of brilliance? I told them if they weren't interested in that, I wasn't interested in being here." He chuckled to himself and turned around. "Of course I was bluffing. I can't afford to lose this job."

He walked back over to Maddalena, still running the loose bow strings between her fingers. "So quiet," he said. "What's wrong?"

Were you sorry you danced with me?

When she did not reply, he continued. "They went on and on about how much they respected my judgment concerning the potential of the figlie, and how freethinking they were to let me spend any time with you. At the same time they told me I am to prepare you to be a third violinist. I seem to be the only one who sees any inconsistency in that, but how could so many great men of Venice be wrong?"

He sniffed. "I am to produce brilliance among the first violinists . . . whether they possess it or not. And make third violinists out of girls like you." He picked up his violin and began to tune it again. "So we will be taking a different approach—that is, if you ever decide to look at me."

Maddalena raised her eyes. "Does *different* mean 'nothing special'?"

"What? So sad? Of course it will be special. I won't let it be grim. And I won't let you turn out to be ordinary, not if I can help it. Even if I have to do it one stolen minute at a time." He cocked his head and gave her a conspiratorial grin.

"Were you sorry you danced with me?" Finally she had said it.

"I'm just sorry I can't do it again." He shrugged. "And besides, I thought about it and they're right. Your imagination isn't helping you become an attiva. You play to please yourself, and that doesn't carry much weight here."

"I want to please you," Maddalena said, her eyes filling with tears.

He exhaled slowly through pursed lips, causing a wisp of his hair to lift off his forehead. "You don't understand. If you were not a ward of the Pietà and I were not a priest, and we lived somewhere in Venice, we could pull out our violins and play to our hearts' delight." His voice tightened as he spoke. "But none of those things are true. The Pietà is not paying me, or raising you, to entertain each other."

If we lived in Venice? Images swirled through her mind. A living room. A fire. Violins. Dancing.

Vivaldi was giving her a quizzical look. "Do you understand?"

The vision dissipated and she was back in the practice room. She felt the cold and shivered. "Yes."

"And if you don't get a third violin chair soon—" He did not need to finish. The Congregazione would not continue to support a failed violinist forever.

Maddalena stared at the floor. "I think if I did not have music . . ." She could not even finish the thought.

"That you would die? I don't suppose you could know how well I understand you." He paused. "I would like to lift your face, but I am forbidden. I want to tell you a secret, but you will have to look at me."

Complying, she saw the strain in his eyes. "I don't remember choosing to be a priest," he began. "My father is a barber who plays the violin with the orchestra of San Marco. He was worried about my future . . ." His voice fell off as he looked across the room.

"I've never been healthy, never been able to breathe well, and my heart pains me. My parents thought I was going to die before living even a month. When I was fifteen, they pushed me toward the priesthood. I can't say I objected strongly—after all, I would always have a job. And we all thought it would suit me. I've carried a breviary with me from childhood. Prayer steadies me, and most days I follow the holy office as much as I can."

He was an adult, a priest, a man, and much as she wanted to know his story, much as she wanted to be the one he told it to, she was uncomfortable hearing it. Still, she let him go on.

He shook his head hard, as if to dislodge an unwanted thought. "After I was ordained, I was very unhappy. I would say mass, and hear confessions, minister to the sick, bury the dead, but I wasn't really paying attention. Please don't misunderstand, it wasn't for lack of love of God, or a feeling the work wasn't important, but I had all these melodies floating in and out of my head. It was like trying to catch a flock of birds with my bare hands. By the time I could write them down, they had escaped.

"One day I was celebrating mass, and just before the Elevation of the Host, the most glorious music came into my head. I swear I thought my life depended on writing it down before it was lost. I felt short of breath, as if I might faint, so I handed the communion wafer to the other priest and ran from the altar. Then I sat in the sacristy and wrote the music down."

"What happened next? Did you get in trouble?"

"Of course." He laughed quietly. "It's odd to call it fortunate to have an illness that causes me so much pain—you've seen that, I'm afraid—but I was able to use my shortness of breath as an excuse, and then I realized it might be a way to get out of being a parish priest altogether. May God strike me dead, but I cannot help but believe He would rather hear my music than my mumblings at the altar."

Vivaldi saw the quizzical look on her face. "Have I offended you, Maddalena Rossa? I don't suppose you have ever heard a priest talk this way."

She shook her head. "It's not that. No one—at least not any adult—has ever talked to me like that. I mean, they tell me lots of things, like stop daydreaming and pay attention, or pick the threads off my skirt." She looked down at her skirt and brushed her hand across it, although nothing was there. "I don't mean to complain, but here, when people look you in the eye or call you by name, it's usually because they're angry, or giving you an order."

"Complain all you want. I won't tell." He winked at her. "We should start the lesson," he said. "It would be a very bad idea not to teach you anything today."

Soon he was lost in his warm-up and no longer paying attention to her, but he was seated so close she could hear the tiny whistle in his throat where his breath caught, and see loose ends of red hair splayed on the shoulders of his robe. She didn't dare reach out and smooth his hair as she did Chiaretta's, but for a second her hands wanted to. Then the world of the Pietà closed back in around her, and she picked up her violin.

DURING THE REST PERIOD THAT AFTERNOON, MADDALENA'S stomach began to hurt, and she felt an awareness of her body at the point between where her thighs met her belly. She had been told all her life not to allow her fingers to stray to that place, but the feeling was so foreign her hand went there without her willing it. Her fingers felt slippery, and she lifted them in front of her eyes, staring at the coating of blood.

Keeping such matters private on an open ward was impossible, and Chiaretta was horrified at what she thought had to be an injury deep inside Maddalena's body. But when the older girls talked about it, Chiaretta understood that if she didn't bleed, her breasts would fail to grow. Her nipples had grown puffy and large, but that was all, and Chiaretta was tired of staring down at nothing while the other figlie di coro had such beautiful, soft mounds pressing out of the bodices of their gowns. Chiaretta wanted something to show off, even if she had to accept the bleeding to get it.

"You can pretend," one of the figlie said to her as a half dozen of the coro prepared to leave for what would be Chiaretta's first private party in a Venetian home. "You take a couple of handkerchiefs and put them like this." The girl shoved her fingers deep into the bodice of her dress. Her breast was so ample the nipple peeked out. Embarrassed, she tucked it back in.

Chiaretta looked down at her own flat chest. "I don't have anything to push up," she said.

"Neither did I," the girl said, tugging at her bodice to straighten it. "Just try it. You'll be surprised."

CHIARETTA LOOKED DOWN AT THE TINY PROTUBERANCES forced upward to the edge of her bodice as she stepped out of the damp gloom of the alley alongside the Pietà. Sunlight bounced off the light stones of the Riva degli Schiavoni and sparkled on the lagoon. Forgetting her self-consciousness, she blinked at the brightly colored clothing and masks of passersby celebrating one of the many festivals of the Venetian year. A large black gondola, polished until it shone like obsidian, was tied up at the dock. The felce had azure velvet curtains, embroidered with the family crest of Antonia Morosini's family. The gondolier was dressed in a brocade jacket of the same blue, his head topped with a black tricornered hat. When he saw the figlie emerge from the Pietà, he jumped off to help them board.

Chiaretta savored every footstep, pretending she was boarding her private gondola to go home to her palazzo after a visit. Her fantasy was interrupted by the commotion on the quay. Someone was calling to one of the soloists. "Agostina! Agostina! Bravissima!" Then another picked up the refrain, but this time for Cecilia.

And then she heard it. "Chiaretta!" She turned to look and saw a cluster of people who seemed to know who she was. They had pulled off their masks and were smiling and waving at her. A flower landed atop one of Chiaretta's shoes from a bouquet someone had dismantled to throw at the figlie, followed by a blue-and-pink mask in the shape of a bird that clattered to the ground in front of her. She bent to pick it up, but the chaperone grabbed her arm and hurried her along with a clucking sound.

As she boarded the gondola, Chiaretta was not sure whether it was the rocking of the boat or the unexpected acclaim that made her so dizzy she had to reach out for the gondolier to hold herself up. As they pulled away from the dock, Chiaretta looked back at the quay. A couple waved, though they could not have seen her inside the felce, and though the sound was faint, she was sure she heard them call her name.

WHEN THEY ARRIVED, THE FIGLIE DI CORO WERE USHERED UP the grand staircase of the Morosini home to the piano nobile. The marble floor of the portego, the reception room that ran uninterrupted the entire length of the house, reflected sunshine from both ends of the hallway, from the loggia overlooking the Grand Canal to the windows that opened onto a courtyard on the other end. Huge gilded mirrors on the walls passed the light back and forth, so the whole room was bathed in a pearlescent glow. Banquet tables were set up at one end, and chairs upholstered in gold damask were scattered against the walls.

Tiny jewels strung on gold threads sparkled in Antonia's hair as she stood with her mother near the middle of the room. Her dress had a bodice of embroidered damask and a lavender silk skirt that rustled and shone as she ran toward the girls.

She pulled Chiaretta aside. Her breath smelled of ginger candy as she whispered in her friend's ear. "There's a man whose family is talking to mine about marriage."

"Marriage to you? You're thirteen!"

"Shh!" Antonia looked around to see if anyone had overheard. "Not now—in a few years. My parents think arranging something now will be best."

She motioned over her shoulder. "Look in the corner—he's wearing a red waistcoat."

Chiaretta saw no young men and continued to scan the crowd. "Don't be so obvious," Antonia said. "He's the one with the black pouch with gold trim, talking to my brother Claudio."

"He's so old!" Chiaretta blurted out. "Do you want to marry him?"

Antonia's expression was blank. "I suppose so. It's a good match, my parents think. It could be worse. He is rather handsome, don't you think?"

Chiaretta had to admit that the idea of marriage was exciting, since married women lived in houses like this one, and gave parties where they wore jewels. She looked at the man again, trying to picture Antonia as his wife. "I guess so," she said.

Bernardo Morosini broke away from his guests and came to greet them. "Chiaretta, cara, so good to see you again. Welcome to my home. Are you in fine voice tonight?"

"Yes, sir," she replied, "and we've been practicing a special treat for you."

"Ah, such a shame I'll have to wait until we've eaten. But you've made the prospect so delightful I won't wait another minute!" Raising his voice, he called his guests to attention. "Please, ladies and gentlemen, these beautiful young women have told me they won't perform until I have fed them."

The guests laughed and began to walk over to the table, chatting among themselves. Chiaretta hung back, uncertain what to do, but Antonia took her hand. "You're sitting next to me. My mother said so."

Antonia led her to a place at a large table that gleamed from years of vigorous polishing. Candles had been lit down the middle, catching the glow of three silver serving bowls spaced along its length, in which an assortment of fruit was heaped.

"We're having oysters first, then soup," Antonia said. Chiaretta's heart fell. *I don't know what an oyster is,* she thought darkly, *but I get soup every day. If that's all there is to eat, they've been lying to me.*

Servants had appeared with decanters of wine they poured into Murano glass goblets. Chiaretta noticed that even the figlie's glasses were being filled, and she nudged Antonia. "We get wine?"

"Half a glass," her friend said, wrinkling her nose. "I don't like it anyway. They'll pour a little water in it if you ask."

More servants came in carrying trays on which shells were arranged. "For the signorine?" one of them said, smiling, as he deposited two oysters on each of their plates. The blob in the shell was the color of the half-digested food that large shorebirds left in splats on the Riva, and just as slimy looking. "We eat that?" Chiaretta asked Antonia.

"It's an oyster! It's delicious." Antonia lifted it to her mouth. "Tastes fresh, just like the ocean."

If the ocean was anything like the canals, it certainly wasn't fresh. Chiaretta poked at the gray blob, watching it quiver, while Antonia polished off her second one.

"Don't chew, just swallow," the voice on the other side of her said. She put the oyster in her mouth and held it for a moment, then shut her eyes and swallowed it down. She gagged. It felt like the mucus sliding down her throat when she warmed up to sing. Her eyes watered, and a burst of saliva stung her jaw.

"Here," the voice was saying, and she felt a napkin brush against her mouth. She looked up at Antonia's brother Claudio. "I suppose it is a bit of a shock that people eat something that ugly," he said.

"And it tastes ugly too," Chiaretta said. "I'm sorry. I guess that wasn't very polite."

"But honest," he said, looking at her as if he wanted to say something more. But the woman on his other side was speaking to him. He excused himself and turned to her.

The soup was being served, and though it was delicious, with tiny bits of meat and vegetables, Chiaretta's mood grew even more glum. A bowl of broth and the disgusting lump in her stomach were not what she had been expecting.

And then the bowls were cleared, and the servants were bringing out one platter after another—pheasant, calves' liver, veal— coming back again and again to ask if she wanted more of this or that, putting colorful mounds of vegetables on her plate, pouring one sauce over one dish and another over something else.

She ate until the food stopped coming, finishing one last bite as Bernardo Morosini rose to his feet. "We have a sweet for you," he said, "but I propose that we save that for later and adjourn now to the other end of the portego. I, for one, have waited far too long to hear our guests perform. If that is acceptable to you?" He gave a perfunctory look around the table, but the guests were already pushing out their chairs.

Claudio was among the first to get up. "Signorina," he said, pulling out Chiaretta's chair. She wanted to feel dainty as she rose and thanked him, but her stomach felt as big as her head. She felt a burp making its way up her chest, but fortunately Claudio had already gone to assist someone else, and it escaped unheard into her hands.

The figlie were gathering, and she and Antonia went to join them. Singing with such a full stomach was not as pleasant as Chiaretta had thought it might be. She felt a little sleepy and was afraid to take in too deep a breath for fear it might explode out of her in a belch. But the music sounded so rich and different echoing off the marble floors than it did from the balcony of the chapel, and the looks on the guests' faces were so approving that within minutes she felt her voice radiating from her, like the heat from a coal.

The time for the surprise had arrived. Antonia had told the maestra what her father's favorite songs were, and the maestra had chosen one that was not too bawdy for the figlie to sing.

After a short introduction on the lute, Chiaretta began her solo.

I saw a dove come from the sky,
And swoop down into my garden
Over its breast two wings were folded
And in its mouth a blossom . . .

Antonia and the rest of the figlie joined in, their voices filling the portego.

Would you like to smell the scent of love?
Its fragrance so grand from a flower so small.

Antonia's father dabbed at his eyes when the girls finished. Chiaretta looked around, dazed by the sound of applause. She tried to to see if Claudio was clapping, but she couldn't find him, and her glance fell instead upon Antonia's intended. In his eyes she saw a different look, a hooded expression she did not understand. Without knowing why, she became aware of the handkerchiefs pressing against her ribs. She averted her eyes and didn't look up again until the applause had stopped.

Night was falling when the figlie di coro descended the stairs and boarded the gondola for home. Several of the guests accompanied them back, among them Claudio and Antonia's intended. The men sat in the open air while the girls clustered inside the felce, shivering from the damp.

Chiaretta was too tired to talk, so she leaned her head on another girl's shoulder and listened to the chatter. Shutting her eyes, she returned to thoughts of being the queen of a house like that, of having a husband who was a younger version of Antonia's father, so kind and generous. She would have pearls in her hair and blossoms tucked in her bosom . . .

She must have drifted off to sleep, because the next thing she noticed was the bump of the gondola against the dock. When she left the felce, she saw that the men who had escorted them had donned black capes and hats, and their faces were covered with white masks. Claudio was on the dock, still holding his mask in his hand as he directed the gondoliers to return without them.

As Chiaretta stepped over the railing to get off the gondola, one of the masked men took her hand. When he lifted her up, she felt his hand slip under her petticoat and brush the back of her knee, his fingers traveling up the inside of her thigh almost to the top. Startled, she wriggled away from his hand and did not turn around until she was on the dock. She looked back at him and saw the red doublet peeking out from under his cape and the gold trim of a black pouch reflecting in the torchlight.

EIGHT

CHIARETTA TOLD NO ONE, NOT EVEN MADDALENA, WHAT the man had done. The next few times Antonia came for a lesson she avoided her, feeling somehow to blame for what had happened. As the months passed, the incident faded from her mind. And then, the subject of his marriage to Antonia was abruptly closed. Her father had been angry and her mother upset, but Antonia was told only that the details were not suitable for a young girl to hear.

Chiaretta breathed a sigh of relief when she learned Antonia was not to marry him. The mocking, frozen grin on the white mask came into her mind from time to time, unbidden, as if to say that with such cover no one would ever be guilty of anything, and that silence would be the price of maintaining her own modesty.

SOON CHIARETTA WAS CAUGHT UP IN THE PREPARATIONS FOR an oratorio the figlie had been told might be Francesco Gasparini's last for the Pietà.

"Is he dying?" Chiaretta asked the girl standing next to her. She had laid eyes on the Maestro di Coro only two or three times because his fame was such that he usually appeared only to rehearse and conduct premieres of his new works. Still, something about the way everyone's voice changed when his name came up made him seem almost as important as the doge.

"No, they say he's retiring," the girl replied.

"Again," snickered an older figlia beside her.

Chiaretta had not been in on the joke, but Anna Maria was. "No one is very happy with him anymore," she told Maddalena and Chiaretta later. "They say he's supposed to be here more often, and the music he sends is a lot of rearrangements, nothing original."

"How do you know so much?" Maddalena asked.

"I just stand near the maestre, and I hear things."

Chiaretta thought for a moment. "I heard one of the maestre say something like 'not this again,' when she was looking at some music, but I assumed I had heard wrong."

"Which one?"

"Fioruccia."

"Well of course," Anna Maria said. "She hates Gasparini. Well, maybe not hates. She's always praying every time I see her outside the sala, so I guess she's not supposed to hate anybody. But I heard her talking to one of the other maestre about how he was taking whores' music—"

"What?" Chiaretta and Maddalena gasped in unison.

"He puts Latin words to melodies he writes for opera singers, and then we sing them. She said people in the audience recognize the music and imagine love scenes while we're singing about God. Like that duet of the Gloria last week—"

"I loved that!" said Chiaretta. "I wish it had been my solo."

"Of course you do." Anna Maria reached up and pulled Chiaretta's cap down over her eyes. "Little 'greedy for attention'! But I guess that was her point. Fancy enough to make us prideful. You know—the kind of music the Virgin doesn't want to hear."

HOW COULD THE VIRGIN NOT WANT TO HEAR HER SING HER best? Chiaretta wondered. Still, she supposed that with the amount Fioruccia prayed she might know more about what made the people in heaven unhappy. Chiaretta started praying with a little more fervor before a statue of the Virgin in an alcove off one of the walkways. Watching Mary's face for a sign of disapproval, after a few weeks she concluded that her stone eyes had softened. Chiaretta interpreted this to mean that the Virgin might allow a little room for her high notes and trills as long as she didn't forget to pray afterward. Still, after each of her performances she cast a furtive look around to make sure she didn't have to pass too close to Fioruccia.

Maddalena gave Fioruccia no further thought, especially when the Congregazione hired Vivaldi as a composer to make up the shortfall in Gasparini's music. Maddalena worried about his haggard appearance and his constant wheeze during her lessons, but he reassured her he had never felt better in his life.

"Perhaps you will be the next Gasparini," she said one afternoon.

Vivaldi shook his head. "It will never happen. There has never been a Maestro di Coro at any of the ospedali who doesn't play the organ. And besides, I'm not sure I would want the job."

"Why not?"

"For the same reason Gasparini seems to be losing interest. It's difficult to spend so much energy on students who have no future."

"No future? What do you mean? The Pietà will always be here."

"But not you, not your sister, not Anna Maria." He sighed.

"Maddalena, think about it. A girl learns to sing or play so beautifully that the whole city is at her feet. She performs for a few years, and then she gives way so those she has taught can have their turn. Or she enters a convent, where the church officials go back and forth on the issue of whether music is corrupting or ennobling for women to hear. So some years she plays music and others she doesn't, or more likely she skulks around doing it on the sly and feeling like a sinner."

Maddalena thought for a moment. "Chiaretta wants to be an opera singer. What about that?"

Vivaldi laughed. "She can forget it."

"Why? Isn't she good enough?"

His eyes grew distant, as if he were remembering Chiaretta's voice. "No," he said. "That's not it. Your sister was born to sing opera." He stood up and walked to the window, thinking for a minute before turning back to her. "You know, there's money in opera, and I'm a priest without a parish. I can't live on the money I make giving violin lessons. This place"— he swept his arm in all directions to indicate the Pietà—"loves its music and starves its composers."

He sat down again and rubbed his brow, squeezing his eyes shut.

"Are you . . . in pain? Do you need me to do something?"

"No. I was just thinking about the opera singers I work with. I would give anything to have someone like Chiaretta. It's not just her voice or how pretty she is. She has such a sense of drama, such a spirit . . ."

Maddalena was confused. "Well then . . . ?"

"The Pietà would never allow it." He sliced his hand through the air in front of him as if he were chopping it in half. "Never. The putte are angels. Virgin angels. Without that, they're just musicians. The balcony says, 'Here stand women who have the special protection of God.' So do you think the Congregazione would ever allow the perception that the figlie are in training to become painted women who lounge in gondolas and gamble at the Ridotto?"

Maddalena looked at her folded hands in her lap and said nothing.

"For most men, what you can't be is far more exciting than what you can." His voice was almost a whisper.

Maddalena's heart was too heavy to try to think about what he meant. "She can marry," she threw out in a tone that admitted defeat.

"Yes, that's true. But did you know that husbands must sign an oath that any bride coming from one of the ospedali will never sing or play an instrument outside her home? And that he also has to post a very large bond, which he forfeits if she does? So some lucky child is sung to sleep by the best voice in Venice, and some husband is entertained by a lute or a harpsichord in his parlor, but that's all that comes from years of training."

Maddalena sat quietly, absorbing the message.

Vivaldi interrupted her grim thoughts. "Surely you don't think the musical education you receive is strictly for the glory of God."

"No," she said, surprised by the quiver in her voice. "They tell us that, but we know it's also to make us more marriageable."

"And it does. But most of you do not marry, is that not right?"

Over her years in the Pietà, Maddalena had seen more figlie end up in convents than anywhere else.

"Well, isn't it?" he demanded. She nodded her head.

"Cara, perhaps I am being too cynical, and perhaps I should say nothing more, but I think you don't understand what the Pietà is all about."

Cara? Maddalena tried to focus on what he was saying, but her heart was racing at having been called "dear."

"What are there now—eight hundred, a thousand girls at the Pietà, not even counting the patients in the hospital? Can you imagine how much it costs to put even a tiny fire in what—a hundred rooms perhaps? Bread and a little soup in every stomach? The Congregazione is not out for profit overall, but that doesn't mean they don't try to make money wherever they can. They're not fools. You appear behind a grille to drive the audience to distraction. You're not nuns, so you can be bought by marriage, or at least borrowed to entertain at their parties. There's no more delicious fantasy in Venice than having one of you for their own, and those who can afford it pay dearly for the privilege of your company for even an hour. Without you, the Pietà would be insolvent. No question about it."

"You make it sound so calculating, like we're nothing more than"—she struggled for a word—"cattle."

"No, no. It's not like that. I think you are using each other." He smiled. "Where would Maddalena Rossa be without the Pietà?"

Where would I be? Maddalena could not form even one clear thought.

Vivaldi filled the silence. "It's terrible to be born to do something you will never be permitted to do. Especially while you watch yourself go through life doing something else." He paused, then added, almost whispering, "I know. Believe me, I know."

❧❧❧

VIVALDI'S NEW TITLE OF MAESTRO DEI CONCERTI BROUGHT little power over the tight-knit world of maestre and coro. Figlie worked their way up, advancing by auditions from third to second to first chair, and no exceptions would be made for someone just because an outsider—especially one who might only be passing through—wished it to be so.

But Vivaldi had another idea. At one of their lessons he handed Maddalena some sheet music, jiggling with impatience as she leafed through it.

"A concerto in F major," she said. "But with five movements instead of three?"

"There are three, with bridges between them," he said. "Play the second bridge. It's the one marked 'adagio.'"

She stared at the music, still unable to understand what she was seeing. The first and second violins were playing an ostinato, no more than a simple repeated phrase.

"Play the third violin part," Vivaldi said. "I'll play the first." At the beginning her notes conformed to those he was playing, but at the end of each phrase, her part floated up and down in graceful arcs and flutters.

It was less than a minute long, and they played it again and again. Maddalena lingered on each note before linking it to the next, not lifting her fingers for fear the music might slip from her grasp.

"Like falling leaves," she said when she finished.

"Or snowflakes." He smiled. "I wrote the third violin part just for you, Maddalena Rossa. For my little poet. You're struggling for your place in the coro today, but when you're older, you'll be the one they'll ask to stay on for life, if that's what you want."

"I want to be here if you are." The music still hovered in her mind and made her voice distant and dreamy.

He looked away from her, and his expression clouded. "I can't promise that, and besides, you will become the teacher and won't need me."

"I can't imagine that."

He looked at her quizzically. "Little one, I'm not leaving tomorrow. But you know, the Congregazione's views are quite mercenary, and if they think they have a good backlog of music and adequately trained violinists, they may feel they can do without me, at least for a while."

The feeling of bliss the music had brought her was gone in an instant. Maddalena toyed with her fingers, trying to will away the sudden fear that had made her heart pound. *The Congregazione may be able to do without him, but I don't think I can.*

"What are you thinking?" Vivaldi's voice had softened almost to a whisper.

"That I don't know what I'd do if you left," she blurted out. *Don't say any more,* she told herself. *Don't sound like a foolish little girl.* "But you're the Maestro dei Concerti now," she said finally. "Doesn't that mean anything?"

"Just a title, and all the more reason to get rid of me, because they have to pay me more. And of course, if and when Gasparini returns, I may seem a real extravagance."

He reached out and took her hand. "I've upset you."

Maddalena nodded and bit her lip to keep it from trembling. She could hear him breathing, but he said nothing, and she was afraid to meet his eyes.

"You must hear me, Maddalena Rossa," he said, breaking the silence. "I don't control what the Congregazione does, but as long as I am here you will always be protected."

Vivaldi was still holding one of her hands. Bending her head, she put the other hand on her forehead to keep him from seeing her tears. "No one but Chiaretta and Anna Maria really care about me," she said. "I mean, other than you."

"I do care," he said. "Perhaps more than you know." He had moved his chair closer and reached out an arm to bring her toward him. She buried her face in his chest, and much as she wanted to control the noisy intakes of air and heaving shoulders that would tell him she was crying, she could not. She felt his lips press against the back of her neck, once and then a second time.

The shock stopped her tears. Only the circles of hot breath on his shirt told her she hadn't stopped breathing altogether. She wanted to lift her face, but terrified of having it so close to his, she stayed rigid against his chest.

"Had enough of crying?" he asked, pulling away.

"I think so," Maddalena said. She was looking at him now, seeing his eyes move in small darts over her face as he took in its details. Self-conscious, she wiped her wet cheeks with her fingers.

His mouth moved to within an inch or two of hers, and she felt a sweet wrenching in her stomach that traveled all the way up to her throat.

He pulled back. "No," he said. "I'm sorry." He stood up and, crossing himself quickly, murmured something under his breath.

She felt as if her insides were being torn out, as if they were somehow connected to him and she could not have them back until he held her again and kissed her. *He's a priest,* she told herself, making a quick sign of the cross. "Hail, Mary, full of grace," she whispered. "The Lord is with thee . . ."

She felt suddenly aware of her body under her uniform. *I'm a woman,* she thought, *not a little girl.* "Mother of God, pray for us sinners," she murmured with an urgency she had never felt before. *It's a sin even to want to kiss him, but I do.* "Now and at the hour of our death. Amen."

She looked up when she had finished her prayer, but he was watching her so intently she had to look away and begin the prayer again, this time silently in her head, just to keep her thoughts from straying.

He picked up his violin and put it in its case. For a moment she envisioned running from the Pietà with him, running from Venice, living with him as man and woman. She put her head in her hands to stop the ideas that were spinning it in circles.

He snapped the case shut. "Please forgive me, but I shouldn't stay even a moment longer."

Maddalena felt her body close in on itself again. "Please stay," she said, grasping for a reason that would appear sensible. "We haven't practiced the concerto nearly enough." Seeing the bewildered look on his face, she added, "The one you wrote for me."

The wheeze in his breathing was growing louder. "Perhaps that was a mistake." His voice was almost inaudible and his eyes were averted, and Maddalena was not sure whether he had meant her to hear what he said. "You practice without me," he replied, hurrying from the room.

MADDALENA STAYED WHERE SHE WAS, GOING OVER IN HER mind what had just occurred, focusing first on this detail and then on that one, until she reached a point where she wasn't sure what had happened at all.

Her first kiss would be a momentous event, but since it hadn't occurred, she didn't know what to think. "Nothing happened," she said out loud, but she didn't believe it. Even the furniture in the sala looked different. And if it were just an ordinary moment for Vivaldi, why did he suddenly start to wheeze, and why did he run away?

She played around with the idea that he wanted her in the way she vaguely understood men wanted women. Perhaps he felt something similar to the brief sensations that had stirred in her own body and knew better what to make of them and how to react than she did. She wasn't sure she wanted anything like that to happen again, it had so thoroughly confused her. But remembering the sweet rising up of something she had not even sensed was alive inside her, she knew she would not turn away a chance to feel it again.

Something big had happened, she concluded, even if she hadn't been kissed. And when anything happened, her first thought was to share it with her sister. Maddalena put her violin case back in the cabinet. She wouldn't see Chiaretta for several hours, and that would give her time to figure out what to say.

As she walked back toward the lace room, she stopped for a moment at a shrine tucked into a corner of one of the hallways. The painted image of Mary holding the infant Jesus looked out at her. Maddalena fixed her attention on those eyes, hoping she might read some kind of message in them. The Madonna stared back.

Is she angry with me? Does she think I did something only bad women do? The idea was so odd it would have made her laugh, if sin were not such a serious matter.

"I'm sorry," she whispered. "I had thoughts I shouldn't have. I won't have them again."

But before she reached the lace room, she stopped in the hallway to conjure up once again the feeling of Vivaldi's lips on her neck and the warmth of his breath on her face.

By the time she saw her sister that evening, Maddalena had decided to tell her nothing. The statue of Mary had offered no reassurance, and she feared Chiaretta's reaction might make her feel worse, and even more confused.

I've always told Chiaretta everything really important, Maddalena thought. *If we didn't know each other's secrets, we'd be like everybody else.* All the way back to the ward, Maddalena rationalized her decision to keep her first big secret from her sister. After all, in the end, what was there to tell? What kind of a story was there in not being kissed?

MADDALENA SOON LEARNED HOW HARD KEEPING ANYTHING from Chiaretta could be. Perhaps she mentioned Vivaldi too much in the next week or so, or perhaps too little, but her sister sensed something was different.

One afternoon, Maddalena and Anna Maria went to the sala dal violino to practice in their free time, and Chiaretta tagged along. When Maddalena commented that Vivaldi had more trouble breathing when the windows were closed and the fires were lit, she thought she had kept her tone casual, even indifferent, but Chiaretta leapt on her words.

"You're like his mother!" she said. "No—no—you're like his wife!"

"I am not!" Maddalena retorted a bit too sharply. Chiaretta puckered her lips and made kissing noises into the air.

"You're being horrid!" Maddalena said.

Chiaretta raised her eyebrows, as if she realized she had stumbled upon something interesting. "Well?" she said, curving her voice upward.

"Well what?" Maddalena growled. "All I did was make a simple comment, and you're turning it into something awful, like I was—" She couldn't finish.

"Like you were kissing in the practice room?" Chiaretta rarely kept teasing her sister when she could see she had hit a nerve, but for some reason she hadn't been able to stop.

Maddalena turned scarlet. "How—" she started to say. *How did you know?* She saw Anna Maria's and Chiaretta's huge eyes and hands clamped to their mouths and realized they didn't know a thing.

"Oh dear," Chiaretta said. "Was it bad what I said?"

"No. I just wish you knew a little better when to shut your mouth." Maddalena's voice was clipped, and even though she saw that the harshness of her tone had hurt her sister's feelings, for once she didn't rush to apologize.

"I'm sorry," Chiaretta said. "I didn't mean—"

Maddalena's color was returning to normal, but Chiaretta could see she was avoiding looking at her. Something had happened, and Chiaretta had to know what it was. "He didn't, did he?" she asked.

Maddalena's eyes glinted with anger. "No!" she hissed, glad it was the truth.

❦❦❦

"WHAT IS THIS?" PELLEGRINA, THE FIRST VIOLINIST SAID, pointing to the music. "Why don't you get a beginner to play it?"

Luciana shrugged. "Maestro Vivaldi has written it this way, and this is the way we will play it."

Maddalena raised her glance from the floor at the sharpness in the maestra's voice ordering Pellegrina to stop complaining and play. Pellegrina was even more unhappy at the end of the first run-through. She began sawing at her violin with her eyes crossed. "There must be some mistake," she whined. "When is Maestro Gasparini coming back?"

Pellegrina was showing willfulness and vanity, two traits that could be best controlled in the coro by making an example of someone from time to time. Her face turned pale as Luciana walked toward her. Everyone froze. Luciana was retiring in about a week and might want to leave a parting legacy. She yanked the lace cap and hood from Pellegrina's head and gripped her hair. The figlie recognized the gesture and held their breath.

Before Luciana could make a move, Pellegrina had begun to blubber her apologies. Then a male voice was heard clearing his throat in the doorway.

"Maestro Vivaldi!" one of the girls said.

"It goes like this," Vivaldi said, yanking Pellegrina's instrument out of her hands. He drew his bow across the strings in a way that freed every note, filling it with the wistfulness and regret Pellegrina had been uninterested in hearing. His face was in profile from where Maddalena was sitting, and she could not stop looking at him. When his eyes shut, savoring something hidden deep in the music, Maddalena felt she was the only person in the world who could hear it too.

Vivaldi had canceled her last lesson, and she had not seen him since the afternoon when he almost kissed her. He looked only at Pellegrina when he came in, and Maddalena was not sure he knew she was there. But how could he not sense her presence, when the space between them felt as charged as the air just before a lightning strike?

Maddalena's violin felt glued to her lap, but the other figlie had picked up their instruments and were now playing along with the maestro. Finally hers moved into place of its own accord, and her bow began to ride across the strings. They were reaching the point where her first solo would begin, and Maddalena felt her heart rise. Her first notes would be a greeting to him, she thought, and he would turn and smile as he watched her play. But suddenly, Vivaldi took his bow from the strings, and within a few notes the sala had gone quiet again.

"Do you think you can manage?" he growled, handing the violin back to Pellegrina without looking in Maddalena's direction.

"Yes, sir," Pellegrina said, and though her eyes glittered with rage, her pale cheeks showed the relief of having been spared the scissors and the shame.

"Good," he replied and stalked from the room.

MADDALENA AND CHIARETTA WATCHED THROUGH A WINDOW as snow fell between the roofs of the building into the alley alongside the Pietà. Christmas Day had been bright and warm, but in the last few days a cold wind had blown in, bringing snow behind it.

The maestra clapped her hands for the figlie to take their places on the balcony. Below them people stomped their feet to remove the dirty slush from their shoes, scraped rented scagni against the stone floor, and rustled their programs.

Maddalena stood at the rail, taking in the scene before sitting down in her new position as third violin. A commotion arose surrounding a man in a Carnevale mask who had just entered the church. A servant was brushing the snow from his cape, and a place was being vacated for him in the best viewing spot in the chapel.

Vivaldi was not on the balcony, having no solo until the concert after the mass, and when he showed up unexpected, he was trembling.

"Do you know who that is?" he asked the sotto maestra, who was standing far enough away from Maddalena for his question to be almost inaudible. "The King of Denmark. He's traveling incognito, and he's come to hear us."

Vivaldi left as quickly as he had come, and within a few minutes Maddalena watched from the balcony as he approached the king's entourage. She already knew today would be out of the ordinary because she would have her first solo, but suddenly it had grown into more than she could have imagined. She was looking at the King of Denmark, and at her mentor nodding and bowing next to him.

Maddalena smiled. He was thrilled, no doubt, but she had no trouble reading what else was on his mind. Even while Vivaldi was saying words of greeting, he was certainly also calculating how much music he could have ready to sell to the king in a few days' time. Maddalena wondered if she could make herself be on his mind as well. Staring at him, she willed him to look up at her, but instead of responding, he shifted his weight in a way that turned his back to the balcony and to her. She felt a pang of rejection just as she had the day of Pellegrina's chastisement, when he had stormed from the room without acknowledging her.

She had been so deeply hurt that she had not even wanted to come to her next lesson. He was nervous when she came in, and it took him a few minutes to recognize that she too was not acting like herself. They had played little music that day, losing track of time as they sat and talked. He hadn't meant to hurt her feelings. In fact, he thought he was being sensitive to her by ignoring her, trying to show her that he was going to be completely professional from then on, and that she wouldn't need to worry about what he might do. He explained that he had abruptly stopped before her solo because, when he realized it was coming up, he thought she might not want to play it after all that had occurred. "But I knew you were there," he had told her. "Believe me, I know when you're in a room."

He cared about her—she knew he did—and he was acting in their best interests. He was a priest, and she was a cloistered young woman. To keep what they had, they had to be perceived as having nothing. He would certainly lose position if anyone knew he had kissed a figlia di coro. If he lost his position, they would lose the chance not just to play their violins together but to talk, which was just as important. Since then Maddalena had shifted her thinking, deciding that not being treated as special was one of the ways he told her she really was.

She was his muse—he had hinted as much—but nonetheless, the bond between them could never be revealed in public, and would have to be sustained when they were alone by only the most subtle of means—a tenderness in the voice, a smile, a touch that lingered when he corrected her technique. These moments had become charged with an excruciating delicacy and depth for Maddalena because they were all she had.

"Here I am," she whispered from the balcony as Vivaldi conversed with the king. "Look up."

Vivaldi turned his body, gesturing in the direction of the balcony. He was pointing to various places, as if describing to the king the arrangement of the coro, and Maddalena thought, although she could not be sure, that his finger had rested, if only for a fleeting moment, directly on her.

Did I make him do that? Vivaldi was still talking to the king, but he turned away from the balcony and she could no longer see his face.

The coro had by now come out, and Maddalena moved away from the railing to take her place. She tried to lose herself in the music, but her upcoming solo loomed before her, making her enter so early on a few bars that Pellegrina scowled at her and stuck out her tongue when the violins rested.

And then the moment arrived. She needn't have feared. As if

hypnotized, her hand caressed the bow and stroked the strings, and though a third violinist probably went unnoticed by the audience, she played the adagio Vivaldi had written for her as if all the heartaches in human history were contained in it. Then she and the others broke into the final bright movement, as if grief could be shrugged off because life, in the end, is so good.

And it was. She grabbed Chiaretta's hand and squeezed it as they left the balcony.

THE FIGLIE BUZZED WITH EXCITEMENT AS THE PRIORA WAVED them down a narrow hallway and through an open door connecting the parlatorio and the cloister. "I'm going to meet a king!" Chiaretta whispered to herself in disbelief.

On the figlie's side of the grille dividing the room was a row of benches, while on the other side, the king and his retinue were seated in chairs near the fire. The coro hung back, watching the king get up to greet the priora at the grille.

"Such a curious custom," he said, gesturing to the wrought-iron barrier. "We can see them, but we cannot move among them?"

"No, Your Majesty," she said. "Not at the moment. It is our way. But if you would like something more intimate, we have a small sala for private concerts, and I'm sure one could be arranged."

Vivaldi entered the parlatorio on the public side, and the king turned to him and applauded. "Bravo! The reputation of the Pietà is most decidedly deserved. A feast for the ears and the eyes," he said, looking back again at the figlie.

The king's tone was stiff, and whether he truly appreciated the music was impossible to tell, but it didn't matter. He was still a king, standing almost close enough to touch. Vivaldi asked first the singers and then the orchestra to come to the grille. The king stretched out his hand and swept it in a long wave in front of him as his eyes passed over each one of them in turn. *"Bravissime,"* he said. "I think that is your word?"

Vivaldi nodded and looked over at the performers. His glance rested for a moment on Maddalena, and he gave her an almost imperceptible nod before looking back at the king. She looked away, but Chiaretta touched Maddalena's shoulder from behind, to let her know that she too had noticed.

THE PRIORA'S QUICK ASSURANCE THAT THE KING COULD HAVE a private concert proved to be a dilemma for the Nobili Uomini Deputati, who had arranged for a potential new donor to have the figlie perform at a party at his home on the sole night the king was available. Denmark was far away and the king had made no mention of payment, so the Congregazione had agreed that changing the plan was imprudent.

To put the most expedient face on the situation, the Nobili Uomini Deputati informed the king that he would have the pleasure of hearing a special performance by the Pietà's great prodigy Anna Maria, along with the noted sisters Maddalena and Chiaretta, who at sixteen and thirteen were upcoming stars. One of the greatest musicians of her time, Maestra Luciana, would also come out of retirement for the concert in his honor. Chiaretta would perform all the vocals, Maddalena would play the violin, and Anna Maria would play whatever else was needed. They had three days to prepare.

A list was drawn up of Gasparini's works that were familiar enough to Luciana to require no more than a quick review in her chambers. Maddalena, Chiaretta, and Anna Maria were excused from other work, and even from chapel prayers, to practice.

Vivaldi was beside himself when he saw the program. "What good does it do me if the king hears Gasparini's music?"

"The music is nice, even if it's not yours," Maddalena offered, "and on such short notice it's understandable."

"Understandable?" Vivaldi snorted. "That's not the point.

A nice concert doesn't pay the rent." He threw some sheet music toward the credenza in the practice room. Most of it spilled onto the floor, and Vivaldi grabbed his hair in his hands. "Aahh! *In te, Domine, speravi, non confundar in aeternum*," he said under his breath as he bent over, still praying, and gathered the strewn papers.

Ignoring him, Maddalena put in order the pages of what she saw was a Nisi Dominus for contralto and orchestra. She began to hum the opening bars, and within seconds he was standing next to her, grabbing the music.

"Do you think you could do this if I rewrote it for you? One violin instead of an orchestra, a soprano not a contralto, and Anna Maria on continuo? The cello—yes, that's good, that's good," he said, without waiting for her response.

By the next morning he had rewritten the whole motet and came to the room where the three girls were rehearsing, spending only a few minutes with them before rushing out again. "I have to go home and start writing," he said. "If I get a commission, I must be ready. I've heard the king is not staying long."

SKEPTICISM HAD BEEN WRITTEN ON MADDALENA'S PALE FACE before Vivaldi arrived and remained after he left.

"It's for a king!" Chiaretta crowed. "Why aren't you more excited?"

The king was not the one on Maddalena's mind. Luciana, with whom she would be playing one of Gasparini's duets, still had the ability to scramble Maddalena's nerves.

"You can show her how good you are now," Chiaretta said. "She's just a devil from hell. Remember?"

Anna Maria was not in on the joke but chimed in. "She's an ugly old witch, and you can play as well as she can now," she said, looking at them with her serious, stark eyes.

Maddalena picked up her violin. "I guess we'll see." Chiaretta and Anna Maria applauded.

THE THREE OF THEM HAD LITTLE TIME TO REHEARSE VIVALDI'S pieces because they had been so intent on preparing Maddalena for her performance with Luciana. Maddalena worried privately about not being ready but said nothing. In the last year or so, Chiaretta had developed a way of looking aside, or even just shifting her weight, and Maddalena would know something was bothering her. She could say "Hmm," in a particular tone, and Maddalena would feel her distaste, especially when they talked about Vivaldi. Though her relationship with her sister was still close and fiercely loyal, it had suffered a little since the day in the sala dal violino, when Chiaretta had sensed that Maddalena was not telling her everything about whether Vivaldi had kissed her.

As a result, any mention of the maestro elicited Chiaretta's full range of disapproving responses. Chiaretta would never believe Maddalena was concerned about rehearsing Vivaldi's pieces only because she wanted to play them well. She believed her sister was fretting about a man—and worse, a man she could never have. It was best, Maddalena decided, not even to mention his name.

ON THE DAY OF THE PERFORMANCE, LUCIANA HEAVED HER BODY up the stairs a few steps behind Maddalena, filling the stairwell with the sound of her labored breathing. When they reached the top of the stairs, they found themselves in a space scarcely wider than a window ledge, one that could accommodate a handful of musicians only if they remained standing throughout the performance. Luciana grunted and fell into the chair that had been provided for her despite the cramped quarters, while the two sisters and Anna Maria peered through the gauze down into the sala.

Gilded cherubs with mischievous grins on their faces held aside the thick brocade curtains of the room below. Scattered on a floor of polished stone were armchairs with soft velvet seats that looked so comfortable Maddalena was not surprised the king had already begun to slouch in one of them. Vivaldi and a member of the king's retinue spoke in a corner. More stucco cherubs played musical instruments as they looked down on the guests from the four corners of the ceiling.

Maddalena felt her heart skip when she saw Vivaldi, out of sudden fear her playing would let him down. Nothing remained, however, but to push on and hope for the best. When the five of them were settled, she lifted her violin and led into Chiaretta's first solo with a three-note gallop, answered by Anna Maria's insistent two-note ostinato on the cello.

"Nisi, nisi Dominus," Chiaretta began, and the music flowed. As Chiaretta moved into the next section, the three girls exchanged grins about the words she was singing. It was futile to get up before daybreak, the psalmist had said, a sentiment that had broken them up with laughter in rehearsal, since they had been getting up before dawn every day of their lives. *"Surgite, surgite."* Chiaretta's voice jumped with excitement, calling on the world to get up, with the urgency of someone who has gotten out of bed to find the house on fire.

Maddalena and Anna Maria's accompaniment was so tight and smooth that it did not occur to Chiaretta to do anything but try to fill the sala with her voice. The small size of the room amplified the music, and she was lost in what felt like an envelope of sound. Near the end of the motet, she cast a glance over to her sister and saw something so unexpected she gasped and had to improvise a few notes to get back in control of the music.

Luciana was hovering over Maddalena, turning the pages of her music. She had seen her struggling and, without a word, had pulled herself to her feet to help her. Chiaretta looked over at Anna Maria, who let her jaw go slack to signal her astonishment.

Luciana sat back down for the rest of the concert, and the violins and cello played one of Gasparini's compositions. Maddalena kept her eyes averted during the first movement, but in the most difficult section, she looked up to work with her partner, just as Vivaldi had taught her, and saw Luciana already watching her. Later, when she looked again, Luciana had shut her eyes, and her face had softened in a way Maddalena had never seen. *This must be what she was like when she was young,* Maddalena thought. *She had a heart then too.*

As applause rang out from below, Maddalena felt suddenly shy, breaking the silence between them with the only words she could think of. "Thank you."

"No. Thank you," Luciana said, but in the dim light Maddalena could not read her expression. The old maestra turned to ask Anna Maria to help her to her room, and without another word, she was gone.

❦❦❦

MADDALENA HUMMED AS SHE AND HER SISTER PUT ON THEIR shoes to go down to the rehearsal room after the midday rest. Chiaretta felt some of the same contentment seep into her, as if she could curl back up in bed and start purring like the stray cats that found their way into the courtyards of the Pietà and rubbed up against the leg of one figlia after another.

Maddalena's high spirits had not diminished in the two gloomy months since the king's visit. She and Chiaretta had several performances a week during the Carnevale season, many of them at lavish parties away from the Pietà. Vivaldi had gotten his commission from the king. His operas were profitable, and the only problem was that they were keeping him so busy he often had to cancel her lessons. Nevertheless, she felt closer than ever to him after the success of the king's special concert, a victory he had told her she was in large part responsible for. So close, she sensed him standing behind her chair every time she performed.

Maddalena and Chiaretta got to the practice room early enough to look out onto the Riva degli Schiavoni and watch the passing spectacle of Carnevale. Below them, mummers and acrobatic clowns ingratiated themselves to masked men in black cloaks. Ladies, disguised under glittering masks with the faces of cats or birds or mythical creatures, paraded in feathers and jewels. Hawkers sold cakes, lemons, toys, flowers, and elixirs for every ailment.

Beyond the din of their voices, the sound of bagpipes and drums mingled with the calls of the merchants in their stalls spilling off the Broglio and down the Riva toward the Pietà. Back and forth on the Grand Canal a steady procession of gondolas took one boatload of revelers to the docks of San Marco and came back with another. Men lay with their legs sprawled over women in the bottoms of gondolas. Others stood urinating in great dramatic arcs into the lagoon, held by their knees to keep them from toppling into the water. Women threw confetti and flowers, while men on unsteady legs launched empty flasks of wine into the canal. Flat-bottomed boats filled with musicians traveled up and down, their music floating up to the windows along the waterways.

For the residents of the Pietà, there would be no venturing onto the streets except under close guard to and from special appearances, such as a magnificent annual concert that would take place in the doge's chambers in a few days' time. Maddalena and Chiaretta went to take their places with the other members of the coro awaiting the beginning of the final rehearsal. The windows were closed against the cold, but the pop of fireworks and the loud voices of people on the street could still be heard.

Maestro Vivaldi had not arrived. After twenty minutes of waiting, the figlie drifted away to look out the window or began playing their own parts in their seats. Then the door opened, and Prudenzia, the new maestra dal violino, came in holding a piece of paper, which she put down on the music stand.

"Girls," she said. "Let's begin. I will lead you today."

For the next two hours, Maddalena watched the door, but Vivaldi did not come. Finally, Prudenzia dismissed them. She collected the music on her stand and placed it in a cabinet. "Make your devotion tomorrow morning and get dressed. We perform for the doge at midday." Her voice was clipped, and she left without saying anything else.

Maddalena sat back down, pretending to practice a difficult section while she waited for the others to leave. When she was alone, she went over to the cabinet and began leafing through the music to see if Prudenzia had left the paper behind.

She found it near the bottom of the pile, a small piece of folded paper signed by Bernardo Morosini, Antonia's father. "This is to notify you that Don Antonio Vivaldi has been relieved of his duties at the Pietà. Please prepare the girls for the doge's concert, as it will go on as scheduled."

Maddalena read the words again and again before sliding the note back in among the sheets of music. *He's gone. Just like that.* She put her hands over her face, squeezing her eyes shut until they hurt.

She moaned inadvertently. It echoed through the empty room, mingling with a woman's shrill laughter wafting up from the street. It sounded like two violins played with rough twigs instead of bows, the shrieks of the woman in the street and the screams inside her skull.

NINE

*M*ADDALENA GOT THROUGH THE DOGE'S CONCERT
by closing her eyes so she would not notice Vivaldi's absence.
Chiaretta was charming enough for both of them as they were in-
troduced to Alvise Mocenigo, the Doge of Venice, after which, begging a headache, Maddalena was able to escape back to the Pietà
before being stuck at a banquet table for hours.

Chiaretta sat down on the bed beside her sister when she returned, hoping the movement might rouse her. When Maddalena
did not budge, Chiaretta stood up with a sigh and went to find
someone else to help her take off her dress. Maddalena opened her
eyes to see if her sister was gone. For the first time since they had
come to the Pietà, she wanted her sister to go away, wanted everything to go away, wanted more than anything not to have to face
the world.

Chiaretta slipped back and lay down on her bed. Maddalena heard her burrowing into her pillow, rotating her shoulders and hips as her breathing turned heavy with sleep. Now almost fourteen, Chiaretta seemed to float from performance to performance with as little effort as it took for confetti to flutter through the air, but at that moment the heaviness over Maddalena was so profound she wondered how she would even be able to lift her bow at her next practice. Just a note from Vivaldi—even a few scribbled words—would have been enough. In her imagination she opened a letter with her name written in beautiful, large letters at the top. He would start by telling her of the sadness in his heart, then go on to say how vigorously he had fought to stay. He would close by telling her he would return, if for no other reason than that he was not complete unless he was playing music with her. For a moment Maddalena wasn't sure how he would sign it. "Your friend Vivaldi" was a possibility, or maybe just his initials.

No, she decided. He would sign it "Antonio."

Only two days had passed since she had read Prudenzia's note. Perhaps he was still in Venice and hadn't yet had time to write. That thought was enough to relax her muscles and quiet her mind. Pulling her blanket up and tucking it in around her neck to keep out the chill, she shut her eyes and fell asleep.

WHEN NO LETTER ARRIVED, MADDALENA RESIGNED HERSELF to the conclusion that Vivaldi had more important things to think about than her. He seemed not just to have been fired from the Pietà but to have vanished from Venice altogether. One day, when she overheard the maestre gossiping, she was sure she heard his name and thought they were casting their eyes over at her.

What were they whispering? Were they blaming her for his dismissal? Maybe they were discussing the violin bow, the dancing, the third violin solo, the special lessons—it could be so many things. Chiaretta had been right to frown when she talked about him. It did look improper. He was a priest, after all, and she was a young woman nearing seventeen.

And if his favoritism had cost him his job? The thought was so distressing to her that she could not bear to eat. She poked at the food on her plate and thought, *I have dinner, but does he?* Each morsel staring back at her seemed like a betrayal of him, and she could not swallow a single bite.

She could put her tumultuous feelings to rest only by telling herself it was for the best. Maybe she was wrong about ever having been important to him. She'd been a fool for thinking otherwise, but she was wiser now. Telling herself the subject was closed let her mind go blank, buying her a few moments of peace. But before she knew it, against her will, her mind was alive again.

What was it he had said? For there to be anything special between them it had to seem as if there was nothing between them at all? It made sense at the time, but looking back, she wondered, had he paid no attention to her because she was special, or because she really wasn't? Somewhere along the line he stopped caring about her, and she hadn't noticed because nothing changed in the way he acted. Since he gave her the third violin solo and then nearly kissed her, he had almost completely ignored her, despite how hard she tried to please him. *Chiaretta was right. I acted like a little wife, and he let me.*

As the months passed, she was less sure whether to resent him or be grateful for what he had offered, even for a short time. Sometimes these two emotions became one, and she despised him for giving her a taste of something he knew she would want more of, but not be able to have. Only the cruelest person in the world would do something like that. Unable to fall back asleep at night, she spun her questions and their changing answers over and over in her head in the hope that this time she would sit up and say "That's it!" and it really would be, and she wouldn't have to think anymore. But instead, with each retelling and reinterpretation, she sank deeper into gloom.

When Prudenzia suggested that Maddalena master a new instrument, she put her violin away without protest and threw herself into learning the cello. Its low and mournful notes dragged her body down until she could barely keep her head up, and she begged to be relieved of the string section altogether. *Maybe just getting through every day is enough of a goal,* she thought, remembering Silvia and the lifelessness of her lessons as she took to learning the recorder again.

Silvia the Rat. The nickname seemed so unkind now. For all her mincing ways with Luciana and all her inflated self-promotion, the obvious inadequacy of Silvia's talent had eventually caught up with her. Soon after Vivaldi's departure—for that was how Maddalena measured time—Silvia had been told that she would not be advancing any further in the coro and that a place had been found for her in a convent on the other side of the city. Maddalena had heard her cries echoing down the hallway.

"God, God, nothing but God," she had heard her screaming until a telltale cracking sound and wounded cry reverberated down the hall to indicate she had been slapped, and slapped hard, to make her stop. "I want to die!" were the last words Maddalena heard, before a door slammed and Silvia was left alone to contemplate her fate.

Maybe it's wisest not to care too much about anything, Maddalena thought. *Maybe music is just another thing it isn't safe to love.*

❦❦❦

BY THE TIME SHE WAS SEVENTEEN, MADDALENA HAD BECOME SO thin her bones protruded and her eyes grew dull. Chiaretta, at fourteen, was shorter than her sister but outweighed her by at least ten pounds. Melancholia had been the diagnosis of the hospital matron, who clucked over the color of Maddalena's urine and treated her with aloe and borage to purge her body of excess black bile.

Even her sister couldn't reach Maddalena. After a performance at the inauguration of Giovanni Corner as the new doge in 1709, Chiaretta tried to describe the crowd, the colors, the food, but she knew Maddalena wasn't listening. And Anna Maria was no longer in the bed next to theirs. Promoted early to sotto maestra when she turned twenty, she had moved off their ward some time before.

On the way to a concert, Chiaretta had seen the gondolier push aside a dead seagull with his oar. She had watched as its bedraggled body took the blow and then continued to bob in the crests and troughs of the canal. Something about the way Maddalena shrugged her shoulders chilled Chiaretta with a memory of that bird.

When the Congregazione offered her a chance to go with a group of figlie di coro to spend a week at a villa outside Venice on the Brenta Canal, Chiaretta turned it down.

"I don't want to leave you here alone," she wrote in her sketchbook.

"You should go if you want to," Maddalena wrote back. "You'll have Anna Maria for company."

"You don't care what I do?"

"Of course I care."

Chiaretta looked at her sister's listless reply, and impatience bubbled up through her concern. "I will then," she wrote. "You don't care about anything. You don't share even one thought with me anymore." Her face crumpled, and she began to cry. "You're scaring me," she added, handing the sketchbook to her sister.

Chiaretta's tears had always gotten Maddalena's attention. Now Maddalena realized she couldn't even remember the last time she had seen her sister cry. Still, she didn't have the energy to try to make the situation better between them. "You have your life and I have mine," she wrote. "Go live yours. Just leave me alone."

"But you don't have a life," Chiaretta whispered, not caring if the warden heard. "You don't even try. I don't remember what your smile looks like!"

"Well, that's just it," Maddalena whispered back. She leaned forward with her eyes wide open, shaking her head as if to convey that Chiaretta was missing something obvious. "This *is* my life. Look at that dried up apple Luciana. How old is she, and how many more years does she have to hobble around with those rotting tree trunks for legs? And Michielina, staggering around blind from copying scores in the dark?" Her voice had risen to the point where the warden hissed at her to be quiet.

She grabbed the book and drew a sketch of an old crone. Underneath it she wrote, "Maddalena—a few years from now."

She stood up and dusted off the front of her skirt as if she had someplace to go, then sat down again.

Chiaretta put the book away. "All right," she whispered. "If that's the way you want it." Her voice trailed off, leaving her ultimatum vague and incomplete.

CHIARETTA SPENT THE WEEK AT THE VILLA ON THE BRENTA Canal wishing it were over. The work was minimal—a short concert for their host and guests each evening—and each day yawned before her with nothing but endless hours to worry about her sister. Every evening at dinner she smiled, bending her neck and looking up through her lashes in a way she had been told made girls look attractively shy. After dinner, she willed herself to lose track of everything as she sang, and then after the concert, as soon as was polite, she begged leave of her hosts and went to bed. "Five more days," she would say as she lay in the dark. Then four, then three.

Anna Maria insisted on dragging her out every day, once for a walk along the towpath and another time for a boat ride on the canal. When they returned, Chiaretta forced a smile and told her friend how much better she was feeling. When two more days remained, Anna Maria arranged for them to take a carriage into the countryside for a picnic lunch. The stable hand driving them spread a blanket in the shade of a large tree next to a cherry orchard and laid out their meal of cold chicken, a square of soft white cheese, a loaf of bread, and a bottle of water to mix with a small amount of wine. His duty done, he walked back to the carriage and fell asleep out of the sun.

When they had finished lunch, Anna Maria and Chiaretta lay on their backs, putting their hats over their faces to protect against the sun filtering through the leaves. After a few minutes Chiaretta turned on her side toward Anna Maria. Resting on her elbow, she put her head in her hand. "I don't know what to do about Maddalena," she said.

"You were so quiet I thought you were asleep." Anna Maria rolled over to face her. "I've been afraid to bring it up. I didn't want to remind you."

"You couldn't have reminded me. I haven't forgotten, not for a minute."

"She wants Vivaldi to come back, that's all."

Chiaretta fell silent, picking at a small spot on her dress to dislodge whatever had dried there.

Anna Maria leaned closer and waved her hand in front of Chiaretta's eyes. "I said she wants Vivaldi to come back."

"I know. I heard you," Chiaretta said. "What do you think about that?"

"Well, he's not like any other priest I ever met. Always looking out for himself. I don't think priests are supposed to do that." She watched a ladybug crawl across Chiaretta's skirt, coaxing it onto her finger when it came into reach. "Do you remember that rehearsal when Caterina had a fever and ended up fainting?"

Chiaretta sniffed. "He was mad she had disrupted the schedule. He was jiggling and jumping around the way he does, and muttering Latin under his breath." A wave of fatigue came over her, and continuing the conversation felt like too much effort. "Would you like some cherries?"

Anna Maria got up and linked her arm in hers. "She thinks about him too much," Chiaretta said as they walked the few steps to the edge of the orchard.

"Can you blame her? She wasn't even an attiva and she got private lessons."

"And was talked about all over the Pietà. He just used her to keep from getting bored. He didn't need her." Chiaretta shook her head in disgust. "He left without saying good-bye, and she is still sitting there in misery. He's selfish beyond imagining. He'll come back if and when he wants to, and she'll be dutifully waiting."

Anna Maria picked two cherries and handed one to Chiaretta. "I don't think you're being fair to him. Did you ever listen to Maddalena play? Truly listen? She was better than anyone in the coro. Better than I am, certainly. She could pull her bow across the strings in a way that made me want to say"—Anna Maria put a fist on her chest—"'Here, take my heart.' And she didn't teach herself that. He brought it out in her. And that's what's missing now. That's what she wants."

Chiaretta reached up into the tree and added a few more cherries to the one that was still in her hand. *That's what she wants.* She finally understood. She stared at the fruit in her hand, not sure how it had gotten there. She put one of the cherries in her mouth and chewed without tasting, while the others fell to the ground.

"Thank you," she said to Anna Maria. "But I'm not sure how much it helps anything." She started walking back to the blanket but stopped and turned to her friend. "Do you ever actually suffer for your music—give yourself to it the way she does?"

Anna Maria gave her a wry smile. "I'm too busy being their prodigy. I don't have the time for that. Or the temperament."

"I don't either," Chiaretta admitted. "I guess I should be glad he trained her, but I see her shriveling up now that he's gone and . . ." Chiaretta buried her face in her hands and began to cry.

Anna Maria put her arms around her. "Cry. It's the first time you've relaxed all week."

Chiaretta stayed pressed against her friend's chest for what seemed like a long time before pulling back. "I feel better," she said.

"Truly, or are you still pretending, the way you have been all week?"

"Truly."

"Good," Anna Maria said. "One last thing, and then we don't have to talk about it anymore. Maddalena has to find her own way, even if it looks to you like she isn't trying. Even if sometimes you want to shake her and tell her to stop pitying herself."

Chiaretta looked at her, then knelt to gather up the leftovers of the picnic. "There are ants all over it. Shall we just leave it for them?"

Anna Maria nodded, picking up bones with her fingertips and flinging them into the grass.

"Here! Here! I'll do that!" The stable hand was running over.

"Want to get some more cherries?" Chiaretta asked.

"Better get there before I eat them all," Anna Maria said, taking off ahead of her.

CHIARETTA CAME BACK FROM HER HOLIDAY WITH A NEW RE-solve to mend the rift with her sister. She arrived as the midday meal was being served, but when she saw Maddalena staring at her plate of food, her plan vanished in a rush of fear. Perhaps her time away had highlighted the wan appearance of her sister, or perhaps something terrible had happened in her absence. Whatever the cause, Maddalena looked so haggard that Chiaretta rushed to her. She sat down next to her and touched her knee, but Maddalena did not return the gesture.

"Not now," she whispered.

The meal was interminable, but finally they were back on the ward.

Chiaretta sat on her bed, looking at her sister. "Is Vivaldi dead?" she mouthed. Was there anything else that could make Maddalena look that way?

Maddalena shook her head, but by then the warden had come to stand by their beds. They rolled on their backs and lay looking at the ceiling, waiting for enough time to pass so they could get up and bring out the sketchbooks.

"The priora told me I can't stay here more than another year," Maddalena wrote. "I have to become a nun or get married."

"WHAT?" Chiaretta's answer took up a quarter of a page.

"Prudenzia said I'm no use to the coro anymore. She said you can tell by my age whether a girl has it in her."

"You were the best they had when Don Vivaldi was here."

Maddalena's face darkened. "She asked me whether he had ever—" She stopped writing for a moment, and Chiaretta grabbed the sketchbook.

"Ever what?"

"Ever touched me," she whispered. "You know."

Chiaretta thought back to the time on the gondola when the man had slipped his hand up her thigh. "He didn't, did he?"

Maddalena picked up the book again. "OF COURSE NOT!" The brush of Vivaldi's lips on her neck had been so small a gesture, and the look on Chiaretta's face was so dire that Maddalena was sure she must be thinking of far more serious acts. It had been so long ago, it would be a distraction to say anything about it now.

Chiaretta saw the flush on her sister's face. "He never touched you here," she leaned forward and whispered, drawing her hand across her bodice, "or here?" She pushed her hand through the folds of her skirt.

"No! He's a priest!" Maddalena slashed two lines into a cross to emphasize the point in a way that said the subject was closed.

Maddalena put the sketchbook away. Chiaretta fell back on her cot, and Maddalena did the same, flooded with loneliness so physical it made her shudder, as lost as a shorebird shrieking in the night fog. *Where does it land?* she wondered. *Where do I?*

THE PROSPECT OF MADDALENA LEAVING FOREVER WAS SO frightening Chiaretta could think of nothing else except how to go with her. Night after night she lay awake concocting wild schemes. They could run away, but where would they go? Would they have to disguise themselves as men, and if so, where would they get the clothes? They could try to find their way back to the village of their childhood, but would they have to marry men there in order to stay? She had been only six when she left, but she still remembered that all the men were ragged, and sometimes her foster father came into the house covered in dirt and smelling so bad she would sneeze and her eyes would water.

We could become nuns together, she thought one night. That was at least possible, and it enabled her finally to get to sleep.

THE PRIORA WAS SITTING AT HER DESK WHEN CHIARETTA WAS ushered into her office. "I understand from the matron that you told her you wish to become a nun?" The priora raised her voice and cocked her head in disapproval. "This is rather unexpected, Chiaretta, coming from one of the attive in the coro."

"Yes, Madonna, I know, but I've given it a great deal of thought," Chiaretta responded. "I want to take vows when my sister does."

"Chiaretta, my dear, dear girl," the priora said. "Your devotion to each other is quite obvious, but do you feel you have a vocation?" She arched her eyebrows and stared at her.

It seemed a simple and appropriate enough question, but something about it hit Chiaretta with the force of a burchiello smashing into a dock. She looked up at the priora and saw the falseness of the smile, the feigned concern in her voice. *Did you ask Maddalena if she had a vocation?*

The plan that had made so much sense in the night began to unravel. She opened her mouth to say that she didn't want to be a nun, that she was sorry she had bothered her, and that all she wanted was for the priora to let Maddalena stay. Before she could do so, the priora's servant opened the door to the study.

"Signore Bembo is here to see you, Madonna. Shall I tell him to wait?"

"No, no, bring him in. I'd like him to hear this."

Antonio Bembo wore the black cloak required of all patrician men in Venice, and Chiaretta recognized him as one of the Nobili Uomini Deputati.

"Signore Bembo, you have come at a most opportune time," the priora said. "Chiaretta, tell him what you have told me."

Chiaretta started to blurt out how it had all been a big mistake, but when she saw the expression on the priora's face she stopped. The priora looked pinned to her chair, shifting her weight as if she were nervous and trying not to show it.

At that moment, a voice seemed to come from some hidden recess of Chiaretta's mind, telling her that even though she was just fourteen and no match for the wits of Signore Bembo or the priora, if she had the courage to play out what she had started, she would not end up with her own path lined to a convent, or perhaps her sister's either.

She took a deep breath. "I told Madonna I want to be a nun." The pleasant expression with which Signore Bembo had greeted her vanished.

Her specially fitted dresses, her invitations to the country and to fancy homes on the Grand Canal, her name on the tavolette? It all made sense. *They have plans for me.*

She turned her gaze from Signore Bembo to the priora. "I want to serve Our Lord," she told her, surprised that her voice could sound so steady when she was telling a lie. She said a quick, silent prayer for forgiveness and added what she thought might be blasphemy to the list of things she must not forget to confess. *But this is my sister I'm talking about. I'll explain to God later.*

When she opened her eyes, she saw that the ease had returned to the priora's face. "There are many ways to do that, my dear. You do it with your voice every week. Not only does God hear you but, just as important, you bring others closer to Him." Signore Bembo concurred with a nod of his head.

I tell her I want to leave and she tries to talk me out of it. Maddalena says she wants to stay and she doesn't listen. I don't need to be honest. She doesn't deserve it. I just have to win. "Perhaps I am just being selfish, Madonna, but I am more concerned about my own soul." She turned toward Signore Bembo, looking up through her lashes at him the way she had practiced at the villa.

"What taint could there possibly be on your soul?" The man's voice exploded with disbelief.

The look of fragile innocence had worked. "It's the music," Chiaretta said, folding her hands in her lap and posing with her eyelashes again. "I sometimes sing just to hear myself, and I am so prideful I often can go through a whole mass without thinking about God at all." *Please God, don't let me die before my next confession,* she prayed. But the faces of Signore Bembo and the priora were so grave, they made her feel reckless. "I think perhaps I should not sing anymore at all."

Signore Bembo chuckled, and Chiaretta felt a sudden panic. *If this milk goes sour, I will drown myself in the canal.*

"That, Chiaretta, is what confession is for," he said. "All God asks of you is that you recognize your shortcomings and ask for His help in overcoming them."

The priora nodded. "The solution, my dear, is to learn to sing with less pride, not to stop singing."

Chiaretta fell silent. She could think of nothing to fight back with. *I'm not going to get what I want, and now I'm going to lose my sister or end up in a convent too.* "Maddalena has no vocation," she said. "I don't want her to go." She covered her face with her hands and tried not to cry.

The priora's face clouded as she watched Chiaretta disintegrate before her. "I have been priora here for nearly twenty years now, and I see what reaching womanhood often does to young girls. It makes them moody, or sometimes just lazy and difficult to control. Chiaretta, look at me."

Chiaretta took her hands from her face and accepted the handkerchief Signore Bembo handed her.

"The priora has kept us informed about your sister," he said. "She showed promise as a musician, but—"

The priora broke in. "You may not know this, but the Congregazione is very much involved with the progress of all the girls. They are the ones who promoted you early, and they also decide who stays and who goes. If you take vows, it will only be because they permit it. Your future's not yours for the asking."

Chiaretta didn't like being told that someone else would make that kind of decision for her, but in this case, she needed the Congregazione's help out of the fix she had gotten herself into. She turned to Signore Bembo. "Please don't send my sister away. I beg you, sir." She paused and the tears welled in her eyes again, this time without a shred of insincerity. "I beg you."

"Our policy is to watch and wait to see if girls of the coro can come out of the problems associated with their"—Signore Bembo paused to look for the most delicate word—"womanhood in a year or two and be useful again. Your sister has done little of any value to the coro for several years now."

That's not why! Chiaretta wanted to scream at him, but more than anything she did not want to make him angry. "It will be hard for me, signore, if she is not here. I am studying for my first big parts now. I have never lived without her."

"There are no plans to send her immediately," the priora said in a tone that seemed a little more sympathetic.

"I know Maddalena is having trouble," Chiaretta went on. "Something inside of her is different now. I don't understand it, and I don't think she does either. But please, don't throw her away like this."

"I hardly think—" the priora said, but Signore Bembo waved her off.

"She doesn't belong in a convent," Chiaretta pleaded. "Can't she be bled? Isn't there a tonic?" And then another idea occurred to her. "Maybe having a pupil would give her something she liked doing. Maybe it would help."

"My dear, no one but the giubilate are allowed to make money by taking on outside students," the priora said. "Surely that can't be what you're suggesting."

"Perhaps she could assist them somehow?" Chiaretta liked the idea more and more. "She's so patient and kind, I know she would be a good teacher. She wouldn't ask for any money."

"With Signore Bembo's permission"—the priora looked at him—"I will talk to Maestra Luciana about the possibility of taking Maddalena on as an assistant with her pupils?"

Luciana! Chiaretta hadn't thought of that. *Maddalena would rather be a nun.* "Maestra Luciana is a very gifted musician," she said, "but she has not recognized my sister's ability for reasons I do not understand." She liked the way she sounded—a mature woman with important business to handle—although she wasn't quite sure where the voice or the manner had come from. "I don't believe she will agree, or be of any help in making it work if she does."

The priora looked at Chiaretta quizzically. She took in a breath as if she were about to speak but changed her mind.

"Well then," she said, getting up from her desk to let Chiaretta know their meeting was over.

*Part Three*_____

CHIARETTA

TRIUMPHANS

_____*1710–1716*

TEN

ELIZABETA CONTARINI WAS SO PALE THE TRACERY OF BLUE veins could be seen under the skin of her hands. Her hair was too fine to hold in the combs that kept it off her face, and little wisps fell across her temple and onto her right cheek as she bent her neck over her violin. She bit her lower lip in concentration, showing the tips of her small and slightly crooked incisors. Her mouth was an almost perfect replica in miniature of the heart shape of her face.

"It's very hard," she said in a tiny, girlish voice.

"Yes, it is," Maddalena said. "Try it again, and remember to keep your hand from rotating out when you're fingering."

Elizabeta's family's wealth was conveyed in the silk brocade of her dresses and the fasteners of gold and pearl in her hair. Her father's importance as a member of the Congregazione caused a stir in the practice rooms when she came once a week for singing and violin lessons.

Maddalena had been her private violin instructor for almost a year, starting as Luciana's assistant. For the first few months, Chiaretta had intercepted the eleven-year-old as she came and went from her singing lessons. Charming her at first by teaching her the same breathing technique Michielina had taught her years before on the balcony, Chiaretta had brought up the subject of Luciana in an offhand way. As she suspected, Elizabeta was terrified of the maestra, so much so that she had made almost no progress on the violin in more than six months. Over the course of a few weeks, Chiaretta had worked on her to get her father to request that Maddalena be her instructor rather than the disfigured and bad-smelling Luciana, whom Chiaretta suggested was the source of the nightmares Elizabeta all of a sudden claimed to be having.

Once Luciana was out of the picture, Maddalena discovered that Elizabeta was not shy at all. In fact she seemed so desperate for someone to talk to that Maddalena often had to tell her to concentrate on the music. When she first talked about her family, Elizabeta had been astounded that Maddalena did not know that among her ancestors were six doges of Venice, the first having ruled as far back as the eleventh century and the most recent having served until his death less than thirty years before. In Elizabeta's world, everyone just knew.

When Elizabeta's father and mother had determined that, for reasons of temperament, her older sister was not suited for marriage, they decided it would be Elizabeta who would marry instead. Her family had only a few years to groom her into a prize for a nobleman, and the lessons at the Pietà were part of that preparation. Elizabeta told Maddalena all of this in a detached way. Parents chose for daughters, and daughters went along without forming their own opinions.

Elizabeta had no particular aptitude for the violin, but she loved her lessons. "Let's play the game," she would plead after strug-gling with her own music for a while. "Petals falling in an apple orchard," Maddalena would say as she improvised, or "bees buzz-ing around a honeycomb," or "a breeze rippling across the la-goon," and Elizabeta would clap her hands in delight.

Over time, the color returned to Maddalena's face, and a small amount of weight began to accumulate around her hips. She was included again in invitations to parties, and most important of all, she was back on the balcony of the Pietà.

Chiaretta was quietly triumphant. Maddalena knew that her sister had gone to the priora and had succeeded in granting her at least a temporary reprieve, but Chiaretta would never share the details. As time passed, the success of her trip to the priora's office was clear. The subject of the convent was never raised again.

JUST AS THE AUGUST HEAT BEGAN TO SETTLE INTO THE ROOMS of the Pietà, Maddalena and Chiaretta packed their bags to go with a small group of attive up the Brenta Canal to spend a few days at a villa in the countryside. Chiaretta, who to that point had only been able to tell Maddalena about such outings, was beside herself with excitement that Maddalena, at eighteen, was coming on her first trip.

"Perhaps you'll have an admirer," Chiaretta told her sister. "You're so pretty you're bound to be popular."

Though Maddalena was not a great beauty, her hair was a lus-trous auburn color, and her cheekbones and angular face gave her a distinctive appearance that some might call appealing, even com-pelling, if not exactly pretty in a conventional way. Indeed, in some families she might have been considered the attractive one, but next to Chiaretta anyone would have come out a distant second.

The figlie went by gondola to Fusina, where they transferred to a private barge and draft horses pulled them along the towpath to

Villa Foscari, the first of the grand mansions along the canal. Chiaretta and the others wanted to protect themselves from the sun and heat, so Maddalena went out on deck alone. It had been almost ten years since she'd left her foster home in the country, ten years without seeing cows grazing, or a dirt path through a field, or the sky unobstructed by rooftops, and she could not make herself go back inside despite the chaperone's warnings that too much sun would make her sick.

Eventually they reached the villa. It looked to Maddalena as if someone had erected a palace on the back side of a Greek temple. The flat roof of the villa was broken up by four towering white chimneys and a small triangular attic with gabled windows. An open porch made of columns covered by a sloped roof jutted out, accessed by two matching white marble staircases leading up from the pathway across the lawn.

The barge came to a stop at a small dock, and several men dressed in livery emerged from the ground floor underneath the porch. They hurried toward the dock to help the girls off and take their belongings to the house. Chiaretta was one of the last off the barge, and Maddalena held back to wait for her, watching the line of figlie scattered along the path like a border of red flowers against the green lawn.

Inside, Maddalena wandered through the portego, which stretched from one end of the house to the other. No tortured saints or sad-looking virgins conspired to make her feel humble, and no depictions of heavenly rewards hinted at what obedience might gain her. Here, the frescoed walls showed banquet tables heavy with fruit and roasted meat, around which comfortably dressed people were caught in the moment of telling a secret, sharing a furtive kiss, or even playing with a dog. Trompe l'oeil windows held curtains that seemed to blow into the room, and painted doors opened into rooms that did not exist. The whole space was an invitation to enjoy life, and Maddalena had never seen anything like it.

Chiaretta caught her sister's elbow. "We need to go up and rest before the guests arrive." She steered her toward a doorway in an alcove at the far end of the room. At the top of a staircase was another portego, off which were sleeping chambers for the figlie. Maddalena and Chiaretta settled in to a sleeping platform elevated a few feet above the floor in one of the rooms. The bed took up almost the entire space in the sparsely decorated room, except for a cassone under the window, in which they found an extra coverlet embroidered with a garland of leaves and flowers.

Maddalena pulled the coverlet over them both and turned to her sister. "Thank you," she said.

"Thank me for what?"

She fiddled with a strand of Chiaretta's hair, not so much because it was out of place but because she felt a sudden surge of love that made her need to touch her sister.

"For everything," she said, nuzzling her head into the pillow and shutting her eyes.

THE FOSCARI FAMILY HAD INVITED A DOZEN DINNER GUESTS IN addition to the figlie, swelling the crowd in the room to a little under thirty. The first evening the concert preceded the meal to accommodate the figlie, who were tired from their journey. Even before the instruments had been put away, servants had lit torches on the walls to illuminate a table topped with green-and-gold brocade. Game and fish brought in that day from nearby streams and fields were heaped on platters, along with vegetables from the garden, and rice flecked with spices from the Levant. After dinner, a heady drink as sweet as syrup had been poured into small glasses, accompanied by panna cotta sprinkled with berries from the forest at the edge of the estate.

When everyone had declared the meal magnificent and pushed away from the table, most of the guests wandered outside to enjoy the cool night air. Laughter and song drifted across the lawn from small boats on the canal, their lanterns making slow trails along the water as they passed.

Maddalena watched as half a dozen people got off a boat and came down the pathway. One of the women squealed as a man chased her. Another man caught her when she tripped over her hem, and as she fell into his arms, he reached inside her bodice to fondle her breast. Another man and woman lingered behind the others. He held a bottle of wine in one hand while he leaned forward to kiss her.

Maddalena quickly slipped behind a pillar to avoid being seen. When they reached the top of the stairs, one of the men noticed the girls in their concert dresses. "Look what we have here!" he exclaimed, lifting his eyebrows in approval.

Alvise Foscari's wife came out on the porch, and the man turned his attention to the woman of the house, kissing her hand before following her inside.

"You can come out now. It's safe." The voice belonged to another guest, who had witnessed the spectacle.

"I'd better go," Maddalena said, feeling suddenly overwhelmed.

"Please stay. It isn't often I get a chance to talk with one of you."

Maddalena had no idea what she was supposed to say, but it didn't matter because he did most of the talking. His name was Marco Valiero, and he was visiting for the evening from his family's villa a few miles away. He was handsome in the way lent to ordinary appearance by immaculate grooming and well-fitting clothing of high quality, but by any other standard he was a slightly overweight man in his late twenties, of middling height and unremarkable face. Still, he was well mannered, and within a few minutes Maddalena had relaxed enough to decide she was enjoying his company.

"Are people always like that here?" she asked him.

"Like them? I'm afraid so. We would die of boredom otherwise."

I mean, we visit each other, but we don't all act like they did." He made a sweeping gesture and bowed as if he were greeting a princess. "Some of us are far better behaved."

Maddalena smiled.

"Good!" he said. "I was wondering if you had teeth. So far your mouth has been so tightly closed I wasn't sure."

She smiled again.

"Even better!" He picked up her hand and kissed it.

One of the chaperones appeared from nowhere at Maddalena's side to tell her the figlie were to go up to their rooms for the night.

"It's been a pleasure," Marco said as she turned to leave, but Maddalena was ushered away before she could reply.

NESTLED INTO THE BED, WITH THE CURTAINS DRAWN, SHE AND Chiaretta whispered about the day. "Who were those women?" Maddalena asked.

"The ones who came on the boat?" Chiaretta replied. "Courtesans."

Maddalena pictured the hand inside the bodice and the indiscreet kiss on the walkway. Years of listening to gossip in the Pietà had exposed her to what went on between men and women, and to the general outline of what some women did for money, but she had never seen any of it played out before her eyes.

"Who was the man you were talking to?" Chiaretta asked.

Maddalena told Chiaretta about her conversation, but when she got to the part about the kiss on the hand, she felt her sister stiffen.

"Maddalena," she said. "I feel like one of the chaperones getting ready to wag my finger. But you have to be careful." Chiaretta sat up in bed and looked at her sister. "Most of these men have wives, and a few are betrothed. That doesn't mean they aren't looking for female company, just that it must not be us. Most of the bachelors can't afford to marry, and they're just looking for a little entertainment."

"But I don't understand. I thought the whole point is that we're virgins."

"And most men don't want anyone to think they disrespect that." Chiaretta thought back to the hand touching her thigh so many years ago and shuddered. "But not all of them. For some, I suppose, we're a form of sport."

Maddalena was by now sitting up in bed also. "You make it sound so sordid."

"It doesn't have to be, if we keep our heads. You remember hearing about that soprano Zanetta a few years back? The one who was caught with a man on one of these trips?"

Maddalena nodded. The scandal had happened before their time, and she had heard only that Zanetta insisted she simply wanted to see inside a gazebo visible from the main house but was afraid to go alone. The man swore on his honor he hadn't touched her, but still, they had been out of sight in a place she had no permission to be. Shortly after her return to the Pietà, with hair scarcely an inch long, she was sent to a convent.

Maddalena grabbed her sister's hand as if to keep herself safe from the implications of Zanetta's story. "I'm not in trouble, am I?"

"No, but I just make sure not to talk to any man for more than a few minutes, except in a group. If I flirt, I flirt with everyone." Chiaretta squeezed Maddalena's hand. "I'm getting up to blow out the candle so we can sleep."

Maddalena had already laid her head down on the pillow. "You have to be very careful," Chiaretta said, tucking the cover in around her sister in the darkened room. "It's so easy to be gossiped about. If he comes back tomorrow, I wouldn't speak to him alone."

He didn't, but in the course of listening to the conversations around her the following evening, Maddalena learned that Marco Valiero had a wife who the year before had produced an heir. She was expecting again at the end of the summer and was confined to the villa awaiting the birth. It had been all in an evening's fun.

It isn't fun for me, she thought as she lay awake after the concert, picturing the ease with which her sister handled the attention. *I'd rather be at the Pietà.*

ALVISE FOSCARI CAME TO THE DOCK TO SAY GOOD-BYE TO THE girls the following morning, making them promise to return. The sky was dark, and just as they pulled away it began to rain. Though Maddalena watched through the windows of the boat all the way back to Fusina, the magic she had felt on the outward trip was lost in the downpour and the sour aftertaste of her interaction with Marco Valiero. They arrived by gondola at the Pietà dock in the afternoon and went to the ward to take a nap before supper.

As soon as Maddalena and Chiaretta dropped onto their beds, Anna Maria came in, without a hint of a smile, to greet them. "Did you hear the news?" she whispered.

Vivaldi. Had something happened to Vivaldi?

"Maestra Luciana died in her sleep last night," she said.

Chiaretta let out an excited cry, then covered her mouth. For a brief moment she chastised herself for her glee but then gave in to it. Her sister had always viewed Luciana with resignation, but to Chiaretta, Luciana was a viper. "God is clearing a path for you," she whispered, but Maddalena was not so sure.

LUCIANA'S DEATH HAD NO REAL IMPACT ON MADDALENA'S LIFE. She still practiced every day and gave Elizabeta her lesson once a week. Then, as the first leaves began to turn yellow, Elizabeta's lessons were canceled. She had fallen ill. At the beginning of September, Maddalena received a note from the priora telling her Elizabeta would not be returning. Her illness had left her weakened in a way that made her parents think it would be better for her not to take on the strains of childbirth that would be part of becoming a wife. They had decided to place her in one of the most luxurious Venetian convents and marry off their third daughter instead. The violin would not be a skill Elizabeta would need after all, the priora explained, and her time was better spent recovering her strength at home.

"You can get another pupil," Chiaretta said, in a rare misunderstanding of her sister's gloom.

"I can get a pupil," Maddalena replied, picturing the gentle child she had grown to love. "But how do I get another Elizabeta?"

Maddalena never knew how Elizabeta felt about getting married. Being a wife was not easy, even for the rich. She had seen as much from the number of times she had been part of a mass sung for a woman dead in childbirth before she was much older than Maddalena herself. In some ways convent life seemed like a better fate. Still, she had difficulty imagining Elizabeta, or anyone else, being willing to enter what was little more than a prison for the rest of her life. Maddalena felt a pang in her heart every time she pictured Elizabeta leaving home, eyes downcast and saying nothing but perhaps harboring thoughts of such desperation and betrayal that she would hope to be struck dead before the convent doors slammed behind her.

In her free time, Maddalena made a lace bookmark, designing it herself with a pattern of birds in flight around the edges, and a *P* in the center she copied from the scar on her heel. She sent it to Elizabeta with a note to remember her and the Pietà. Then she picked up her lace cushion again and made another just like it for Silvia. "From your friend Maddalena," she wrote. "I hope you are well."

THE FIRST COLD SNAP OF FALL HIT VENICE A FEW WEEKS LATER, and the city began preparing for another annual round of Carnevale. The nights grew longer, and Maddalena felt with growing dread the approach of another winter. She took out her warm cloak and kept it drawn around her long in advance of her sister pulling out her own. Chiaretta watched with mounting anxiety as Maddalena grew quiet again and her steps slowed.

Then at the end of September, when Chiaretta came into the choir room, she sensed a buzz in the air. "What's happening?" she asked, but before she could get an answer, the door at the other end of the room opened. The body of the maestra partially blocked the figure in the doorway behind her, but there was no mistaking who it was. No one else had such red hair.

"Most of you know Don Vivaldi already," the maestra said. "For those of you who don't, he is our former and now"—she nodded in the direction of the priest—"our present Maestro dei Concerti."

But Chiaretta heard none of this. Though she would be punished with a diet of bread and water for a week for leaving rehearsal without permission, she had already bolted from the room to find her sister.

※ ※ ※

VIVALDI'S DEPARTURE FROM THE PIETÀ WITHOUT A WORD TO her still stung Maddalena when she thought about it, but such thoughts had become rare over time. She long knew it had nothing to do with her. The Congregazione were not displeased with him, but just as he expected, they thought his salary was an unnecessary extravagance. Recently, whispers about a stinging rebuke to the coro had reached the priora's ear. At a concert during Carnevale, one of the maestre overheard a member of the Council of Ten saying that the coro of the Pietà was now the least accomplished of those of the four ospedali. Worse, the others with him agreed. Since Gasparini had already been granted another leave, the Congregazione moved quickly. Vivaldi's services, it appeared, were needed after all.

Maddalena's memories were stored away like a pile of letters around which a ribbon had been tied to keep them from coming loose. Vivaldi had plucked her away from what looked like a bleak fate and set her on the road to becoming an attiva in the coro. For that she was grateful, although she owed more to Chiaretta for everything that had happened since. In fact, she wasn't sure she should attribute anything to Vivaldi except her skill at an instrument she rarely got to play. Retirees continued to exert a great deal of influence over promotions and placements in the coro, and even after the concert for the King of Denmark, Luciana never gave her a chance. Though she had given violin lessons to Elizabeta and practiced on her own, Maddalena still played the recorder at concerts.

And now Luciana was dead and he was back. Maddalena wished she could attribute her excitement only to the possibility of playing the violin in the coro again. She wished she didn't care for him, but as much as she wanted to control her imagination about what his return might mean, she couldn't. She allowed herself to remember their lessons, his winks, his touch, his endearments, and she pushed aside the hurts, wanting nothing more than to have him back in her life.

DISAPPOINTMENT SETTLED IN WHEN SHE WAS NOT AMONG THE violinists he called for a private audition. Since he would be composing a great deal of new music for the coro and wanted to tailor it to the musicians and singers he had, his first step was to hear each attiva for himself. He had worked his way through the string section to the woodwinds before Maddalena received word of her turn to play for him.

"He called for you first among the recorders," Chiaretta wrote, and though she meant to cheer her sister up, it sounded hollow even to her.

"He didn't notice I wasn't on the violin list," Maddalena wrote. "I wish I didn't have to see him at all."

"He's here and he's in charge now," Chiaretta wrote. "Are you going to take a violin?"

"Why? It's been decided, hasn't it?"

Chiaretta circled the word *decided* and drew a line to the margin. "Did *you* decide? You have to say what you want, and sometimes you have to fight. If you really want it. Maybe you don't."

Maddalena retrieved a small knife in a leather case from the cassone, and taking time to absorb Chiaretta's remark, she sharpened the pencil.

"I thought I could tell him what happened if he asked," she wrote.

"It's not good to wait for people to notice. They usually don't."

Chiaretta leaned forward. "Take the violin!" she whispered.

WHEN MADDALENA ENTERED THE SALA, SHE SAW THE EYES OF Prudenzia, the new maestra, dart to the instrument case she carried, and Maddalena's face burned with the sense that she had somehow betrayed the maestra. Vivaldi's face seemed to color a little when he saw it, but Maddalena wasn't sure because she felt so self-conscious, she looked away.

Vivaldi greeted her with the aloofness of an impartial host. He listened to her play the recorder, and when she finished, his brow was furrowed. "You are quite good," he said. "Very technically proficient. But I'm confused. Your name was not on the list of violinists, but I see the case you brought."

Maddalena felt prickles of sweat under her arms. Then, remembering Chiaretta's words, she plunged in. "I am told there are enough figlie dal violino, and I am needed on the recorder." She struggled to lift her eyes to look at him. "But I love the violin."

Vivaldi held his gaze on her for a few seconds, cocking his head slightly, as if he were trying to find in her eyes the rest of what she wanted to say. He turned to the maestra. "I would like to hear Maddalena play the violin."

Maddalena opened the case, her hands trembling so much she had difficulty tightening the bow. She began one of Elizabeta's favorite pieces, climbing upward until the notes were so high they drifted away before fluttering back down again.

She stopped. "I'm sorry," she said. "I was in such a hurry to play I'm afraid my instrument isn't well tuned. I can begin again if you'd like after I—"

Vivaldi's eyes were bright, and a smile played at one corner of his mouth. "No, that won't be necessary. I thought the recorder . . . that perhaps you had settled into it, and I didn't want to presume."

He turned to Prudenzia. "I hope you will not be too bothered by losing her, but I believe her services are more needed among the violins." He gave Maddalena a perfunctory nod. "That will be all." Looking back at the maestra, he asked, "Is there anyone else to hear today?"

As long as I am here, you will always be protected.

Maddalena stopped in an alcove on the way back to the rehearsal room. "Thank you," she whispered to the statue of the Virgin. *I should have listened to Chiaretta,* she thought. *God was clearing my path after all.* "Thank you," she whispered again, touching Mary's cool stone robe with her fingertips. "Thank you, thank you, thank you."

ELEVEN

THE SHEET MUSIC BEGAN WITH A VIOLIN SEESAWING BE-
tween a few notes. A second violin picked up the same melody,
leading into a pulsing repetition, which then lengthened and
slowed until the music resembled the rocking of a boat on a still
night.

Maddalena sat in the practice room at the beginning of her lesson with Vivaldi, turning the pages and imagining the sounds.

"Laudate pueri Dominum," she said, tracing the words written
over the music. "This looks beautiful."

"My first motet for soprano and violin written specifically for
the Pietà," Vivaldi said. "It's a surprise for your sister." He paused.
"And you."

"This is for a first violin."

He smiled in amusement at her confusion. "Don't you get it?"

he asked. "You've been promoted. You have to be a first violinist. No one else can play my music the way I want it to sound."

"But it's going to look—"

He cut her off. "Like favoritism? Let it. Prudenzia agrees with me about you, and as long as the maestra dal violino goes along, who could argue? Especially now that Luciana's not around to frighten the poor woman out of doing her job." He grinned. "I'm not just a violin teacher, like before. I'm really in charge now. And that means things are going to change for you."

A FEW WEEKS LATER, MADDALENA SAT IN THE CHAPEL BALCONY and drew her violin to her chin. Excitement built in the orchestra as the bass viol player threw herself into the notes, making the grille of the balcony reverberate. The strings pulsed loud and then soft, over and over again, building up to Chiaretta's entrance.

Her voice rang out, full and rich as drops of nectar oozing from ripe fruit. "Children, praise the name of the Lord," she sang in Latin, changing keys and ornamenting her voice to keep the music dazzling and new. After a run of high notes, she pounded the words before plunging to the low end of her range and merging into the staccato reprise of the instruments.

This was no dry biblical text in Vivaldi's hands. He stormed, tiptoed, skipped, and blasted through the words of the psalm. *"Sit nomen Domini,"* Chiaretta sang, with the sweetness of a mother helping a sleepy child finish bedtime prayers. *"Suscitans, suscitans!"* she called out breathlessly, as if God's arrival was as imminent as a bolt of lightning in a dead black summer sky, before her voice took off in a flight of notes that danced with joy.

The end of the motet began with slow, melancholic notes on the low strings of Maddalena's violin, accompanied by a cello and a delicate pizzicato on the other strings. *"Gloria Patri, et Filio . . . "* Chiaretta began. When they reached the next words of the doxology, *"et Spiritui Sancto,"* she hung on to the last note, allowing

Maddalena to pick up the beginning of the melody before her voice fell off. Then, when Maddalena reached the same point, she held her last note while Chiaretta picked the melody up again in the same fashion, making transfer after seamless transfer between voice and violin, over, under, around, like fabric woven by an invisible hand. Chiaretta's voice climbed higher, and Maddalena went with her like an echo. Then they were together again, finishing in unison, their music rising and falling like the sound of God breathing.

AFTER THE ACCLAIM OF THE *LAUDATE PUERI*, VIVALDI PUSHED himself with such ferocity that he often had to stop rehearsals to collapse in a chair and struggle for his next breath. Aromatics were kept in each of the rooms where the maestro worked, and nurses from the hospital were dispatched with steaming towels and salves if the attacks were prolonged. Not much else could be done, and though any of the coro could have held a sachet to his face, the unspoken understanding was that Maddalena would do it if she were there.

Less than a year after she and Chiaretta had performed the *Laudate pueri*, she was promoted to sotto maestra dal violino, sharing those duties with Anna Maria. Though a few eyebrows were arched at Maddalena's quick rise, the issue faded when Vivaldi favored everyone in turn, writing nothing more for Maddalena for several months and producing new works for recorders, mandolins, lutes, violas, and cellos, as well as the full range of voices.

With the appointment as sotto maestra, Maddalena left the lace room forever. Even with the additional time she gained by not making lace every day, Vivaldi's delay in starting another piece for her came as a relief, because her new workload was crushing. She was now responsible for overseeing the lessons of the iniziate and instructing two advanced pupils herself. In addition, all the sotto maestre were expected to ensure music was copied properly and on time, maintain the instruments, attend auditions, rehearse the coro, and conduct in the absence of the maestre.

And then, just as the first leaves began to curl and turn brown at their edges, and the trees wore a full coat of summer dust, music for a *Salve Regina* arrived for the copyists. Maddalena was the first to see it. In the left corner above the title Vivaldi had written two names. "Maddalena Rossa—violino," it said, and "Chiaretta—Soprano."

Maddalena ran her fingers across each of the pages as if touching something sacred. At the beginning of the third movement, she stopped. Above the first bar Vivaldi had written a single word. "Dance."

THE BOLDNESS OF HIS *SALVE REGINA* ANNOUNCED ITSELF A FEW weeks later as the first notes floated over the chapel. The orchestra was silent throughout the first movement. Maddalena played a soft and flowing melody before Chiaretta entered, repeating it in a higher octave. They shared the music back and forth, as if they were drinking from one goblet, lingering at the end with the reluctance of someone who knows that the time for such sweetness is almost over and the glass will not be filled again.

After a short orchestral opening, Chiaretta launched into the second section. *"Ad te, ad te clamamus, exsules filii Hevae,"* she sang, "to you we shout, we children of Eve in exile." Only half in jest, she had accused Vivaldi in rehearsals of torturing her by making her sing for all of the exiled children simultaneously. Vivaldi was pleased. "You understand perfectly. You *are* the clamor," he said. "You have to do it with your voice."

The tripping syllables, the tight melismas, the drawn-out vocalizations dissolving into cascades of sound were exhausting, and Chiaretta signaled to Maddalena to let her take a few breaths to recover when she finished.

Then she nodded, and it was time to dance.

Maddalena had rehearsed the coro for the *Salve Regina,* and on their first day she told the figlie to put their instruments away. Handing them the sheet music, she had them hum their parts. Their voices were thin with self-consciousness, and the tempo slowed down until the last of them gave up and fell silent.

"Try wagging your head back and forth," she said. "Now try rocking from side to side." Pulling up a chair between two of the figlie, she put her arms around their shoulders and began pushing them back and forth to the rhythm. "La, la la la—now keep moving but try vocalizing," she said, and the figlie sang out, butting shoulders until they dissolved into giggles. "All right," she said. "Now, take out your instruments again."

AT THE PERFORMANCE, THE FIGLIE'S MOUTHS WERE STRETCHED to the limit with smiles. The cellists and bass violists bobbed their heads as they plucked strings, and the other figlie swayed back and forth to the lively rhythm. And then the music turned serious again. In the last section, the violins began a wheezy melody, like a lullaby played on a shepherd's bagpipes. Then they all fell silent except for Maddalena's violin and a theorbo in the background.

"Et Jesum benedictum," Chiaretta began, wrapping her arms around herself as she melted into the beauty of the simple tune. *"O clemens, O pia, O dulcis Virgo Maria."* The most sincere of love songs to the Virgin Mary filled the chapel, though it felt no louder than a whisper, and at the end the music simply evaporated.

Chiaretta felt drops of perspiration making their way into the small of her back as she opened her eyes. The fading last note of a composition always sucked something out of the air in the chapel, creating a momentary vacuum before the music was entirely gone and the ordinary world restored. But this time that void in sound was not there. Rising up from the floor of the chapel was not the sound of shuffling feet, clearing throats, or murmured exchanges of approval in a place where applause was not allowed. She looked through the grille and saw the entire congregation on its feet clapping.

Maddalena came up and put her arms around her sister. "You were perfect," she said. "Look at them!"

"So were you," Chiaretta said, her voice hoarse with emotion. Together they left the balcony while the audience, having recovered its decorum, watched in silence as their silhouettes disappeared.

AMONG THOSE AFFECTED BY CHIARETTA'S SINGING OF THE Salve Regina was Claudio Morosini. He had come back early from the family's villa on the Brenta Canal to handle some business in Venice in the muggy heat of summer and had decided to make the best of an unpleasant situation by going to the mass and concert at the Pietà.

The following two weeks, he went to the parlatorio for visiting hours, but Chiaretta was not there. Eventually the priora directed her to go, saying that her reputation was now such that guests were hoping for a chance to see and talk to her. Chiaretta complied every week after that, coming downstairs with the other figlie and standing at the grille. She engaged in aimless conversation and offered meager refreshments to the guests, without noticing the young man in a mask who came and went without speaking to anyone.

A month later, Chiaretta was summoned by the priora. "You have an admirer," she said. "The family has begun discussions about the suitability of a marriage."

"Marriage?" Chiaretta sat back in her chair. "Who is it?"

"A man from one of the old houses of Venice. His family has served on the Congregazione for generations. I believe you know his sister, Antonia."

"Claudio?" *He gave me his napkin after I swallowed my first oyster,* she thought, *and pulled out my chair as if I were a lady.* And then memory shifted and she was getting off the gondola while his companion fondled her thigh.

She put her hand to her mouth. "Priora—" She didn't know how to continue. "Is he a nice man?" she asked, almost in a whisper. "I mean, he seems to be, but . . ."

The priora laughed. "I have it from his father that he is, but who is not going to say that about his son?" She gave Chiaretta a puzzled look. "It's an odd reaction, yours. Occasionally girls will be upset, but for the most part they are so excited they forget to ask any questions. Other than how old and how wealthy he is—and whether he is handsome, of course."

"I already know those things."

"Yes, of course," the priora said. "To answer your question, he has been well raised. It's a good family—a remarkable one, really—but of course that is no guarantee of character. I can at least add that he is not one of those nobles who spends his family's money without replacing it through his own efforts. It's good, I think, when wealthy men find some productive use for their time."

"He has a job?"

"Not exactly. He owns a business selling paintings of Venice. He has a workshop for the artists and a little shop near the Rialto Bridge. And he's an investor in one of the opera houses—the Teatro Sant'Angelo, I think it is." She motioned toward the far wall of the study. "That's a veduta—it's what the paintings are called. It was a gift to the Pietà from his father. Would you like to see it?"

As they walked over to the painting, the priora continued. "It's rather small, but Signore Morosini tells me most of the vedute are. Apparently that's the idea." They were now standing in front of the painting, and the priora was tracing her finger along the bottom, not quite touching the surface. "The charm is the details—so tiny but so clear, so lively."

Chiaretta leaned forward. "That's the dock at the Pietà."

"Yes. And did you look at the gondola?" There, no bigger than painted ants, was a group of figlie being helped onboard. The priora smiled. "Are you looking to see if he included you?"

"They're too small to be anybody," Chiaretta murmured, taking in the stretch of the Riva degli Schiavoni on both sides of the Pietà—the hat maker, the apothecary, the butcher, just as in real life—and the lagoon swirling with dozens of boats. Above the buildings the sky was immense and threatening, as if it were preparing to swoop down and send all the people running for cover.

The priora stepped away, as if to continue their discussion, but Chiaretta didn't notice. Her eyes were digging deeper into the painting, trying to force it to reveal what would happen to the tiny girl in the red-and-white uniform who was taking the hand of the gondolier while the world spun around her.

Chiaretta had been so focused on the painting that when she looked up she thought for a moment she was going to faint. "I—" she said, reaching out to steady herself on the back of a chair.

The priora took her arm and led her back to where they had been sitting. "I know this is quite a shock."

Chiaretta nodded. "May I sit and think for a minute?"

"Of course."

Chiaretta shut her eyes and listened to the pop of the fire, the rustle of pages being turned in a ledger, the clink of a pen in an ink-well, the priora's soft breathing. Her mind filled with images of chests full of beautiful dresses and servants hovering over her. She would have her own gondola and come to visit at the Pietà . . .

Visit. The thought stopped her cold. She would have to leave her sister. And her singing. With her eyes still shut, and in a voice so subdued and distant it didn't sound as if it could have come from her own throat, she asked, "Is it true that I can't sing anymore if I marry?"

She heard the rustle of the priora's skirt as she got up to come sit next to her.

"You may sing in your home for family, but public appearance is impossible. Whether family can include other guests is a matter of interpretation, and the best I can say is that sometimes enforcement has been quite strict. There's trouble from time to time when a husband tries to exploit his wife by turning their home into a private concert hall, and no one wants that. But other times, our brides have sung or played at parties in their homes as long as there's no hint money is being made from their efforts."

Chiaretta had opened her eyes and was watching the priora with a troubled expression.

"My child, it is your decision," the priora said. "But you are almost twenty now, are you not? And you know as well as I do what happens when you turn twenty-two."

Chiaretta nodded her head. At the Pietà, musicians had to survive two promotions. The first was at sixteen, when girls who did not have promising futures were put to other work or sent to convents. She and Maddalena were among those promoted to the next level, which involved six more years of training and performances. About a year ago, Maddalena had reached twenty-two and had been required to sign an oath that she would remain in service to the coro for ten more years in exchange for the investment the Pietà was making in her. Even if she had a suitor and wanted to marry, she would now have to wait until her obligation was finished.

"It would be a shame if you were to leave," the priora went on, "because you have many good years ahead of you—your best years, I imagine, since your voice is just now coming into fullness. And the Pietà will lose too, but there are others to take your place. There are always others. Right now we are very rich in voices— Caterina, Barbara, Anastasia . . ."

Caterina. Almost enough reason to stay, just for spite. Sometimes it took everything Chiaretta had just to sing side by side with her. Although Vivaldi had written several pieces for Chiaretta, he had written as many for Caterina's silky, low voice, and even after the success of the *Salve Regina,* several times Caterina's name had been higher than Chiaretta's on tavolette. To make it worse, Caterina and Barbara both seemed to enjoy insinuating that Chiaretta was lucky to be pretty because her voice was thin and her repertoire narrow, and if it weren't for Maddalena's relationship with Vivaldi, she would still be in the chorus.

"They're just jealous," Maddalena had written in her sketchbook. "And even they don't believe it." But it bothered Chiaretta, especially the way Caterina and Barbara never discussed Vivaldi without mentioning Maddalena, and never brought up Maddalena without including Vivaldi, smirking as if the two were a couple, with all that that might imply.

It was true, in the past she had worried that Vivaldi was taking advantage of her sister's naïveté and loyalty, but since his return and Maddalena's promotion, their relationship seemed to be strictly business. The private lessons, which had been the cause of most of the smirking, were no more frequent than those with any other musician preparing for a difficult solo.

The priora's voice brought Chiaretta back to the subject at hand. "You are a beautiful young woman, and you have an admirer who is not likely to wait. You wouldn't have to marry right away. In fact you might be here another year or more, because the Congregazione will probably insist you stay on to benefit the Pietà a while longer."

"Can they refuse?"

"Refuse to let you marry? Of course. They would if the suitor was inappropriate." She laughed. "Claudio Morosini is the son of one of the Nobili Uomini Deputati. I think it will only be a matter of the price his family will have to pay to persuade the Congregazione the Pietà has not taken too severe a loss in the matter. But if you're amenable to meeting with him, you will have a chance to talk here in my study, and if you agree that negotiations can begin—"

"Negotiations?"

"Your dowry, and the family's bequest to the coro to compensate for losing your services."

"But I don't have a dowry. I have a few things in a cassone."

"Our wards are not paupers. We're proud when they make good marriages, and we give everyone a dowry."

Chiaretta's temples were pounding. "May I think about it some more?"

"Of course, but the family would be very surprised to hear that there is any girl in Venice who would not jump at a proposal from Claudio Morosini. I would at least like to be able to say that you have agreed he may stop by."

"All right—yes, then." Chiaretta nodded, in part because the idea did appeal to her, and in part because it would end a conversation that had left her exhausted. To have the power to decide was a nice feeling, but it was a far cry from being asked what her wishes were. *My wish is to sing wherever and whenever I want for as long as I want,* she thought. *And I don't want to leave my sister.* But in a world where much of what she wanted was not possible, perhaps she had made the right decision to agree to meet him.

And perhaps not. She shuddered. *I don't want to think about it,* she said to herself. As she walked back to the ward, she thought about nothing else.

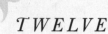

TWELVE

CHIARETTA PUT DOWN HER NEEDLE AND SIGHED. THE bell would be sounding any minute for Sext, and then it would be time for the midday meal. "Why aren't they here?"

"Maybe they'll come this afternoon," Maddalena replied, looking up from her own work at her sister. They had been given permission to spend the morning in a small room near the priora's study. Chiaretta had rubbed her face and neck with a coarse piece of cloth and pinched her cheeks until her skin glowed. She had been told to wear her black concert uniform, dressed up with a lace collar Maddalena made for her several years earlier. Maddalena had played with her hair until it shone against her face and was caught up in a neat roll at the back of her neck.

"Are you sure you're all right?" Chiaretta asked her sister.

Maddalena laughed. "I should be the one asking you that!"

"No. You know what I mean."

Just a few years ago, Chiaretta had begged the priora not to send Maddalena away, and now it looked as if Chiaretta might be leaving instead. Minutes after she had given her consent to meet Claudio, anxiety pummeled her, and she had almost gone back to the priora to call the meeting off.

Sitting on her bed afterward, Chiaretta had drawn a sketch of herself with tears running down her cheeks. "I made a fuss about letting you stay because I needed you, and now—what kind of a sister am I to leave you?" she wrote, before going to wait in silence outside the maestre's chambers, where Maddalena now lived. When Maddalena came out, she handed the sketchbook to her.

Maddalena pointed toward Chiaretta's ward, and they went to sit on her bed. "This is different. I'm satisfied here," she wrote back. "And you're not."

"But you'll be alone!"

"Alone at the Pietà? Sometimes I wish I could be! And I have always known you would leave." Maddalena drew a butterfly, labeling it "Chiaretta." "You can't stay your whole life on one flower," she wrote below it. "You would be wasting your true life if you stayed here."

"Wasting my life?" They'd looked around to see if the ward matron had heard, but they could not see her in the room. "Maddalena, you hear the applause!" she whispered. "You see all the parties I go to. The doge greets me by name! I've done quite well."

"I said 'your true life.' There are so many other things you love besides music. Wouldn't it be nice to be free to move around the city? To be the woman of the house, with your own big bed and private room? To have beautiful children and watch them grow?"

It was, Chiaretta knew, exactly what she wanted.

And so the two of them had agreed. Chiaretta would meet

Claudio with an open mind, and if she liked him, she would marry him.

And now, all she had to do was wait.

THE BELL WAS RINGING. THE TWO SISTERS CROSSED THEM-selves and began their prayers. Before the last peal of the bell had sounded, a girl from the priora's office came to fetch Chiaretta.

"The priora gives you permission to miss Sext," she said. "There are visitors waiting for you."

Chiaretta turned toward Maddalena, who threw out her arms to embrace her. After a moment, Maddalena pulled back and looked at her sister at arm's length.

"Go!" Maddalena said. Chiaretta flushed with excitement, but fear caused her eyes to dart, and she made no move to leave.

"Go!" Maddalena said again. She touched her fingers to her lips and placed them on Chiaretta's cheek. "Make him love you as much as I do."

ALTHOUGH SHE HAD SEEN HIM ON SEVERAL OCCASIONS, ALL Chiaretta remembered was that Claudio had brown hair and was average size. What she saw in the priora's study was a sturdy, broad-faced man of roughly thirty, with smooth skin shaven to a ruddy glow. His eyebrows were thick but nicely shaped, and his teeth were straight and healthy. His eyes were the rich brown of walnut wood, with a hint of puffiness underneath that added to their warmth. They were kind eyes, she decided, and the little lines at their edges turned up in a way that suggested he found much to smile about.

He has a gentle voice, she thought, after he spoke. It would not be bad to hear that voice every day. But even if he were not as attractive, this encounter was not just with a man but with the world he represented—a life outside the Pietà. What she most liked about singing was calling out from the balcony to the people in the world beyond, and Claudio had heard.

Behind her in the priora's study, she felt the presence of the painting of the figlie on the dock. This time she was not the hesitant girl in the painting getting onto the gondola. She was the one the artist hadn't painted, the one who had slipped away from the chaperone's gaze and was already heading off down the quay to see what life had to offer. And so, when the priora sent for her the next day to ask if she had an answer for Claudio Morosini, with only a slight hesitation Chiaretta agreed to marry him. *Let life start,* she thought. *Let my own painting begin.*

FOR SEVERAL WEEKS CHIARETTA HAD NO FURTHER CONTACT with Claudio. The priora told her only that discussions were under way, ones that did not involve her, and that until they were complete, no engagement could be announced. With each day, Chiaretta grew more worried, and she answered a summons to the priora's office with such great trepidation that by the time she arrived she was in tears.

There, in the middle of the floor, was a large wooden cassone. On the side and top, in gilded relief, was the coat of arms of the Morosini family.

"It's a gift for you," said the priora. "An engagement present."

Chiaretta covered her mouth with her hands. "Does this mean—"

"Yes."

Chiaretta sank into a chair. *"Virgo Dei genitrix,"* she said, crossing herself. The priora did the same, bowing her head and praying along with her. When they had finished, Chiaretta opened her eyes and stared at the priora. "I am going to be married," she said, trying out the thought.

The priora smiled. "Claudio has been very worried you would think he was not sincere when the negotiations took so long, but I have his permission to explain to you now. The terms of your departure from the Pietà were by far the least of the difficulties, though the Congregazione will be paid handsomely, I assure you. But Claudio is a member of one of the noble families, and a marriage involving any of them cannot take place until the betrothal is registered with the Avvogadori di Commun. If both bride and groom are not both from noble families, the registry rarely happens."

"You mean it might not have worked out? Why didn't you tell me that before?" Chiaretta felt the heat seeping into her cheeks. "It's been—" *Torture,* she thought to herself but restrained her anger.

"Because to Claudio, the outcome was never in doubt. The members of the Avvogadori change every year, and this year his family has many supporters. It just took time to work around the rules." The priora sat down across from Chiaretta and leaned forward for emphasis. "Nevertheless, it is a great accomplishment. A registered marriage means that your children will be recognized. Your sons will be part of the senate, and your daughters will be able to make good marriages. Without that"—she shrugged—"it would be quite simple. We would not permit you to leave, and he would not ask."

The priora looked Chiaretta in the eyes. "Claudio is a good man. He will make a fine husband. You will face difficulties, I'm sure, from people who believe he should have chosen one of their own daughters. And I have heard Claudio's mother is unconvinced. You will have to be strong, but I know you are. I've seen that your whole life."

The priora got up and walked over to the cassone. "Just keep reminding yourself that registry ends the matter. If the Avvogadori di Commun says you are good enough for Claudio Morosini, you are." She bent over and inserted a key into the lock. "Would you like to take a look?"

Inside the cassone, all Chiaretta could see was a black cloak and veil, on top of which had been laid a prayer book with an elegant tooled leather cover. "This is for a bride?" she asked. "It looks more like I'm becoming a nun."

"Your white gown will come later, for your wedding." The priora put aside the cloak and veil, revealing a black dress in the bottom of the cassone. "Take it out," she said. "Let's have a look." The dress had a heavy velvet skirt and a bodice and sleeves of damask embroidered in black with hints of gold. The placket in the middle of the bodice was made from tucked white silk trimmed with lace that extended up to her collarbones. "It's beautiful," Chiaretta whispered, holding it up in front of her. "Is it mine?"

"Of course." The priora laughed. "Suitable for a proud bridegroom to introduce you to his family. He will be coming tomorrow to take you to your betrothal party. You'll need to cover yourself with this"—she held up the cloak—"and until you've been married one year, you'll also wear this." The priora picked up the veil and put it over Chiaretta's head.

When the priora pulled the veil away, she saw Chiaretta's face was flushed. "It's all so strange," Chiaretta said, covering her face with her hands and feeling her breath bathe her fingers.

"Come along now," the priora said. "Let's try on this dress. That should make any pretty young bride feel happy."

CLAUDIO'S FACE SHOWED HIS DELIGHT WHEN HE ENTERED THE priora's study the next afternoon and saw Chiaretta standing in front of the fire, waiting for him. Antonia, who had recently been married, had come that morning with lotions and oils, rubbing them into every inch of visible skin until Chiaretta glowed and smelled like something between a forest and a flower arrangement. Then she had brushed Chiaretta's hair, securing it at the sides with some ornaments she had brought from home, before rubbing the smallest hint of color onto Chiaretta's lips and cheeks and helping her into her dress.

This time the gondola had indeed come just for her. A small oil lamp cast a glow over the colored pillows and patterned throws Claudio had put in the felce to keep them warm. Seated inside, they kept a nervous distance from each other while Antonia, wiggling with enthusiasm, chattered on about the good fortune that was making a sister of her best friend.

When they arrived at the dock at the Palazzo Morosini, torches had been lit even though the afternoon shadows had just begun to deepen. On the piano nobile, the reflected glow of candelabras on side tables gleamed in the mirrors behind them. Servants moved among the guests with small glasses of wine while a trio of male musicians, sitting where Chiaretta had often performed, played in the background.

"Here they are!" Bernardo Morosini boomed. "Where is my wife?"

A stout woman with a fleshy neck spilling out around the edges of her bodice started across the room toward them. Her hair, lightened to blond, formed a ruff around her face. The gold threads in the green brocade on the sleeves and front placket of her dress caught the torchlight at an odd angle as she came toward them, creating an acid glow that vanished only when she stood in front of them.

"Giustina," Bernardo said, "meet your new daughter."

"I've heard you sing," Giustina Morosini said, in a tone devoid of emotion.

"Thank you." Not until after she said it did Chiaretta realize Giustina's words were not actually a clear compliment.

"Tell me, dear, is there a firm date yet, for the wedding? I feel so poorly informed," Giustina said, casting a cold glance at Bernardo.

Claudio intercepted the question. "The Congregazione insists that we wait a year. I'm sure I told you that." Whether Giustina sensed it or not, Chiaretta could hear his annoyance, and the thought cheered her up considerably.

"Oh, that's plenty of time, then. I am sure you will find there is a great deal to learn." Giustina's smile seemed to have more practice than sincerity behind it and was followed by a quick departure to greet an arriving guest, but nevertheless Chiaretta decided that, overall, the first encounter had not gone as badly as it might have. Bernardo took her arm, and telling Claudio that he was abducting the bride, he led her across the room to introduce her to some of his guests.

After a few minutes Claudio came to tell his father that dinner was ready to be served. "But don't worry," he said to Chiaretta, "my one contribution to the menu was to make sure there were no oysters."

Claudio went over to the musicians to help him bring the guests to attention. "Before we sit down, I'd like to share a moment with all of you," he said, gesturing to Chiaretta to join him.

When the guests were quiet, Claudio smiled. "I am a very happy man," he said. "I am marrying an angel." He kissed Chiaretta on the cheek. "And though there are many customs we will be forgoing, there is one too important to overlook."

As he spoke, Antonia came up next to them and held out a long, flat case that he opened to reveal a strand of pearls. "For my bride," he said.

Chiaretta's hand flew to her mouth in surprise as Antonia came up to her. "Aren't they beautiful? Put them on!" she said. "You wear them from now until your first anniversary, like mine." She reached up to touch the strand around her own neck.

Claudio came up in front of her, moving to one side so the guests could see better. "May I?"

Chiaretta nodded, and Claudio fastened the clasp. As the guests applauded, she reached up to stroke the pearls, lined up one after another circling her throat, heavy, perfect, and cold.

WHEN CHIARETTA CAME BACK TO THE PIETÀ THAT NIGHT, SHE was intercepted at the door by a figlia di commun who told her not to go to the ward but to report instead to the priora's quarters.

The priora was dressed in a wool robe, her hair tied loosely back for bed. "I have had your things removed from the ward," she said. "It invites daydreaming for the other figlie to see you coming and going in these clothes. And jealousy too. While you are here, you will need to wear your uniform and follow your regular schedule."

The priora gestured to the pearls. "They're beautiful. If you'd like to keep them yourself you can, or you can leave them with me for safekeeping."

Chiaretta had already put her hand to the back of her neck. Unused to the weight, her neck had grown stiff over the course of the evening. "I'd like you to keep them here," she said. Her eyes burned with fatigue, and she tried to suppress a yawn.

"May I go to bed?" she asked, looking around as if her new bed might be found in some corner of the priora's study.

"I'm sorry," the priora said. "It's late. I'll take you there now."

As they went out the door, she turned in the opposite direction from the ward that had been Chiaretta's home, taking her into another wing.

"There are several empty rooms on this hall," the priora said. "This used to be Luciana's. You will stay here until your marriage."

Large even at half the size of the priora's study, the room had a neatly made bed against one wall and a sitting area with a chair and table in the middle. In another corner were several cabinets and a small writing desk. A prie-dieu stood nearby, centered under a niche in which stood a small statue of the Virgin clasping her hands over her heart and looking heavenward.

"I'll light the lamp for you and help with your dress," the priora said. "And tomorrow I'll instruct the figlie di commun who serve the giubilate to look in on you to see if you need anything."

The priora left, and Chiaretta crawled into bed and fell asleep. When she woke up later, the oil in the lamp was gone and the room was black. She cried out in terror of the dark and got out of bed to feel her way to the door. In the hallway, the moon shone through the windows, making the pieces of furniture look like beasts. She shut the door and got back into bed, pulled the blankets over her head, and lay awake until morning.

CHIARETTA BEGGED TO BE ALLOWED TO GO BACK TO THE WARD, but the priora was firm. "It's not just the clothing, or the hours you will be keeping," she told her. "The figlie aren't entirely ignorant of such matters, but it isn't healthy for them to be focused on"—she searched for the right words—"on what marriage means." She sighed. "I'm sorry to say this, but even though you are still a virgin, there is still some sort of"—she put up her hands and exhaled in frustration at the limitations of language—"taint. I guess that's the best word for it. So, much as I sympathize, going back to the ward is out of the question."

"Then please let Maddalena come and stay with me! I've never slept alone. Maybe she could leave her things where they are and just come at night. There's plenty of room for another bed."

BEFORE THE DAY WAS OVER, CHIARETTA FOUND HER PLEA HAD been answered.

"I'd probably never see you otherwise," Maddalena said that evening as she got into the bed that had been moved into the room.

As it turned out, Maddalena saw Chiaretta almost as often as she had before. Chiaretta's daily schedule was affected less than they expected during the first few months of her engagement. The

Carnevale season started the first week in October, with a short break the two weeks before Christmas, and then built in intensity in the weeks leading up to Ash Wednesday and the beginning of Lent. Carnevale was a time of sanctioned debauchery and excess, altogether unsuitable for the wards of the Pietà, even the betrothed ones. Chiaretta's invitations were scrutinized, and the merest hint of exposure to the unsavory meant she would not be going out at all.

Most of the approved invitations were to the afternoon conclaves of the Morosini women and their friends. Claudio rarely made an appearance, and Chiaretta often went days without seeing him. Antonia had not been at all concerned or surprised by her brother's absence. "He's getting married," she said, "but he still wants to get commissions for paintings from everybody who sets foot in Venice for Carnevale, and he talks as if the Teatro Sant'-Angelo and the Pietà are always ten ducats away from bankruptcy. And you have no idea how much work this Venetian Republic is. Every man in the city is in one meeting or another half the time they're awake." She rolled her eyes. "Besides, these parties are so overrun with gossipy old hens that a man with any brains at all would pretend to be busy even if he only had an appointment with his tailor."

Neither Claudio nor Antonia could understand how excruciating these visits were for Chiaretta. The conversations were lost on her. She didn't know any of the people being gossiped about, and she often couldn't understand what they had done that was worth so much discussion. This one had gone to a party with foreigners. That one was seen far too often in the company of his wife in public. This one was so drunk he fell down the stairs of the Ridotto. Chiaretta hated the false affection even more. "Dear Chiaretta can't possibly know what we mean," the women would say from time to time. The point was clear. She was not one of them.

One afternoon at Antonia's house, Giustina and several others excused themselves to go to another floor to examine fabric samples from Antonia's husband, Piero's, export business. Antonia and Chiaretta went up to her apartment to talk privately.

"He's a Morosini and you don't even have a last name," Antonia said as they discussed yet another snub. "What do you expect? It's not just you getting used to them. It's the other way around too."

Antonia had a point. When the time came for Chiaretta to return to the Pietà, she told her friend she wanted to find the other women to say good-bye. On a lower floor, they heard the voices of Giustina and her friends drifting into the portego through a door left ajar.

"Such a disappointment," one of them was saying.

"And of course so many of us had hoped—"

Antonia held Chiaretta back.

"I know." The voice was Giustina's. "So many marriageable daughters of good families to choose from. And of course Bernardo was so busy fawning over her, he was no help."

"Let's go," Antonia mouthed.

Chiaretta shook her head and resisted the pull on her arm.

"Claudio is quite the stubborn one. I suppose that's why he's such a good businessman," said another of the women. "And actually, I find her charming. She may surprise you."

"My aunt," Antonia whispered. Relieved that she had at least some support, Chiaretta drew nearer the doorway. "She's quite modest—certainly not spoiled," the aunt went on. "They raise them well there."

"To marry a butcher, perhaps," Giustina said, and several of them laughed.

Chiaretta stepped back as if to avoid a bludgeon. Antonia whisked her up to her apartment again to give her a chance to compose herself.

"Why is your mother so mean?" Chiaretta sobbed. "I can't help who I am."

"My mother is a she-wolf," Antonia replied. "I couldn't wait to get married and leave home. Everything offends her."

"Why didn't you tell me this?"

Antonia was perplexed. "Tell you what? And what difference does it make? Would you have said to Claudio, 'No, I can't marry you because your mother is a witch who stirs a pot in hell'?"

"I'll have to live in the same house."

"It's a big house. And don't worry. Leave it to me and Claudio. We have practice with this. Years of it." Antonia laughed, but then her brow furrowed and she fell silent.

"Chiaretta, do you know anything about your parents?" she finally asked.

"Nothing. Why?"

"Well, it's just an observation, but everybody knows that many abandoned babies are fathered by our illustrious Venetian noblemen." She shrugged. "Sorry to say, I even noticed a few at the Pietà that looked a lot like some people in my family." She wiggled her high, broad forehead. "The Morosini brow, you know."

Chiaretta looked at her, puzzled. "My point," Antonia went on, "is that there's a pretty good chance you—a lot of you—have a noble father. Maybe that's why Claudio was able to get the Avvogadori to go along with the marriage. Maybe there's been some information shared in secret. Or maybe not, but it's a possibility."

At the Pietà, the figlie did not know enough about their parentage to make it much of a subject for thought, and Chiaretta had not considered the possibility that either or both of her parents might be among people she had passed on the canal, or even sung for.

"Look," Antonia said. "Don't let your heart get sad about my mother. The next time you see her, just say to yourself that you might not be able to name your father and grandfather and God knows how many generations back, but there's a good chance they're as noble as hers."

CHIARETTA PONDERED WHAT ANTONIA HAD SAID AS THE MO-
rosini gondola took her back to the Pietà. When she came to the
priora's study to leave her pearls, she asked for a few minutes of
her time.

"I'd like to know what records there are about me," she said.
"About how I came to be here."

The priora gave Chiaretta a fleeting smile, as if she had suspected the question might come. "Normally we refuse such re-
quests," she said. "That knowledge has no bearing on a figlia's life
here, and could cause more harm than good. But I suspect I know
why you're asking. I can't promise I'll share everything with you,
but perhaps I can find out something."

A few days later, Chiaretta had her answer. "Your mother ap-
pears to have been a courtesan," the priora said, "and from the
condition in which she left you, she probably lived quite well.
From that I think we can conclude her patron—presumably your
father—was either a nobleman or a wealthy merchant, but my
guess would be the former. She was ill and knew she couldn't raise
you and your sister. I read the letter she left, and I can tell you with
certainty that she loved you."

Tears sprang to Chiaretta's eyes. "She left a letter?"

"Yes, a beautiful letter, full of concern for you and your sister.
The money she left made it possible for you to stay together. Otherwise, I imagine you would both be here and not even know you
were sisters."

Chiaretta was too overcome to speak.

The priora picked up an embroidered bag on her desk. "I've
made a decision not to show you the letter at this time. Perhaps
someday. But I have something else you may want to see." She
took out two cream-colored objects and placed them in Chiaretta's
hand.

Chiaretta ran her fingers across the carved flower on each one.
"I don't understand."

"They were with the things your mother left. She broke a comb in three to have a way to prove she was really your mother if she came back for you. One piece for each of you."

Chiaretta traced the ragged edges of the ivory, trying to comprehend. *My mother broke this with her own hands.* Her mother had always been an abstraction before, but now she was a presence in the study. Chiaretta looked up as if to catch her ghost before it vanished, surprised to see that the room was still the same and only the priora was standing in front of her.

"We prefer the figlie not to know such objects exist," the priora said. "Under the circumstances, I could probably allow you to keep yours, but I don't see how we can let Maddalena have her piece."

Chiaretta had not stopped crying since the priora told her about her mother, nor had she stopped caressing the two pieces of ivory since she first held them in her hand. *I want my piece. I want to know this is tucked away somewhere. I want to know my mother is with me.*

The priora was still talking. "I considered not letting you see this, because of the problem with Maddalena, but I thought perhaps I could persuade you not to show her or tell her about it."

I can't do that, Chiaretta thought. She put the ivory flowers back in the bag and handed it to the priora. "Thank you," she said. "But I won't agree to keep this a secret from Maddalena, so you should keep both pieces, if that's all right with you." Chiaretta did not take her eyes off her as an unnerving length of time passed.

"All right," the priora finally said, as a smile that started in the corners of her eyes spread over her whole face. "You've stood your ground well ever since you were young. I pity anyone outside the Pietà who tries to get you to do anything you don't want to do."

She handed the bag back to Chiaretta. "I'm sure you will keep these safe."

"And I can show them to my sister?"

"Yes, but only if she agrees not to discuss it with anyone else. And I think it's best if you keep her piece for her. Would you promise that?"

Chiaretta nodded and tucked the bag away in the pocket of her apron. "I'd rather have this than my pearls," she said, patting the lump it made.

She turned to go, but the priora stopped her. "I have one more thing I want to say. My dear child, if you are wondering whether your parentage gives you anything to be ashamed of, it most certainly does not. The Pietà exists because Venice has a problem, for which you are not to blame. Those who, I assume, have hurt you are the ones whose sons and brothers continue to create new wards for us each year because they can't find anyone they're permitted, or can afford, to marry." She paused and shut her eyes. "Sometimes I think the Mother of God must weep for us, for how our city has destroyed the bonds of parent and child through the pride of a few who care only about keeping their place at the top."

WHEN THE CHRISTMAS HIATUS IN CARNEVALE ARRIVED, CHIaretta began seeing Claudio more often. On Christmas Eve they attended a service under the golden domes of the basilica of Saint Mark, and afterward they strolled through the Piazza San Marco.

"I've never seen anyone who prays as hard as you do," Claudio said as they left the church and stopped to admire the rows of candles in the windows around the square.

"What do you expect? With all the silence at the Pietà, God and the Virgin are the easiest ones to talk to." Chiaretta's laugh quickly sobered. "Do you want to know what I was praying for?"

"I would be honored."

"I want your mother to accept me."

"What makes you think she doesn't?"

She said I should marry a butcher. "I thought it was obvious.

Antonia is waiting for me to say it's all right for her to bring the problem up with you."

"Oh dear," Claudio said. "I'd be surprised if I'm left with any ears at all after she's finished burning through them." He smiled until he saw Chiaretta's crestfallen face. "It was just an attempt to be funny, my love. A rather poor one, I admit."

They started to walk across the piazza again, and Claudio went on. "Antonia is one of the most forthright people I know. Rather blunt sometimes, but I prefer honesty over subtlety anyway." He stopped again and drew Chiaretta to him. "You're shaking. Are you cold, or afraid of something?"

"Both, a bit."

"I'll take you back now, get you warm. And I'll work on my mother. I promise."

❦❦❦

WHEN CARNEVALE BEGAN AGAIN, CHIARETTA ACCEPTED WITH relief the renewed seclusion at the Pietà, throwing herself into her singing and treasuring what she knew were her last months of living with her sister. And then Carnevale was over, and the last rounds of parties and outings intensified before the heat of summer set in, and the nobles once again escaped the city.

In May, Chiaretta was permitted to go with Claudio and his father on the family gondola to participate in Ascension Day, known in Venice as the Sensa. The day the doge made his annual trip from his palace to the mouth of the lagoon was the grandest festival of the year, but until this year Chiaretta had always stood in the upper windows of the Pietà to watch with the rest of the coro the passing of the doge's official gondola, the Bucintoro. This year she would be on one of the hundreds of boats crowding the lagoon to follow the Bucintoro to the edge of the ocean for the ceremonial tossing of a gold ring into the water to symbolize the marriage of the Venetian Republic to the sea.

The Morosinis' gondola had been polished until the lacquer glowed. Embroidered silk cushions were flung on the seats, and coverlets and tapestries decorated the felce. Claudio had bought her a parasol, which he held over her head as they settled in and pushed off from the dock of the Pietà. Chiaretta waved to Maddalena, Anna Maria, and the other figlie di coro when she saw them in the window. When they waved back, they caught the eye of a woman wearing a pink silk dress and a Carnevale mask, seated in a gondola next to a man who was kissing her on the neck. Seeing the girls, the woman blew kisses, and the man stood up and waved at them, just as the sound of cannon fire erupted near the Doge's Palace.

"Do you see it?" Claudio was pointing in the direction of the Broglio, a few hundred yards up the Grand Canal. He stood her up, holding Chiaretta by the waist so she could get a better look at the Bucintoro. The size of a floating palace, it stood several stories high, painted bright red and trimmed in gold. Massive red banners embroidered with the doge's emblems hung from a golden bowsprit that jutted into the air. The figureheads, a pair of golden cherubs about twenty feet high and weighing several tons, peeked out from behind banners fluttering in the breeze.

"I can hear the fanfare," Bernardo said. "They're bringing out the doge from his palace. They'll be pulling up the anchor any moment."

Fireworks exploded, and loud shouts erupted from the nearby boats as forty-two massive oars manned by hidden oarsmen on the Bucintoro began stroking in unison. As it started down the canal, men in black capes and Carnevale masks, and women in dresses that shimmered in the sunlight, stood up to watch. Families cheered from flat-bottomed peote and burchielli that just the day before had been cleaned of fish heads, lettuce leaves, or the remnants of whatever else they bought and sold for a living, and were now draped with banners of bright cloth and garlands of flowers.

Small barges carrying chamber orchestras bobbed in the wake left by the Bucintoro as it passed.

The gondolas of foreign ambassadors and the papal nuncio were the only ones not required to be black. Golden apparitions as much as fifty feet long, they were festooned from bow to stern with tangled curlicues, scallops, and braiding. Their felces took the shape of Greek temples, adorned with carvings of gods and goddesses, dolphins, and legendary creatures of the sea. Curtains of silk damask, embroidered and fringed with gold, created shade and privacy for the passengers inside.

A lifetime of participation in the Sensa had made Bernardo indifferent to the spectacle. "I don't know about you two," he said, "but I think it's damned hot out here. I'm going inside." He stumbled a little from the effects of the wine he had been drinking since they left the dock. "If I fall asleep, don't wake me up for the ring. I've seen it."

"I'm sure the Pietà would not be impressed with their appointed chaperone," Claudio said, "but I'm delighted." He pulled her to him, moving his lips along her jaw toward her mouth. "May I?" he asked.

"The gondolier," she whispered.

"Don't worry about him. Their job is not to notice, but even more important, their job is not to tell." He looked up at the gondolier, who was straining to keep them in open water away from other boats. "Tell her, Biasio. Tell her about your oath."

The gondolier laughed. "Don't worry about me, signorina. If I see, may I not remember, and if I tell, may I die."

"It's true," Claudio said. "If they can't be completely trusted, they won't have a job. Anyone who reveals what he sees or hears is likely to end up floating in the canal with his throat slit by his fellow gondoliers."

Chiaretta shivered. "How awful."

"In a few years you'll be saying 'how wonderful.' Still, for you, a little privacy." He tilted the parasol so it hid them from the gondo-lier's view. He moved his face closer to her, and she turned her head so that his lips grazed hers. He had kissed her several times before, and she felt what was becoming the sweet, familiar pang that traveled from her jaw to her ribs and made it hard to take a deep breath. His lips pressed against hers, and the ache became a pleasant stab. One hand reached behind her shoulders, and the other traveled down to her waist as he drew her to him.

Such a loud clamor broke out that he pulled back and moved the parasol aside. "Look," he said, standing her up. "The doge is throwing the ring in the water. It's supposed to make the sea happy enough to bring us a year of peaceful weather."

"Peaceful weather. I hope so," Chiaretta said, reaching up to brush his cheek. She turned to look at the gondolier, who grinned and put his hand over his eyes.

THIRTEEN

Y MIDSUMMER THE WEALTHY OF VENICE HAD MADE their escape to the countryside, in the annual event known as the villegiatura. Though the tidal currents washed the Grand Canal of most of its polluted water, those left behind had to endure the stench of sulfur and rotting garbage that wafted up from the smaller waterways and squares of the interior. Being situated on the lagoon, the Pietà was free from the worst of it, but the figlie still sweltered in the heat, trying to take what refuge could be found in the shady overhangs of the courtyard, or in rooms penetrated by a breeze.

Despite the torpor, Maddalena had never seen Vivaldi so agitated. The white silk shirts he stripped down to in the thick sea air were translucent with perspiration, showing the pale skin of his chest and back. He stamped in frustration at the time wasted with broken reeds and frayed strings at rehearsals and kept up a stream of Latin in a tone that sounded more like curses than like prayers.

His worst outbursts came when he was out of view of the attive and had only the sotto maestre as witnesses. Unlike the others, Maddalena had seen Vivaldi's temper before, especially when he was trying to balance a new opera season with his obligations at the Pietà. She had long ago reached the point where she knew the best response was to busy herself with whatever work could be done at the moment and wait for him to settle down.

The sotto maestra of each group of instruments sat down alone with Vivaldi to run through each new piece of music before beginning rehearsals. When Maddalena's turn came, she was usually so distracted by her various duties that she had no chance to ponder how different the tone of their meetings had been when she was younger. And so it came as a shock one morning when he laid his violin on his lap and told her he did not know what he would do without her. "When I played this in Padua," he said of one piece, "the musicians were always a half beat behind, and I had to fight them to play it the way I wrote it."

His eyes softened. "It's always better with you," he said. "I count on it." The tenderness in his voice caught Maddalena by surprise, and for a moment the wall of defenses she had erected against him—her professionalism, her responsibilities, her maturity—disappeared and she felt again like the young girl who had lived for his compliments and his intimacies. *That was then and this is now,* she told herself, trying to will away the uneasiness that was making her heart pound. *I don't want to care about him like that again.*

He pulled his violin from its case. "Do you see something different?" It took Maddalena a few seconds to notice that he had altered his instrument so the fingerboard came down nearly all the way to the bridge. "Can you see what that would do?" he asked, picking up his bow and playing the highest pitch on a regular violin, then jumping interval by interval until his fingers could go no farther.

"And look at this." He traced his fingers across the wood of his bow to show how the arch had been flattened out. "I've been experimenting at home," he said. "Try to do this with yours." He jumped back and forth from the lowest to the highest string.

"I can't," she said. "You know the bow will bounce right off."

"But not with mine!" His face was flushed with excitement. "I am going to show Venice something so incredible they'll wake up the next day wondering if it was a dream. Just wait, Maddalena Rossa, just wait."

THE CONCERTO WAS DRAWING TO A CLOSE IN THE SWELTERING chapel when Vivaldi began the cadenza he had bragged to Maddalena about. It started routinely enough with a flight of quick notes, leading to a few bars of what sounded like a country jig. He played a short musical phrase, repeating it at increasingly higher pitches, going up and up and up, closer and closer to the bridge, turning his bow until the sounds were not those of a violin at all but of birds chirping in a tree. He reached over to the lowest string, adding a single syncopated hooting note before easing the violin back down, leading the rest of the orchestra into the exuberant closing bars.

"Did you like it?" he asked her afterward.

"I think I held my breath through the whole cadenza."

"Good," he said, closing his violin case and giving it a triumphant pat.

Maddalena was relieved he did not notice she hadn't answered his question. The cadenza was less a thing of beauty than a challenge to the listener, more brilliant than pleasant. It rang in her ears for days.

VIVALDI HAD BEEN RIGHT. HIS CADENZA WAS THE TALK OF VENice. But though he came to the Pietà the following week with the light step and square shoulders of the triumphant, he soon was buried again in work.

Chiaretta's wedding was in a few months, and the opportunities to write music for her were growing short. For her last public performance, he was writing a role for her in a new oratorio. All five solo roles, male and female, in *Juditha Triumphans* had to be sung by the figlie di coro. The rest of the singers would form a chorus of Hebrew women if they had high-pitched voices, or the enemy soldiers of Babylon if their voices were deep. Every musician and singer in the coro, even many of the retirees and iniziate, would be included, so mighty Nebuchadnezzar's army and the heroic resistance of Judith would not sound insubstantial. The halls of the Pietà echoed with the sounds of figlie not just playing the usual assortment of woodwinds and stringed instruments but pounding on drums and blowing on trumpets as well.

Two months of concerts were scheduled to precede this grand finale in November, and the stress on the leaders of the coro was greater than anything Maddalena had yet experienced. Vivaldi was close to collapse. A few days before the opening concert of the season, a nurse tiptoed into the sala and whispered to Maddalena to come with her. The maestro had left the rehearsal about an hour before and had been found, apparently not breathing, in the hallway. He was taken to the infirmary, where the nurses revived him with aromatics, but since they had heard that Maddalena knew more about how to treat his attacks, they sent for her to help.

Vivaldi's color had already returned to normal and his breathing had improved by the time she got there. The nurses were tidying up, but just as she walked in they got a call to attend to a patient having a seizure. They bustled out of the room, leaving their clutter behind. Suddenly Maddalena and Vivaldi were alone.

"There is no one who cares as much for me as you do," he said, still a little breathless. "Look at how quickly you came."

Maddalena did not sit down next to him, though he motioned for her to do so. She went to the nurses' counter, where she began folding the damp towels and separating the bottles and boxes of aromatics into neat groups. Since his return she had managed never to be alone with him without business to keep them occupied.

He doesn't need me. I should just excuse myself and go, she thought, but curiosity kept her waiting for what he might say next. "The nurses seem very capable," she said. "I'd say they cared for you quite well."

"They're nurses. They'd do the same for anyone." He exhaled loudly enough for Maddalena to stop her work and turn around. He was watching her.

"I live alone," he said. "Except for a servant who fixes my supper and cleans up after me for wages." He got up and busied himself adjusting his clothing, deliberately avoiding looking at her. "I often wonder what it would be like if I had not taken vows, if I could have someone who took care of me because she chose to."

Why is he telling me this?

"So when I come to the Pietà . . . Perhaps I should not tell you this—" He turned back toward her. "I look forward to seeing you. You are the truest and most sincere person I know." Maddalena saw his eyes take her in as she stood facing him, her back pressed against the counter. "And I see you now, so mature and accomplished, and . . ." His eyes glistened and his voice broke, only slightly but unmistakably. "And I am just so proud."

He sat down and motioned again for her to come sit next to him, but she stayed where she was. He splayed his hands on his knees and began to rock back and forth in small, nervous movements. "Don't get me wrong," he said. "What's done is done. But I cannot help envying the man who would have you for a wife."

I should leave, she thought. *I should chastise him for daring to be so bold, and then I should walk out.*

Vivaldi looked up, acknowledging her long silence. "I have said too much."

"Yes, I think so."

"Forgive me. After my attacks, I often find myself being more honest than I would be otherwise. As if perhaps I recognize that the next one could mark my last moments in this world and I don't want to leave the record incomplete."

"Perhaps."

"Maddalena, look at me." He stood up to face her but did not move in her direction. "I will say nothing more, I promise. But I want you to know I treasure the moments I have spent with you more than any in my life. It would make me sad beyond repair if what I have said caused you to feel uncomfortable being with me."

"No," Maddalena said. "It won't. I'm needed at rehearsal." With no more than a nod, she turned her back and left the room.

For the next half hour, Maddalena missed her cues, misread her part, and finally put her bow down. Pleading a headache, she asked to be excused. As she lay on her bed in the quiet room, she could not decide if what bothered her more was what he had said, or that he had promised never to say it again.

MADDALENA SHARED NOTHING WITH CHIARETTA ABOUT WHAT Vivaldi had told her. She remembered how uncomfortable he had made the relationship with her sister at times in the past, and she didn't want to revive what was best left behind them. But confiding in her sister would have been difficult for another reason. Even before the meeting in the infirmary, an awkward silence had set in between the sisters over a dispute between Chiaretta and the maestro.

The lead role of Judith needed a voice dramatic enough for the audience to envision her cutting off a head with the swing of a sword, and Chiaretta's voice was far too sweet for that. She accepted that her last role would not be the title one, but the conflict began in earnest when she learned that Vivaldi had not written even the second most substantial role for her. Vagaus, the eunuch servant of Nebuchadnezzar's general, Holofernes, would be performed by Barbara, whom Chiaretta was convinced Vivaldi was already grooming to take her place.

Chiaretta was astonished. "My farewell performance and I'm playing the maid?" she had said, brandishing the music in front of Vivaldi's face.

"I'm sorry," he told her. "I can't take any chances with a larger role. You have no time to rehearse. Even this will be difficult for you, I'm afraid."

"I'm the best sight reader of all of them," Chiaretta countered. "You could adjust the range a little. I could do Barbara's role, or sing Ozias. He doesn't even show up until the end, and it's less to learn. And I'd be last. I'd be remembered."

"True." Vivaldi nodded his head. "But it isn't just the number of notes you have. What impression do you want to make? Do you want the audience to listen to you sing the role of a manservant? Even worse, a eunuch?"

Chiaretta had to concede that she wanted her final impression to be as an attractive woman, and the matter was settled, at least temporarily, when he sent her back to the apocryphal story to point out that he had invented the character of Abra to have a role suitable for her at all.

Her second explosion came when she saw the sheet music for her four arias and wanted to sing only the first two. "Boring" was her verdict on the third, and "wretched" was the nicest word she had for the last piece of music she would ever sing in public.

"He promised he would write the role for me, but listen to this!" She made a hash of the last aria one evening in their room. Maddalena, who had struggled for weeks to be the peacemaker, had to agree that it did sound like the marches the boys in the village had made up when they were playing soldiers.

Chiaretta could barely make her way through rehearsals without dropping her voice to a growl and stopping altogether in annoyance before finishing. Maddalena tried to get her sister to see it from Vivaldi's point of view, that there was a story to tell and she had one of many roles to play, but Chiaretta lashed out at her for defending him.

The soloists received just their own parts to rehearse, and the war broke out again when Chiaretta saw how all the pieces of the oratorio fit together. Her final aria was followed by one that would be sung by Barbara. A figlia named Giulia was playing Ozias, the governor of the besieged Hebrew city of Bethulia, and she would have the final aria and recitative.

"These are the last notes I am going to sing!" Chiaretta flung the music to the floor at her next private rehearsal with Vivaldi. "I hate them! And you make it worse by making the next aria so much better they'll forget me before I've had time to step back from the railing!"

"Chiaretta, how can a servant girl sing the last words of an oratorio? The story matters." Vivaldi spoke with the flat emphasis used to explain unpleasant facts to a child. "The characters matter."

"The audience won't care if Holofernes sings through his severed head," Chiaretta retorted. "They come to hear the singers."

Vivaldi's face reddened. "They come," he said, "to hear the music. It is the entire composition that counts, not just you."

Chiaretta refused to attend the next rehearsal, and when Vivaldi filled in with an understudy without comment, she sent word to him that she would not sing in the production at all.

"Caterina swaggers around acting like she really is Judith and I'm her maid. And don't you see the way Barbara smirks at me?" Chiaretta wept into her hands as she sat with her sister in their room. "And Giulia too. Why did he do this to me?"

Maddalena knew Chiaretta's threat not to perform was an empty one. Her final performance would already have occurred at a mass the week before, and not singing again would have been too much for her to bear.

"Your sister has been impossible," Vivaldi said to Maddalena at a break in one of the full rehearsals, while Chiaretta fumed in her room. "But threatening not to sing? It's ridiculous. Figlie di coro do what they are told. Deciding whether a part is good enough for them? That's no different from the divas at the opera house." He shuddered. "And besides, how much of a chance is there that the Congregazione will pass up the opportunity to make money on a farewell performance just to coddle your sister's ego? And her new family is unlikely to take kindly to her tantrums either." The annoyance in his voice was tinged with bitterness and anger. "No," he said. "She'll sing."

"It sounds as if you don't like her anymore," Maddalena said.

"That's not it at all," he said. "I feel terribly sorry for her. And for me, and for you, and for everyone. You won't ever play with her again. I can never write for her. No one who comes to the chapel will hear her voice. And that's nothing compared to what it must be like for her to know what she will lose. She has a gift she's scarcely had time to develop, and a decade or maybe more of fame she'll never see."

He shook his head. "No, even these last few weeks when she has been throwing tantrums and insulting my music, I have felt sorry for her. I wondered what I would be doing if the church had told me I couldn't play the violin." He paused. "I honestly can't imagine it. God help me, I think I would rather be dead."

THE FAINT SOUNDS OF DRUMS AND TRUMPETS GREW LOUDER as Chiaretta and Maddalena walked down the hallway toward the stairs leading to the chapel balcony. At the door to the staircase, Chiaretta stopped for a moment. "This is the last time I'll walk up these stairs."

Maddalena said nothing. She reached up and pretended to straighten her sister's sleeve, just for a reason to touch her. A girl of about ten came down the hall carrying a pitcher of water. She stared at Chiaretta until she came abreast of her, at which time she lowered her head, murmured a pardon, and started up the stairs.

"I must have looked like that," Chiaretta said, watching the girl protect the water from sloshing on the steps as she ascended. "The time I snuck up the stairs and found Michielina. So long ago I can hardly remember."

"We need to get upstairs," Maddalena had to say a second time. Chiaretta's lips were parted, and her eyes widened and then narrowed almost imperceptibly, as if her thoughts were so numerous and contradictory they had battled themselves down to none at all. She took in a breath as if to speak but then did no more than hold out her hand to Maddalena and pull her close in a long embrace.

Finally the two of them made their way onto the balcony. Below them the chapel was already nearly full. Maddalena began tuning her violin, but stopped for a moment. "Has Claudio arrived?" she asked.

"I don't know," Chiaretta said, peering through a break in the black gauze draping. "I don't see him."

She hadn't really looked. It felt as if the crowd was gathering to witness her execution. "I think I've made a mistake," she whispered, not sure whether she wanted to be heard.

"This place is more crowded than heaven!" Anna Maria grinned at them and crossed her eyes before sitting down at the harpsi-chord. As the other musicians filed in and took their places, she began to run her fingers across the keys. The singers came out next and lined up nearest the grille. Mechanically, Chiaretta went to join them. The last to come onto the balcony was Vivaldi, carry-ing his violin. He stood for the opening notes at an angle where he could be seen by the brass and string sections, and when the figlie nodded readiness, he lifted his bow to cue them.

The brass blared a fanfare, setting the scene in two warring camps, before Maddalena and the others burst into wild bowing, supported underneath by the cellos and bass viols. By the end of the sinfonia, every instrument had been heard. The timpani pounded until the music stands rattled. The woodwinds tootled, while in the background an ensemble of lutes, mandolins, theor-bos, and archlutes strummed furiously.

The music died down and Vivaldi began a wild solo, with the maestra, Prudenzia, joining in as principal violinist, followed by Maddalena, playing lead second violin. Together they wove a story of mounting excitement, ending in a final thunderous crescendo of drums and brass.

And then the story began. After Holofernes rallied his troops, his servant entered to tell him a beautiful woman from the Hebrew camp wanted to make his acquaintance. Caterina stepped forward and, without a bar of recitative, began to sing. Her voice was soft and fluid as she sang of Judith's fears and hopes, caressing each phrase with grace and a hint of melancholy.

Although the November cold had already begun seeping through the windows and hallways of the Pietà, the crowded bal-cony quickly grew hot. The figlie who had no other role than to swell the choruses began picking up pieces of music that had al-ready been played and used them to fan the musicians, who were glistening with sweat.

And then the music turned to Chiaretta. *"Ne timeas non,"* she sang. "Don't be afraid." Accompanied by Anna Maria at the harpsichord, Chiaretta's voice hovered over the chapel, the notes rising and falling, ebbing and flowing with perfect ease. Maddalena rested her violin on her lap as she watched her sister. Though Abra was supposed to be singing about Judith's beauty, it seemed to Maddalena as if not just the music but also the words were perfect for her sister. *"Cedit ira, ridet amor,"* Chiaretta sang. "Seeing the beauty of your face, anger fades and love begins to shine, and everyone applauds your noble spirit."

Before she finished, the violinist next to Maddalena fainted, and a crash of timpani at the rear suggested that another musician had fallen to the heat. The youngest figlie brought towels, dipped in hastily procured pails of water, for musicians and singers to wipe their brows when they had a few bars of rest.

Chiaretta shifted her feet back and forth, filling her lungs and exhaling in quiet sighs as she waited for her turn. Judith was calling Abra to support her in her hour of need. "Like a turtledove I speak to you, my trusted friend," Caterina sang, cooing like the bird itself. The music was so beautiful, so perfect, that despite her jealousy Chiaretta felt herself succumbing to it. When the solo was over, one of the newest iniziate gave Caterina a towel to wipe the sweat away, and exhausted, she buried her face in it without noticing the girl's adoring look.

Vivaldi had given Chiaretta a spectacular aria to counter with, but to her horror, in the recitative leading up to it, her voice came out sounding uncertain and a bit shrill. She fought to open her throat while Maddalena played the melody she would pick up. The last time they played together had to be perfect, and her voice settled. Within a minute Caterina's aria was put behind them, and the audience belonged to Chiaretta.

Maddalena's accompaniment fell silent, and Chiaretta's voice soared alone over the chapel with the heartbreak of farewell. Everything a voice could promise was delivered as her notes rose and fell, warbled and trilled. She sang as if she could fly off the balcony, straight out the back of the chapel and directly to paradise, before coming back to earth to bring the aria to a close.

"Abra! Abra!" Judith cried a few minutes later, after she had cut off Holofernes' head. Chiaretta brought her character to joyful life at the success of their mission, sliding her voice up and down as if drunk with happiness. And then she launched into the hated last aria, milking it for every likable bar as she went along. She took one last breath and made her voice soar once more, bidding it good-bye as she sent it into the rafters. And then it was over.

❦❦❦

IN THE WEEK REMAINING BEFORE THE WEDDING, EVERY MOTION Maddalena and Chiaretta made, every step they took, felt unnatural. Though Maddalena had relished the luxury of being able to practice with only her sister for company the last few months, playing her violin inside their room now felt like twisting a broken arm, and she kept it locked inside its case.

One night Chiaretta began to hum and then fell silent.

"Go on," Maddalena urged.

Chiaretta looked at her sister with a wan smile. "I guess I need to practice what it's like to have nothing to practice." She put down the mending she had been doing, and they went to bed in silence.

CHIARETTA'S WEDDING DRESS AND VEIL WERE LAID OUT IN A room adjoining the priora's study. Maddalena was brushing her sister's hair, which would be left loose, according to Venetian tradition, when Antonia and her mother arrived. Antonia, whose waist was growing thick with her first pregnancy, clapped her hands with excitement as Chiaretta's dress was laced up. Even Giustina was caught up in the moment, as she helped fasten a family heirloom, a jeweled pendant she herself had chosen, around Chiaretta's neck.

Venetian women were always married in their families' churches. The Pietà was the family for their own brides, but to control the excitement and imagination of the rest of the figlie, they were normally not permitted to attend. For Chiaretta's wedding, Anna Maria and the rest of the coro were given special permission to watch in silence from the balcony. Maddalena alone was allowed on the floor of the chapel, with Claudio's immediate family. They stood inside a small candlelit area near the altar, while all around them the chapel was deep in shadows. The priest's colorless voice disappeared into the gloom as he mumbled his way through the nuptial mass.

When she had been officially pronounced his wife, Chiaretta walked on Claudio's arm through the dark, quiet nave. Bernardo rushed ahead to open the door, and they stepped out into a flood of golden sunlight. The Riva was crowded with spectators jostling for a glimpse of her. "Chiaretta! Chiaretta!" they shouted over and over again.

Though her face was veiled, she could see their faces as she made her way across the flower-strewn walkway. *They're crying,* she realized.

And then, as she boarded her gondola, she heard what else they were saying. *"Addio!"* they called out. "Good-bye, Chiaretta. *Addio!"*

The gondola, festooned from the silver ferro to the stern with ribbons and flowers, pulled away through water turned pink and yellow and red by thousands of petals, getting smaller and smaller until it disappeared from view.

To Maddalena, standing on the empty dock, the boat seemed to be crossing the river Styx. It felt that much like dying.

*Part Four*_____

MASKS

_____*1716–1719*

FOURTEEN

CHIARETTA AWOKE ALONE IN HER BEDCHAMBER THE morning after her wedding. She sat up, pulling back the bed curtains to see feeble sunlight reaching into the room from a tiny glazed window. *I've missed prayers,* she thought. *"Domine, labia mea aperies,"* she murmured as she crossed herself, then paused, uncertain whether it was so late in the morning she should be saying Terce instead of Prime. She pulled back the velvet coverlet to get out of bed and continue her prayers at the wooden prie-dieu in the corner of her room. The tenderness between her legs made her wince, and she looked down to see a bloodstain on the sheets.

She draped the coverlet over the sheet to hide the stain from view and sat down on the bed again, her prayers forgotten in the enormity of where she was. At the Pietà, Maddalena would be murmuring encouragement to an attiva struggling with a new technique, and Anna Maria would be fretting about getting music copied in time for rehearsal. The sweet familiarity made her heart twist in her chest. *It's over,* she thought. *There is no going back.*

Chiaretta had been told by the priora what in general to expect on her wedding night, but alone in her room, she reviewed the details with bewilderment, as if she wasn't sure it had actually happened to her. At the Pietà dressing was simple, but when Claudio dropped her wedding gown below her waist and then helped her step out of it, her corset made her still feel almost fully clothed. As he loosened it, she took in what felt like her first deep breath since that morning. Standing behind her, he reached around to hold her tight, then turned her toward him and embraced her so firmly that by the time he pulled away and her breasts were left bare to his view, she hadn't felt as vulnerable and exposed as she had expected.

He took her into bed without removing the rest of her underclothing and then got up to blow out the candle. When he came back into bed, he was naked and pressed against her the unimaginably large thing she had been told would break the seal of her virginity and make her officially and completely his wife. It took some coaxing for her to relax enough to let him push between her legs, and then, as he whispered reassurances through her whimpers of fear, he pressed harder until she cried out and felt him burning inside her. It was less painful than she had been warned about—more of a shock than anything else—and when he began to moan, she was terrified that something inside her was hurting him. When he stiffened and then fell down next to her with a groan, she thought for a moment he might be dead, until he reached over and wiped his forehead on the sheet.

"Are you all right?" she asked, to which he burst out laughing. "I'm the one who should be asking," he said. "Did I hurt you too much?" She told him he hadn't, but then, unexpectedly, she started to cry, and though he wanted to know why, she could not explain.

He held her in his arms until she fell asleep. And then, when she woke up, he was gone. Chiaretta had no idea what she was supposed to do next. She went to the prie-dieu and knelt. *Blessed Mother of God, please forgive me if I don't pray properly today. I don't really feel like me.* She pressed her palms against her face and let their coolness seep into her flushed skin. "Please help me to be a good wife to Claudio," she whispered. "And help me understand this world I chose to live in."

Next to the prie-dieu was a large gilded cassone. Its lid was open, and she could see the small bag containing the pieces of ivory comb resting on top of a pile of linens. She picked the bag up and held it for a moment, feeling the two shapes inside, before kissing it and secreting it near the bottom, away from other eyes.

Despite her promise, Chiaretta would have given her sister her piece when she left the Pietà, but Maddalena did not ask for it. When Chiaretta first showed her the bits of ivory, Maddalena looked at them for a long time before handing them back, saying she didn't want to see them again. "They'll just get me thinking," she said. "I'd rather not be reminded." But Chiaretta wanted to be reminded. She felt like enough of an oddity among the Morosinis. It helped a little to know that her past was as populated with real human beings as anyone else's. She just didn't know who they were.

As she buried the pieces of comb in the cassone, her other hand rested on top of a set of lace-trimmed pillowcases Maddalena had made for her as a wedding gift. Seeing them, Chiaretta felt a rush of fear at how leaving the Pietà would change her relationship with her sister. But still, as she looked around the room, the future didn't seem bleak, just unknown. Her bed was so big and comfortable it felt like sleeping on a cloud, and the adjoining sitting room, which Claudio had told her was hers also, was larger than the room she and Maddalena had shared until the day before. Claudio had his own rooms on the same floor, and because his parents lived on the floor below, the portego onto which their rooms opened would be theirs alone. And Claudio? She would have to learn to deal with a life in which everything, including her husband's habits, was new. Nevertheless, she had thought he would be there when she woke up.

In the way Antonia had taught her was required of patrician brides, she pinned up the back of her hair, sliding a thin gold band from her hairline to the crown of her head. "Chiaretta Morosini," she said aloud to herself in the mirror. *I have a last name.* "Chiaretta Morosini," she said again, trying to smile the way she would when she greeted the world.

She put on a plain dress she had been told would be suitable for days when she would not be venturing from the house. Its scoop neck was trimmed with a ribbon woven from gold thread and accented with tiny glass beads. From just below her breasts, a voluminous silk skirt dropped to the floor, and the tight sleeves, in a matching blue chosen to accent her eyes, ballooned out at the elbows to enable her to move her arms. When she had laced on a pair of soft-soled shoes, she opened the door.

The portego was silent. The natural light had been almost extinguished by the deepening gloom of a rainy day. "Claudio?" she called. The echo died without a reply. She knocked on the door of his study, and when she got no answer, she pushed it open to see that the lamps were unlit.

Drawn toward the light of the window at the end of the portego, Chiaretta went out onto the loggia overlooking the Grand Canal. Gondoliers passed by, not appearing to notice the raindrops falling into the water, as they called out to one another. She took in a deep breath and felt the strange sensation of being outside alone.

"What are you doing out there?" Giustina Morosini stood in the portego, motioning Chiaretta to come back inside. "You're shivering," she said, in a way that for a change sounded more concerned than critical. "Claudio is away on business for the day," she said, anticipating her new daughter-in-law's question. "You are all right?"

"Yes," Chiaretta said quickly. Then, realizing Giustina was referring to what had occurred between her and Claudio on their wedding night, she blushed.

"Now that I know you're up, I will instruct the servants to change the sheets," Giustina said, motioning toward the staircase leading down to the piano nobile. "You will come with me and listen, so you will know how to speak to them yourself in the future."

She rang a bell. "Zuana will be here in a minute. Our servants stay out of sight, but you'll find they are not far away and they come promptly.

"The sheets in the signora's bedroom need changing," she said to the young servant who had hurried into the room. "And make sure it is done properly so there will be no stain."

"Oh dear," she said when the servant hurried off and she turned and saw Chiaretta's scarlet face. "I've embarrassed you. Well, you will learn there is no way to avoid having servants know your business. The important thing is that they keep your secrets. Will you have breakfast in your quarters today?"

Chiaretta had no idea what the answer should be. "I don't know," she said. "Is that what—?" *What we do?*

Giustina cut her off. "Do whatever you wish," she said with a forced smile.

"I"—Chiaretta stammered—"I'm sorry, but I don't know what to wish."

"All right." Giustina's clipped tone implied that Chiaretta was wasting her time. "Today I will ask Zuana to bring breakfast to you in your chambers. After that you can decide about dinner."

"Zuana?"

"The servant girl who was just here. She is yours. Quite young, but I think you'll find her adequate."

Giustina said nothing more, and in the silence that followed Chiaretta heard a quick murmured interchange between two servants on the floor below them and the squeaky hinge of a cabinet as something was put away. Somewhere outside the house a church bell pealed.

"Will Claudio be here for dinner?" Chiaretta broke into the quiet as pleasantly as she could manage.

"I doubt it, although he might surprise us. It is the day after his wedding after all. He often takes his dinner elsewhere, though, and you shouldn't count on him."

Chiaretta thought she saw the hint of a smirk on Giustina's face, as if knowing more about her son than Chiaretta did was a weapon her mother-in-law intended to keep polished and ready. *What had Antonia called her mother? A she-wolf.* Claudio and Antonia had probably done their best to help, but if Giustina did not have it in her to be any kinder than this, Chiaretta would have to learn to deal with her mother-in-law on her own.

Though she had been up only a short while, suddenly she felt exhausted and excused herself to go back to her room. She lay down on her bed, her eyes burning so intensely it hurt to shut them. Then she heard a soft tapping on her door.

"Madonna?" a small voice said.

She opened the door to see Zuana, holding a tray. "Your breakfast," she said as if it were a question. Noticing Chiaretta's red eyes, she asked, "Madonna is all right?"

"Yes," she said. "Do I take the tray?"

Zuana gave her a bemused grin. "No, Madonna, I put it down for you." She set up a place for Chiaretta to eat and then disappeared with no more than a nod.

Overwhelmed by even the simplest things she did not know, Chiaretta stared at the plate in front of her. She chewed without tasting, then put her napkin down and crawled into bed, noticing that the sheets were clean. When she awoke, the food had been removed without her having heard a thing.

BY NIGHTFALL CLAUDIO WAS STILL NOT HOME. CHIARETTA PUT on a shawl she had found in the cassone and went out onto the loggia to watch the last of the rain clouds drifting over the moon. A boat with a group of musicians trailed behind a gondola in which Chiaretta could make out the silhouette of a couple embracing.

As another gondola passed the loggia, she heard the melody of one of her solos at the Pietà. She began to sing, at first almost in a whisper, but her voice soon rose unaware. The gondolier came back into a position just under the balcony. The light from his lantern danced on the dark waters of the canal as he began to harmonize. A night heron added its cry to the music as it flew by.

"What are you doing?" Claudio's voice reverberated in the portego and his boots clicked against the marble floor as he strode toward her. "Get away from there! Don't you understand?" He pulled so hard on her arm she cried out. "I told you never to sing in public!"

He dragged her away from the loggia and shut the door behind him, his brow knit in anger. "Sing inside for me, for my family. Sing if I say you can. But until then, keep your mouth shut!"

Chiaretta's face, white with terror in the dim light of the portego, caused him to release his grip. He lowered his voice and tried to explain. "I took out a bond. I signed an oath. Do you know what that means?"

She squeezed her eyes shut, shaking her head.

"Chiaretta, a denunciation is a terrible thing. I could spend my life in prison. I could lose my business. People even lose their lives—"

Choking on a sob that exploded from deep within her, Chiaretta broke away from him. She ran into her chamber and flung the door shut behind her.

THE DAY BEFORE, AFTER CHIARETTA'S GONDOLA DISAPPEARED among the other boats near the Doge's Palace, Maddalena went back inside the church. The candles around the altar had already been blown out, and as her eyes adjusted to the darkness, they were drawn to the balcony, where a single oil lamp was burning. A lone figure was silhouetted against the dim light.

"Anna Maria?" Maddalena whispered. "Is that you?"

"Maddalena? Where are you? I can't see anything."

"I'm sitting on one of the benches. I'll stand up. Can you see me now?"

"Barely. What are you doing?"

"Just sitting here thinking."

"I came to practice on the organ. Do you mind?"

"No." Maddalena sighed and sat back down. By rote, she crossed herself, but no prayers came, only a blankness as dark as the chapel itself.

Maddalena heard the bench scrape as Anna Maria sat down, and then the first wheezy notes broke through the silence. She rested her elbows on her knees and put her face in her hands. The oppressive sound of the organ grated on her nerves like a tongue exploring a toothache.

She got up and stole out of the church. Night was falling, and fog was settling into the courtyard. *It looked like this the first time I saw it,* she thought, shutting her eyes and remembering. Inside the chapel, the organ fell silent. For a moment, time stopped and there was no future to concern herself about, no life without

Chiaretta to contemplate. Then the music started up again. Her feet moved unbidden, telling her it was time to go on.

THE ROOM WHERE SHE HAD SLEPT WITH HER SISTER WAS drained of life. Maddalena herself would be leaving, having been told to return to the quarters where the maestre lived. *Best to do this quickly,* she thought, going to the cassone to collect her things. Inside, left behind in the rush, was Chiaretta's sketchbook. Maddalena sat on the bed and caressed the cover before opening it.

> *I saw Antonia today and she is comming to the party. She says there will be games and more food than I have ever sen.*
>
> *I walked along this cannal and saw kinfishers.*
>
> *I didn't know what some of the foods were.*

Maddalena leafed back a few pages, knowing what she would find. "Susana cracked her bow," she had written, "and Luciana gave the one I use to her. She told her to leave it in the cabinet so I could use it too, but she didn't look like she cared if she did or not."

She turned the page. "Luciana is a devvil from hell."

Maddalena traced the dent that Chiaretta had made in the book with those words. Then she got up and wiped her eyes. Smoothing out the blanket where she had been sitting, she noticed a golden hair. She tucked it into the pages of the sketchbook and kissed the cover before closing the door behind her.

THE STONE WALLS OF THE ROOM WHERE THE MAESTRE AND sotto maestre lived were covered by threadbare tapestries that kept out some of the cold, and the room was small enough for the coal stove to do the rest. In the middle was a carpet, on top of which were several chairs and a table. Anna Maria was sitting on

Maddalena's bed and jumped up to greet her. "Where did you go today?" she said, putting her arm around her and leading her to one of the chairs. "I called out when I was finished playing, but nobody was there."

"I've been packing up, and"—Maddalena sat down and winced, although she hadn't felt any pain—"I guess, here I am."

She got up and gave Anna Maria a wan smile as she put Chiaretta's sketchbook in the cassone by her bed. As she shut the lid, a sudden rush of memories forced her down on her bed as hard as if she had been pushed. She put her hands over her face and began to cry.

CHIARETTA KNELT AT THE PRIE-DIEU UNTIL HER CANDLE WENT out. Then, feeling her way around the unfamiliar room, she found her bed and lay in it, staring into the darkness. *I don't belong here,* she thought. *I will never belong here.* But what could be done about it now? Was her mistake enough for Claudio to annul their marriage? He had as much as said she was a danger to him. And if he did annul the marriage, where would she go? Not back to the Pietà, not after what had happened the night before. *Perhaps I could move away, go someplace where I could sing. I could support myself somehow, maybe find work singing opera. I have savings at the Pietà. I can go tell them to give me my money and leave Venice.*

For the first time since she had woken up that morning, she felt something other than fear. But the plan would not work, and she knew it. The Pietà would not turn over her savings to let her do anything like that. And even if they did, what would she do then?

Do I just walk up to a gondolier and tell him to take me—where? Out of town? She had never walked around Venice alone, never once held coins in her hand. And even if she got out of the city, where would she go? She knew the names of a few other places— Rome, Milan, Florence—but not where they were. She lay in bed, punishing herself for everything she did not know, until she fell asleep.

A FEW HOURS LATER, SHE WOKE UP TO FIND CLAUDIO SITTING in a chair beside her bed.

"I was watching you sleep," he said. "And feeling like an ass." He held out his hand, inviting her to sit up. "You are the first person I've ever known who wasn't raised just as I was," he said. "I'll have to stop assuming you understand things you don't know anything about."

Chiaretta sat on the edge of the bed. "I'm so sorry," she whispered.

Claudio pulled her to her feet. "Come to my room," he said. "Zuana couldn't stoke your fire because she was afraid to go in when you wouldn't answer." Putting his arm around her, he guided her toward the door. "It's warmer there, and the lamps are lit."

Claudio's study was paneled in wood ornamented with designs in scarlet and gold. A bookshelf covered one wall, and a window with heavy velvet curtains took up another. A small fireplace gave off enough light to illuminate a portrait of a stern-looking man hanging above the mantel.

"My great-uncle Francesco," Claudio said when he saw Chiaretta looking at the painting. "Commander of the Venetian fleet when he wasn't busy being the doge." He gestured toward a chair. "This is the most comfortable place to sit. I can call for some tea if you'd like."

Chiaretta shook her head, sitting and arranging her robe around her, as Claudio continued. "I keep this portrait here to remind me who I am. Being part of one of the old families of Venice makes me a little of everyone else before me." He sat down, pulling his chair closer to her. "Every Morosini at least—good or bad."

"Claudio, I—"

He took her hand. "You don't have to say anything. I was not a gentleman. I've acted disgracefully, and it is you who are owed an apology. I'd just like to make a better start now."

"I just don't know . . ." Chiaretta's voice trailed off.

"Don't know what?"

The words tumbled out. "Whether you think you made a mistake. Whether you want me. Whether I can do this."

Claudio stood up and walked behind her chair, leaning forward to put his arms around her. "I wouldn't have asked to marry you if I wasn't sure you could do it in grand style." He put his head down and buried his face in her neck. "You are as strong as you are beautiful," he said, kissing her again and again until she slapped his hand and told him to stop tickling her.

"That's more like it," he said. "I want to see you smiling." He came around and pulled her to her feet. "You are my wife," he said, looking in her eyes, "and I am so proud, and so happy." He grinned. "And all of Venice is jealous."

THE FIRE HAD DIED DOWN AND THE DAWN LIGHT HAD BEGUN to filter into the room before Chiaretta and Claudio were too tired to talk anymore. His mother, they agreed, would be difficult to get around as long as they lived in the same house. But families had an understanding that each floor in the home was separate and private, and Giustina was as unlikely to invade their space without warning as they were to walk unannounced into hers. The circumstances that morning were unusual, and she wouldn't be making such appearances a habit. If she did, Claudio, not Chiaretta, would take it in hand.

The situation might change, but seeking Giustina out now, they agreed, would gain Chiaretta nothing. She would probably end up feeling worse every time she tried. Though Giustina might see herself as in charge of her daughter-in-law's education, Chiaretta would be better off making herself as unavailable as possible for her mother-in-law's kind of lesson. Tomorrow Claudio would stop by Antonia's house and ask her to come over as often as she could to spend time with his wife. Chiaretta could learn from her friend how everything was done, and when her pregnancy forced Antonia into confinement, Chiaretta could keep her company at home.

"I just hope she doesn't turn you into a monster." Claudio laughed, pulling Chiaretta to her feet. "But for now, I need to get you to bed. I've kept you up all night."

In her bedchamber, he removed her robe, revealing her body beneath a thin silk shift. "Ahh," he said, running his eyes over her as she reached out her arms. "But I would be a cad to lie with you again so soon." He pulled back the coverlet. "Sleep now. It will all work out. Just give it time."

FIFTEEN

HE MASK WAS MADE OF LEATHER, STRETCHED AND molded into the shape of a cat's face and painted in pearlescent shades of white and blue. A filigreed design in gold mesh and wire sprang out like angel wings from the nose bridge, as if the cat itself were wearing a mask.

"It's beautiful," Chiaretta said, running her fingers over the faux pearls and tiny glass beads that rimmed the mask's edges. Handing it to Claudio, she stood and turned around. "Will you help me put it on?"

When he was finished tying the ribbon, she went out to the portego to look at herself in one of the gilded mirrors along the walls. At the Pietà, Chiaretta had seen her reflection only when she studied maniera and in the few minutes before a concert, when the figlie passed around a hand mirror. Two months after her wedding she was still getting used to the sensation of seeing herself in her new clothes and hairstyle as she walked through the portego or looked into the silver-backed mirror on her dressing table. *This is what I look like with my hair down,* or *This is what I look like when I wake up in the morning,* or *This is what I look like walking,* she would think to herself, not so much out of vanity as curiosity and amazement.

Chiaretta stood in front of the huge mirror, watching the masked figure copy her movements. She felt a little queasy, as she sometimes did getting on or off a gondola when the canal waters were stirred up. She untied the mask and the feeling vanished, then she held it up to her face and took it away over and over again, in a slow process of reassurance.

It does look beautiful with my new dress, she thought. The bodice of shimmering silver and aquamarine brocade showed off her full breasts over a skirt fashioned from yards of taffeta silk that swished when she moved.

Turning to find Claudio to have him put the mask back on, she gasped to see a man in a tricornered hat over a black hood and mantle watching her from a few feet away. "Did my bauta scare you?" Her husband's voice was muffled beyond recognition by the edge of the plain white mask resting on his upper lip.

The blood rushed from her head, and she put her hand on a chair to steady herself, ambushed by the sudden memory of the man in the white mask so many years before. "I don't like this," she said.

"Nonsense! Everyone loves Carnevale. It just takes a little getting used to."

"But what if we get separated? How will I find you?"

Claudio had taken off his hat and mask, and stood before her in a silk hood that covered his head except for a small hole for his face. He leaned forward to kiss her cheek. "Some other man in a bauta will put you in his gondola and take you to his house and I'll never see you again."

He watched to make sure she knew he was joking before adding, "It won't happen. You will be glued to my arm. Or even better . . ." He disappeared into her bedroom and came back with the square of purple silk the mask had been wrapped in. "Help me fold this and pin it on my hat."

When Chiaretta handed him her mask to tie it back on, he shook his head. "That's for parties." He disappeared into his study and brought out a bauta identical to his own. "You have to wear this."

He helped her put on the hood and mantle, and after tying on her plain white mask, he went back into his study and returned with a tricornered hat identical to his.

Chiaretta looked out at herself and felt the nausea returning. Two figures stared at her from the mirror. One was tall and, except for the white mask, was garbed in black from head to foot. The other was smaller and, below the mantle, was wearing a taffeta skirt. She shut her eyes and exhaled through her nostrils. The mask heated up in response, and as she shifted her shoulders inside the bauta, she reminded herself that as long as she didn't look in the mirror, she was just herself.

She took Claudio's arm, and together they descended the stairs and walked out the dock. Chiaretta glanced up at the purple rosette pinned onto his hat as they boarded the gondola. Seeing it, a surge of affection overpowered her, making her want nothing more than to run with him back up to her bedchamber, throw off their costumes, and make love.

The gondolier cast off the lines, and they slipped out onto the Grand Canal toward the Rialto Bridge. Around them in the darkness, boats glided through the water, filled with figures in black, their masks a ghoulish white in the lamplight.

WHERE CLAUDIO WAS TAKING HER WAS A SURPRISE HE DIDN'T want to spoil. Not until she saw the brightly lit facade of the Teatro

San Giovanni Grisostomo did Chiaretta understand that she was going to her first opera, not at the Teatro Sant'Angelo but as the guest of boxholders at the most lavish theater in Venice.

"I'm afraid you're going to be totally spoiled and you won't even want to come to my poor little theater after you see this one!" Claudio spoke almost at a yell to be heard over the cries of people hawking refreshments and selling tickets. "*Scenario!*" he called out, holding up a small coin to catch the attention of a young boy selling programs.

As they moved through the lobby, Chiaretta saw the majority of the people in attendance were wearing cloaks identical to theirs and the same white masks, although a few wore black ones with wrinkled brows or bulging eye sockets.

"What are those?" she asked, mumbling her words under the lip of her mask.

"Characters from the commedia dell'arte," Claudio said. "In a year you'll recognize them all."

"And who is that bird?" She nodded in the direction of someone hobbling toward them wearing a mask with painted-on spectacles and a long beak.

Claudio lifted his mask slightly to speak more clearly. "During the last plague, a doctor stuffed his mask with herbs he thought would keep him from getting sick while he treated his patients."

"Did it work?"

"Not for long, but everybody loved the mask."

The person wearing the plague doctor mask brushed Chiaretta's shoulder in passing, offering excuses in a soft, high voice before continuing on.

"Was that a woman?" Chiaretta asked, amazed.

Claudio turned around to look. "You never know in Venice," he said, scrutinizing the figure as it disappeared around a corner. "She—or he—is wearing pianelle. They're these ridiculous high clogs hardly anybody wears anymore. Women today would rather get their feet wet than walk on stilts, and I for one am glad." He hugged her around the shoulder. "I like you just the height you are."

Claudio took her arm as they reached the staircase. After ascending several flights, Chiaretta found herself in a curved hallway. Men in livery were standing in front of a dozen or more gilded doors, and when Claudio reached a particular one, the servant ushered them inside.

The box in which Chiaretta found herself was divided into two parts. In the back, just inside the door, a couch and matching armchair were arranged around a table on which playing cards were strewn. On a credenza to one side were several bottles of wine and silver trays with cheeses and preserves. A mirror was positioned on one wall to reflect the view on the stage for those who were too far inside the box to see it directly. In the middle of the box, a curtain had been pulled back. Through it Chiaretta could see a gilded balcony rail and a scattering of half a dozen or more seats with red velvet upholstery.

The owners of the box had not yet arrived, but within a few minutes Claudio was greeted by a man who removed his mask to reveal himself. Marco Grimani, whose family owned the opera house, was making the rounds of the boxes to greet his friends.

"I heard you would be here," he said to Claudio. "And I wanted to meet your bride, the famous Chiaretta della Pietà." He bowed to her and took her hand. "Blasted Carnevale! For years I tried to see your face, and now you're wearing a mask!"

"You can take off your bauta," Claudio told her, reaching up to remove her hat. He untied her mask and helped her pull the hood and mantle over her head.

"Brava!" Marco said. "Proof that the putte are angels after all!" He lifted her hand with a flourish and kissed her on the wrist.

Their conversation was cut off by the arrival of the owners of the box. While Claudio sat on the sofa and chatted, Marco escorted

Chiaretta to the front. She looked out across at the tiers of identical boxes ringing the sides and back of the theater. Gilded reliefs of shells, flowers, and leaves decorated the pillars. Human figures carved in marble held up each box from below.

She leaned out to look over the railing down to the floor, where dozens of people were milling around. "Where are they going to sit?" she asked Marco.

"They're not," he said, "unless they rent seats. Just like at the Pietà." He pointed to a few people carrying benches to the front. "There's still an hour to go. It will be packed down there by the time it starts."

"But how will they see?"

Marco chuckled. "No one pays much attention anyway." He pointed up. "Watch the ceiling!"

On one end was painted the Grimani coat of arms and a figure that Marco told her represented Glory, surrounded by cherubs and divinities holding garlands of flowers. Toward the other end was a tableau depicting Venus.

"It's beautiful," she said.

"Oh, you haven't seen the best part yet," Marco crowed. "It's one of the wonders of Venice!" Just then the tableau of Venus began to retract and a chandelier almost thirty feet across was lowered. Four gold and silver branches, on which dozens of white candles burned, came together at the center in the coat of arms of the Grimani family, from which emanated gilded rays encrusted with balls painted like pearls.

"Bravo!" Claudio said, coming up behind them and pulling up another seat. "For my bride," he said, handing Chiaretta a small glass of amber-colored wine. "The Grimanis put on the best show in town even before the opera starts."

"And while we're waiting, we can watch the pre-opera entertainment." Marco pointed across to the boxes on the other side. "There are the Gradenigos, enjoying the first course of their dinner." His eyes scanned the boxes. "What have we here?"

He pointed to a box where a man in a bauta cupped the bodice of a masked woman's dress before they closed the curtain behind them. "We'll just pretend we can't imagine who they are," Marco said. "After all, they're wearing masks. Who could tell?"

"No idea at all," repeated Claudio, his eyebrows raised as the two men passed a look between them that Chiaretta did not understand.

Below, on the main floor, she saw two men arguing. They pulled the masks from their faces and began to rain blows on each other. Soon others joined in, until a pile of bodies kicked and flailed on the floor while a few women fanned themselves wildly and people in the first tier of boxes threw whatever they could find at them.

The orchestra had been tuning up for the last five or ten minutes but could not be heard over the din until the conductor signaled them to play as loudly as they could. As the chandelier rose and the tableau of Venus slid back through the hole in the ceiling, they played the first notes.

Chiaretta watched the curtain go up on a set evoking an ancient Greek harbor. A vessel sat at a wharf midstage, while in the foreground on one side was an open-air temple. Chiaretta looked into a palace courtyard with a marble staircase, leading up to a mezzanine bedchamber on the other side of the stage. In a manner so seamless there appeared to be no back wall to the theater at all, the set blended into a painted backdrop depicting a coast with an armada of ships in the distance.

The audience on the floor applauded before going back to what they had been doing. Dancers came onstage to perform a ballet, setting the scene for the entrance of the hero and his entourage of soldiers. After a few minutes of recitative, a voice pierced through the noise in the theater and brought the crowd briefly to attention. Though the pitch was in a woman's range, the same as Caterina's when she sang Judith, the sound resonated off the back wall and ceiling with what seemed to Chiaretta to be several times the volume.

"Do you know who that is? You're seeing one of the great castrati of our time," Claudio told her. "It's Senesino. He's on his way to Dresden after this opera closes, but word is he plans to sing for Handel in London."

The heroine was going to fall in love with a short little man with rolls of fat spilling out over the collar of his costume? *He looks like a walnut with arms and legs,* Chiaretta thought. As he continued his aria, the magnitude of his voice began to make anything, even love with a walnut, seem possible.

"The lungs of a man and the voice of a boy," Claudio said. "But quite a price to pay."

Senesino's voice grew louder, leading into a cadenza filled with trills and swoops and runs of notes growing ever higher in pitch until the whole audience was watching him. Cued by a flourish of his pudgy arms, the orchestra joined in, and the aria ended, to an explosion of applause.

Then the stage was filled again with soldiers, and women waving them off to war. Senesino got on a boat at midstage. Around him painted rows of waves moved back and forth, and his boat began to rock. A god flew down from the rafters, and they performed a duet before the god disappeared above the stage. As the boat moved offstage, Senesino raised his voice. Brandishing his sword, he brought the curtain down on the first act.

Except for a naval battle, complete with cannons and smoke and a ship that sank by disappearing under the stage, the audience ignored most of the rest of the opera. The seats on the other side of the theater were empty except when Senesino sang, and below Chiaretta, the people in the lowest-tiered boxes were more engaged in a contest to see who could spit farthest into the crowd.

As she watched the other singers struggle over the noise,

Chiaretta thought about the rapt audiences seated below her as she sang from the chapel balcony. Tonight, a soprano had already stopped in the middle of an aria and rushed into the wings screaming at the audience to stop throwing things onstage, and another let her voice drop as if the effort wasn't worth it, but most just went gamely on.

Finally, even Chiaretta grew bored and went to join Claudio. His face was flushed with wine, and he was losing jovially at cards. She stood behind her husband, resting her fingers on his shoulders. He reached up and patted her hand. "My good luck has arrived," he said to his friends, and won the next three hands.

The curtain dropped for the final time, the chandelier came back down, and the audience began to drift out. Hiding a yawn, Chiaretta put on her bauta, and as she took Claudio's arm, they descended to the lobby and out onto the street.

The square in front of the theater had been transformed into a wild scene of masked Carnevale revelers, jugglers, street musicians, and vendors of food and trinkets. Claudio led her through the crush and down side streets, shielding her with his body from the crowds of people trying to force their way through in both directions.

Then she and Claudio were at the Rialto Bridge. Above them, the stone arch was full of people, reminding Chiaretta of the day she had witnessed the fights at the Ponte dei Carmini when she was a little girl. Drunken choruses of bawdy songs drifted through the night air, but tonight the occasional loose feather from a mask or empty flask of wine was all that fell from the bridge.

Still, Chiaretta leaned into Claudio's arm and held it tight. She wanted to be home. *Home.* Palazzo Morosini, her own bed, her own room, with her husband beside her.

MADDALENA LISTENED TO THE SOUNDS OF THE FIRST NIGHT of Carnevale from behind the walls of the Pietà. Earlier that evening she had been in the parlatorio as group after group of people passed through. The figlie chatted and giggled with their faces close to the grille, offering pastries and small glasses of wine across the barrier to their guests, and clapping their hands as the revelers entertained them with hand puppets and magic tricks.

Maddalena had watched to see if perhaps Chiaretta would be among them. She had come twice with Antonia since her wedding, but the experience of talking to each other through the grille was so unnerving they had both been glad when the visits ended. But tonight Chiaretta had not come, and although Maddalena wasn't surprised, she was still disappointed when she left the crowded parlatorio and went up to bed without a glimpse of her sister.

A few days later, Vivaldi arrived for a conference on two concerti Maddalena would supervise. His hair was stringy, and his eyes were rimmed with red. His hands were trembling as he took the violin from its case, and she saw his arms jerk several times in the way hers sometimes did when she woke from a bad dream.

"Are you all right?" she asked him.

He shrugged it off. "It's just nerves. *L'Incoronazione di Dario* is opening next week, and the scene painting is still not done, the castrato acts like he's God, and the investors think I can produce an opera without money."

Vivaldi didn't wait for a response. "I got an order for ten concerti," he told Maddalena with a conspiratorial grin, "and I delivered them in three days."

"How could you do that?"

"I didn't sleep! And they weren't entirely new, but what does original mean anyway? I took works I'd already done and changed them a little here and there. Everyone does it."

His laugh came out as a snicker. "Sometimes I just rip off the title page and write a new one, dedicating the work to the person who bought it. No one knows the difference. The client I sold them to is leaving Venice anyway."

It didn't sound very honest, and Vivaldi noticed the dubious expression on Maddalena's face. "I have no choice," he said. "Music pays very badly. I have a house and two servants. I have to eat and so do they. And my father is not well and may be moving in soon."

He lifted his palms up and gave her a helpless look. "Maddalena, for you music can be whatever you want—dreamy, luxurious, sentimental, passionate, who knows? For me it's a business, and when I'm sitting at my desk composing, most of the time I am strictly a mercenary, I'm afraid."

He saw her somber face. "Don't despise me," he said. "It's not my choice. That's just the way it is."

His words spilled out with tics and wild gestures. Without a word, Maddalena put down a pewter cup full of water on the table next to his violin case and waited.

I have better things to do, she thought, picking up the new music he had brought. *I could be getting this to the copyists. I have a concert to rehearse. I have a pupil to visit in the infirmary.*

He took a sip without comment. "The Congregazione isn't very happy with me, because I'm spending almost all my time on my operas."

"Operas?" She pulled herself back, trying to sound more interested than she felt. "There's another besides Dario?"

"*Penelope la Casta.* You know, the story of Ulysses' wife." Vivaldi took another drink and thought for a moment. "A little like you, she is. Patient. Always there waiting."

Waiting? He thinks I have nothing to do but wait for him to show up? Maddalena began loosening her bow. "You need to sleep," she said, trying to control the annoyance in her voice.

Vivaldi leaned forward and, resting his elbows on his knees, he covered his face with his hands. "You are always so good to me. I think you're right."

The endearments that had once sustained her now rubbed her raw. *Go,* she thought. *Just go.*

He was already packing up. "If I'm not sick already, I should be," he said, "and they are all so unforgiving. So unforgiving." He snapped his violin case shut. "I'd better go home."

Maddalena watched from a window as he walked along the alley next to the Pietà, clutching his chest, whether from pain or habit she was not sure. She felt her stomach turn the way it had years before as she tapped in the cabinet for the missing bow. He was a difficult man, but ever since his return, the music the coro played had been divine, sometimes so exquisite she felt as if her heart were hovering just outside her body, experiencing music unmediated by any boundaries at all.

"I didn't mean it about you going," she whispered, but even as she said it, the other part of her was glad to see his back disappear around the corner.

WHEN MADDALENA NEXT SAW VIVALDI, HE CAME BEARING THE news she didn't want to hear. *Dario* was a financial success, but the opera itself had not received much praise, and the job of impresario in the cutthroat theater environment of Venice was more than he had bargained for. Even before the first performance of *Penelope,* he had made a decision to leave for Mantua as soon as Carnevale ended, to try his luck there. He was finished at the Pietà by mutual agreement, and he had just stopped in to say good-bye.

As Maddalena lay alone in bed that night, she thought back to his last departure. It had almost destroyed her life, and it struck her as odd that she could no longer remember what she had been thinking and why she had been so distraught. *I don't recognize that girl now,* she thought to herself.

She rolled onto her side and looked around the room. *As long as I am here, you will always be protected,* she remembered him saying, but here she was, sleeping among the leaders of the coro, and she didn't need that reassurance anymore.

But why do I feel so empty? She had spent several years since his return bustling around pretending she didn't care, and she had believed it herself. But now she envisioned a carriage on the road to a new city, with Vivaldi inside, his head full of music, and she wished she were beside him.

She sat up to think. The covers fell to her lap, leaving her bare shoulders exposed in the cold air of the dormitory.

He is the most brilliant musician of his time.

He is a priest.

I am an orphan who can play the violin.

That was all. The rest was kindnesses and good fortune and no more.

No more? She doubted it. She was an adult, and her judgment in such matters was better than the last time he left. He did care about her, of that she was sure, but why bother lying awake thinking about it, or about how she felt about him? Maddalena lay back down. It felt good to be where she was, and who she was. What difference did it make if he wanted to be with her? Why bother even wondering if she wanted to be with him? What would be the point of holding her past up to the light and asking herself whether the right word for whatever she had felt for him was love, or infatuation, or something else?

He was gone, and even thinking about him would drag her down as surely as unwanted things tied to rocks went to the bottom of the lagoon.

What is wrong with me? Her hands were cold and clammy as she held them to her face. Anna Maria was murmuring in her sleep, and Maddalena could hear a bed creak as one of the sotto maestre turned over. *Perhaps my humors are out of balance. Maybe I should ask to be bled,* she thought, *to get rid of this war in my veins.*

But another feeling washed over her also, a surprising lightness, almost a giddiness. Vivaldi was exhausting, with his moods, his fragile lungs, his cutting of corners, and his little frauds. Life would be easier now, without him to take up so much space. She could concentrate only on the coro now, surrounding herself with music and with the next generation of putte. She would become the maestra in a few years, when Prudenzia retired. There would be more Elizabetas among her pupils, and she could love them for their purity and their simplicity.

That should be enough, she told herself, but when she pictured her future, she thought she should feel more of a glow. And then it struck her. *I want to love someone and be loved back in the same way. Not like sisters love each other, not like I love the putte and they love me but like—* She stopped for a moment before acknowledging what she was thinking: *like a man and a woman.* Perhaps being around Vivaldi had given her a glimpse of something people in other circumstances got to feel, got to act upon. She noticed something was missing in her life only when he was absent from it. But it couldn't be love she had for him. Love should feel different from the ache inside her.

How would it feel to be drawn inside the warm aura emanating from another person, to crawl in and live there? She lay down again and tried to imagine it. The only person she had ever thrown her arms around and held tight was her sister. Now she was gone, and Vivaldi too. She felt something inside begin to fold in around her, the stirrings of despair and self-pity.

"No!" she whispered into her pillow. *I am never again going to feel as bad as I did the last time he left.* Her breath was hot in the pillow. *Never.*

SIXTEEN

ANTONIA'S BELLY WAS BIG AS A LUTE IN HER EIGHTH month of pregnancy. Every morning Chiaretta secretly brought the sweets and other delicacies Antonia's doctor and husband had forbidden out of fear of her mounting size.

"When they have the babies, they can starve themselves if they want," Antonia said as Chiaretta arrived one day toward the end of Carnevale. She beckoned Chiaretta to take the contraband from her pockets and lay it on her lap. Then, leaning forward as much as she could from the cloud of pillows arranged against the headboard of her bed, Antonia unwrapped the parcel. "Sugared nuts! And fruit candy!" she squealed, popping a square of dried, sweetened lemon into her mouth. "You are so good to me, but do you think you could smuggle in a little wine tomorrow? Some of that sweet stuff I like?"

"Antonia!" Chiaretta slapped the knee that was poking up under the covers. "It's a little hard to hide that, and what am I supposed to do? Go to the kitchen and say I need a bottle of wine?"

"Why not? They're your servants. They aren't going to talk."

"Except to your mother."

"Oh please, don't remind me." Antonia groaned. She clutched her stomach. "Sancta Maria, this hurts. I can't wait for it to be over." She leaned back and took a few deep breaths. "So," she said, "tell me what my brother's been up to."

Chiaretta's face clouded. "He didn't come home again last night."

"And how many times is this?"

"I don't know."

"Good. You're not counting anymore. That's progress. You didn't say anything to my mother, did you?"

"No, of course not!" The first time she'd found Claudio's bed undisturbed, Chiaretta had gone to Giustina in a panic, certain he had drowned in the canal or was lying in a prison cell after being denounced and arrested. Giustina had been merciless. Chiaretta was foolish and ungrateful. Claudio would do what husbands had a right to do, and she would know this if she had been raised to be a patrician's wife. Chiaretta had vowed from that day forward that, even if Claudio didn't come home for a week, Giustina would not hear about it from her.

"I wouldn't know if Piero was home or not. And I don't care either." Antonia's discomfort made her whiny and cross, eager to launch into tales of her husband's gambling, his whores, and his unforgivable dullness.

Today she just shrugged. "Help me into my chair, would you?" When she was settled, she started. "Believe me, the unusual part is how much attention Claudio pays you, not how little. You don't have your own friends yet, but by next Carnevale you will, and I'd be surprised if he takes you out at all—or if you want him to. Husbands aren't very much fun."

"But I see married women out all the time!"

"Not with their husbands!" Antonia looked at Chiaretta as if she had lost her mind. "When I have my figure back, I will find myself a cavaliere servente, or maybe two or three, to bring me presents, and take me to the opera and dinner, and go gambling at the Ridotto."

"A cavaliere servente?"

Antonia opened her eyes and dropped her jaw in feigned amazement.

"Antonia, don't mock me."

"I'm sorry," Antonia said. "I'm just an old crab." She winced and pressed her hand into the side of her belly. "The baby moves around, and sometimes it really hurts. Do you want to feel?"

She reached over and pressed Chiaretta's hand against her side. Chiaretta felt the baby move away from the pressure and settle again on Antonia's other side. "What's it like?" she asked.

"Being pregnant? It's horrid, but I think I will like having my little accomplishment around the house." She fell back in her chair and lifted her swollen feet onto an ottoman of velvet and brocade. "God, I hope it's a boy. I pray for a boy every night."

"Why?"

"Chiaretta, *maritar o monacar?* You can't have failed to notice that!"

Marriage or the nunnery. *If Bernardo were my father, I could have been forced into a convent or married to a man almost twice my age whom I didn't love at all,* Chiaretta realized. It was no exaggeration. That was exactly what he had done to Antonia and her sister. In some ways, odd as it seemed, she and Maddalena had been lucky to be abandoned. At least they had made some choices for themselves.

Antonia's tone when she spoke about Piero was already tinged with sarcasm and bitterness. Still, she exuded optimism, a sense that, though marriage was a disappointment and a bore, life didn't have to be. Behind all her grousing lay the specter of the alternative, Antonia's sister's lifeless face looking out from the grille of the parlatorio in the convent of San Zaccaria when the women of the family made their visits.

Antonia was still talking. "When I am out of my confinement, I'm going to have all new dresses made. You never get your waist back, they say, and I am going to cost Piero a fortune." She had already shown Chiaretta swatches of a dozen fabrics she had chosen for herself from the most expensive in her husband's inventory. "And then, I am going to put on my bauta and go show off those beautiful dresses to my lover!"

"Lover? You have a lover?" This day was turning out to be full of surprises. "Is that what they are then, these—what did you call them?—cavalieri serventi?"

Antonia looked at her with astonishment. "You really don't know any of this, do you?"

Chiaretta shook her head.

"A cavaliere servente is a man who's always there to take you out, and buy you little gifts, and come calling so you don't get bored. Much more useful than a husband. And they don't expect sex. In fact, it all depends on them not getting any."

She reached over and patted Chiaretta's hand as if she were reassuring a child. "And of course you do know what a lover is, don't you?"

"That I have figured out, thank you." Chiaretta leaned forward and whispered, "You have one of those too?"

"Not yet, but I will. Honestly, Piero . . ." She wrinkled her nose as if she had just smelled rotting garbage, completing her thought by crossing her eyes.

Chiaretta went to the window to gather her thoughts. *I don't want a lover, or a cavaliere servente. I want my husband.*

"Chiaretta?" Antonia was looking at her quizzically, and Chiaretta realized she must have been lost in thought for quite a while.

"Sorry," she said. "It's just—sometimes I wonder if I should ever have married Claudio."

Antonia was shocked. "You seem so happy."

"I *am* happy. I love him. He's very good to me."

For once Antonia didn't fill the silence with jokes or teasing but waited for her to continue.

"I just want Claudio to be with me. I didn't know about all of this. Nothing makes sense to me. Maybe I should have stayed at the Pietà."

Antonia laughed. "You can't actually picture yourself an old crone there, can you? And besides, it's done now." She leaned toward Chiaretta as far as her large belly permitted, and her voice became solemn. "Marriage isn't what you think it is. It's what gives you the freedom to amuse yourself in this world, that's all. Trust me, Claudio is doing that."

Seeing Chiaretta's stricken face, she rushed to explain. "The only real mistake you could make would be to expect Claudio to be different from the others. You'll be miserable if you do. And it's a waste of time not to get busy learning how to play the game yourself. Life in Venice is meaningless without risk. Are you going to sit on your loggia alone for the rest of your life, trying to figure out which of the couples on the gondolas is your husband and his lover?"

Chiaretta covered her mouth with her hand. "How did you know?"

"I just guessed. I did it myself, until I decided I didn't care."

The afternoon sun was lighting the other side of the canal, and Antonia needed to rest. For once, Chiaretta was glad the late hour gave her an excuse to leave.

WHO IS THIS PERSON WHO CRIES ALL THE TIME? CHIARETTA wondered as she rode home in the darkened felce. *What has happened to me? And what am I going to do about it?*

She rubbed her forehead to rid herself of the torment of what Claudio's secrets might be. Perhaps he would be there when she got home. Perhaps she would not have to spend another evening picking at her supper and trying to banish thoughts about what he might be doing. Perhaps Bernardo would invite her down to share their meal. Having to put up with Giustina was worth it for a dose of her father-in-law's humor, even if Claudio's chair was empty. But Bernardo also was rarely there, perhaps for the reasons Antonia had begun to explain.

Claudio was at home, and his face brightened when he saw her. He kissed her and spent half an hour before supper in her sitting room talking with her about his business and the next opera season at the Teatro Sant'Angelo. He accepted a vague response from Chiaretta about her time with Antonia, and then he jumped to his feet.

"I almost forgot!" he said, pulling from his jacket a small box containing two large pearls attached to hairpins. Bending over her to place them in her hair, he kissed each ear, nibbling on the lobes until she squealed and pulled away.

This is what I want from you, she thought. *This is what makes my life perfect.* She felt a familiar tingling in her breasts as her nipples hardened, and she turned her face up to place her lips on his, lingering to play with the tip of her tongue on his mouth.

"Shall I tell the servants we'll eat later?" he asked.

"Please do," Chiaretta said, taking his hand as she rose and turned her back to him so he could loosen the laces of her dress.

LATER, THEY STOOD OUTSIDE WATCHING AS A CHAMBER GROUP on a burchiello serenaded someone in the house next to theirs. A young man holding flowers stood up and sang in the direction of a balcony, although Chiaretta could not see if anyone was there.

"You are made for kisses," he sang. "A man would die of rapture if he could but glimpse your face tonight." He raised his voice and pleaded in a repeated chorus, "For pity's sake, don't say no."

Chiaretta snuggled up next to Claudio in the misty air of the spring night. "What do her parents think of that?" she asked him.

"Her parents? He's singing to the woman of the house."

Chiaretta turned to look at him, astonished.

"It's nothing really, just flattery. He'll probably come around tomorrow to get his thank-you for the serenade. He'll bring the flowers, wilted a little, and recite a poem he's written about how they are as downtrodden as his heart because she won't have him."

"And then what?"

"Nothing. Though he might hope she'll eventually say yes, she won't. As long as she teases him, he'll come around, but it would be a big mistake for her to let it get out of hand."

"What does her husband think?"

"He doesn't mind. In fact, as long as everyone follows the rules, he's glad for it. It makes his wife happy." He pulled her closer to him. "She probably has more than one cavaliere servente. You will too." He pressed his mouth into her hair. "I'll even help you choose your first one, someone who won't take advantage of you."

He turned to her. "Why the sad look? You need to have friends. You need to have admirers. It's just the way it is. I don't mind." He pulled away. "Shall we go inside?"

An hour or so later, as Chiaretta lay in her bed, she heard Zuana's voice in the portego saying good night to Claudio. His boots clicked as he crossed the marble floor, the sound disappearing as he went down the stairs to the dock.

THE FOLLOWING MORNING, FOR THE FIRST TIME SINCE HER marriage, Chiaretta did not look to see whether Claudio was in his quarters. Instead, she sat at her dressing table with her jewelry chest, holding up this earring, that comb, this pendant, tipping her head from side to side and smiling as if at an admirer.

She called for Zuana, who arranged her hair, put on her pearl necklace, laced her corset, and helped her into one of her prettiest dresses. She would have to wear a veil, but underneath it, she would have powdered skin and beauty spots, and if she should meet someone to flirt with, she was going to do it.

"I want to visit my sister," she told the gondolier. "Take me to the Pietà." What she needed to learn to do could not be practiced at a cloister full of virgins, but she could think of no other place to go. Setting out alone was enough of a start.

DESPITE THE FACT THAT SHE HAD GROWN UP THERE, AS A MAR-ried woman Chiaretta was not allowed to be anywhere in the Pietà except the parlatorio. In her beautiful dresses and her coiffed hair, she felt deep discomfort on the other side of the grille, corseted and painted into something she was not, and separated from the girls in their red and white dresses because she had permitted a man to lie between her legs. *I don't belong anywhere anymore,* she thought as she waited for her sister to come downstairs.

Maddalena looked more serene than she had ever seen her, and Chiaretta had the odd sensation that she was the one on the captive side of the grille. Her beauty spots and makeup might have impressed the other figlie, but Maddalena saw right through them.

"What's wrong?" she asked. Though Chiaretta denied and blustered through the first few minutes of their time, they soon had drawn to one corner and bent their heads together.

Chiaretta could think of nothing to say. Where could she start? Maddalena reached through the grille, and Chiaretta laced her fingers through her sister's. Minutes passed in silence while she dabbed at her eyes to keep her makeup from spotting.

"Shall I go get the sketchbook so you can write?" Maddalena's voice was gentle, with just enough teasing in it to make Chiaretta manage a smile.

"No. I just want to sit here with you, if that's all right."

Maddalena squeezed her hand. "Of course."

They sat without speaking for a while longer, until Maddalena broke the silence. "You know Vivaldi is leaving. He will finish up Carnevale and go to Mantua."

"Claudio told me. Are you all right?"

"It isn't like last time," Maddalena said. "I'm a grown woman, a sotto maestra. I know who I am now."

Chiaretta searched her sister's face for signs it wasn't true, and found nothing.

"I mean it," Maddalena said. "I don't need him anymore."

❦❦❦

ANTONIA'S BABY WAS A BOY NAMED ALEXANDRO, AFTER PIERO'S father. In the Venetian custom, during the days after the birth, Antonia was propped up on pillows as a steady stream of well-wishers passed through her bedroom. The baby was sent to a wet nurse, who brought him to Antonia for daily visits while she tended to the more important task of regaining her figure.

Months later, laced into a tighter corset, Antonia was making up for having missed all of Carnevale the year before, as well as the other spring festivals. Piero had made good on her new wardrobe, and on the feast day of Saint Mark in April, she stood with Chiaretta in front of the great mirrors of the portego in Palazzo Morosini admiring herself as they finished getting ready for the celebration.

Chiaretta's first anniversary had come and gone, and her pearls had been put away, but she had waited until Antonia was ready to go out in public again to begin putting in motion her plan for a life independent of Claudio. Antonia had been right that he would spend little time with her at her second Carnevale, and if it were not for a night at the opera with Bernardo and a few parties with Antonia's friends at small private casinos, she would have seen nothing of Carnevale that could not have been observed from her balcony. Now she was ready to set foot outside again.

Claudio and Piero had announced several weeks earlier that they would be on a barge with investors in the Teatro Sant'Angelo, watching the regatta that was the highlight of the festival. Because they were not taking their wives, they suggested that Antonia and Chiaretta go out together to see the gondoliers in their annual race across the lagoon.

Before Claudio left, he presented Chiaretta with the traditional gift for Saint Mark's Day, a red rosebud known as a bocolo that men gave to the women they loved. He had kissed her and wished her a wonderful time with Antonia before donning his bauta and leaving the house. Chiaretta broke the stem of the bocolo and tucked the flower into the bodice of her dress, shrugging off a twinge of guilt that she would be using it to accentuate her breasts for someone else. Not only did Claudio know what she was doing, but he had had a discussion with Piero about it. His wife needed a companion, Claudio had said. She spent too much time alone, and she would be happier if she wasn't missing out on so much. Piero passed on this information to Antonia not as a broken confidence but as a way for Chiaretta to know her husband's thoughts without the need for an awkward conversation.

Antonia had invited two others to join them on a burchiello she hired for the day so her own gondolier could be part of the race. They were bringing sparkling wine, and Antonia was supplying the lunch. The two guests were the men among Piero's cousins Antonia thought most suitable for practice at flirtation.

"Luca and Andrea know who you are," Antonia said as the two women walked down the broad stairs from Chiaretta's quarters. "They heard you sing at the Pietà. Andrea plays the harpsichord and has a very nice voice, but he hardly ever lets anyone hear him. He practically has to be dragged out to play at parties."

They passed the piano nobile, and Antonia barely broke stride to look in the door. "Good. My mother's not here. I don't have to say hello."

She resumed her chatter as they walked down the remaining stairs to the dock. "Luca is one of those people whose best talent is being easy to be around. You'll like him. Everybody does."

Chiaretta wasn't listening, still pondering the last words Antonia had said as they left her room. "Claudio thinks our plan for the day is perfect," she had said. *If it's perfect for him,* Chiaretta vowed, *I'll make it perfect for me too.*

"Did you hear me?" Antonia asked as they paused in the damp and musty boathouse under the palazzo. "Anyone who's heard you sing is ready to be in love, especially after they lay eyes on you. Just remember two things. Don't let my cousins kiss you on the mouth, even if they try to make it seem casual, and not even a note from that pretty little throat. Anything they want, they should have to beg years for."

The men stood on the dock with their hoods on, holding the masks and hats of their baute in their hands. Luca Barberigo was short and round in the middle, with a hairline that was beginning to recede even though he was still under thirty. A guileless quality about his face put Chiaretta at ease. Andrea Corner was tall and solemn, with gray-blue eyes and features so angular they suggested scars that were not actually there. His hair was thick and almost black, without a hint of the gold or red found in many Venetians.

They sat in the sunlight with the women as the boat crept out among the hundreds heading toward the lagoon. Luca opened a bottle of wine from the Veneto and handed a small glass to each of them. "To the tragedy of marriage," he said. "It has taken away two more of the beautiful women of Venice."

Antonia grimaced at Luca's awkward attempt at charm, but

Luca was unfazed. He picked up Chiaretta's hand and kissed it. Chiaretta let his hand linger, giving him a coquettish smile.

Luca poured wine before their glasses were even empty, and Chiaretta made a joke of hiding hers so he wouldn't give her any more. Soon shouts rose up from the far end of the lagoon to signal that the race was on. She watched as dozens of gondolas decked with flowers and banners approached. Antonia lifted her mask and peered into the distance, trying to spot the banners of Piero's family and her own. As the gondolas streaked toward them, she picked out the Morosini banner among the boats in the lead and called to Chiaretta to watch.

The crowd was screaming as the boats passed by, and by the time the first ones reached Chiaretta, the Morosini gondola had a small lead. As the gondolas passed, a man cheering from a barge on the other side of the racecourse pulled up his mask and bent over the woman at his side. A red rosebud fell from her hand as he kissed her before covering his face again. One glimpse was enough. Chiaretta felt her heart slam into her stomach. It was Claudio.

WHEN THE REGATTA WAS OVER, CHIARETTA PLEADED A HEAD-ache, and much to Antonia's disappointment, she asked to be taken home. When Claudio returned that night, she heard his footsteps in the portego with dread. *What can I say to him?* she wondered, but he went to bed without stopping in to say good night.

By the time Chiaretta got up the next day, Zuana had left a note from Luca on a tray in her dressing room. He thanked her for her company and asked if he could be her escort the next time she went out, wherever she wished to go.

Luca was nice and easy to be with, but Andrea interested her more. He had a sense of himself that emanated from every pore, an intensity that shot into Chiaretta's bones when she first saw him. He didn't speak much, leaving Luca to do most of the socializing, but the entire time on the boat she had been wishing he would nudge Luca aside and focus on her alone.

Zuana knocked on her door and brought in another note in a sealed envelope and a red rosebud.

"A day late, but sincerely felt," Andrea had written in a bold hand.

"Is there anything Madonna wishes?" Zuana asked.

Chiaretta's heart was pounding. "Yes," she said. "I am feeling much better. I'll be going out this morning." Antonia would know what she should do next.

Antonia's advice was simple: encourage them both. Luca would be the ideal cavaliere servente—obedient, convenient, and not prone to let his adoration get out of hand. He would be a good escort for the theater and the opera and would cover her losing hands at the casinos as if it were a pleasure to have his pocket emptied. As for Andrea, hadn't Chiaretta noticed how he couldn't take his eyes off her?

"Even better than Luca," Antonia said. "For that little extra . . ." She imitated a shiver of erotic excitement. "It's better than sex," she said. "Not to have it, I mean, and wonder about it the whole time you're with someone, don't you think?" She looked at Chiaretta's uncomprehending face. "No, I guess you don't," she said. "You're still in love with your husband."

Later, Chiaretta sat on the balcony of Palazzo Morosini reading the two notes again. What was it that Antonia had said? *Life in Venice is meaningless without risk.* She went inside and rang the bell for Zuana. *Marriage is what gives you the freedom to amuse yourself in this world, that's all.* "Bring me some writing paper and two envelopes," she told the maid.

SEVENTEEN

*T*HE ENDLESS REVELRY OF VENICE WAS SOMETHING TO be endured as far as Maddalena was concerned. Especially during the main Carnevale season, several times a week groups of the figlie di coro were sent off to perform in the mansions, churches, and other institutions of the city. Inattentive the few days before, impossible on the day of, and silly with giggles afterward, the figlie made rehearsals a nightmare for all their teachers. Every year Maddalena looked forward to the start of Lent, and her only hope until then was that her duties might from time to time be light enough to allow her a few moments in a quiet practice room with her violin.

When Ash Wednesday brought an abrupt end to the festivities, the Pietà settled back, like a reveler sinking into a familiar chair after a long night out. The mood in the sala dal violino was calmer, offering palpable relief to the figlie, who whether they would admit it or not, had seen enough of the outside world for a while. Even the iniziate, who shared in the excitement although as a rule were not invited out, calmed down when their fantasies were no longer fueled by new gossip.

This particular Lent, however, Maddalena was not expecting many chances to relax. Anna Maria had been promoted to maestra dal violino a few months earlier, when Prudenzia had become one of the two maestre di coro—the highest position among the women of the coro, second only to the male director and, among the women, to the priora herself. Maddalena, now twenty-eight, had long been one of two sotto maestre dal violino, but she was by herself for the time being. Soon another one would be appointed and Maddalena would become the supervisor only of the attive in the string section, but at the moment she was trying to do the tasks of two.

Despite the work involved, the beginning students brought something precious to her life. They were so small and thin that sometimes she wanted to pull them under her cloak and let them hold her until they felt like coming back out into the world. Some of them scowled with the intensity of warriors as they battled against what their hands would not let them do. Others spent much of their lessons sighing and drooping their shoulders as their teachers, figlie barely older than themselves, explained something for the third or fourth time. Left alone for a few minutes, some of them, particularly the youngest ones, would fall asleep, clutching their violins while the bows clattered to the floor.

That's me, Maddalena would think, watching one of them, and *there's Chiaretta, there's Anna Maria,* as she moved through the room beaming at something done well, or putting a hand on the shoulder of a child crying from frustration or exhaustion. But one ghost from her past she had vowed to banish. In her sala, there would be no Luciana.

Within a few months of becoming a sotto maestra, she had seen a little girl reduced to tears by her teacher, a thirteen-year-old named Gerita. Her first reaction had been to scold Gerita, but she pulled herself back. *They're all little girls,* she told herself. After the lesson, she pulled her aside.

"Why were you scolding Cornelia?"

"Because she did it wrong. I told her what to do and she didn't do it."

"Do you think she was trying?"

Gerita stopped for a moment to think. "I guess so. She was doing it over and over again."

"Did scolding her help?"

"No," Gerita growled with annoyance. "Maybe she's just not very good."

"But if she learned how to do it, she would be good, especially for someone who can't have been playing even a year," Maddalena replied. "So what do you think we should do?"

"I don't know. Maybe just let her keep practicing?"

"Why don't you give that a try? And if she still doesn't improve, let me know, and we'll think of something together." Maddalena reached up and straightened Gerita's hood, although it hadn't needed it. "But try not to let Cornelia know you're disappointed. It won't really help."

They just do it the way they've been shown, she thought as she watched Gerita leave the practice room. *All of it. How to hold the bow, how to finger, how to scold.*

IN HER SECOND YEAR AS A SOTTO MAESTRA, MADDALENA'S TURN came to rehearse the orchestra for a concert. The weather had been gloomy and cold for weeks on end, and many of the figlie were weak with chills and coughs. The music was some that Vivaldi had written, patched together from several works the coro had already performed. The first movement was light, with an infectious rhythm, but the figlie were dragging through it. Frustrated, Maddalena was about to send them off to practice on their own when an idea occurred to her.

"Girls!" She tapped her bow on the music stand. "I want to ask you something." She looked at them each in turn. "It's a simple question. What makes you happy?"

Some of them screwed up their faces, but others sat looking stupefied.

"What do you mean?" one of them said.

"Just what I said," she replied. "Kittens in the courtyard? Meat for dinner? What makes your heart jump up and say, 'Now this is a good day!'"

Gerita, now a pretty sixteen-year-old, sat up straight. "I know! I'm happy when they throw flowers at us on the quay."

Another girl giggled. "I'm happy when they give us wine at the parties."

"I'm happy when my blanket is warm enough." The voice was almost inaudible. Several of them turned to look at Benedetta, a tiny, dark-haired viola d'amore player with a cleft palate that made her so self-conscious she rarely spoke.

The mood turned solemn for a second, before the figlie looked away from her. "I like the fireworks on the lagoon!" one of them cried out.

"All right," said Maddalena. With a downturn of her mouth, she played their music as a lugubrious funeral march. A few of them giggled. Then she stood up straighter. "Fireworks!" she said, playing the music again, clean and bright. "Now it's your turn."

The figlie picked up their violins. The notes were crisp and the pace was lively, and when they were finished the figlie exchanged happy, secretive glances before she called them to order again.

Maddalena nodded to Gerita. "Stand up and show us how you feel when someone throws flowers at you. Use your violin."

Without prompting, Gerita began to play, bending her waist

from side to side and shifting her hips as she gave a flirtatious smile to her friends in the coro. She bowed and sat down while the others applauded.

Maddalena picked a few more and asked them to demonstrate, and then she called on Benedetta. "You're warm in bed, and you're drifting off to sleep." Picking up her own violin, she played the languid opening of the slow movement. "You play your part, and I'll play mine."

Benedetta shut her eyes and began. The air in the room stilled. The phrases flowed from her viola as easily as breathing, as intimate as a rising lump in the throat. *My bed is giving back the heat it has stolen from me. My legs and arms are unfurling like a flower when the sun shines.* Maddalena knew what was in Benedetta's music.

By now Maddalena had stopped playing and was hugging her violin close to her body as she watched Benedetta finish. The little girl's sigh was the only sound in the room as she opened her eyes to see the rest of the coro staring at her, still completely absorbed in the story she was telling.

The time for rehearsal was over, but no one wanted to leave. "The music will be here tomorrow," Maddalena said, as she told them to put away their instruments. "All it needs is you."

❦❦❦

WHEN CLAUDIO CALLED THE ARRANGEMENT WITH LUCA AND Andrea perfect, Chiaretta wondered how she would handle the blow. By the time another year had passed, Antonia was pregnant for a second time and too nauseated to go out, but the three of them had commemorated the occasion of their first meeting by watching the gondola race on Saint Mark's Day. This year, Chiaretta leaned back and laughed all afternoon, trailing her hand in the water, looking down from time to time at the three rosebuds in her bodice.

She had progressed in three Carnevale seasons from fear to enthusiasm to even a measure of abandon. "Forget all that nonsense they told you at the Pietà about how God wants you to be good all the time," Antonia told her. "I mean, wouldn't you rather have people lining up to beg for forgiveness than sit all alone in heaven because nobody had done anything wrong?"

Chiaretta still knelt at the prie-dieu when she woke up, but by that point she had lost track of the daily office, substituting her own morning prayer consisting of an entreaty to the Virgin to give her a sign if she was displeasing her that day. Evening prayer was often little more than crossing herself as she crawled into bed, and asking for forgiveness if the mother of God had sent a signal she missed.

"I don't feel any less religious," she told Maddalena a few days after Easter. "Now that I actually have to worry about sinning, I pay a lot more attention to it."

Maddalena smiled. "There's not much chance to sin here. And I'm not sure why God should be impressed with how much we pray here, because they make us do it." She thought for a moment. "If I were God, I'd only count what a person chooses to do."

Chiaretta looked a little relieved. "Well, I confess every week. That's a choice. And I go to mass every Sunday." She thought for a moment. "Except in the summer, when I'm in the country." She furrowed her brow. "Maybe I don't go so often after all. But I do go every day during Lent."

She made this last point in the bright voice Maddalena treasured from their childhood. She motioned with her finger for Chiaretta to move her face closer to the grille, and when she did, Maddalena reached through and stroked her on the cheek. "You haven't changed at all. And I can't think of any reason God wouldn't love you just as much as we all do." She looked across the parlatorio toward the door. "Including them."

No one was there, but Chiaretta knew who she meant. For

nearly a year, Luca and Andrea had been bringing her to visit Maddalena each week before the three of them went to dinner at one of the restaurants nearby. That day, because the weather was better than it had been in several weeks, the two men had gone for a stroll on the quay to give her some time alone with her sister.

"Especially the tall one," Maddalena went on. "Your back is always turned so you can't see the way he looks at you, but I can."

"Andrea? It's Luca who adores me. But Andrea—well, he seems to find me amusing, that's all. He's very quiet."

"He's also very handsome."

Chiaretta blushed.

"You like him," Maddalena said.

"More than Luca actually. Luca's a lot of fun, and awfully sweet, but sometimes he's a bit boorish." Chiaretta looked down at her hands and began adjusting her gloves. "I like Andrea—in a different way."

Maddalena gave her a quizzical smile. "I know a little about having feelings for a man it's wrong even to hope to have."

Chiaretta looked up. "Vivaldi?" Now Chiaretta was the one waiting for an answer, but before Maddalena could reply, the door to the parlatorio opened, and Luca and Andrea came in.

"Brrr!" Luca said. "It's cold out there for April." He came over to the grille. "May I steal this gentle lady from you, just for a week?"

Maddalena smiled. "Only if I have your word you'll bring her back safely."

"Safely," Luca said, clicking his heels like a soldier. "And on time."

He helped Chiaretta to her feet while Andrea held out her cloak. "Are you ready for dinner?" Andrea asked in a voice so quiet it turned a routine question into something private and tender.

"Umm." Chiaretta nodded, looking back at Maddalena to avoid his gaze. The change in her expression was too slight for anyone but a sister to notice. Her brows had come together and her eyes narrowed in the way they did when she stood on the balcony of the Pietà waiting to sing new music for the first time—determined, self-confident, and a little afraid.

🐝🐝🐝

BY ASCENSION DAY IN MAY, ANTONIA WAS FEELING WELL ENOUGH to go out to watch the Bucintoro in a burchiello Luca rented for the day. The wide, flat-bottomed boat provided enough room for three musicians to come along to play for them as they bobbed in the lagoon, and for a servant to fill their glasses and serve their lunch. The four of them took seats under a bright red canopy and pulled off their masks. Chiaretta's face was damp with sweat, and she handed a napkin to Antonia, moving her face toward her as a signal to daub it dry without disturbing her makeup.

"May I?" Andrea asked. Chiaretta's heart jumped.

"Certainly!" Antonia answered for her, handing Andrea the napkin with a sly look.

Andrea patted a corner of the napkin over Chiaretta's forehead and cheeks, and when he reached her mouth he traced its outline. She cast her eyes down, uncomfortable with his touch, and then looked up to see Andrea's eyes locking with hers. He examined her face inch by inch, and whether this took a few seconds or a few minutes, Chiaretta could not have said. Then he took the napkin and daubed her throat, moving his hand down until he had swept across the tops of her breasts at the edge of her bodice.

For Chiaretta, the boat was a swirl of faces. Antonia's was grinning triumphantly, Luca's was rigid with an attempt not to scowl, and Andrea's was solemn as ever, but opened up somehow, as if a door had been left ajar through which secrets and intimacies might escape, or enter.

After the passage of the Bucintoro, the servant began to lay out lunch as the burchiello moved to a quieter part of the lagoon, near the island of Giudecca. Food had been brought for everyone, and when the musicians had their fill, they went back to their seats to play again.

"I feel like singing," Antonia said, calling out to the musicians. "Do you know this one? *Quando fra l'altre donne ad ora ad ora.*"

"Ah, Petrarch," one of the musicians said, picking up the melody on the violin. "When Love shows herself in a beautiful face among other women from time to time," Antonia sang, and Luca joined in, his voice rising and falling with the effects of the wine and the lolling water. "The less beautiful each face is than yours, the more my love for you grows."

Antonia and Luca had moved their faces close together, exchanging the soulful looks of lovers before breaking away in laughter. Antonia turned in Chiaretta's direction. "Why don't you sing something for us?" she asked.

"Me? I can't. You know that!"

"Oh, nobody cares about that anymore!"

"Nobody on this boat at least!" Luca answered, looking at the musicians. "Do you know who this is?" he asked, gesturing to Chiaretta.

"Certainly," the leader said. "Chiaretta della Pietà. Who could forget?"

"And would you denounce her if she were to honor you with a song?"

The musician looked at the other two and made a slitting gesture across his throat. They grinned and returned the gesture.

"So what will it be?" Luca asked. "Nothing religious I hope."

"I don't know," Chiaretta said. "I need to ask Claudio first."

"Oh, please!" Antonia wheedled. "He's always in Vienna or Rome or somewhere. That could take months!"

"Antonia, I can't," Chiaretta pleaded.

"Leave her alone." Andrea's voice was firm. "She said she can't."

Antonia and Luca groaned, knowing it meant the subject was closed.

"I'll sing," Andrea said.

Antonia's jaw dropped. "You never sing!"

"I like to sing, I just don't like to perform. Today, in honor of the occasion—" He turned to Chiaretta. "Do you know Veronica Franco?"

"No. I don't think I've met her." She turned to Antonia. "Have I?"

"It's not likely," Andrea said. "She's been dead for over a hundred years. She was a beautiful courtesan here in Venice—and a poet so intelligent she probably drove our great-grandfathers wild. Would you like to hear something she wrote?"

"Please."

Andrea began to sing, nodding to the musicians to join in. "Desire gives pain to the heart," he sang, "from which springs both hope and worry." His voice was soft and rich as a bow gliding across the strings of a cello. "Out of suspicion I make mistakes that grow into lasting ills. And from my stubborn delusions come a thousand deceits, which later I must accept as damage I've done."

They all applauded when he finished, and Chiaretta said, almost in a whisper, "That was beautiful."

"A little dark," Andrea said. "I don't know why that one came into my head."

"It does sound quite fatalistic," Chiaretta replied.

"I suppose, but I think it's more a warning," Andrea said.

"Not to get caught!" Antonia reached over and took a gulp of wine from Luca's glass.

"No, not that," Andrea said. "When we love someone, we have to be careful of the harm our crazy thoughts can set in motion. That's what I think she meant." A gust of wind rippled over the water, and Andrea looked up to the horizon. "Storm coming," he said to Luca. "It will be raining in an hour. We should get these ladies back home."

OVER A PRIVATE SUPPER IN THEIR QUARTERS A FEW DAYS AFTER Claudio's return, Chiaretta brought up Antonia's request to hear her sing.

He shrugged his shoulders. "So what happened?" he asked. "Did you do it?"

"No!" Chiaretta answered, shocked at the suggestion. "I said I couldn't. Andrea defended me, and it was over."

"Bravo for Andrea!" He raised his glass in a toast. "And doubly so for my sensible and loyal wife."

Chiaretta could see he was thinking, and she waited for him.

"Venice is changing," Claudio finally said. "Things aren't as strict as they used to be. I'm not going to say a denouncement isn't serious, but it's nothing a person can't get out of these days. More of an inconvenience than anything else, probably an expensive one, but no one's going to be picking up my dead body at the prison over a song."

"What about the bond? There was something about a bond with the Pietà, wasn't there?"

He reached across the table and touched her hand. "The Pietà wouldn't even suggest I forfeit the bond. They aren't going to antagonize the Morosini family over something like that. Look at my father. He makes more money for them every month with his parties than that pitiful bond would pay." Claudio thought for a moment. "In fact, I think that's a wonderful idea."

"What?"

"Your singing again. How do you like the idea of the Pietà sending over your sister to put on a recital with you, just for a few friends? If they say yes, the question of whether you can sing for other people is decided, wouldn't you think?"

"Claudio, I haven't sung in years."

His face glowed in the candlelight. "Except for me. And the world hasn't heard your voice in far too long." Though the lines of age on his face and the hints of gray in his hair were unmistakable, he was at the moment, Chiaretta thought, the most beautiful man who had ever lived.

AND SO IT WAS RESOLVED. JUST BEFORE THE PATRICIANS OF Venice began departing to their country villas for the summer, several dozen guests gathered on the piano nobile of the Palazzo Morosini for an intimate evening, with entertainment by the former Chiaretta della Pietà and her sister.

Andrea had agreed, once again to Antonia's shock, to accompany the sisters on the harpsichord. The week before, when Maddalena visited the Palazzo Morosini to rehearse, she told both of them about her plan to bring Benedetta and Cornelia to their first private party. Maestra Prudenzia had questioned the wisdom of sending Benedetta rather than someone more attractive, but Maddalena had been adamant that when the selection of performers was up to her, the invitations would go to the hardest workers and the best musicians. And besides, Maddalena thought to herself, no figlia di coro was easier to love than tiny Benedetta, with her sweet, scarred face. If Maddalena were a rich Venetian nobleman, Benedetta would be the one to loosen her purse strings.

Maddalena had not spent much time face-to-face with Andrea before, and she could see why Chiaretta liked him. He was the kind of person who smiled when something was funny, and didn't when it wasn't. He watched Chiaretta in a way that was neither gawking or intrusive, but out of concern that she be warm enough in a drafty room, that she get enough to eat, that she stop to rest when she was tired. The effect on Chiaretta was unmistakable. She glowed whenever he was around.

"I'll have to be careful what we serve." Chiaretta laughed, telling them the story of the oysters. "I love them now, but they *are* rather frightening to look at."

"Probably fish with big staring eyes wouldn't work either," Andrea said. "They've always seemed a bit accusatory to me."

"And no little animals either," Maddalena added. "At some party we went to, they served thrushes with the heads still on, and one of the figlie vomited right there at the table. The others started crying about the poor little dead birds, and they made quite a hash of the concert afterward, I'm afraid."

NO SUCH INCIDENT OCCURRED AT THE MOROSINIS' PARTY. Benedetta and Cornelia sat wide-eyed at the table, taking second and third portions of the foods they liked and exchanging furtive glances about the amount of wine in their glasses. "No seconds on that," Maddalena whispered from her seat next to them. "Don't forget, you have to perform."

After dinner, Maddalena played a trio sonata with the two figlie and then asked Chiaretta to join her. At the first notes, the audience stirred, as if they thought they should know but couldn't quite place the melody. Then Chiaretta began to sing.

"*Salve Regina, mater.*" Her voice rang out across the portego. "*Vita, dulcedo, et spes,*" she sang. "Our life, sweetness, and hope, greetings to you, Queen, mother of mercy." Benedetta and Cornelia, who were playing a simple continuo, could not take their eyes off her as they listened to a voice they had only heard stories about.

When they finished, Claudio stood up. "You have just heard the music that made me fall in love with my wife." The men applauded and the women sighed.

"Knowing that, Chiaretta has prepared another surprise for you." Andrea got up and sat at the harpsichord. He and Maddalena played the opening notes, and Chiaretta broke into her favorite aria from her last performance. "Seeing the beauty of your face," she sang, "anger fades and love begins to shine."

When she finished, Claudio went over to the window. "Come and look." He gestured to the guests. Having heard the music, a dozen boatmen were hovering on the canal under the window. Chiaretta shrank back, but Claudio nudged her to stay in front of the window. "It's all right, now," he said. "It's all right."

As the crowd went back to their seats, Andrea spoke up. "There are more surprises tonight," he said, looking at Chiaretta, "and this one is for you." He sat down at the harpsichord, and Antonia and Claudio stood next to him.

"Andrea tells me you have a special liking for Veronica Franco," Claudio said, "and it seemed to us as if this poem could have been written for no one but you."

Andrea began to play. *"Occhi lucenti et belli,"* they sang in harmony. "Beautiful shining eyes, how could be conveyed in one moment so much that is new? Such tender feelings—sweet, biting, and wild—they enter this scorched heart, which wants to give you whatever you wish." As they sang, both Claudio and Andrea were fixed on Chiaretta. "One who would live and die for you wishes only that your dear and beautiful eyes will forever be serene, happy, and clear."

Maddalena stood with her arm around her sister's waist. Chiaretta's knees softened, and Maddalena tightened her arm to steady her. *They both love her,* Maddalena thought. *If she didn't know it before, she knows it now.*

EIGHTEEN

THE PLAN CONCOCTED IN A ROWBOAT ON THE BRENTA Canal that summer was so bold it could only have come from Antonia. She had traveled out to the Morosini villa for the summer, with her two children, servants, and a nanny, and every day she and Chiaretta snuck away for a little time together. That day they were joined by Luca, who made the short trip from the Barberigo villa, a little farther up the canal.

She had first raised the subject on the dock, but it had been temporarily forgotten while Luca clumsily rowed toward the opposite bank and then, in an unintentional zigzag, headed back in the direction of the dock at a speed that threatened to toss them all in the water when they crashed.

"I wish that Andrea were here to hold my parasol," Antonia

pouted when Luca had gotten the boat straightened out. "Or that Luca had more hands."

"That reminds me, have you seen Andrea at all?" Chiaretta tried to look nonchalant while waiting for a reply.

"Not much," Luca said. "He stopped in for a day or two when he was doing business in Padua, but he says he's too busy for the villegiatura this summer."

"That bookbinding investment?" Antonia asked.

"That, and something else about a process to print music— Damn!" Luca had rowed so close to the bank that willow branches stroked over him, knocking his cap from his head.

Once he was again in the center of the canal, Luca looked at Chiaretta. "So what do you think of Antonia's idea?"

Chiaretta groaned. "I was hoping you'd forgotten about it."

"Well, why not?" Antonia asked.

"Because it's insane. I can't sing in an opera!"

"Well of course not, if they know it's you," Antonia said. "But those women are so buried under their paint and their wigs, they could be your own mother and you wouldn't know." She put her hand to her mouth. "Sorry," she said. "I forgot you don't have one."

Antonia's thoughtless remarks were so frequent and so benign in intent they had become one of her most endearing traits.

"That's not exactly true. I do have one, I just don't know who she is. So you're right—she could be standing up there singing her heart out and I wouldn't know. On the other hand, I think I would recognize *your* mother if she were dressed as the King of France."

"With a mustache and a beard!" Antonia shrieked. "Now that would be a sight! But seriously, why not, if you were sure you wouldn't get caught?"

"Well, it would be a lot of work, for one thing."

"You wouldn't have to do the whole opera," Antonia said. "We could find one where the soprano has a long break between scenes and you could change clothes with her. Then when you're done,

264 🐌 *Laurel Corona* _____

you change clothes again, and we're off to the Ridotto with our delicious little secret."

The chirps from birds playing in the air around them and the small splashes of the oars were all that could be heard as the two of them waited for Chiaretta's answer.

"It does sound like fun," she said.

"Fun?" Luca broke in. "It sounds like so much fun that if you don't do it, I'll die feeling my whole life has been a waste."

"Oh, stop exaggerating." Antonia slapped the top of his hand. "It will just hurt desperately for—well, maybe ten years or so, that's all."

Chiaretta leaned over the edge of the boat, watching a frog kick alongside before disappearing into the brown water. Two horses grazing in a pasture came up to the bank, expecting a handout. Hearing them whinny, she sat up, brought back to the moment. Antonia and Luca were staring at her.

"Well?" they both said.

"It's silly to discuss it. Claudio would have to agree."

"It might be best if he didn't know," Luca said. "In case there was trouble."

Chiaretta stared at him, astounded. "If there might be trouble, he most certainly has a right to know."

Antonia sighed. "You're no fun. And besides, what if he actually wanted you to do it, but he didn't want to know about it. You'd be the one who wrecked the whole thing by mentioning it. He might have to say no then, even though he wouldn't have minded."

"I'll take that chance."

"But if he says yes, you'll do it?"

Chiaretta sighed. "I'll give it some thought. Honestly, I will."

Antonia clapped her hands. "So here's what I think. It should be at the Teatro Sant'Angelo. Nobody who works there will risk his job by saying anything even if he does figure it out. Claudio's an investor, and you don't denounce an investor and his wife unless you're as brainless as a crayfish. And Vivaldi is supposed to be back for Carnevale."

"To the Pietà?" *Not again.*

Reacting to the alarm in Chiaretta's voice, Antonia gave her a quizzical look. "Not that I've heard," she said. "Just for the opera season, I imagine. Hard to picture him going back to the Pietà when he's getting so famous. Anyway, do you think we could get him to go along?"

"I was pretty horrible to him before I left," Chiaretta said.

Luca cocked his head. "First I've heard about this."

"He wrote four arias, in this order. Wonderful; wonderful but right before and after something even better; ridiculous; and horrible."

"I loved it," Antonia said. "Especially the one that sounded like a turtledove."

"I didn't sing that one. That's my point. I had to sing the one after—"

"He'll go along," Luca interrupted. "He could never pass up a chance for you to sing in one of his operas. I think the little Red Priest will have to change his pants after he's told the idea."

"Luca!" Feigning shock, Antonia started to chide him when two huge dragonflies buzzed past her cheek and hovered in the air near her ear. "Get them away from me!" she screeched, waving her arms until the boat rocked. Luca stood up, and the boat lurched. "No! No! Sit down before we capsize!"

By the time Luca dropped back to his seat, the dragonflies had vanished and the subject of the opera, to Chiaretta's relief, seemed to have gone with them.

❦❦❦

EVERY TIME CHIARETTA THOUGHT SHE UNDERSTOOD LIFE IN Venice, she was proven wrong. She hadn't given the opera another thought, so certain was she that Claudio would refuse. Antonia and Luca were the ones who had brought it up again at the first of Bernardo's fall parties. Claudio had been hesitant at first about Chiaretta's going onstage, even once, and in disguise, but by the end of the evening he was enthusiastic.

"You'll remember it the rest of your life," he told her that night as they lay in bed. "And it's Carnevale, so if anyone says they saw you, we'll just say they'd had too much to drink and you were home that night." He propped himself up on his elbow, tracing her belly with his finger. "And even if you told the truth, the police would probably ask you to change your story, so they wouldn't have to do anything about it."

"Would you come if I sang?"

Claudio fell back down onto the mattress and exhaled. "No, I think that's a little too risky. I'll make sure I have business out of town, but my God, how sad I am to miss it."

"I don't know if I want to, if you aren't there watching me."

"I'll be watching you. I'll remember what day it is and when you're onstage, I'll sit in a café wherever I am and imagine you up there." He turned over and began stroking her hair. "I just have one question."

"What?"

"Is it all right if I imagine you naked?" He threw his arm around her and launched himself on top of her, burrowing into her neck and making sounds like a bear. She shrieked with delight until he silenced her with kisses.

WHEN VIVALDI ARRIVED BACK FROM MANTUA FOR THE FALL Carnevale season, Andrea and Luca approached him about the plan. They were still shaking their heads a week later.

"He was so happy he started speaking Latin, and thanking God, as if *He* had anything to do with it," Luca said over dinner with Antonia and Chiaretta.

"Luca, you shouldn't talk that way," Chiaretta chided.

"About Vivaldi or God?"

"Both! Aren't you afraid of making God angry, saying things like that?"

Andrea smiled in amusement. "Perhaps you've never heard the saying that we are Venetians first and Christians second."

Chiaretta fell silent, not sure how to respond to what seemed like a dangerous thought.

"Well, how religious is this anyway?" Luca added. "He tried to sell us a copy—more than one if we wanted—of what you would sing, and for a little extra he would transpose it to suit your voice. Oh, and then he said for a little more money, just for that performance he'd put in some songs you already knew, with different words to fit the plot, such as it is."

"And at first he insisted on coming over to give you lessons," Andrea added, "but when we told him we'd changed our minds and got up to leave, he said never mind, that he was sure you remembered all he'd taught you."

Luca was laughing. "I thought if I stayed a few more minutes he might have tried to sell me his bed, or maybe his manservant."

"Stop it," Chiaretta said, in a voice so uncharacteristically harsh that Luca fell silent and they all sat staring at her. "What can you do that is anything close to what he does? Sometimes when I looked at the music he'd written for me, I would tremble so hard I had to put it down. Even though there's nothing much to like about him, that's what I remember." Her voice trailed off to a whisper. "He wrote with something in him beyond anything I've ever known."

"Like tapping the music of the spheres." Andrea's eyes grew distant as he spoke. "Like pulling beauty out of the stars and handing it to you, saying, 'I found this in heaven. Here. It's for you.'" He held out his empty hand, as if offering Chiaretta a gift.

How could he know about that? How could he be so exactly right? Chiaretta wondered.

Andrea had left Luca and Antonia with nothing to do but clear their throats and start wondering what liqueur they wanted before leaving.

"A little sweet wine from the South would be nice," Chiaretta said, looking away from Andrea while he motioned for the waiter.

❦❦❦

VIVALDI HAD ONLY ONE OPERA IN THE FALL SEASON, BUT THE role of Rosane in *La Verità in Cimento* was perfect for Chiaretta. The soprano playing Rosane would have enough time between her scenes to slip out of her costume before Chiaretta went onstage late in the first act, and then to put it on again for the second. Chiaretta would sing as part of an ensemble, have some lines of recitative, and finish with an aria that would bring the act to a close.

As far as Antonia, Luca, and Andrea were concerned, no event in the fall Carnevale season was more exciting than spending afternoons on the piano nobile of the Palazzo Morosini helping Chiaretta prepare.

At first, her misgivings came out in the form of spluttering resistance. "I hate Rosane," she said. "Zelim's a nice man who loves her and she used to love him until Melindo came around. He's the heir to the throne, so all of a sudden she's cut Zelim to tatters, saying she's in love with Melindo. But the minute it looks like Zelim is the true heir, suddenly it's Zelim, Zelim, Zelim again?"

"It's just an excuse for singing," Antonia said. "If you want real life, stay home."

"But she's such a tart!" Chiaretta waved the sheet music. "Listen to this: 'I love Melindo, but if it's going to cost me my happiness, and if pleasure lies with Zelim, then good-bye, Melindo.' Who says those kinds of things?"

"Rosane does." Luca shrugged. "I think she sounds like fun."

"Come on, Chiaretta, sing the music in Latin if it will make you feel better." Antonia rolled her eyes. "Just let's hear it."

Andrea took the sheet music from her and played the melody on the harpsichord. It swirled and undulated in the air of the portego, and within a few bars Antonia was swaying, holding her hands in front of her as if she were feeling the chest of a lover. "Dio mio!" she said. "The little priest wrote that?"

Antonia stood next to Andrea and sang the first few bars. By the middle of the melody, Andrea was singing along with her. Luca grabbed Chiaretta's elbow and nudged her toward the harpsichord. "You don't want to sing this?" he asked, his voice rising in disbelief. "It's terrific!"

"Well," Chiaretta said, "I guess I'll try." Before she could hesitate further, Andrea began playing the introduction.

"My love, you are my hope and delight," she sang. Her voice echoed off the floor and danced in the golden light of the portego. She stopped at the end of the first section and turned to Antonia, expecting approval.

But Antonia was scowling. "It's not a lullaby! The little slut thinks nobody's listening, so she's crowing about how sexy she is, and how she should be able to have all the men she wants."

Chiaretta looked at Andrea for support, but instead he nodded. "I'm afraid Antonia's right."

"Try it this way." Antonia sang the melody, pulsing at the beginning of each bar and ending it with a breathy sigh. "It doesn't sound very good when I do it, but that's what it should be like."

Andrea started playing again, and Chiaretta imitated Antonia.

"Much better!" Luca said.

"But still not enough." Antonia lifted her shoulders and made circles, using her elbows to massage the sides of her breasts to push them up. "Watch me."

"Amato, ben tu sei la mia speranza," she sang, turning to Luca.

The tops of her breasts spilled forward as she dropped her shoulders and leaned her head toward him. *"Tu sei il mio piacer."* Putting her face only inches from his, she emphasized each word with her lips, as if she were daring him to kiss her.

"Ma per serbare a te costanza, non vuo turbare il mio goder." She turned away and danced in a slow circle before coming back to face him. Standing now at arm's length, she put her hands on her hips and swayed. "But I don't want to interrupt my pleasure just to be faithful to you," she repeated with a wink at Luca.

"Brava!" Luca clapped.

Andrea joined in the applause. "That was quite something, Antonia."

"Makes me wish you weren't my cousin's wife," Luca said, putting his arm around Antonia's waist and drawing their hips together in a friendly hug. "Especially when there's a bedroom nearby."

Andrea turned to Chiaretta. "What's wrong?"

Her eyes were huge in her solemn face. "I can't do that."

"Why not?" Luca asked. "You stuffed the head of Holofernes in a bag at the Pietà."

While he and Antonia laughed, Andrea stared at her. "You are a beautiful, sensual woman. Surely you must know that."

Chiaretta felt her skin prickle and her face grow hot. "I—"

Antonia and Luca had stopped laughing. They all watched her, waiting.

"I don't really know why not. I've just never done it before. At the Pietà no one could see me. And the music wasn't like this."

"You'll have to learn how to act," Andrea said. "At least a little."

"Luca, do you remember a few years back the fat one who stood there like a cow and we were supposed to believe she was so sexy that men would die for her?" Antonia asked. "Did she ever come back to Venice?"

"I don't think so. Not after someone threw a bench at her in the last act."

"Luca, stop," Chiaretta said. She had seen enough singers booed without mercy at the opera houses around Venice, and the reminder was giving her second thoughts.

Andrea stood up. "We all talked Chiaretta into this, and I don't think it's right for us to come over here and tell stories that can't help but scare her." He looked Luca and Antonia in the eyes. "We have work to do."

Antonia took Chiaretta's hand. "I'm sorry. Sometimes I still forget that, in a way, you're not really from here, not from Venice at all." She looked at Andrea. "Play it again."

Although she could never manage to forget the presence of the two men in the room, Chiaretta was soon able to put her self-consciousness aside enough to move her head, her shoulders, her hips, her mouth to the patterns of the aria. Little by little the embarrassment faded until it was gone.

"You're enjoying this!" Antonia said one afternoon after watching Chiaretta flounce and prance around the portego as she practiced her recitative.

Chiaretta gave her a wicked smile. "I can't believe how much fun I'm having."

"Well then," Andrea said. "Let's try the ensemble."

Chiaretta picked up the music and was leafing through it without a word.

"I played it already at home," Andrea said, reading her mind. "It's not just beautiful, it's sublime." He began to play.

"Aure placide e serene . . ." Chiaretta's voice rose like the tranquil breeze she sang of. She held the high notes for a moment before letting her voice down gently and passing the melody to the others in turn.

"You echo my laments," all of them sang at the end, in harmony so tight it ached. When they finished, the music seemed suspended in the air for a moment before it died off.

"Mater Dei," Chiaretta whispered under her breath. "That

is—" She let her voice trail off. No word could describe the beauty of what they had just sung.

"I've never had music go straight into my soul like that," Andrea murmured. "Never."

His eyes bored into Chiaretta's. The lucid and pristine harmonies had stripped away all pretense and laid her so bare that, instead of looking away, she found herself staring back.

Staring longer.

Antonia cleared her throat, breaking the spell. "So what did you think?" she asked Luca.

For once, Luca was speechless. He motioned with his chin toward Chiaretta, who had covered her face with her hands while Andrea pulled her to him and rocked her in his arms.

ONE MORNING TWO WEEKS BEFORE THE PERFORMANCE, ZUANA came up to Chiaretta's apartment to tell her Andrea was waiting for her on the piano nobile. No practice had been arranged for that day, and worried that something had gone wrong, Chiaretta patted down loose strands of hair and put on a dressing gown suitable for receiving a frequent guest at home. Then she hurried downstairs, where she found Andrea at the harpsichord looking at some sheet music.

Seeing her in a dressing gown with her hair undone and an apprehensive look on her face, Andrea got up from the bench. "I'm sorry to come unexpectedly. I've frightened you, haven't I?"

"Has something bad happened?"

"No, actually something quite wonderful. I thought you would want to know about it right away. This is a gift for you from Maestro Vivaldi." He handed the sheet music to her. "Entirely without charge, I might add," he said with a grin.

"De due rai languir costante," Chiaretta read the title aloud and then began running her eyes over the music. "It's lovely. But I don't understand."

"It's a little something I've heard the gondoliers sing. He's fancied up the melody a bit and used the words in an aria for you. I ran into him near the Broglio yesterday afternoon, and he asked if I could deliver it to you, since he wasn't feeling well."

Chiaretta put the sheet music in a neat pile on the harpsichord. "It's a very nice gift, and I'll look at it as soon as I can, but not until after the opera."

"No," Andrea said. "I came over because it can't wait. He's written it for you to sing in the opera. That is, if you can manage one more piece of music."

Chiaretta picked up the music and began looking at it again. "I don't know . . ."

Andrea held out his hand for her to give him the pages as she finished with them and began working the music out on the harpsichord. " 'To languish constantly for two eyes should be a pleasure and is instead a torment,' " he sang along as he started the music again. " 'Archer of love, lessen my ardor and leave me more content.' Not many words to learn, mostly vocalizing, and the essential melody is simple."

Chiaretta handed him the last few sheets of the music. "Perhaps he doesn't realize how out of practice I am."

"Perhaps all he realizes is this golden opportunity to hear you sing one more time something he's written just for you. If I were you I'd be immensely flattered."

"I am. But it doesn't sound like Rosane. I don't understand how it fits."

"That doesn't matter. Operas change all the time—a castrato says he wants to sing something from last month's opera in Rome because it suits his voice better, or a diva will complain that the notes are too high or too low, or that she wants something more dramatic or more tender—who knows?—and the poor composer has to go along. This time, for a change, he's doing it because *he* wants to."

Chiaretta began playing with the keys on one end of the harpsichord. "I suppose it wouldn't hurt to try," she said, sitting next to Andrea on the bench. "And if I find it's too much, I'll tell him I can't do it."

She was sitting so close to him she sensed a faint odor of lavender and myrtle in his clothing and could see where flecks of dust had accumulated along the seams of his coat. Since the day he had held her in his arms, Chiaretta had been grateful for Antonia's and Luca's constant presence because she had not wanted to be alone with Andrea. Now, without thinking about what she was doing, she had sat so close to him in her dressing gown that she could feel the press of his thigh against hers.

She got up quickly. "I'll turn the pages," she said, stepping to one side of the bench and reaching around him to line up the music.

With his right hand, Andrea played a simplified version of the woodwind accompaniment while his left played the string continuo. It sounded like a tree full of songbirds, chirping a happy chorus while people below them danced, and Chiaretta fell so in love with the piece that she implored him to stay longer to practice.

Finally, he had to go. "I'll come back tomorrow, if you'd like," he said, getting up to put on his cloak and hat.

The sound of a throat being cleared startled them, and they turned to see Giustina at the other end of the portego. She walked toward them. "I wondered who was here." Her eyes scanned Chiaretta, noting her dressing gown and loose hair.

Chiaretta's heart sank. What time was it? And why had she not thought to go upstairs and dress before they began?

Giustina's mouth was a thin line. She greeted Andrea with frigid cordiality and said nothing to Chiaretta at all.

"I must apologize," Andrea said. "I have imposed most terribly this morning." He turned to Chiaretta. "I'll leave the music here for you, and come back tomorrow, if you'd like." Chiaretta nodded, too unnerved to speak.

GIUSTINA WATCHED ANDREA WALK ACROSS THE PORTEGO, AND when he was gone, she turned to Chiaretta. "I will not have this in my house."

Chiaretta opened her mouth to apologize but stopped herself. "I don't know what you mean."

"So if my son were to walk in now and see you in your bedclothes with another man, you'd expect him to be pleased?"

I haven't done anything wrong and I don't owe her an explanation. "This is my husband's house also—and mine," Chiaretta told her. "I believe he would trust me to know how to behave. And, I might add, these are not my bedclothes."

Giustina's eyes narrowed, but she said nothing, continuing to stare at Chiaretta, who struggled not to look away first. Then she spoke. "It is one thing to have male friends. People expect it. And Andrea has my son's approval." She looked toward an open door off the portego. "I need to sit down, and I would like you to come with me."

Chiaretta followed her into a small parlor. The hearth was cold, the lamps were unlit, and the one small, high window did no more than cast shadows across the room. "No point in calling the servants to light the fire. We won't be long." She motioned to Chiaretta to sit in the chair opposite hers.

"I've seen how Andrea looks at you, long before what happened today, and though he knows what's appropriate with a married woman, it's still clear he has . . ." She paused as if not sure how to phrase it. "His passions."

"Andrea has shown no passion to me."

"He's a gentleman. That doesn't mean he won't hope for a signal from you that you might be receptive to him."

"I love my husband, Giustina."

In the gloom, Chiaretta could not read the expression on her mother-in-law's face, but she heard her take in a breath and let it out with a sigh that seemed to contain a mixture of annoyance and resignation.

"In Venice many people love more than one person," Giustina said. "And as long as they keep their secrets, no misery is likely to come of it. But make no mistake, Chiaretta, those who are indiscreet pay dearly for it."

"Are you suggesting I've been unfaithful?"

"I want to make very clear to you how serious an error you would be making."

Chiaretta stood up. "I appreciate your concern for me," she said, trying to disguise her anger. "But I don't need to be told this."

"Oh, really? Did you know that divorce is possible in Venice, and that adultery is cause for it? And did you know that divorced women rarely have the means to live on their own? And returning to your family—that would be a bit of a problem for you, wouldn't it?"

Chiaretta felt the blood rise in her cheeks and was grateful the room was too dark for Giustina to see the effects of her words. *Could I be abandoned?* she wondered, but she did not want to give her mother-in-law the satisfaction of answering her question.

"Thank you for the advice," she said. "But as you've so graciously pointed out, I still haven't had time to dress today." She turned and left Giustina sitting in the dark.

☙☙☙

"I DON'T KNOW WHY SHE'S STILL SO HORRID TO YOU," ANTONIA said two weeks later as they entered the stage door for Chiaretta's performance. "She knows what she's saying isn't true."

"Antonia, I've heard people talk about divorce. It *is* possible."

"Not in your case. If it would cause you to be abandoned, the court wouldn't allow it. She's just trying to scare you."

"Well, she did. I even thought about not singing, but then I decided I couldn't let her have that effect on me."

"You've become a real Morosini!" Antonia grinned at her. "Let's find your dressing room."

"Maestro Vivaldi said he would meet me," Chiaretta said, looking in confusion at the warren of hallways and doors in front of her. Scenery and props cluttered the passages as she and Antonia wandered single file in what they assumed was the direction of the stage. The light was so dim that they had taken off their masks in the vain hope of seeing a little better. They pressed against a painted backdrop as two stagehands passed in the opposite direction, carrying a rolled carpet under their arms.

"Excuse me," Antonia called after them. "Where is Signorina Strada's dressing room?"

"Ahead and to the right," one of them called over his shoulder.

Antonia shrugged and kept walking. They came to a wider corridor where a half dozen people in costumes were chatting with two police guards. Antonia inquired again, and one of the guards left the group to take them to the diva's dressing room.

"Are you friends of hers?" the guard asked.

"No—" Chiaretta started to say, but Antonia's "Yes" drowned her out.

Just as he raised his hand to knock on a door, he stopped. "Wait a minute," he said. "I know you—you're Chiaretta della Pietà, aren't you? I saw you in the parlatorio at Carnevale and a few times on the Riva when you were going out."

"No, you're mistaken," Antonia rushed to say. Chiaretta had never heard fear in her friend's voice before. Her own heart was pounding too hard to speak.

"Wait here," the guard said. "I'll be back in a minute."

"*Sancta Maria,*" Antonia whispered. "I think we might be in trouble."

Chiaretta looked up and down the hallway. "Should we try to get out?"

They heard a familiar voice from inside Anna Maria Strada's dressing room, and Vivaldi opened the door. "Ah. You're here!" Seeing their frightened faces, he ushered them inside. The diva sat at her dressing table warming up her voice while putting on makeup. She nodded to them but made no move to get up.

"The police know she's here—" Antonia said.

Vivaldi clutched his chest. *"Deus in adjutorium,"* he stammered. "I should never have agreed to this!"

Chiaretta had collapsed in a chair. *It's Claudio who could go to jail. What would happen to me then?* Vivaldi crossed himself, and even though she hadn't been praying, by rote Chiaretta's fingers moved to her forehead to do the same. *I should never have let them talk me into this.* She crossed herself again.

Someone was knocking on the door. "Should we answer?" Antonia whispered, but Anna Maria had already gotten up. She threw open the door with a smile, as if she were expecting an admirer. Her face fell again when, instead, two police guards walked in.

"Chiaretta della Pietà?" the second one said. Chiaretta's stomach turned over. Antonia's hand on her shoulder tightened like a vise.

"My God, you're right!" He slapped the first guard on the back. "It really is her!" He fished in his pocket for a few zecchini. "You win," he said, handing over the coins.

"My brother was crazy about you," the first guard explained. "And when you got married, it was like the end of the world. So when I saw you—"

"You scared us to death!" Antonia stood in front of them, shaking her finger.

"Oh, I'm sorry. I forgot—"

"So you're not going to say anything?" Vivaldi cut in.

"You mean about how she's not supposed to sing?" the first

guard said. "We want to hear her, not arrest her! We won't breathe a word."

The second guard laughed. "For once I'm glad to be at work."

Vivaldi's relief was obvious. "Then as impresario, I give you permission to watch the first act from my box." Bobbing his head as he thanked them, he ushered the two guards to the door. He shut it behind them and checked the latch.

"Dio mio." He pressed his back against the door. Chiaretta cupped her hand over her mouth. "Dio mio," she repeated.

CHIARETTA HAD GONE TO SEVERAL PERFORMANCES OF *LA VE-rità in Cimento* to memorize the blocking for her scenes, and one afternoon she had met with Vivaldi to tour the set. Despite her preparation, now that it was brightly lit and crowded with actors in the wings, she found the stage almost unrecognizable.

Anna Maria Strada was larger than she was, and the costume hung on Chiaretta in a way she could not imagine people would fail to notice. Fortunately, once she had gotten past the stagehands, she could wait in the shadows unobserved. With only a few minutes to go, Antonia left to watch from the box with Luca and Andrea. Chiaretta rubbed her hands together and jiggled her knees to try to calm her nerves, as she waited alone for her entrance. Sweat trickled from her armpits, and her head felt swallowed up by a huge wig so hot her scalp felt as if it were burning. Her makeup was so thick it wrinkled whenever she tried to move her mouth.

La Mantovanina, the mezzo-soprano playing the Sultan's wife, Rustena, came up before her entrance and stood next to Chiaretta in the wings. Onstage the Sultan, Mamud, was having a long conversation in recitative with his mistress, Damira.

"The Maestro told us you were someone from out of town who wanted to sing," La Mantovanina said under her breath. "Are you any good?"

Before Chiaretta could answer, Mamud left the stage, rushing by her so fast she had to step back to avoid him. "Stupid bitch up-staged me again," he growled before disappearing.

When she turned back to La Mantovanina, the mezzo was already onstage, agitated at Damira's plot to unseat Rustena's son as heir in favor of her own. Finally Damira stepped into the wings, leaving La Mantovanina onstage alone.

"Oh," she said, looking Chiaretta over. "You're the one who's singing for Anna Maria tonight." She shrugged. "I wish you were singing for me. I have an awful headache." She went over to a stool and sat down without saying anything more.

"Too much wine at dinner again, Margarita?" Girolamo Albertini nodded to Chiaretta before going over to knead the diva's shoulders. He was dressed in a gold turban and a brightly patterned jacket with red pants that ballooned out before being tucked into high boots. His soft and fatty-looking face confirmed what his voice had already given away, that he was the castrato in the role of Zelim.

Albertini looked around. "Where's La Coralli? We have to go on in a minute. The delicate flower's almost dead."

Margarita snickered. Onstage, La Mantovanina was singing about how joy was as short-lived as a flower. Albertini sang the last few lines in a low voice to open his throat. "My miserly life has never handed me pleasure without an equal dose of bitterness and pain," he sang, stopping to look around. "Where is that girl?"

Just at that moment another singer in the costume of a Turkish prince slipped up beside them.

"Late, late, late," Albertini said.

"Sorry, sorry, sorry." Though Chiaretta knew a woman was playing the role of Melindo, she was still taken by surprise when she saw La Coralli's trousers and bound chest. Embarrassed to have stared, Chiaretta looked away.

La Mantovanina swept offstage on the other side, and Chiaretta felt La Coralli push her from behind.

"Don't look at the audience," she whispered. "Just pretend they're not there."

Chiaretta blinked in the bright lights. *I'm onstage. They can see me.* Her music vanished from her head.

La Coralli grabbed her wrist, as if she knew Chiaretta might be tempted to run. Then the familiar first sounds came up from the orchestra, and before she had time to think, she had already sung her first notes. "Serene and peaceful breezes," she sang. The notes had come out well, but her heart was beating so fast she could scarcely take in air to project her voice.

"Pleasant babbling streams." The castrato's voice was so huge that for a moment Chiaretta was too startled to remember to act. Then she arched her neck and looked haughtily away from him toward Melindo.

"Boughs, lovely and innocent," La Coralli sang, and though it felt odd to flirt with a woman dressed as a man, Chiaretta leaned toward her, touching her cheek the way she had seen Anna Maria Strada do.

"Whispering, murmuring, you echo my laments." Chiaretta's voice soared over theirs, strong and full and clear. *I'm doing it,* she thought. *I'm doing it.*

The others left the stage, and the chortling sound of flutes rose up from the orchestra, beginning the aria Vivaldi had inserted into the opera for her. Much as Chiaretta loved the lilting melody, she had at first been wary about including it. She would be alone onstage for the aria, and after she heard about benches being thrown at divas who couldn't act, it had taken some effort to convince her that wouldn't happen to her.

"To languish constantly for two eyes seems a pleasure and is a torment," she sang. Sometimes the flutes played alone, sometimes in the background, and sometimes with her, like a flock of larks landing in a meadow. Toward the end of the aria, Chiaretta could ornament her voice to answer the flutes however she wished. She warbled and trilled with as much confidence as if she were looking over Andrea's shoulder while he played, and though the lights were hot and the room in front of her was dark, she thought of nothing but his graceful fingers on the keys.

The bass viols plucked the last notes of the continuo, and with only a single arpeggio from the harpsichord, Chiaretta transformed herself into Rosane again. *I'm almost done,* she thought, feeling a weight lift from her. *This is it. Go out and treasure it.* She came to the edge of the stage and looked out at the dim outlines of the crowd. *"Amato ben tu sei la mia speranza,"* she sang, stretching the *ah* in the last word as if each one of them were the lover she was imagining.

She twirled away. Pretending Luca and Andrea were onstage with her, she beckoned and teased, invited and pushed away each one in turn. Then, as the orchestra played the accompaniment one last time, she walked to the edge of the stage and traversed its length, looking out into the audience and blowing kisses. As the last notes sounded, she sauntered offstage, as confident as a courtesan with a trail of admirers in her wake.

LA CORALLI WAS WAITING IN THE WINGS. "WHO *ARE* YOU?" SHE asked, before waving Chiaretta toward the stage. "Go out for a bow."

Applause rolled toward her in torrents from the boxes. *"Brava! Bravissima!"*

"Anna Maria, I love you!" someone shouted, as cries of "Viva La Strada!" erupted all over the theater.

Chiaretta stood in the lights, feeling tiny and huge at the same time. "Brava, Chiaretta," she whispered, just to hear her own name once. She stretched out her arms as if to embrace the crowd, and then with a wave she left the stage.

La Coralli was still waiting. "Who are you?" she asked again.

"I live in Venice," Chiaretta said, and then remembering Antonia's words at their rehearsal, she corrected herself. "I'm from here." *Finally,* she thought, *finally that feels true.*

"You're not an opera singer?" La Coralli shook her head in amazement.

"No."

"Why not?"

"My husband won't let me." Chiaretta smiled inside at the little lie.

"Lucky for us," La Coralli said. "I think Anna Maria would be out of a job otherwise." She laughed. "And me too, if you didn't mind strapping your tits and wearing pants." She motioned to Chiaretta. "Come on. I'm supposed to get that costume off you."

ANDREA ARRIVED ALONE AT CHIARETTA'S DRESSING ROOM AFter the performance. His eyes were glittering. "You were magnificent," he said. "Did you hear the applause?"

"It seemed awfully loud from the stage, but I've only heard it from the box before."

"Louder than for any of the other singers. You even broke up a couple of fights. They stopped to listen, and then I guess they forgot what they were fighting about."

"Did you like it?"

He shook his head in disbelief. "I thought for a moment you had lost your courage and it was Anna Maria after all, because I couldn't imagine how anyone could walk out with such confidence, and just"—he clenched his fists in front of his chest for emphasis—"just grab the audience the way you did. And then of course I knew it wasn't her because I know your voice so well." He drew in a deep breath and, without taking his eyes off her, let the air out slowly.

"I don't even know where it came from. All of a sudden I was just up there doing it."

He was still looking at her.

"Where are the others?" she asked, turning toward the door to avoid his eyes.

"Luca and Antonia are off to the Ridotto preparing the celebration." He laughed, and the tension was broken. "Antonia makes a most indelicate noblewoman, but she certainly compensates for it in her loyalty to a friend. She was the loudest person in the house after your arias. Luca had to restrain her or it would have been worse, I'm sure, and we didn't want anyone to wonder why in the world she would have cared so much." He paused. "Can I help you with your dress?"

Chiaretta had already removed the costume and put her own dress back on, but she had not been able to close it in the back. Though the suggestion of such an intimacy unnerved her, the backstage maids had all run off with Anna Maria, finishing her costume change.

She turned her back to Andrea, and he began connecting the hooks and pulling the laces tight. "I heard about the guards," he said. *The guards. Was it still the same night?* "It seems like a lifetime ago," Chiaretta said. "I'd already forgotten."

His motions were enough to buffet her slightly, and she felt his strong fingers pushing into her back. She shut her eyes and tried to concentrate on something else.

"Finished," he said, and she turned around. The look in his eyes had grown intense again, and she felt her corset tighten around her ribs as she took in a secretive gulp of air.

"We should go," she managed to say. "Luca and Antonia must be at the Ridotto by now."

Andrea stood, taking in her hair, her eyes, her cheeks, her mouth, before sweeping his eyes briefly and discreetly from her head to her feet.

"Both of them losing Luca's money, I presume," he said. "Let me help you with your bauta."

HE PUT HIS ARM AROUND HER WAIST TO GUIDE HER THROUGH the crowded Piazza Sant'Angelo. Boys were setting off firecrackers, and two intoxicated women exposed their breasts to the cheering crowd. Impromptu bands played on each corner of the square, while jugglers, mummers, and magicians competed for space on the church steps. The aromas of caramelized sugar and roasting nuts filled the air from a booth where a man stood holding a bear cub on a chain while children darted in to taunt it.

"Don't they ever get tired of this?" Chiaretta asked, pressing closer to Andrea.

He tightened his hold around her waist. "It's the last night before the break for Christmas. I guess they want to make sure they have enough to tell their confessor for two weeks."

As they passed the church of San Moisè and turned in the direction of the casino, the sky lit up with fireworks.

"Let's go watch," Andrea said, as they passed by the entrance to the Ridotto and walked the few remaining steps to the Riva. Oil lamps on boats scribbled lines of light in the darkness as they were jostled by the water of the lagoon. The dome of Santa Maria della Salute glowed in the moonlight, and Chiaretta could see the outline of the crowd gathered there. Then the sky was lit again with golden sparks that fell in burning cinders into the canal, dying with hundreds of little hisses.

A shower of embers fell close to them on the walkway, and Andrea drew her closer. "Let's move back a little." He pulled her aside into a sheltered corner between two buildings, and though she no longer needed protection from the crowds or the sparks, Andrea did not pull away. Instead, he turned toward her.

"Chiaretta," he said. "Take off your mask. I have something I can't wait any longer to say." His eyes softened when he saw her face, and he lifted his hand to brush her cheek. Another burst showered down nearby, but he didn't seem to notice. "Claudio is my friend and so are you. But I find myself in such pain over my feelings for you, and I just want to say that if you ever felt that you wanted to— If you wanted there to be more between us, I would guard your honor with my life."

Chiaretta put both hands to her mouth and stared at him. He reached behind her neck with one of his hands, and gently taking her fingers away from her face with the other, he pulled her toward him and kissed her. His lips were thinner than Claudio's, but his tongue traced the corners of her own with a delicacy that sent spikes of sweet pleasure through her shoulders and down her arms, through her neck and to the bottom of her spine.

He pulled away. "I'm sorry," he said. "I took something from you that you hadn't offered."

She lifted herself up on her toes and looked into his eyes. "I'm offering it now," she said, kissing him again.

SHORTLY AFTER DAWN THE FOLLOWING MORNING, CHIARETTA was woken from a restless sleep by a wave of nausea so strong she barely made it to her washbasin before she vomited. For the last week she had fought down the same feeling, dismissing it as nervousness about the performance and forgetting about it by midmorning.

When Zuana came in to inquire if she wanted breakfast, she stopped short at the smell coming from the basin and the figure of her mistress fallen back on the bed like a discarded cloak. She rushed to remove the basin, and when she carried it back dry and clean, Chiaretta was sitting up.

"I don't know what came over me," Chiaretta said. "I woke up sick, but I seem to be better now." Her nipples felt like hot coals, and her breasts seemed to be made of stone; when she reached down to touch them, she winced at the pain.

"Would Madonna like me to ask the lady of the house to come attend her?"

Giustina? Why would she want Giustina? Her quizzical look

made Zuana smile. "At these times, Madonna, a woman might like to talk to another woman. Or perhaps I should call for your husband?"

At these times? Then it dawned on her. Her hand flew to her mouth. "Zuana. Does this mean—?"

"Yes, Madonna. It is the first sign."

All thoughts of Andrea vanished. *I'm going to have a baby.*

*Part Five*_____

BLESSINGS

_____*1723—1726*

NINETEEN

ONATA MOROSINI HELD UP THE BLUE AND WHITE cat's mask in front of her face. "I want to wear this one!"

"Cara, it's too big. It belongs to your mother. Be careful with it!" The gold filigreed wings had bent a little over the six years since Claudio had given Chiaretta the mask, but it was still beautiful. Besina, the young nanny, grabbed it away.

The little girl's face crumpled. "But it's a kitty. I don't like mine. It isn't special."

"It isn't supposed to be. You're supposed to look like everybody else. It goes with the bauta your father bought you."

"But this is a party. I want to wear a mask." Donata twirled in her silk chemise and long slip and practiced the new dance she was learning, shutting her eyes and whispering the count out loud as she concentrated. "I'm four and I'm singing at the party!" she crowed.

"Almost four, and not if you don't take a nap first!" Chiaretta came in, holding a one-year-old boy. She put him down, holding him up by one arm and linking her finger through a tape sewn into the back of his jacket to help him learn to walk. "Go to Besina!" The child gurgled, his broad face wet with the drool of a new tooth. Still holding him, she moved forward as he put out each foot in turn.

"Good boy, Maffeo!" she said as she passed the tape to the nanny.

"He won't need his girello soon," Besina said, picking him up and slipping him into a polished wooden walker carved with leaves and flowers. Maffeo babbled as he patted the designs on the girello with his wet fingers before pushing himself across the room toward his sister.

"Yes, I think you're right. Another week or two and he'll be walking. Is my husband back from the Pietà?"

"No, Madonna, I don't believe so. Would you like me to find out?"

"No, but would you leave a message that I'd like to see him before the guests arrive?"

"Of course." Besina looked over at Maffeo, who had begun to suck on his knuckles. "Excuse me, Madonna, but I think it's time for him to be fed. Shall I take him to the wet nurse?"

"Yes, please. I can get Donata into bed." Chiaretta watched as Besina pulled the baby from the girello and bounced him in her arms. He whimpered, and Chiaretta came over to him, smoothing his hair and kissing him on the forehead. He reached out his arms for her, but she moved just out of reach. "Go with Besina, my darling. I'll see you after your nap."

Donata was in one corner of the nursery, rocking her dolls in the carved wooden cradle generations of Morosinis had slept in as infants.

"Do I have to take a nap?" she asked her mother.

"The party isn't for a few hours. It will make the time pass."

"Can I sleep in your bed?" Donata turned around and gave her mother a calculated smile. "With you?"

Chiaretta laughed. "I suppose so. I may not fall asleep, but I'll lie down with you until you do."

She helped her daughter up into the high bed and got in after her. Donata turned toward her, and Chiaretta cradled her head in the hollow of her shoulder.

"When will my aunt get here?" Donata asked.

"Which one?"

"Maddalena. Who else is coming? Antonia?"

"Maybe." Antonia had just given birth to her fourth child, and the quick succession of pregnancies and a stillbirth had made her so heavy and listless that she rarely went out. *A third girl,* Chiaretta thought, playing with Donata's fine blond hair as her breathing grew shallow and she took in the little snuffles of air Chiaretta knew meant she was falling asleep.

It had taken Antonia several weeks to think of a name for her new daughter, and she had sent her away with barely a glance after her birth. "Convent fodder," she had said. "Piero won't be happy."

Claudio, Chiaretta thought with pleasure, had been delighted with his perfect little daughter and son. Piero was not anywhere near as good a father or provider. Antonia hadn't gotten a new wardrobe after her last two babies, and Chiaretta had noticed with dismay how stained and worn some of the new baby's bedding looked. Though Piero's family was once among the wealthiest in Venice, he was not particularly intelligent and had not shown a good head for business. In the last two years the rumors about his gambling losses had gotten so bad it was hard for Chiaretta to look Antonia in the face.

When the story circulated that, in order to make one last bet, Piero crawled under the gaming table to find a few zecchini he had dropped, he denied it had been him. The rumor eventually floated away, replaced by another about someone else. The masks everyone except the banker wore at the casinos gave Piero his cover and Antonia the ability to put the best public face on her husband's growing shame. For that and other reasons, in the last few years Antonia had become reclusive, rarely wanting visitors, even among her oldest friends.

I have my beautiful babies for company, Chiaretta thought. *Antonia will come around. Someday she'll look at her children and see what a blessing they are.* When she saw her own features and personality reflected in Donata, she wanted to pull her daughter to herself and never let go. The ferocity of her love overwhelmed Chiaretta at times, and she was adamant that nothing would separate her from her children, even if it was the Venetian way.

SOON AFTER HER BODY HAD FIRST STARTED TO SWELL WITH Donata, a Morosini property in one of the small squares of Venice fell vacant after the family leasing it went back to Austria. Chiaretta insisted that she and Claudio make it their family home. She took only Zuana with her to Ca' Morosini, and Claudio retained only his own personal servant. A new staff worked for them, without loyalties to the Palazzo Morosini or to the troublesome woman who lived there.

The house looked out onto a lively square, where Besina often took Donata to look in the shops or chat with the vendors, bringing home their small gifts—an apple from the grocer, a bright feather from the milliner. Twice a week, Chiaretta took Donata to mass at the church on the other side of the square, followed by a treat at a café.

The portego on the piano nobile was about half the size of the one they had moved from, ideal for the smaller kinds of entertainment Chiaretta favored. The portego on the next level, where the family lived, was perfect for her daughter to dance in her stocking feet and listen to her voice echo off the terrazzo floor as she sang.

Though she might have chosen larger personal quarters, Chiaretta had taken a corner of the new house where, next to her own rooms, there was another suitable for a nursery. Besina lived downstairs with the rest of the servants, but she had a bed in the nursery as well.

Donata mumbled something in her sleep, and Chiaretta realized she too had dozed off. Much remained to be done in the hours before the party, so she slipped her arm out from under her daughter and got out of bed. She knocked on the door to Claudio's quarters, but he was still not there. His father had died after a brief illness the year before, leaving Claudio to take over his role on the Congregazione. It took up more hours of his time than Chiaretta could ever have imagined. This year Claudio was also serving on the Council of Ten, often returning home so exhausted he fell asleep within minutes of getting his boots off.

By now Chiaretta had adjusted to the fact that the floor where his boots dropped was sometimes not in their home. Antonia had been right. The woman on the boat was a courtesan, and though occasionally a nobleman was foolish enough to fall in love with one of them, their company was a diversion no one gave much thought to. Claudio asked nothing of his wife but to look out for his wants and needs, and be discreet about private matters. Chiaretta expected and got the same from him. Perhaps the Venetians were right after all, that not expecting one's spouse to be the source of all happiness and pleasure led to a more contented life.

Tonight, her husband would be lucky to get even a few minutes' rest before the guests arrived. Among the dozen or so invitees was an elderly man Claudio was encouraging to remember the Pietà in his will, and another donor who appeared to be moving his favor to the coro of another ospedale, the Mendicanti. If all went well, a private concert led by the illustrious violinist

Maddalena della Pietà would lead to two favorable commitments in one evening.

As she started back toward her quarters, Chiaretta heard Claudio's footsteps on the stairs. He was sweating in his black patrician cloak in the sultry heat of a June evening.

She took his cloak and followed him into his study. "Did you get it?" she asked, gesturing to a small package he was holding.

"Yes. They stayed open for me. Where is she?"

"Asleep in my bed. Why don't you lay it on the pillow?"

Claudio tiptoed into the bedroom and bent over his daughter for a moment before leaving the package next to the arm she had flung outside the coverlet. Chiaretta felt a sweet pang in her heart as she watched him. Claudio loved his children more openly than any other father she knew. He found time for them whenever he could, and tolerated being interrupted in his study just to get a kiss or a view of a new tooth. *I am so glad to be married to him,* Chiaretta thought.

Donata stirred and opened her eyes. "Papa!" Her hand touched the package, and she sat up to see what it was. "A present for me?" she said, her eyes opening wide. She pulled at the wrapping and extracted a tiny pink and gold papier-mâché half-mask with an attached stick to hold it in front of her eyes.

"Your mama told me you wanted a kitty one to match your new dress for the party," Claudio said. "Do you like it?"

Donata had already gotten up to run to the mirror, and Claudio turned to his wife, taking her in his arms for a moment before they both broke away to get ready for their guests.

CHIARETTA BARELY HAD TIME TO DRESS BEFORE MADDALENA arrived from the Pietà with a small group of figlie di coro dressed in their black concert dresses. Chiaretta watched as some of them hung back at the far end of the portego, just as she had done when she was their age. Maddalena stopped in the middle of the room and turned around. "Come," she urged. "Meet your hostess." The figlie, most of them in their early teens, approached Chiaretta shyly.

"Is it true you were once in the coro?" one of them asked, her eyes taking in the brocade and velvet of Chiaretta's gown and the sparkling jewels tucked in her coils of hair.

"Yes, it is," she said, reaching out to remove a stray thread from the girl's shoulder. The girl looked down, her cheeks coloring with surprise at the tender and unexpected gesture.

Donata had monopolized Maddalena from the moment she saw her, showing off her new mask and begging her to come see the doll she had named after her. "Maffeo can almost walk!" she said as they headed toward the stairs that led to her bedroom. Maddalena looked over at Chiaretta, whom she had not yet had a chance to greet. Now promoted from sotto maestra to maestra dal violin, at thirty-one Maddalena had hardly changed in appearance in years. Her hair had begun to dull from the rich reddish chestnut of her youth, but her face was only faintly lined and still radiant from within. She gave Chiaretta a helpless smile as Donata whisked her away.

The figlie di coro had gone to the other end of the room to put their instruments in the corner, and Chiaretta watched them while keeping an eye on the servants putting the first course on the table. A hand touched her elbow, and she turned to see Andrea.

"Hello," he said. Chiaretta looked over her shoulder to see if Claudio was watching. "He's in the sala d'oro with a couple of your guests," Andrea said. "How are you?"

Andrea had been away on business for over a month, and she hadn't been certain whether he would return in time to come that evening. She felt the familiar sensation in her loins that always came over her when she first saw her lover.

"You're back," she whispered. Then she pulled away and

arranged her body and face to look the same as it would for any other guest. "Can I offer you a glass of wine?" she said with a feigned tone of impartiality. "Soon?" she whispered, her eyes pleading. "I've missed you terribly." She turned around and motioned a servant toward him, then walked away to greet another guest.

AFTER DINNER, CHIARETTA SAT DOWN AT THE HARPSICHORD at the far end of the portego, and Donata stood next to her while they sang a children's song for the guests. Maddalena stood to one side, watching her niece move her new mask over and then away from her eyes as she sang. Time would tell if Donata had inherited her mother's talent along with her blond hair, but her coquettish grin and her loud and confident voice left no doubt she had her spirit.

Then Chiaretta sang a solo accompanied by her sister. *"Benedetto sia il giorno, et il mese, et l'anno,"* she sang. "Blessed be the day, the month, the year, the season, the time, the hour, the moment, the beautiful country, and the place where I first felt bound to the two beautiful eyes that still hold me." Chiaretta looked over at Donata, who was standing next to her father holding his leg, and gave her a wink to tell her she meant the words just for her.

Maddalena played an interlude, and then Chiaretta picked up the melody again. "And blessed be the sweet pain I had in first knowing love, and the bow and the arrows that pricked me, and the hurts that went deep into my heart." At these words Chiaretta turned away from everyone else in her life, looking only at her sister, whose eyes acknowledged everything they both felt.

After the figlie performed, Chiaretta and Maddalena linked arms as they walked back toward the banquet table, where plates with small pieces of nougat and candied fruit were being laid out for the guests.

"Oh, Maddalena, you'll be interested in this," Claudio said, pulling out her chair. "Vivaldi's coming back to the Pietà. It was just decided today."

Maddalena reached out to grab the edge of the table. A spoon clattered to the floor, and a servant rushed to pick it up, murmuring apologies that Maddalena did not hear. She stared at the wine being poured into her glass. Reflected candlelight had turned its gilded rim into a tiny halo and illuminated the crimson liquid from within, but Maddalena saw nothing.

Blessed be the season, the time, the hour . . . So much had changed since she had seen him last. Enough time had passed to reshape her memories and put them safely away. And now he would be coming back to shatter her tranquillity again.

TWENTY

*I*N THE CORNER OF THE ROOM WHERE MADDALENA SAT working, the coal in the stove popped and rustled as it settled into embers. On the wooden desk lay a thick pile of sheet music, and in front of her was a piece of paper on which she had copied a few notes. The oil lamp flickered on the desk, and she reached out to adjust the flame, moving it closer to get a little more light.

She looked at a line of the music. "Viola," she said, humming each note as she wrote it down. Vivaldi had written something beautiful for Benedetta, and as Maddalena dipped her pen in the inkwell, she told herself to concentrate only on how beautiful it would sound. She told herself not to think about the composer at all, although his familiar hand leapt out at her on every page.

Claudio, she learned later, had not meant to imply that Vivaldi would be returning in person as Maestro dei Concerti. The

Congregazione had contracted with him to supply two new concerti a month, which he was free either to send by post or to deliver in person. He had chosen the former and had not, as far as she knew, set foot in Venice in the nearly two years since Claudio's announcement at the party.

It didn't take much to bring back the knot in her stomach and the heaviness in her head when she thought about him. *Just copy the music,* she would say to herself. *Just copy the music.*

But sometimes she couldn't make herself listen, especially at moments like this, when her fingers stiffened in the cold and she had to stop work to warm them. As she held her hands near the stove, her thoughts wandered to the way she and Vivaldi would stare at each other, perspiration beading on their foreheads, when they finished a piece of music. The way he would lean over her to show her how to adjust her fingering, his red hair catching the light and making the whole room glow.

She missed him, missed the crackling energy of the coro when he played with them. She even missed his moods and his tantrums. They were to be expected from a man whose being was so suffused with music it left little room for good manners. He was a genius. The coro played the music he sent, and played it well, but it wasn't the same as having him there.

How old is he now? Closer to fifty than forty, Maddalena thought. She wondered how age had changed him. It certainly had changed her. The clamor of her humors when she was younger was gone, and she exulted in simple pleasures now—seeing Donata and Maffeo run toward her with outstretched arms, or giving her students a comforting hug when, facing a setback, they struggled to be brave. Though life was exciting when Vivaldi was at the Pietà, his presence and absence were a fair trade, she decided. Less energy, more calm. Less passion, more peace.

No, she thought, it would be fine if he came back in person, fine if they played music together again, and fine if none of it happened.

At first Chiaretta had been angry at Claudio for not better judging the impact of his announcement, but Maddalena had pointed out that he could not have known what Vivaldi meant to her. "If I explain, I know he'll want to apologize," Chiaretta had said, but they both knew without saying that Maddalena would be embarrassed to have her childhood feelings revealed.

Maddalena held her hands over the stove, opening and closing them like pincers. She rubbed them together to keep them warm as she went back to her desk.

Just copy the music.

"Viola," she said picking up her pen.

A FEW WEEKS LATER, SHE WAITED ON THE BALCONY OVERLOOKING the chapel to catch a glimpse of Chiaretta and Donata, who were coming with Andrea to hear Benedetta play. Maddalena herself was not performing, and rarely did so in the chapel anymore, having time only for the occasional recital in the grand homes of Venice. Making sure the figlie were well taught and well treated gave her a different kind of pleasure than a solo on the balcony, and a far more lasting one.

Chiaretta, Donata, and Andrea came in, and she watched as Andrea got the mother and daughter seated. The three of them crossed themselves and prayed. *How odd it is that they aren't a family,* Maddalena thought. *How strange a place this Venice is.* She far preferred to be on the gauze-draped balcony, where everything was so much simpler, but she was also glad her sister had a man next to her who tended to her so well. And one whom Donata adored, at least if the way she was tipping her head and smiling at him as she walked her fingers over his jacket was any indication.

THE THREE OF THEM CAME TO THE PARLATORIO TO SEE HER after the concert. Donata's mouth was sticky with crumbs from the treat she had been offered by one of the figlie, and she smelled of honey as she pursed her lips to kiss Maddalena through the grate.

"Benedetta was very good," Donata said. "Someday I'll be part of the coro too!"

"You sound just like your mother when *she* was six, my precious little one," Maddalena replied.

Now even Andrea came to the grille to speak with Maddalena when they visited. She had known for some time that he and her sister met once a week in rooms he rented in a palazzo off one of the smaller canals. It had a doorway that opened just off a tiny square, which led to a private entrance. The rest of the house was unoccupied at the moment, making the arrangement as safe as possible.

When Chiaretta first whispered to her about her affair with Andrea, Maddalena did not know what to think. Marriage was sacred, but Venice had its own ways, and she was glad she did not have to try to understand them. Nor was there any need to judge. She trusted Chiaretta to know what she was doing and gave Andrea the respect owed to someone her sister had chosen. It really wasn't any of her business, she decided, as long as no one she loved was harmed by it.

She saw, in her frequent trips to Ca' Morosini, that Chiaretta's relationship with Claudio did not appear to be suffering. Whether he knew the truth about his wife and Andrea, Maddalena couldn't tell, but if he did, he gave no sign of being displeased. Maddalena liked Andrea's somber bearing and his gentle heart. She liked Claudio also, for giving Chiaretta the life she wanted and keeping her safe in it. Two men loved her sister, and Maddalena was grateful for it.

Today the parlatorio was crowded on both sides of the grille. It had been the first concert of the fall season, and the figlie and their guests were noisy and animated. Donata had gone off with Andrea to watch someone doing card tricks in one corner, and

Maddalena leaned closer to the grille to hear what her sister was telling her.

"I said," Chiaretta lifted her voice, "that Maestro Vivaldi has been hired as the impresario for an opera at Claudio's theater in November."

Vivaldi? In Venice? Maddalena knew he came through Venice occasionally for his operas, but not since he'd officially become an employee of the Pietà again. *Is he coming back here?*

Chiaretta had turned to locate Donata and Andrea, and didn't see the anxious look that crossed her sister's face. She turned back and went on. "According to Claudio, it's about time. The Congregazione is disgusted with him. He writes about half of what he agreed to."

Chiaretta noticed Maddalena's furrowed brow. "Are you worried about it? I don't think he's planning on spending much time at the Pietà."

Maddalena shrugged. "I guess I've just reached a point where I think I prefer him at a distance." She thought for a moment. "But it has been a long time. I'd like to see him, and I'd like him to meet Benedetta, and Cornelia, and all the other figlie who play his music now."

Her heart was racing as she spoke, and she could hear the tightness in her voice. *Anticipation or dread?* she asked herself, knowing her mind could not be trusted to give her an honest answer.

THE TAVOLETTA ANNOUNCING THE OPENING OF VIVALDI'S PRO-duction of *L'Inganno Trionfante in Amore* was already posted outside the Teatro Sant'Angelo when Chiaretta came to pay him an angry visit. She had just returned from taking Donata across the canal for a music lesson at the Pietà and in a brief conversation with the priora had learned that Vivaldi had not been in contact with anyone there since his return to Venice for rehearsals of the opera a full month before. Maddalena insisted that she had no expectations, but Chiaretta knew her sister well enough to recognize the telltale signs of hurt as the weeks passed without a word or visit from him.

"Insufferable man," she muttered to herself as she went through the door of the theater. Vivaldi was waving his arms and yelling at the actors on the stage, and when one of them stalked off, he turned, started toward the exit, and nodded to the patrician woman seated on a bench inside the doors to the lobby without recognizing who it was.

"Maestro Vivaldi," she said, following him out into the lobby and lifting her veil.

"Chiaretta! Forgive me. I didn't know it was you." He inhaled sharply with a familiar wheezy hitch.

"You look well," Chiaretta said in a stiff voice. In truth, he looked as harried as ever. His complexion was the color of skimmed milk, and his hair looked as if he had cut it himself, but he moved with the same jittery intensity she remembered, as if something too powerful to hold back lay just below the surface.

"I should have inquired about you when I arrived in Venice," he said, "but I have been so busy. We open next week—but I suppose you know that."

"I plan to be there." Her tone was icy, but he didn't seem to notice.

"It isn't very good. It's just a pasticcio, and I only arranged the music. Have you heard Anna Girò at the San Moisè? She's really spectacular."

Chiaretta ignored his question. "I'd like to talk about my sister."

"Maddalena? How is she?"

His tone was so offhand she colored with anger. "She's fine, but it's hard to imagine why you could have let so much time pass since you returned to Venice without acknowledging she is here." She took a breath to say more but decided against it.

Vivaldi's face clouded. "Surely your husband has informed you of the Congregazione's dissatisfaction with me? I don't believe I would be welcome at the Pietà, even as a visitor."

"They would certainly welcome you if you were carrying new music with you."

Vivaldi stepped back, surprised by the curtness of her reply. "I'm afraid that's impossible for a while. You can see how busy I am."

He gestured toward the stage, where a few singers and members of the orchestra chatted among themselves and stagehands erected scenery. Her gaze followed his, and they both stood silent for a moment watching them. Chiaretta thought of Maddalena alone in her room copying his music. He couldn't possibly imagine how much time there was to think at the Pietà, how anything out of the ordinary was played over and over again in the dark on sleepless nights, how the past was plumbed for the smallest forgotten details, and how much any pleasure to come was anticipated.

Chiaretta wondered whether he was having the same thought she was. How different the Teatro Sant'Angelo and the Pietà were! In one, he didn't seem to command much respect at all, but at the other the musicians treated him almost as if he were the doge himself. *Does anyone admire him here?* she wondered. *It doesn't look like it.*

"When you wrote music for my sister and me, it meant more to us than you could imagine," she said, surprised at the tremor in her voice.

"I'm flattered." He touched his chest in the way she had seen so often when he had tried to ingratiate himself with dignitaries visiting the Pietà. "You are very gracious to come here to tell me that."

Insufferable man! "Maestro Vivaldi, do you think I have come all this way just to deliver a compliment?" She swallowed hard to calm her voice, thinking about how to convey what she had come to the theater to tell him.

"My sister is maestra dal violino now. She owes that in part to you, I know. But even after all these years, her memories of playing with you are important to her. I just came over to ask whether they were important to you at all." She gave an indignant sniff and looked away. "Perhaps you have had too many students just like her."

"Chiaretta, it's not that I have forgotten. But—"

She cut him off. "I've said what I wanted to say. Do with it what you will." She turned and walked out the door.

Within a week, two concerti were delivered to the Congregazione along with a letter requesting the assistance of the maestra dal violino in the preparation of a major new work for the Pietà.

"Did you have anything to do with this?" Maddalena asked Chiaretta.

"I saw him briefly at the theater," Chiaretta said. "But we didn't discuss this." *Close enough to the truth,* she told herself.

❦❦❦

ANNA GIRÒ'S BREASTS PUSHED THEIR WAY UP AND OVER THE top of her corset as if they were plotting an escape. Although she was not fat, her body gave off a general sense of fleshiness that most agreed was unlikely to be conducive to virtue. Her face was pretty enough to be a tool to charm wealthy and influential men, although at the moment her stage makeup was caked on so heavily she could have disguised an acute bout of the pox. She had been billed as a twenty-year-old sensation when she came to Venice from Mantua the year before to star in Albinoni's *Laodicea*. Scornful reviews of her singing from some quarters were countered by such lavish praise from others that most Venetians had shrugged at the obvious conclusion to be drawn: that La Girò might be offering more than her musical talent to some of the cognoscenti of Venice.

Despite differences of opinion about the extent of her talent, from the moment of his arrival in Venice, Vivaldi began pressuring Claudio and the other investors in the Teatro Sant'Angelo to put up the money necessary to secure a commitment from the diva. Claudio had attended her Venetian debut and was not sufficiently impressed to change his plans for a business trip just to hear her sing for the first time at the Teatro Sant'Angelo, so Chiaretta and Andrea were in the Morosini box with only Luca and Antonia for company.

At that moment the effects of a great deal of wine taken with only the first course of their dinner had made them giddy and more than a little caustic about the spectacle taking place on the stage. Anna was flinging her arms out to hold a sustained note and offering up great heaving sighs to cover her difficulties when the music suddenly slid downward. Though Anna was a contralto and thus not prone to screeching on the high notes, Chiaretta heard the quick key changes the orchestra made so she could manage the lowest notes without sounding rather like a dog growling over a bone.

Antonia had managed to pass nearly two years without a pregnancy and had recovered some of her old spirit. "Look at her flapping her arms! You could get up there today and sing better without even practicing," she said to Chiaretta after Anna finished an aria and swept off the stage to great applause.

"Ah, but it's not all about the voice," Andrea said. "She's obviously hard to ignore, and one could argue she's great if people say she is." He turned to Chiaretta. "What do you think?"

Her only response was a shrug of her shoulders. She hadn't really been listening. When she had gone to the theater to speak to Vivaldi about his failure to acknowledge Maddalena upon his return to Venice, he couldn't wait to talk about Anna. *I had to remind him I had a sister,* she thought. *Who is this Anna Girò to him?*

They adjourned to the back of the box and were eating another course of their dinner when Luca made a reference to the Duke of

Massa. Antonia, wanting to be in on every joke, asked Andrea why he was laughing.

"It seems that Anna wanted a harpsichord and used some money her good friend the duke had given her to buy it." Andrea arched his eyebrows. "And let's just say it was more than enough money to cause one to question the nature of the friendship."

Luca coated a forkful of meat with sauce and popped it in his mouth. "I've heard Anna is a very friendly girl," he said with a leer. "Anyway, the man who sold the harpsichord to her somehow got the idea he had been duped, and he went to court."

He put his fork down and wiped his mouth with his napkin. "I'm surprised you haven't heard about this, Chiaretta," he said, picking up his wineglass. "It involved your old friend Vivaldi."

Chiaretta's heart thudded. "What did he have to do with it?"

"He was the go-between. It was Vivaldi who was sued. Seems the old duke gave Anna twice as much money as she spent on the harpsichord. The man who sold it got the idea he had been swindled by the good priest."

"An amusing little scandal made of nothing," Andrea said. "So what if she didn't spend all she had on his harpsichord? He agreed on the price."

"The court saw it that way too, but it makes you wonder why Vivaldi had gotten involved in the first place," Luca said and then cocked his ear. "Isn't that La Girò?" They got up to watch her sing, and the conversation was over. Chiaretta stood with them looking down at the stage, not hearing another note.

BY AGREEMENT WITH THE PIETÀ, MADDALENA WAS TO TAKE THE unusual step of going to Vivaldi's home to work with him. He had been having a long run of bad health and convinced the Nobili Uomini Deputati that it would be in their best interests if he did not have to move around town unnecessarily during the winter. At home, he could have what he needed at hand while he labored on what he had assured them would be the greatest instrumental work of his career. To sweeten the proposal, the violin Maddalena used when she was there would become the property of the Pietà when the work was complete, an expensive gift not to be sneered at by the cash-strapped Congregazione.

Fioruccia, who had so openly disdained the coro's use of melodies from Gasparini's operas, grudgingly agreed to be Maddalena's chaperone when it was pointed out that her dislike for opera composers was the best guarantee that nothing immoral would happen. Even so, it took a month to reach an agreement whereby a woman from the Pietà could go to a man's home, even if the man was a priest.

Vivaldi lived in a part of Venice that Maddalena had never seen. The canals and the fondamenti lining them narrowed with each turn, until the crumbling buildings loomed overhead like rows of beggars in tattered clothing. A woman stepped outside to fling the contents of a slop bucket into the canal, startling a scrawny cat that ran for cover in a dark alley no wider than a wheelbarrow. On the other side, two rats inspected a small pile of garbage, ignoring the curses of a man who kicked at them as he passed.

Is this where he lives? Maddalena wondered, looking up at the houses. *How could any music come from here?*

They crossed under a bridge and entered a wider canal, lined with well-maintained houses whose bright colors glimmered in the sunlight reflecting off the water. *This is better,* Maddalena thought, but her heart sank again when the gondolier stroked across the canal toward another one too small for a walkway and into which so little light penetrated it would be difficult to tell night from day.

He stopped within seconds at a small landing on the side of a pleasant, although rather poorly maintained, rose-colored house that looked out on the larger canal. The gondolier banged on the door with the top of his oar, and while they waited for a response, he turned to them. "Madonne, it's very cold," he said. "If it pleases you, I'll wait at the shop we just passed, where there's a fire." He gestured across the canal to a small saloon, outside of which two men were talking, stamping their feet to keep warm.

Seeing Fioruccia's expression, he added, "I won't be drinking, if that's what you're wondering. Just staying in against the cold. They can send a servant to get me when you're ready."

Just then the door swung open. The chance for Fioruccia to argue with him passed as a manservant held out his hand to her and assisted her inside. When he lifted Maddalena onto the dark landing, her nostrils stung from the smell of mildew in the frigid air. The servant opened another door into a hallway lit with a single oil lamp that cast dim light on a carpet worn through in several places.

"This way," he said, gesturing to a door at the far end. Through it they passed into a parlor in which a small fire cut slightly into the darkness and the cold.

"I'll tell him you're here," the servant said, knocking on a closed door.

Maddalena heard a chair scrape back, followed by footsteps moving to the door. It opened with a squeak of the hinges.

Vivaldi was smaller than she remembered, and his eyes were cloudier. The skin had loosened below his chin, and the bones in his face were even more pronounced.

"Ah!" he said, by way of greeting.

Maddalena was taken aback that he said nothing about how long it had been or even that he was happy to see her. "It's nice to see you again," she said, but he nodded as if he were too distracted to hear and said nothing in reply.

He was wearing a housecoat of moss green wool, over which his untidy hair fell onto his shoulders. Fioruccia scowled at his appearance. "Forgive me," he said, interpreting her expression. "It's the cold. I can put on my priest's cassock, if you insist, but it is still damp from when I got caught in the rain yesterday."

"That won't be necessary," Fioruccia said, staring at his slipper-clad feet with such disdain that he ordered his servant to bring him a pair of stockings and shoes.

He motioned them into his study. The room was almost as large as the parlor, but so cluttered they could scarcely move around. The walls were covered with bookcases, stacked with materials in no apparent order. The floor space was divided between a harpsichord, a large desk, and a music stand. On each were piles of music scores and stacks of paper. Next to a fireplace in which a minuscule fire was burning was an ornate chair with fraying upholstery and a small, mismatched table on which a tray was perched holding a teapot and a crust of bread smeared with the oily remains of some butter.

"It's beyond straightening up," Vivaldi said, motioning to his servant to take away the tray, "but it's the way I work, I'm afraid." He went to the far side of the desk and picked up a rosary, muttering a prayer as he kissed it and put it in a drawer. With a sweep of his hand, he moved the clutter aside.

He turned to Fioruccia. "I've had a fire laid for you outside, where you can be more comfortable while we work. I'll have my servant light the lamp."

Fioruccia scowled, as if she were about to resist leaving them alone, but after a second glance around the cluttered room, she sighed in resignation.

When Fioruccia was settled, Vivaldi retrieved his violin from its case and went straight to the point. "Do you remember years ago when I asked you what this sounded like?" He played a few warbling notes and looked at Maddalena.

"Birds singing in a tree," she said. "And then you made it sound like they were flying away." Her words were chopped and flat.

Small. She felt that way again, as she sat ignored in his study while he wrapped himself in his music.

"That gave me an idea I've been thinking about ever since." Still holding his bow, he pressed down with his fingertips on a page of an open notebook to hold it flat. "Listen to this." He cleared his throat and began to recite.

> *Spring has come in all its gaiety*
> *And the birds welcome it with joyful song*
> *And a zephyr's breath inspires the brooks*
> *To murmur as they flow.*

He closed the notebook while he played the birds' song and began reciting from memory when he had finished.

> *The air is filled with black clouds,*
> *And then the arrival of lightning and thunder,*
> *But when it is once more quiet*
> *The birds come back to sing again.*

He played a wild cadenza depicting the birds' flight. "Do you know who wrote the poem?" he asked.

She shook her head. "I don't recognize it."

"I did," he said. "I've written four sonnets, one for each season, and I'm going to write a concerto to go with each one. I'm calling it *The Four Seasons.* Do you like the idea?"

"I don't understand what you mean."

"I thought of all people you would." His brow creased with annoyance. "I need you to." He picked up his violin and began to play. "It goes like this."

He played a bright melody quickly, tapping his foot to provide a continuo. "That's what the orchestra will play. It's setting the mood of spring. Then the solo violin will do this," he said, launching into the song of the birds. "Then"—he switched into a lower, more flowing melody—"we'll hear the sound of a brook flowing in the spring thaw. And then thunder will frighten the birds." He shut his eyes and began a wild flight of notes. "But they'll come back to their branches, and we end the first movement like this." He played the opening phrases again but in a more muted key, with a hint of melancholy in it.

Maddalena's spirits had lifted with the music. It seemed as if no time at all had passed since he had last sat and played with her. *Nothing in my life is like this. Nothing can take its place,* she thought, accepting the fact that if she wanted the music, she would have to deal with the self-absorbed and often thoughtless man who created it.

"The problem is how to find anyone to play it the way I want," he went on. "There's rain, and wind whistling outside a door, and a man falling down drunk, and a dog barking while his master sleeps."

His breath had begun to catch, and his words were coming out in short phrases between shallow gulps of air. "You're the only one I know who can possibly understand. Everyone else will argue with me, or just play it however they want. I need someone who feels it—and can make the other musicians feel it too. Maddalena Rossa—"

They both turned their heads at the sound of a shrill voice outside the door. Fioruccia's snoring in the parlor was interrupted by the voice of a younger woman.

"Who are you?" Maddalena heard the voice say to Fioruccia before the door to the study was flung open the rest of the way.

"Anna!" Vivaldi's voice rose in alarm.

The woman was wearing a wig and an ornate hat not at all in the Venetian style. Her face was made up as if for a party, and the top of one of her nipples had begun to work its way out from the bodice of her dress.

She flicked her chin in Maddalena's direction, and scowled at him, her hands on her hips. "Who's that?"

He took in a deep breath, but it caught in his throat and he coughed to the point of gagging. His inhalations turned into staccato whoops as he grabbed his chest and fell into a chair.

"Paolina!" Anna cried out. "Come quickly!"

Within a few seconds another woman, a few years older than Anna, hurried into the room. She was dressed similarly, but she had taken off her wig and the brown hair matted next to her skull gave her powdered and rouged face the appearance of a Carnevale mask.

She didn't seem to notice either Maddalena or Fioruccia, who was by now wide awake and standing inside the doorway. "Is it bad?" Paolina asked.

"I think so," Anna said. "I'll go get the servants."

Paolina went to a cupboard and pulled out a small pouch. She sprinkled a spoonful of herbs into a handkerchief, then twisted the top and rubbed the contents in her palms to release the odor.

"Breathe in," she said, holding the sachet to his face and securing him around the back with her other arm. "Anna will be back with the steam." Vivaldi nodded, wide-eyed, but he did not speak.

"Take this," Paolina barked, handing the sachet to Maddalena. Standing so close to him, Maddalena could see his lips had gone blue. Paolina came back with a poultice, and when she loosened Vivaldi's coat and tore open his thin shirt, Maddalena saw how his flesh pulled in under his ribs as he struggled to take each breath.

The smell of camphor and mustard filled the air as Paolina applied the poultice to his chest. By the time Anna got back with a servant carrying a bowl of hot water and squares of steaming cloth, he was breathing more easily. Still, Paolina ordered him to lean forward and breathe through the cloth until it cooled.

She went to the cabinet again and rifled through a box in which were at least a dozen marked packets of herbs and powders. "Lavender, licorice, ginger, chamomile, hyssop," she said under her breath.

Paolina turned to the servant who had carried the cloths and bowl. "Boil water with a spoonful of honey. No—make it two spoonfuls. Then bring it to me in a teapot." She chose two of the packets. "I'll do the rest."

Maddalena stood aside and watched as Vivaldi's manservant took him back to his quarters to change his clothes while Paolina prepared herbs for his tea.

When the women were alone in the study, Anna turned once again to Maddalena. "And who are you?" she asked with the proprietary air of someone in her own home.

Fioruccia already had Maddalena by the arm before she could answer. Her shoulders heaved as she led Maddalena through the hallway and across the dark portico to the back of the house. When she flung open the door, she saw only the water of the canal below her, and she raged back through the house, demanding to be taken to the front door.

"With pleasure," Anna said with a smirk and an exaggerated curtsy. "Follow me."

Outside, the cold assaulted them before they could stop to put their cloaks on. Fioruccia stormed into the saloon and pulled the gondolier to his feet, spilling the cup of warm wine in his hand. "Take us home," she ordered.

INSIDE THE FELCE, FIORUCCIA PULLED THE CURTAINS CLOSED and flung herself back onto the seat. Making the sign of the cross, she moved her lips in prayer, touching her fingers together as if rosary beads were slipping between them.

Who were those women? Maddalena wondered. They knew where everything was and ordered the servants around as if they lived there. But that wasn't possible. Vivaldi was a priest. A priest who had broken his vows—that seemed obvious. Maddalena had watched men and women interact enough by now to recognize that this Anna was no student, no casual friend.

Why didn't he choose her to break his vows with, if his vow of celibacy wasn't sacred to him? The betrayal left Maddalena so numb she was frozen to her seat.

Pictures spun in her mind of Vivaldi and her as man and wife or lovers sitting next to each other in a carriage as they traveled to a new city, or sharing tea and pastry in their house robes in front of a fire. The pictures shifted in her mind, and she saw Vivaldi and Anna in the carriage, Vivaldi and Anna in front of the fire, and she knew that those images were probably true. Why had he told her he wanted her but they could never be together, when he then turned around and had that kind of life with this other woman? *I should hate him for being so false to me,* Maddalena thought. *He's a hypocrite. I should say she's welcome to him.*

Then a revelation hit her so quickly she put her hand over her mouth so Fioruccia wouldn't hear her gasp. *Maybe it isn't because he was a priest that he pulled back from kissing me. Maybe it's because I am who I am.*

If they had become lovers, what then? She couldn't leave the Pietà except as a wife or a nun, and priests couldn't have wives. If he had left the clergy, the Pietà would not have permitted her marriage to a defrocked priest. It wouldn't be moral, and worse, in the eyes of the Pietà, the scandal would be terrible. If she ran away to be with him, what kind of a life would she live, going from town to town with an opera impresario, whispered about wherever she went and not able to play professionally because she was a woman?

He acted as if he were protecting his job, but really he was protecting me. It was my honor he was defending.

Her head was spinning. She had just seen someone caught and disgraced in his own home, someone whose deceit had given her ample reason to despise him, and all she could think about was that she might have misunderstood everything all these years—why he didn't send a letter the first time he left, why he failed to acknowledge her presence so many times, why he didn't visit when he came back to Venice. Anyone else would dismiss him as the most despicable of men after the tawdry scene she had witnessed, and instead—

She had trouble even letting the word form in her head, the word she had driven out so many times before.

I love him.

I can't have him, but I still love him.

Fioruccia had stopped praying. "I hope you've come to your senses about that man," she spat. "Shameless, he is! You know what people say, don't you?" she demanded. "Well, don't you?"

Maddalena shook her head, but she barely heard. She was picturing Vivaldi, wondering what he really had been thinking all those times she had decided he wasn't noticing, all those times she had concluded he didn't care.

"Honestly, how can anyone reach your age and still be so naïve?" Fioruccia went on. "Consorting with harlots! Hah! That man is a disgrace to the church. And why they let you get away with coming here, I don't know." Her voice dropped to a mutter about the whores of Babylon and the fall of Venice as she turned her shoulders toward the side of the felce as if to remove herself from Maddalena's presence altogether.

Blood slammed in great coursing pulses through Maddalena's temples. "Please . . ." she begged.

"Please, what?" Fioruccia hissed. "Don't tell? Hah!" she cackled, and Maddalena felt her life falling away from her again.

TWENTY-ONE

*I*T WAS QUITE A CRISIS," CLAUDIO SAID TO CHIARETTA a day or two later, as they ate supper in their quarters after the children were asleep. "The chaperone has yet to get out of bed, although I suspect that's more to enhance the quality of her gossip than anything else."

"What did Maddalena say?"

"Not much. She said that Vivaldi frequently had such attacks and that she didn't know who the women were, but one of them appeared to be his nurse and handled it all quite competently."

Claudio thought for a moment. "I've seen this 'nurse,'" he said, taking a sip of wine. "Paolina Girò, Anna's sister. They're quite a pair. We called in the Maestro to talk to him, and he insisted the relationship was entirely professional. They leased a house of their own when they came to Venice, but we have reports that they go in and out of his house freely at all hours as if they actually live there. It could become quite a scandal."

"Maddalena in a scandal?"

"No, not her. We're seeing to that. But a priest with an opera singer and her sister—it's all a bit too much for Venetian tastes, although I'm sure everyone is scrambling to be the first to be shocked by every last detail."

Chiaretta pushed her food back and forth on her plate, unable to swallow. Claudio didn't notice. "Still, I'm afraid Vivaldi will have to go," he went on. "Not that it will much matter. We're barely getting a note out of him, with all the commissions he's getting elsewhere. And maybe he'll pay a little more attention to the Teatro Sant'Angelo if we fire him from the Pietà."

Chiaretta had not been listening. "I know tomorrow is a lesson day and they're not supposed to have visitors at the Pietà," she broke in. "But I must see my sister. I need to know if she's all right. Can it be arranged?"

MADDALENA LAY IN BED UNABLE TO SLEEP, GOING OVER EVery detail of that afternoon with the horrified detachment of someone waiting for blood to rise in a wound. The woman he'd called Anna had breezed in as if she belonged there. And then the other one had come in and taken over the role that used to belong to Maddalena. She had done it much more skillfully, pulling out this drawer and that little package and ordering servants to go here or there. She had torn open his shirt, and Maddalena had seen for the first time the naked chest of a man. Not just any man, but one into whose heart the events of the day had caused her to see deeply and, in so doing, confront what was hidden in her own.

It had all the crazy qualities of a dream. Fioruccia raced to the priora's study almost before the gondola was tied up at the dock, not even waiting for Maddalena to disembark. Maddalena was sure that whatever horror Fioruccia claimed she had suffered was more than offset by her glee at having such a story to tell.

What's done is done, Maddalena told herself. *I'll know what to do when I see what happens next.* And though as a rule she preferred thinking through problems to praying about them, she crossed herself as she lay in bed. *Even if this pushes him forever out of my life, I don't want to lose the music,* she whispered. *Just let me have that.*

❦❦❦

"WHAT HAPPENED?" CHIARETTA ASKED, ALARMED AT THE LACK of sleep evident in Maddalena's face as they sat across from each other in the parlatorio.

"I don't know," Maddalena said. "Two women came in as if they lived there, and the next thing I knew, one of them was pulling out one trick after another to cure him, and the other one was acting like I was guilty of something."

"Claudio told me the Congregazione is canceling Vivaldi's contract and forbidding him to associate with the Pietà ever again."

"No! They can't do that!" Maddalena pushed back her chair and stood up. "No!"

"Maddalena, do you hear yourself? You have let that man mistreat you for years. And you're defending him?" Chiaretta's tone was so sharp her words seemed to shatter like glass between them.

"It's not like that," Maddalena said. "You don't know."

Chiaretta was too agitated to hear her. "You look horrible. No one believes you could possibly have done anything wrong, but look what he's done." She waved her hands in front of her as if dispersing a pestilence creeping into the space between them. "He should never have asked you to come to his house, knowing those women might come around! I'm surprised he hasn't been denounced long ago. A priest and his talentless little opera singer, and her sister thrown in too?"

"I'm not defending him. I know it looks bad. But, Chiaretta—" Maddalena gave her a pleading look. "The music!"

Chiaretta shook her head slowly, glaring at her sister without saying anything more.

"He was showing me something before she came in," Maddalena said. "I think it might be the greatest piece of music ever written, if what he played for me . . ."

Maddalena was not one to exaggerate. Though Chiaretta wasn't finished with her scolding, she decided to listen.

"I want to play that music more than anything I have ever wanted in my life." She clasped her hands together. "Can you help?"

Chiaretta hated what she was hearing, but she heard the passion in her sister's voice. "You know it might be too late," she said. "I wish there were a way to help you without helping him, but I imagine there isn't." She stood and patted down her dress. "I'll talk to Claudio."

A FEW DAYS LATER MADDALENA WAS CALLED FOR A PRIVATE meeting in the priora's office. "The Congregazione has given a great deal of time to the matter of Maestro Vivaldi," she told her, "and they asked me to tell you their decision. We wish to maintain control of the first performances of his new work, and he has told us he doesn't feel he can go forward without knowing if you will be playing the first violin. For that reason we have decided to let you continue to work with him."

Maddalena let out the breath she had been holding with such evident relief that she had to struggle not to flinch at the penetrating stare that followed. "You are too attached to him," the priora said after a minute of silence. "It isn't seemly."

"Priora, put whatever restrictions you wish on my work with him. I don't want to be embarrassed either. I just want to play that music."

The priora looked down at her desk before looking up at Maddalena again. "You know, my dear, any kind of passion, even passion for music, has the potential to affect your judgment, and the Maestro is clearly now not in a position to protect your reputation." She leaned forward to look at Maddalena more intently. "You are immensely talented, but perhaps you should hold back more."

It isn't about holding back, Maddalena thought. *Music is about surrender.*

The priora moved in closer as if she were letting Maddalena in on a secret. "To open the fall season with such a work will give us an edge over the other ospedali that will last all year. The Congregazione is planning receptions for donors after the concerts, and your sister's husband has volunteered to sponsor the first performance at his villa this summer. Needless to say, the donations from that will help the coro considerably."

She went on. "The Congregazione feels it is better to give the impression there is nothing to any rumors that might circulate, and the best way to do that is to maintain the association with Don Vivaldi, at least for now. But there will be strict rules."

The priora went through the list on her fingers. Despite his ailments, Vivaldi would come to Maddalena at the Pietà. Paolina Girò would supply a list of her tinctures, teas, inhalants, and poultices to the hospital administration of the Pietà, who would have them ready in case of a problem. In the event of an attack, Maddalena was to ring a bell for the nurse and leave the room when she arrived. She was not to administer any care herself so as to avoid physical contact. They were to work with a minimum of two chairs' width between them at all times, in a part of the room that could be viewed by anyone passing in the hall. Even so, a chaperone would sit inside at all times.

"It is only our faith in your virtue," the priora said, "that makes this possible. I hope you know how much your contribution is appreciated," she said, standing up to signal that the conversation was over.

❦❦❦

BY THE MIDDLE OF JUNE, THE GIRÒ SISTERS AND THE EVENTS of that afternoon had vanished from Maddalena's mind as she worked to near exhaustion to pull the performance of *The Four Seasons* together. She had required the figlie to memorize Vivaldi's sonnets so they would know what they were trying to convey when they played, and sometimes, when her mind would not rest, she recited the poems to herself in the dark, envisioning the spring grass rippling in the breeze, the buzz of gnats and flies in the summer heat, the drunken harvesters and hunted beasts of fall, and the gales and chattering teeth of winter.

Tonight sleep had again refused to come, despite her exhaustion. "We walk on the ice with slow steps," she whispered, "watching intently for fear of slipping." The words were swallowed up by a yawn. "To step hard is to fall, but we go across anyway, until the ice breaks and slides away under our feet."

Tomorrow she would have the coro go over the staccato eighth notes that mimicked walking on ice. It had to be just right to set up Vivaldi's fantastic solo imitating the out-of-control sensation of slipping and falling on the ice, but the figlie had not yet gotten their imaginations involved enough to make it work.

Though Maddalena still wasn't satisfied, Vivaldi was pleased by how well the coro was doing. The musicians were better than he remembered, he told her, and she was the best leader of an orchestra he had ever worked with. She accepted the praise, but her heart no longer yearned for it. She had spent time thinking about what love meant at her age, and decided that it played out not in any great burst of passion but in a new and deep fondness for someone she now saw had been both a protector and a friend. And most of all, love made her want to see his music played exactly as he wished.

The first performance, at Chiaretta's villa, was a month away, and even the most divinely inspired music still came down to hours and hours of hard work, broken strings, and sore fingers. She rolled over and shut her eyes, and soon drifted off to sleep.

TWENTY-TWO

THE DOORS AT BOTH ENDS OF THE PORTEGO OF THE Morosini family's summer villa were thrown open to encourage whatever wisps of breeze might find their way into the room. The moisture from the lawns and the waterways had made the July day suffocating, and by the middle of the afternoon it was unpleasant to be either inside or out.

Chiaretta went out on the front steps to peer up into the sky in hope that a quick thundershower might cool the air before the guests began to arrive. She was carrying a copy of the four sonnets that would accompany the music at that evening's concert, and she looked down at the one for summer. "Under the heavy season of a stifling sun," she read, wiping a damp strand of hair from her forehead, "Man and beast languish and the pines are scorched." Vivaldi had gotten it exactly right.

She watched as a rowboat tied up at the dock on the canal. Donata jumped out first and ran onto the grass. They were too far away to hear, but Chiaretta saw Besina call out to her, and Donata made a wide turn, her arms flung out like the wings of a bird, and headed back toward her nanny at a run. Meanwhile the manservant who had rowed the boat took Maffeo from Besina's arms and put him down on the dock. Chiaretta saw her son, now barely four, look at his feet as he adjusted to the unmoving dock beneath them. Then he took off across the grass, catching up with his sister as she pranced the last few yards back to Besina.

Chiaretta could see that the nanny was reprimanding Donata for running off. She knew her daughter's every gesture and watched from a distance how she hung her head and moved one toe back and forth as she accepted the scolding. Then Besina said something and Donata took off again, this time encouraging Maffeo to run beside her. Besina followed, catching up as the children stopped to pick flowers from one of the beds along the walkway. A butterfly flew up from one of the bushes, and they all ran after it, close enough now for Chiaretta to hear their laughter.

Donata stood facing the house as she extended her finger to give the butterfly a place to alight, and Chiaretta stepped behind one of the columns of the porch. If they saw her, they would run to her, and she wanted to watch them awhile longer. Besina was a blessing, young enough to be light in spirit but clear about what liberties could and could not be taken in raising patrician children. Claudio's mother had not approved of Besina at all, pressuring Chiaretta to hire a sour old nursemaid someone else had recommended. She would know how to raise children properly, Giustina had said, a process that seemed to Chiaretta to be little more than a human version of breaking a horse. People had a role first and a personality second, Giustina believed, and it only caused problems to encourage the second at all. *Everyone ends up with a personality anyway,* Chiaretta thought. *Unfortunately, it's too often like yours.*

Donata was jumping up to try to put a flower in the dangling hand of one of the statues lining the path to the house. Maffeo lifted his arms for Besina to pick him up so he could do the same. Maffeo was too young to do anything now but chase butterflies, say please and thank you, and be quiet most of the time he was told to. But someday this little boy with the broad and happy face that so resembled his father's would join the Grand Council, become a member of the Congregazione of the Pietà, bring guests to his box at the Teatro Sant'Angelo, and be in every respect the Venetian nobleman. *In every respect,* Chiaretta thought, including a life on the side and a gracious acceptance that his wife had one too. Picturing the little boy on the grass growing up to face the disappointments and the tainted pleasures of adulthood was hard and a bit painful, but like everyone else, he would have to do it.

At seven, Donata was passing through her childhood at a pace that amazed her mother. In a few more years, she would have to decide her destiny. Claudio agreed with Chiaretta that, although Donata's choices were limited, they were still her own, and if she wanted to marry, she had the right to be taken seriously about who her husband would be. *What a lucky woman I am,* Chiaretta thought. *A strong, good husband and two beautiful children to love.*

And she did love them. Why so many Venetians considered it vulgar to show too much affection, she didn't know and didn't care. She would have nursed her children herself if Giustina and even Claudio had not been so adamant that this was something a Morosini simply could not do. The compromise they reached was that neither child had been sent away to be wet-nursed. Hardly a day had passed since their births that she had not been able to spend time with them, and their proximity gave Claudio the chance to become deeply attached as well. He often marveled, somewhat wistfully, at how different their childhood was than his own had been. To this, Chiaretta always smiled inwardly but said nothing. No one with a mother and father could really understand what having neither was like, even if some parents' ideas about child rearing did leave something to be desired.

She watched as Maffeo reached the first step to the house, struggling to clear the height of the stairs. Donata lifted her dress to her thighs and was jumping up the steps, counting each one as she went.

"Mama!" she said, catching a glimpse of Chiaretta's dress from behind the pillar where she had been watching. "Why are you hiding?"

Donata hid behind another pillar, looking out at her mother and giggling. Maffeo ran straight to his mother and grabbed her skirt, looking back at Donata as if he had won a race. Chiaretta bent down to put her arms around him, and he saw her wet face. "Are you sad, Mama?" he asked.

"No, my love," she said, wiping her cheeks and giving him a kiss. "Mama is very, very happy."

Dark clouds had been gathering, and the first thunder cracked like the sound of a bough falling from a tree. Both children pulled closer to Chiaretta, grabbing at her skirt. Besina hurried them inside, but Chiaretta stayed on the porch to watch the storm.

A small barge was tying up at the dock. On its deck were two women in bright summer colors and large hats with netting that obscured their faces. As they looked up at the threatening sky, a man in a priest's frock emerged from the cabin of the barge, his red hair showing under his tricornered hat. Just as he jumped ashore, the sky brightened with a bolt of lightning and rain began to pour down. The women disappeared into the cabin while he scurried through the rain.

"Maestro Vivaldi," Chiaretta said when he arrived. "I see you were able to get a ride from Venice." Though she tried to sound like a gracious hostess, she could hear the accusation in her tone. Maddalena might be enraptured by his music, but as far as she was concerned, the man was making a shambles of his life, and the sooner this concert was over the better.

"Yes. It was quite a coincidence. Anna—La Girò," he hurried to add, "is singing in Padua tomorrow. She and her sister suggested I accompany them this far, and I am just a poor musician—"

Stop, she thought, cutting him off by turning to a servant just inside the entrance to the house. "Show Maestro Vivaldi to his room, and see that his clothes are dried."

"I really must go," she said to her guest, and without asking him to excuse her, she walked across the portego and disappeared up the stairs.

MADDALENA WAS WAITING TO TAKE TEA WITH CHIARETTA IN her quarters.

"The Maestro is here," Chiaretta said.

"Good," Maddalena said.

"He got a ride here with those women."

The stricken look on her sister's face was so brief Chiaretta missed it altogether. "That was convenient," Maddalena said as she composed herself.

Chiaretta rang for Zuana and ordered their tea. After Zuana left, she turned to her sister. "How are you and Don Vivaldi getting along since the . . ." She paused, not sure how to phrase the question.

Maddalena shrugged. "I'm fine," she said. "I don't have any trouble working with him."

Chiaretta was taken aback that her sister could talk so casually about him, even if the red in her cheeks betrayed at least a little feeling. "I've never understood how you can be so calm about someone who's hurt you so many times. I guess it's lucky you never fell in love with him. You'd probably hate him now."

Maddalena didn't know what to say, and she toyed with the idea of brushing aside Chiaretta's comment. But in such rare circumstances, sitting in a comfortable room in her sister's home, without a grille between them or anyone to listen in, she suddenly wanted Chiaretta to know everything.

"When I was a little girl, he was like a crusader, galloping through the Pietà to save me." She looked up at Chiaretta. "And he did, you know. Don't ever forget that. Whatever it is with those Girò women, don't ever forget that."

She didn't notice that Chiaretta had taken her hand. "But I think as I got older I realized that my life belongs to me. It's not an extension of somebody else's. Even though the Pietà claims almost every hour of it, it's still mine."

Maddalena noticed her sister's hand and began to play with Chiaretta's fingers as she collected her thoughts. "When I went to his house and La Girò showed up . . . It sounds strange to say, and I can't tell you exactly how it happened," Maddalena continued, "but I knew deep down for the first time that afternoon that he truly cared about me. I feel such loyalty to him, despite having to admit he's essentially a rather foolish man with a great gift."

"You do love him, then, at least a little." Chiaretta's face was solemn.

"Is there such a thing as a little love? That's not how I ever imagined it. So that's hard to answer." Maddalena took a moment to think. "I feel safe with him now," she said. "I don't see how he could hurt me again, because I don't need him, and that makes it easier to open my heart. And I don't think he has any idea how dear he is to me."

She looked at Chiaretta with a long, loving smile. "You know the horses we took the girls to feed the other day when we went on the picnic? If you hold up your hand with food, the horses will run over, but the rest of the time, do they care? And if someone has food for them, does it matter to them what kind of person he is?

For me, it's like that with Vivaldi. I don't want him around, particularly, but I can't imagine ever not coming to him, whatever the circumstances."

They both fell silent. "I need to rest," Maddalena said, pulling her hand away gently. "Chiaretta, what you're going to hear tonight is the most remarkable music ever written, I'm sure of it."

"Hmm," her sister said. "Maybe so, and I'm glad you're at peace with Vivaldi, but I have to admit I'll be glad when he's gone." She stood up. "I have a lot to do. Can you find your room, or should I take you there?"

"I'll find my way," Maddalena assured her. "I always do." Seeing Chiaretta's puzzled look, she added, "Find my way. You taught me how, you know."

A RAUCOUS CHORUS OF BIRDS SANG OUT FROM THE TREES AS the last guests arrived under a blue and white afternoon sky. Vivaldi had insisted that the concert start while the audience had enough light to look through the windows behind the orchestra, where the gentle breeze tousling the leaves would suggest spring. Timed properly, they would finish up the winter concerto as the sky began to bleach out at dusk.

He had changed out of his priest's robe into a black velvet jacket over a lace-trimmed shirt, tailored pants, and white stockings. Maddalena wore a plain dress in the red of the Pietà, and the figlie wore gauzy white dresses, with sprays of colorful summer flowers tucked into their bodices.

Vivaldi played the opening notes with the rest of the violins, while the bass viol hammered out a driving continuo. The figlie repeated the opening melody once without him, and then he was off, imitating the sound of a bird with Maddalena and Cornelia joining in a cheerful reply.

Behind them, on a potted tree on the loggia, two goldfinches perched, bending their heads and looking around as if they had been called by the music. The clouds moved slowly across the sky as the orchestra mellowed into the flowing sounds of a stream. The bass viol, too heavy for the scene, gave way to a tinkling harpsichord continuo. The figlie drew out the nuances of each note before returning to the main melody in a minor key and moving, with dramatic bowing, to a depiction of a spring shower. Just as they began to slide their notes upward to suggest the birds' flight, the goldfinches outside flew away, and the audience murmured in recognition of the moment. Vivaldi began his next solo section, contrasting the birds' flight with the still agitated sounds of the orchestra before calm was restored and the birds, at least the musical ones, returned.

As the first movement closed and the second began, the audience consulted the copies of the sonnets they had found on their chairs. The violins played a soft and undulating ostinato, suggesting a light breeze through the grass, while Vivaldi played a languid melody describing a shepherd stretching out his arms and shifting his body as he slept under a tree. Only the bark of his dog, played by the cello, broke into the perfect calm of the scene.

The music of summer sweltered, evoking the torpor of a hot afternoon, hounded by gnats and flies. A cuckoo, a turtledove, and a goldfinch fluttered and sang in the trees. A sudden storm, cracking and violent, drove the summer concerto to its conclusion.

Fall was a time to celebrate. The violins played a scratchy imitation of bagpipes, and wooden flutes mimicked peasants dancing. Wine soon gave way to drunkenness, and Vivaldi's solo traced a staggering peasant leaving the scene and tumbling to the ground unnoticed while the revelry went on.

Chiaretta and Claudio stood together in an alcove. Near them, their son and daughter stood in front of a newly frescoed section of wall where Chiaretta had commissioned a scene of the two of them peeking through a trompe l'oeil door. Donata and Maffeo were trying not to giggle as they leaned against their own portraits, imitating their painted gestures. Claudio motioned toward them to see if Chiaretta had noticed, and she replied by taking his hand and squeezing it.

Though some members of the audience were still consulting their programs, by now more than a few seemed annoyed at the challenge posed by the sonnets and the unusual and unpredictable sounds from the orchestra. A few turned to look at the banquet table to check on the progress toward dinner. By the fourth concerto, the rustle of bodies shifting in their chairs was unmistakable.

The basses entered first, followed by the violins in jittery trills that weren't meant to be a melody at all, but mimicry of shivering in the cold. Vivaldi's solo sent a north wind swirling through the music, leading to shaking legs and chattering teeth. The second movement evoked the sensuousness of being warm by a fire while rain fell outside, an effect achieved by the soft, rhythmic plucking of strings. The work concluded with people making their way across the ice, to the protection of a shelter before a storm. Vivaldi's violin screamed and whistled like wind howling around the edges of buildings and through the trees. The orchestra amplified the sound into a blizzard, swirling downward into the basses before rising again, the violins picking up in unison the solo melody for a moment before the basses drove the music downward again. Then, without allowing the audience even a moment to anticipate the end, the figlie put their instruments on their laps.

The guests sat for a moment, not understanding that the concert was over. A few began to clap, and then the rest followed politely, but the applause soon drifted off. The guests headed for the table, looking for Claudio to see if it was time to sit down and eat.

Chiaretta had made her way to the orchestra with her husband. She hugged Maddalena, feeling the heat of her body through the damp fabric of her dress. "You were magnificent!" she said. Turning to Vivaldi, she said, "Maddalena was right. It is remarkable."

She had chosen the word with care. *The Four Seasons* was stunning, but she would have to hear it again to know how much she liked it. And whenever small clusters of guests murmured after a concert, as her guests were doing at the moment, criticism was probably outrunning praise. She could imagine what they were saying. The music describing each season was soothing and bright, but never for long. Even if the artistry in the discordant notes was unmistakable, it was not pleasant to listen to. Summer did have gnats along with the breezes, and winter had far more ice than crackling fires, but people didn't want to hear music about such things. For someone always so anxious to please, Vivaldi had offered to an audience expecting the light fare of a summer evening quite a surprise, and not an altogether pleasant one.

As Chiaretta left the orchestra to attend to her guests, the music was already less on her mind than two of the musicians. Her sister had risen to a level Chiaretta could not really understand or ever have imagined. No one except Vivaldi played better than she did. Maddalena and Vivaldi were a world of two, although an odd one—a sullied priest of undeniable genius and a cloistered virgin who played as if she knew everything about the world.

VIVALDI FELL ILL THAT NIGHT. BY MORNING HE HAD RECOV-ered, but the lack of sleep after the intensity of the performance left him too exhausted to return to Venice with the rest of the coro. The best plan, they all decided, was for him to return the following day with Chiaretta and the children, who were accompanying Maddalena back to the Pietà.

The weather was cool enough the day of their journey for Donata and Maffeo to sit with Vivaldi on the deck of the barge, but they soon grew tired and went down below to eat the small meal the servants had prepared and to take a nap out of the hot sun.

When they lay down, Maddalena went out to sit with Vivaldi while Chiaretta stayed below.

"What did you think of it?" he asked her the second she sat down.

"The concert? The figlie played magnificently, I thought."

"That's not what I meant. What did you think of the reaction?"

"I think some of them saw it for what it was."

"And what is it?"

"A masterpiece. Perhaps too much so."

He sniffed. "I like some of the melodies. Perhaps I can use them again in something easier to understand."

"I wouldn't give up so easily. Maybe you can do a little explaining before the performances. Stand up with your violin and play a few bars. Say 'This is the dog,' or 'This is the breeze.'"

Vivaldi didn't seem to hear. "I overestimated the people of Venice," he said in a voice so low and discouraged it was almost inaudible.

"Perhaps. But overestimation isn't always bad." On impulse, Maddalena reached out and brushed the top of his hand. "I'm glad you overestimated me."

His eyes darted from his hand back to her face. "What do you mean?"

"Picking me out when I was little, and insisting that I get a chance. Give the people of Venice a chance too."

"I've given them so many. The coro is in Venice, you're in Venice, but there's not much other reason to stay. My music gets a much better reaction almost everywhere else."

"My being in Venice has never kept you there before."

"And how would you know that?"

"Because you left. Twice."

"I also stayed when I didn't need to."

Maddalena stared at him, uncomprehending. He went on.

"There were times when I felt so humiliated by my treatment at the Pietà that I considered quitting, but I didn't, because I had a lesson with you coming up, or a solo I wanted to write for you. I wrote music for you in Mantua and in Rome too, but you never knew about it because someone else played it."

He looked away. His eyes followed the plodding movements of the draft horses pulling the barge, but he didn't appear to be seeing them. "Sometimes I wonder why I didn't realize, before I took my final vows, that I was wrong for the priesthood." He took in a breath and let it out in a sigh. "That I had too much of the wrong kinds of passion in me."

He looked at Maddalena with an expression so sad she felt her eyes begin to sting with tears. "I was very taken with you—I still am. The church would call it 'tempted.'" He tried to smile. "There. That's my big confession."

"I was too young to understand," Maddalena said softly. "I realize now that every time you hurt me, you were trying to keep from hurting me worse."

He leaned forward. "I couldn't ever show you, but that's exactly how it was." He cupped her hands in his. "When I was fired the first time, I went home and wrote you a letter, and when I was finished, I realized I couldn't send it without creating problems for you. I knew you wouldn't understand my leaving, but what could I do? And when I was rehired and your name wasn't on the list of violins, I wondered how I was going to bring you back without looking like I cared about you too much. It felt like a miracle when I saw you walk in with your violin case. There were so many times like that when I knew you must be misinterpreting, but . . ."

He fell silent, and for the first time he seemed to realize he was clasping her hands. He pulled his hands away, but she took them back and held them in hers.

"You're the best thing that ever happened to me," she said.

Glancing at the closed door to the cabin of the barge, she added, "Except for my sister."

Vivaldi's head had sunk halfway to his knees, and she felt the misery emanating from him. "You bought me a bow when I wasn't even an attiva," she whispered.

He looked up. Her attempt to cheer him seemed to have had an effect. "I loved watching you play," he said. "The first day I came into the sala, do you remember what I told you?"

Maddalena shook her head.

"I said you were not afraid of the difficult. What I didn't know at the time was that the difficult would turn out to include me."

She smiled. "I think I'm old enough to handle it now." She thought about stopping there but decided to say more. "Sometimes when I thought about how life might have been different, I would picture us without the Pietà, without the church, having nothing to concern ourselves with but music. Two people playing the violin and growing old together. And I would tell myself that sometimes what seems meant to be doesn't happen. But here with you now, I'm thinking that things are exactly as they're meant to be, and it's good. You've become one of my most treasured friends, and I have a life I love."

His eyes shone as he watched her speak, and then they grew sad again. "I wish I could say the same about my life."

They pulled apart and sat back on opposite sides of the barge, letting the conversation die away.

Eventually Vivaldi spoke again. "I'm sorry for any problems my"—he reached for a word—"my actions have caused you."

He brushed away an insect that had landed on his sleeve and followed its flight toward the riverbank. "You know, the Girò sisters have their own home. I need a nurse, and you saw Paolina is a good one. And Anna—I write some of my best operatic music for her. But she's so young, and she can be so . . . demanding."

"I saw." Maddalena had not intended her tone to be so curt after the conversation they had just had, but the Girò women were not people she cared to think about. "I think she diminishes you."

Before he could reply, Maffeo and Donata opened the door of the cabin. "We're almost there," Donata said. "We looked through the window."

Chiaretta came up too, with the basket they had packed for the day. While Vivaldi chatted with the two children, she cast a quizzical look at Maddalena, and Maddalena gave her a fleeting smile to say she was all right.

The barge bumped the dock at Fusina, and within a minute they were ready to disembark. Vivaldi helped Maddalena off first. Standing on the quay while he was assisting Chiaretta with the children, Maddalena heard a woman's laughter coming from the entrance to a tavern. Two men were walking with Anna Girò and her sister, who were both dressed in traveling clothes.

Anna stopped short. "Tonio?" she said, walking unsteadily toward Vivaldi. "What is this?" She flung her arm in Maddalena's direction. "Her again?"

Vivaldi looked around to see who might be watching. "She's my performing partner," he hissed.

"I bet she is!"

Chiaretta came up and put her arm around Maddalena, who was frozen to the spot.

"Mama, who's that woman?" Donata asked.

Anna put her face inches from Vivaldi's. "I've had enough," she said, her voice slurring heavily. "Get yourself another singer. Get yourself another nurse." She swaggered as she spoke, so unsteady she had to reach out for his arm to avoid falling.

"Anna. Annina!" he pleaded. "Stop!"

Anna Girò gestured again in Maddalena's direction with the practice of a diva. "Choose, Tonio! Her or me."

Chiaretta grabbed Maddalena by the elbow. "Let's go."

Maddalena nodded but pulled away. "Wait."

She stood directly in front of Anna, looking her in the eyes. Anna took a step back, and her eyes flickered as if she wasn't sure what Maddalena was going to do.

"Signorina Girò," Maddalena said. "I am not his to choose."

She turned back to Chiaretta and took her arm. They walked toward the dock where the Morosini gondola was waiting, without looking back.

INSIDE THE FELCE, MAFFEO WAS WHIMPERING. "I DIDN'T LIKE her, Mama."

"I didn't either."

"Maddalena?" Donata turned to kneel on her seat so she could see her aunt better. "What did you mean? Why didn't you want him to choose you? Doesn't he like you more than her?"

Maddalena looked over her niece's shoulder in Chiaretta's direction, and Chiaretta recognized the plea for help. "He does like Maddalena more, my darling. But her life . . . and your life, and Maffeo's, and mine—"

"And my papa's and Andrea's," Maffeo added in a solemn voice, as if he were reciting the list of people he prayed for every night.

"Yes, my love. Papa's and Andrea's too. The point is that everybody's life belongs to them. Nobody should say 'I choose you,' if you don't want to be chosen."

"But I want to be chosen." Donata had come over to sit next to her mother.

"I know," Chiaretta said, putting her arm around her. "It's nice to be noticed, isn't it? And it's nice to see that someone thinks you're special. But there's something that's a much bigger blessing than being chosen."

"What is it?"

"Choosing for yourself."

Part Six _____

SEASONS

_____*1730–1732*

TWENTY-THREE

HE LUMP IN MADDALENA'S BREAST HARDLY SEEMED worth noticing at first. Though the hair at her temples had dulled to a translucent gray, and some mornings her joints were stiff, at thirty-seven she walked with a light step and still played the violin with a passion that left her dazed and drenched with sweat.

In less than three years, on her fortieth birthday, she would retire and join the giubilate. She would perform if they needed, and be part of a ripieno from time to time, and she could keep the money from outside pupils if she wished. A nice life, she supposed, although imagining how to fill it was difficult.

But the lump kept growing, and when she felt another in her armpit, she went to the hospital wing of the Pietà to ask one of the nurses about it. The nurse ran her fingers over it through Maddalena's dress. "Does it hurt?" she asked.

"No. I notice it sometimes when I start to play, but other than that, it doesn't seem to be anything to worry about." The tone of her voice folded the end of the sentence into a question. "I just thought I should ask."

"This kind of ailment is caused by a blockage in the flow of the humors," the nurse said. She went to a cabinet and looked through bottles and small boxes, pulling out a few and taking them to a table. "I'm going to make you a salve to rub on it," she said. "It should be black to match the bile which has collected in your breast."

In a marble bowl she broke apart clumps of minerals into a fine powder and ground them together with herbs. "And to get the humors moving properly, I'll mix in wet and warm elements, because black bile is cold and dry." She went back to the cabinet to retrieve something else. "Were you born under Saturn?" she turned to ask.

"No."

"Good, because this would be much harder to treat if you were." The nurse came back with a dark tincture. "Drop your dress down," she said as she mixed the contents of the bowl into a rough, inky paste.

"It's going to sting a little, perhaps, as it settles in," the nurse said as she smeared it on. "But don't worry. It has to travel to the lump so it can neutralize it." She fashioned a pad and tied a strip of cloth around Maddalena's chest to secure it. "You'll have to stay in the hospital overnight because we have to give you a purgative to clean out your bowels. Without it, the poultice won't be enough."

The spot became pink and tender to the touch and grew raw and inflamed over the course of a month, but the nurse saw this as a sign that the treatment had been overly effective and had imbalanced Maddalena's humors toward fire rather than earth. The tender and swollen skin, the nurse said, was now in perfect condition for cupping.

A local surgeon was to administer the treatment. He arrived with a small case, inside of which were a set of small knives and several glass cups. He inverted one of the cups over Maddalena's breast and lit a candle. Holding it at the bottom of the cup, he waited for the air inside the cup to heat, creating suction that pulled the skin tight enough to create a seal. The heat continued until blood began to rise in a blister under Maddalena's skin, and when the proper amount had collected, he loosened the seal with his fingernail. He picked up one of the knives and broke the blister, draining the blood into a cup and swirling it as he contemplated it.

"The cupping should help," he said. "This blood is clearly tainted."

Over the months, sachets of basil and lemon were laid under Maddalena's pillow and tucked in her bodice. She swallowed arsenic, myrrh, wormwood tea, and ground mandrake root dissolved in wine that had been reduced to syrup. Special prayers were uttered over her prostrate body in the chapel. She lay on a hospital bed while leeches sucked at her nipple. She became dizzy from bleedings at the prescribed spot on her arm where the particular imbalance of her humors was said to be most effectively influenced.

Maddalena told Chiaretta only that she had an inflammation in her breast. What more was there to say? But every night in her bed, she touched it with growing alarm. *Nothing to worry about,* she tried to convince herself, pulling her hand away and laying it outside the blanket in an effort not to let it to wander back to the spot again. *Just something to live with,* she decided, probably no different than a knot on the knee or an irregularity of the skull. *It doesn't hurt, and that has to mean it isn't serious,* she said to herself every night, with the same monotonous regularity with which she said her prayers. *And besides, with all these remedies, something is bound to work.*

A YEAR LATER, SHORTLY AFTER HER THIRTY-EIGHTH BIRTHDAY, MAD-
dalena slipped on the wet steps of the chapel and broke her leg. "It
was strange," she said to Chiaretta, who visited her in the hospital
of the Pietà. "It wasn't much of a fall. Maybe I'm just getting old."

When Maddalena was able to return to her quarters, Chiaretta
stopped visiting. Six months into a pregnancy, she had grown
prematurely huge and, like her sister, was having trouble getting
around. The reason was apparent two months later, when she gave
birth to twins, a boy named Tomà and a girl, Bianca Maria. When
she had recovered, the family left to spend the summer at the villa,
where she was reduced to exchanging letters with her sister. Chiaretta thought it odd, but not a source of worry, when Maddalena
said she was too busy to visit. Her letters gave no hint of trouble,
filled as they were with cheerful talk about the figlie and their concerts, and questions about the children.

THE FIRST TIME SHE VISITED AFTER HER PREGNANCY, CHI-
aretta watched with horror through the grille of the parlatorio as
her sister came toward her with Anna Maria holding her arm. Chiaretta put her hand to her mouth to avoid having anyone hear her
gasp. Maddalena was leaning on a cane, and her skin was the color
of fireplace ashes.

She's dying. Chiaretta shook the thought away as she greeted
her. "A cane?" she asked, trying to sound lighthearted.

Maddalena sat down and sighed with relief. "Lucky I just have a
little over a year until I can retire and sit in my room all day," she
said with a tiny laugh. Chiaretta could hear how the one sentence
had left her breathless, but Maddalena's voice was cheerful, as if
her comment was meant to be taken as a joke.

"I've been telling her to take better care of herself," Anna Maria
said. "She doesn't eat enough, and that's no way to help a leg heal
properly." Chiaretta recognized the same annoyance in Anna Maria's tone that she had heard in her own just that morning when

Donata pushed aside the mush of lentils and beets the cook had made to cure her stomachache, saying it looked too ugly to eat.

"You're too stubborn for your own good," Chiaretta scolded.

Maddalena looked at both of them with a hint of a glower. "I don't want to talk about me. Tell me about the twins!" she said in a way that announced that the previous subject was closed. "They're what—five months old already?"

"I can't wait for you to meet them. Tomà is a little mischief maker," Chiaretta said, trying, despite how much she loved talking about her children, to accept the change in subject.

"Like his mother when she was little." Anna Maria laughed.

"And Bianca Maria is a little version of you," Chiaretta said to Maddalena. "The sweetest thing. Dark hair with a little red. Doesn't cry much at all." Her face grew solemn. "Are you all right, really?" she asked. "I know how you hold everything in."

"I'm fine." Maddalena took a breath as if she were going to say more but didn't. Chiaretta waited, and eventually her sister went on. "I don't know why I feel so sick all the time. I'm having some trouble breathing at night, and I don't feel much like eating. It's probably all the disgusting things I have to swallow to make me well."

"You would tell me, wouldn't you?"

"Of course."

The light through the windows had begun to dim, and Chiaretta got up to put on her cloak. Maddalena motioned her back to the grille. "The stairs," she said. "You know how dark the stairwells are, and how slippery they can be, and it hurts to go up and down them. You know I love your visits, but can we write for a while until my leg is better?"

Chiaretta looked at Anna Maria to see what she was thinking. Her friend's expression was blank, as if she too was not sure why Maddalena was making such a suggestion. "But how will you see Donata and Maffeo then?" Chiaretta asked. "And the babies?"

"It will just have to wait. But not for long."

Chiaretta shook her head. "I know you, Maddalena. You don't look well at all, and all summer you let me think you were fine. I want to see you for myself."

"Chiaretta, please. The pain . . ."

I don't know what to do, Chiaretta thought. She stared into Maddalena's eyes as if she could force them to give her an idea. Neither said a word.

Then Anna Maria broke in. "I could come down every so often to tell you how she's doing," she suggested.

Maddalena and Chiaretta broke their stare. "That's a wonderful idea," Maddalena said.

Chiaretta was not so sure. After all, Anna Maria had gone through the whole summer without writing, when obviously something was wrong. Still, Chiaretta knew her sister well enough to think she had probably pressured Anna Maria not to worry her. At least this way she might find out something. "All right," Chiaretta said. "But it had better not be for long."

The time had come to leave, and Chiaretta moved her cheek close to the grille for their ritual good-bye. Maddalena kissed her cheek and then turned her own to Chiaretta. Nothing remained between the flaccid skin and her skull, and Chiaretta once again fought back panic.

"Next week. The same time," she said to Anna Maria. "Or sooner. Send word and I will be here, no matter what I'm doing."

Anna Maria nodded her head. Her brow was furrowed, and she could not manage to meet Chiaretta's eyes for more than a second without looking away.

BACK AT HOME, DONATA AND MAFFEO WERE AT THEIR LESSONS and the twins were asleep. Chiaretta stopped in the portego to look in the mirror, leaning forward to examine her reflection. Around her temples the hair was growing even finer, and though the hints of gray did not contrast enough with the blond to be noticeable, she could see how in her thirties her appearance was changing. The skin had begun to crinkle around her eyes, and her lips were thinning. The face looking back at her was still pretty but clearly older, and now strained with worry about her sister.

Claudio was not there to confide her worries in. He had been gone for more than a month on business. Giovanni Antonio Canal, a former scene painter for the Teatro Sant'Angelo, now painted vedute in Claudio's workshop under the name Canaletto, and his paintings were becoming so fashionable all over Europe that Claudio was staying away longer, gathering commissions in more and more cities. His last letter predicted he would be home within a week or two, and Chiaretta tried to brush her anxiety about her sister away until his return, busying herself mothering her new twins, and watching over her eight-year-old son and eleven-year-old daughter.

Maffeo had grown into a dark and handsome child, with the same strong build and thick eyebrows as Claudio. Donata's hair, as blond as Chiaretta's when she was a baby, had turned a strawberry hue, somewhere between her mother's and her aunt's. She had not inherited Chiaretta's blue eyes but something closer to Maddalena's hazel ones, which surrounded by long, dark lashes, gave her coloring of the kind Titian had gloried in.

Donata had already been studying the harpsichord for more than half of her life. Almost every afternoon, she sat contented and dreamy at the keyboard, moving her fingers with growing assurance, her thighs touching Chiaretta's as she listened to the sounds that emanated from some secret wellspring inside her mother. Andrea joined them often, and occasionally Luca did as well, and Donata would squirm with delight as they shared the bench with her and sang one harmony after another.

A few months after her last visit with Maddalena, Chiaretta and

Donata were sitting alone at the harpsichord when Zuana came in to tell her that one of Claudio's business associates was waiting for her downstairs in the sala d'oro.

"I'm not dressed," she said. "Ask him to wait."

"He says it's urgent, Madonna."

Donata felt her mother's body tense. "Mama?" she asked.

"Keep playing, cara," she said, smoothing her skirt and checking her hair in the mirror before hurrying from the room.

A man was standing at the window of the sala d'oro. The light poured in, bouncing off the gilded walls and making the red brocade curtains glow. He jumped when he heard her voice. When he turned around, Chiaretta saw that his face was grave.

Maddalena, she thought. "Is it about my sister?"

"Maddalena della Pietà?" He looked confused. "No, Madonna, it's about your husband."

WITHIN AN HOUR, CHIARETTA CALLED DONATA AND MAFFEO into her apartment. With a swollen face and a barely audible voice, she told them their father was dead. Somewhere outside Munich the coach in which Claudio was riding had lost a wheel. The carriage and horses had tumbled down an embankment, and his neck had snapped. Claudio's body was on its way back to Venice for burial.

She held them each for a long time and then got up. "You'll both sleep in my bed with me for a few days, until after the funeral. Right now, I need to go to the Pietà."

She went to her dressing table and stared, unable to connect herself with the face in the mirror. She picked up a pot of rouge and began daubing it on her cheeks, but she had taken too much and it smeared into the hollows of her skin. She rubbed at it, uncomprehending. Donata came to her side and took her hand, pulling it away from the garish blotches.

"Mama," she said, "let me do it." She took a handkerchief and rubbed until Chiaretta's face was clean. "Just wear a veil," she said in a choked voice. "You'll be pretty again some other day."

THE PRIORA USHERED CHIARETTA INTO HER OFFICE. "WE'VE just received the news," she said. "I am so sorry."

Chiaretta thanked her with the stiffness of a novice actress reciting lines for the first time. "I know there's a great deal to discuss, but right now, I want to see my sister."

The priora flinched almost imperceptibly and drew in a quick breath. "I'll call her down, but you know she is not well."

"I know. I was going to ask Claudio about her when he . . ." Her voice trailed off as she began to weep into her hands.

The priora put an arm around Chiaretta's shoulder and led her to a chair. "Wait here," she said. "I'll have Anna Maria help her down."

A few minutes later, Maddalena walked into the room. It took a moment for Chiaretta to understand that the ghostlike figure on Anna Maria's arm was her sister. Broken wisps of brittle hair had come loose from the bun at the nape of her neck and lay like cobwebs around her cheeks. Her eyes had grown huge in her thin face.

"She made us promise," Anna Maria said, almost in a whimper.

Chiaretta did not hear her or see the priora acknowledge the truth of what Anna Maria had said. Throwing her arms around Maddalena, Chiaretta felt the sharp bones of her sister's shoulders under her limp dress. The enormity of all that was happening swallowed her up, and she began to sob in Maddalena's arms.

"Chiaretta, I—" Maddalena's voice broke off as she began to cry as well.

They held each other for a long time. Then Chiaretta pulled

back to look at her sister. She spoke with a tone that was simultaneously an order and a plea.

"Come home with me," she said.

CLAUDIO'S PRIVATE EFFECTS WERE MOVED INTO HIS STUDY, and his bedroom was prepared for Maddalena, to keep her as close as possible to Chiaretta. Another bed for a nurse was put in a small anteroom. Maddalena's appearance frightened Maffeo, who at first shrank back and for a week would not come near enough to kiss her, but Donata came and sat on her bed every day to read to her, and Besina brought the twins for a daily visit.

Donata made an event of fluffing Maddalena's pillows and turning them to their cool undersides. One day, while Maddalena was sleeping, Donata's fingers touched a small bag under one of the pillows, and she pulled it out. "What's this?" she whispered to her mother.

Chiaretta removed the pieces of comb and gave them to Donata to hold. "It's just something pretty that got broken. I wanted to put it there."

"The little flowers are so perfect," Donata said, stroking her fingers over them just as Chiaretta had when she saw them the first time.

"She doesn't know it's under her pillow," Chiaretta said. "Let's keep it a secret. Our mother and daughter secret."

WHEN DONATA AND MAFFEO MOVED BACK INTO THEIR OWN beds, a week or two later, Chiaretta was able for the first time to be alone. She had sent word to Andrea that she did not want to see him for a while. Much as she longed to be held in a man's strong arms, she wanted those arms to be Claudio's, and since they could not be, she would honor him by remaining uncomforted.

When the day came to read Claudio's will, Antonia and Piero picked her up in their gondola and took her to the solicitor's office. Giustina had died not too long after her husband, Claudio's other sister was in a convent, and his older brother had permanently relocated in Antwerp, so the group hearing the will would include only the three of them. Piero and Antonia could barely sit down for the ride. They shifted in their seats and worried in clipped, spiky voices about Claudio's assets, and what it would mean if he had followed convention and left his brother, whom none but Antonia even knew, in control of them.

In his office, the solicitor pulled out the thick vellum document. Antonia was the first to be provided for. Piero relaxed when he heard that his wife would receive a small annual allowance, but his face went grim as the solicitor read on. No one but Antonia could draw the money, and the commissare of his estate was to ensure it went to meeting her personal needs and running the household. The insult was clear. Piero was not to be trusted.

His cloistered sister would have continued to receive her current annual stipend until her death, but Claudio added a small amount to it. She would live out her days in her well-furnished room at the convent of San Zaccaria, with money to host parties, buy perfume and other luxuries, and remain fashionably dressed.

Claudio left nothing to his brother, declaring that their patrimony had been allocated fairly by their father and each was free to dispose of his portion as he wished. His decision, he said, was to leave it all to his family. Astonished, Chiaretta listened as Claudio's words were read aloud.

"To my beloved wife, Chiaretta, who has been the great pleasure of my life, I leave my entire estate, and I appoint her commissare over it. I direct her to ensure that our children receive equitable patrimonies of sufficient worth to allow my daughters, Donata and Bianca Maria, to make their own decisions when they reach adulthood as to whether they will marry or enter convents. Likewise, my sons, Maffeo and Tomà, are to be provided with patrimonies sufficient to enable them both to marry, to carry on the family businesses, to enter new ventures as they see fit, and to fulfill their obligations to the republic. May my beloved sons be as fortunate as I have been in having loving and capable spouses by their sides, and to my daughters, if they marry, I hope for the same.

"As to my wife's handling of my businesses, it is my strong suggestion that she accept the assistance I am sure will be forthcoming from Luca Barberigo and Andrea Corner. They are excellent businessmen whom I trust always to have the best interests of my wife and children at heart."

The solicitor was still talking, but Chiaretta could not take in anything more. Claudio had left it all—the houses, the partnership in the opera house, the veduta workshop, all of it—to her. And he had invited her to keep Andrea in her life.

Did he know?

The solicitor went on, but Chiaretta heard nothing more. As he folded and put away the will, Antonia and her husband got to their feet.

"Will you be coming back with us?" Piero's voice was hollow and stiff.

The solicitor answered for her. "We need to talk alone for a while," he said. "I'll see that she gets home."

When they had left, the solicitor pulled out another piece of paper. "There was a codicil to the will," he said. "It didn't involve anyone else, so I thought I would share it with you privately. There is one more bequest, this one to the Pietà."

He took a deep breath before continuing. "Chiaretta, this is difficult to say. Your husband had another child, a daughter, by a courtesan who is well known here. She did not wish to raise the girl, so Claudio saw to her admission to the Pietà. He has watched over her as best he could, but her parentage has been kept a secret."

"How old is she?" Chiaretta whispered.

"I believe she's roughly the same age as your older daughter, perhaps a little older. I'm afraid I am not at liberty to tell you her name, or anything other than that she is a healthy girl, a figlia di commun." He managed a brief smile. "Apparently not blessed with musical talent, but pretty enough. At any rate, the codicil provides an annual stipend for dowry enhancement, and you'll need to see to the payment, since you are now the commissare."

He watched as Chiaretta sat staring at nothing. "I'm sorry, but I thought you needed to know." He waited for her to speak, but she still did not respond. "Your husband was a remarkable man," he went on, "perhaps a man of the future when it came to his confidence in you." He picked up the codicil for emphasis. "He loved you. I hope the matter of the child doesn't cause you to question that."

"No," Chiaretta replied, coming back to the reality in the room. "No, it doesn't. It's just so strange to know there's a girl at the Pietà who knows as little about where she came from as I do, and that I can't tell her, or even know who she is."

"It's the way he wished it: I'm sorry. I suppose if you insisted on looking at the records—"

Chiaretta cut him off. "I intend to honor my husband. He has certainly honored me."

The solicitor's face grew somber. "You're going to need a great deal of help in many ways, not just now but for a long time. It isn't easy for anyone to handle as much as Claudio did, and most of the people you'll deal with are not used to listening to women." He paused and then asked, "Do you plan to ask Andrea to help?"

She noticed he mentioned only Andrea and not Luca. She searched for a delicate way to phrase what she wanted to ask. "Was my husband aware of . . . ?"

Seeing her discomfort, the solicitor broke in. "Your relationship with Andrea?"

"Yes," she said. "I need to know before I decide whether to accept his assistance."

"He knew. And as much as a man can approve of such a thing,

Claudio thought you had chosen well. I believe he was trying to say that to you in his will. And of course he also knew you would be learning a difficult secret about him."

He leaned forward. "Chiaretta, if you ever wonder if you were a good wife, or if any other woman competed for his heart, remember what he did for you today. You changed him. I think if he had married anyone else, it would be his brother stepping in to manage not only his estate but the rest of his wife's and children's lives as well. Instead, as of today, you are one of the most powerful women in Venice."

He let it sink in. "It isn't going to be easy, but if you need me . . ."

She had buried her face in her hands, mourning for her husband, for the season, the time, the hour, the moment, the beautiful country, and the place that had brought her such blessings and such pain.

TWENTY-FOUR

*I*N SPITE OF HER FAILING CONDITION, MADDALENA TRIED her best to pull herself out of bed to help Chiaretta, but even the simplest aspects of caring for the children and seeing to the household were too much for her. Her bones hurt so much she could not take a step without crying out, and even breathing had become difficult. She went back to her bed, ashamed at the additional burden she was placing on her sister, and wishing death would come faster, to relieve them both.

Chiaretta was so exhausted she was becoming frantic. Claudio's associates came through the sala d'oro in a near steady stream, and though she had asked Luca to spend a good part of the day meeting with them to assess their concerns and to learn about Claudio's business ventures, even his summaries at the end of the day required more attention than she had to give. Chiaretta had not only two children grieving for their father but twins less than one year old as well, whom she was determined to make as much a focus of her life as Donata and Maffeo had been. And on top of it, she was spending what she knew would be her last weeks with her sister.

I can't do it, Chiaretta thought. She cried every night, her tears soaking into her pillow. But every morning she got up and spoke pleasantly as Zuana did her hair and helped her into her dress. Over the years, Chiaretta had come to love Zuana, who was herself beginning to show the encroachment of age. Chiaretta then went in to see her sister. When Maddalena felt well enough, Chiaretta ordered a light breakfast for both of them, and while they waited she brushed her sister's hair, fluffed her pillows, and helped her change her nightdress.

After breakfast Chiaretta went to the nursery to find her twins. She talked and played with them for a while before going into the library to check on Donata and Maffeo, who were working with their tutor. Time for a pat on the shoulder and a kiss on the cheek was, more often than not, all she had before going off to spend the rest of the day attending meetings of the investors in the Teatro Sant'Angelo, the supervisors of the painting workshop, and others with whom her husband had done business.

The evenings were for Donata and Maffeo, and after Chiaretta ate supper with them, they gathered in Maddalena's room to play games and make music while Maddalena watched. Chiaretta sent the gondola to fetch Anna Maria at least once a week, but she always came alone. She had suggested bringing Benedetta and some of the other figlie, but Maddalena refused. Much as she would have loved to bask in their presence and their music one last time, Maddalena preferred that they not be burdened with a sad memory that might crowd out other happier ones.

Chiaretta had still not resumed her relationship with Andrea. Her grief was too fresh for that. From time to time, Chiaretta invited

Luca and Andrea to a family dinner, both out of gratitude for their support and because she wanted Maffeo to see the way noblemen acted. Both men had promised they would take Maffeo under their wings when he was a little older, to teach him what he could not learn at home—how to hunt, how to win at cards, and how to treat the women who were sure to fawn over him.

As a woman, Chiaretta was not allowed to become a member of the Grand Council. *Anything more to do and I would die,* she thought, recognizing even more clearly how hard Claudio's work had been. But she had one desire that would honor his memory as well as Maddalena's: She wished to take Claudio's place on the Congregazione of the Pietà. The priora at first sputtered at the thought. Although women ran the institution on a daily basis, the only woman who ever served on the board was the priora herself, and she was there more to be directed than to direct.

Slowly, though, she warmed to what she came to see was a remarkable idea—a figlia di coro, now the head of one of the oldest noble families, returning to provide her unique perspective to the board. Though the Congregazione might squirm, the priora was now determined to see it happen. And so a compromise was struck. For many generations the Morosini family had contributed both large sums of money and service as directors of the institution. Maffeo was still too young to begin his involvement, and Chiaretta would serve as his representative until he reached his majority.

"And by the time that happens," the priora said in a private moment with Chiaretta, "who can tell?" Venetian attitudes were changing so fast that perhaps she would be invited to stay in her own right and Maffeo could find another cause. "Just as long as it isn't the Mendicanti," the priora added with a sly grin.

Only one task remained unfinished, and as Maddalena slipped closer to death, Chiaretta knew she could not wait much longer.

She ruined piece after piece of writing paper as she debated how to phrase the letter. And then one morning Maddalena was difficult to rouse, and Chiaretta saw a smear of blood on her pillow. No time remained to search for words. Chiaretta took the pen and wrote: "Come quickly. Maddalena is dying."

THE LETTER REACHED VIVALDI IN MANTUA, WHERE HE WAS working on a new opera. Within a few days, he was standing in the portego of Ca' Morosini.

"Am I too late?" he asked.

"No," she told him. "But it won't be much longer."

Vivaldi looked tired, beyond what might be expected of a middle-aged man after an unexpected and uncomfortable journey. Chiaretta heard his characteristic wheeze and asked, "Did you bring what you need if you are taken ill?"

He pointed to a valise on the floor, next to his violin case. "Paolina packed what is required."

He saw a coldness come over Chiaretta's face at the mention of Paolina Girò's name. "It's not true what they say about me," he said, a bitter edge in his voice. "Rumormongers, all of them! They think nothing of ruining a man."

He inhaled and winced as if he were in pain. "I am a sick man. I need a nurse. Anna, on the other hand—" He shook his head and snorted. "Anna is a mistake I can't seem to rid myself of."

Chiaretta stared at him, wanting to tell him how little she cared at the moment about his problems but not wishing to use the energy it would take to do so. She reached for his hand. "Thank you for coming," she said.

"I came straight here from the coach station. If you are concerned about your reputation, I can stay elsewhere."

Despite the tone of self-pity in his voice, Chiaretta looked again at the aging, vulnerable, unhappy man in front of her, and years of annoyance and anger lifted from her in a surge of memories so strong they overtook everything else she thought about him.

"Let people talk," she said. "You are an old friend." Motioning to the servant to take his things, she hooked her arm in his and walked with him to the staircase.

THOUGH VIVALDI WAS A PRIEST WITHOUT A PARISH, HE HAD been on hand from time to time to give the last rites to the dying. Even so, he recoiled in shock when he saw Maddalena, shrunk to almost nothing in the middle of the huge bed. She seemed to be sleeping, but when he moved across the room, she sensed the presence of someone and opened her eyes.

Seeing Vivaldi as if through a thick mist, she murmured, "Did the bell ring? Am I late for my lesson?" She struggled to sit up. "I don't have my violin! Chiaretta!"

Chiaretta rushed to her sister's side. "I'm here. Look who's come to visit you!" She helped Maddalena sit up and brushed her hair out of her eyes. "It's Don Vivaldi. He's come from Mantua."

"Susana's taken my bow. And I'm too sick to play." Maddalena's voice was barely audible even in the quiet room.

"He hasn't come for that. He's here to visit you."

Vivaldi had moved closer to the bed. "Maddalena? Maddalena Rossa? It's me."

"Maestro," she murmured, then shut her eyes again and appeared to have fallen asleep.

Chiaretta motioned Vivaldi to an empty chair in the corner, and after arranging Maddalena's covers, she went to sit beside him. "She sleeps for hours from the laudanum. If you'd like to rest, I can show you to your room and call you later."

"Will you play something for me?" The request from the bed was so soft neither of them heard it the first time. Maddalena turned her head in the direction of their voices. "Play something."

Chiaretta hurried to the door to summon a servant to bring the violin from Vivaldi's room. When it arrived, he pulled it out of its case and began playing the first bars he ever wrote for her.

"Do you remember this?" he asked. "You were the third violinist, and the others were so angry."

A smile flitted across her lips.

"And then there was this," he said, launching into another piece he had written for her, twirling and pirouetting on the high strings before sliding down to the sad, low ones. "I remember them all," he said, in a deep, choked voice.

Maddalena's eyes were shut again. "Do you want me to play something else?" Vivaldi asked.

"Not now," she murmured. "I need to sleep."

VIVALDI WAS EXHAUSTED AS WELL, AND BOTH HE AND CHIaretta slept until early afternoon. She was woken by the nurse, who came in to tell her that Maddalena's breathing was close to imperceptible and she was unresponsive even when shaken. Chiaretta sent word to Vivaldi, who arrived within minutes with a small bag and a breviary.

"I brought what I needed to give her the last rites," he said.

Chiaretta looked at her sister, lying motionless in the bed. "You'd better start now."

Vivaldi crossed himself, and Chiaretta followed suit. *"Pax huic domui,"* he said.

"Peace to this house and all in it," Chiaretta replied.

Vivaldi ran his finger over a few pages before continuing. "Lord, I am not worthy," he began, "that thou shouldst come under my roof; but say the word only, and my soul shall be healed." Hearing the familiar phrase, Maddalena stirred and opened her eyes.

Vivaldi went to her. "Are you strong enough for the Eucharist?" She nodded, and he placed a piece of wafer between her lips. Then he pulled out a small vial of oil and anointed

Maddalena's eyelids, ears, nostrils, lips, and hands, saying a prayer over each. After he was done, he asked Chiaretta to help him pull the blanket from her feet, and he anointed each of them as well.

"What is this?" he asked, tracing oil over the silvery scar on her heel.

"It's the mark of the Pietà." Chiaretta's voice trembled. "They put it there so they could find us."

He looked at her for a moment, not comprehending what she meant. *"Kyrie eleison,"* he began, putting the oil away as Chiaretta joined him in the prayer. He handed her a small cloth to daub the excess oil from Maddalena's face.

"I'm finished," he said.

Maddalena's lips parted and her eyes were blank, but she seemed to be trying to say something.

Chiaretta leaned forward, making out only one word.

Sing.

She looked at Vivaldi. "Salve Regina. The last section."

Vivaldi picked up his violin and began to play Maddalena's part. Chiaretta got up on the bed and leaned her back against the pillows.

"Et Jesum benedictum," she began. Lifting Maddalena's limp and almost weightless body, she took her in her arms, rocking her to the sway of the music. *"O clemens, O pia, O dulcis Virgo,"* she sang. *My peaceful, holy, sweet virgin sister,* she thought, as tears stung her eyes and smothered her voice in her throat.

A faint smile came over Maddalena's lips, just as it had whenever she played that piece, her favorite of all the music they had played together. Perhaps that was what she was trying to say when she murmured something Chiaretta could not understand. As Vivaldi finished the last notes, Maddalena's shoulders went heavy.

"Go," Chiaretta whispered, as she rocked her sister toward the music.

AUTHOR'S NOTE

This is a work of historical fiction, based in part on real people. The archives of the Ospedale della Pietà record Antonio Vivaldi's purchase of "a bow for Maddalena Rossa," and although I was unable to ascertain a date, this notation gave me the first plot element for *The Four Seasons*. Because the figlie di coro used only first names, it is likely that this distinguished her as "red-haired Maddalena" at a time when more than one figlia named Maddalena performed in the coro.

Chiaretta is the name of a famous soprano of the coro, but of a later era. One of only three elements of the plot known to me to be inconsistent with fact is giving Chiaretta the part of Abra in *Juditha Triumphans,* a role actually sung by someone named Silvia. I tried changing Chiaretta's name to Silvia, but I already had created Silvia the Rat, and an image of her kept cropping up as I rewrote. In the end, I decided that Chiaretta told me her name, and that was that. To my amusement, I learned later that a registry for the Pietà shows that this particular Silvia was in her sixties when she sang Abra, so it turned out that her name was actually the least of my problems.

Anna Girò is a real person, and Vivaldi's relationship with her caused great scandal, although its nature is unknown. From the time of their meeting in Mantua until his death, she and her sister, Paolina, were Vivaldi's almost constant companions, although he claimed Paolina was no more than his nurse and Anna simply one of the stars of his operas. Contemporaneous reports of her voice call into question whether the quality of her singing was high enough to warrant this kind of attention.

Anna and Paolina did have their own home in Venice, but anecdotes, including one by the noted writer Carlo Goldoni, suggest that they actually lived with Vivaldi. The scandal was sufficient to cause him to lose important commissions because of questions about the seemliness of a priest having what appeared to be a sexual relationship with one or possibly both of them. I have steered clear of making any concrete suggestions about this possibility, for if Vivaldi did keep his vow of chastity, creating a plot that had him doing otherwise would be a terrible disservice to someone who cannot now defend himself.

The other important Anna, Anna Maria della Pietà, is also a real person about the same age as Chiaretta and Maddalena. Abandoned as an infant, she remained at the Pietà all her life, living into her eighties. She served as principal violinist from 1720 to 1737, and Vivaldi wrote as many as thirty-seven concerti for her. One admirer wrote a poem praising her skill on the harpsichord, violin, cello, viola d'amore, lute, theorbo, and mandolin. Of her violin playing, he claimed,

> *The clever Anna Maria,*
> *True incarnation of goodness and beauty*
> *. . . plays the violin in such a manner*
> *That transports anyone who hears her to Paradise,*

If possibly it is true that even up there
Angels play like that.

The second time I am aware that I strayed from the facts was to adjust the dates of Anna Maria's life. She was born in 1694, two years after the character of Maddalena, but because I felt her story was so deserving of being part of this book, I moved her age forward to make her slightly older than Maddalena, so she could be already on the adolescent ward when Maddalena arrives there.

The third point at which I strayed slightly from fact was back-dating the performance of *La Verità in Cimento* from its true premiere in fall 1720 to fall 1719. I did this to improve the chronology for the birth of Chiaretta's children and the premiere of *The Four Seasons* in 1726. No one has yet been able to determine for what opera Vivaldi wrote the aria *"Di due rai languir costante,"* but since it was a common practice to alter the material of an opera to suit the singers, I saw no problem with using it here.

About Vivaldi himself, only a handful of reports exist. This nearly total silence sheds light on the richness of the musical environment of eighteenth-century Venice, where even someone of his caliber could not manage to stand out clearly from the rest. His health problems (probably asthma, although some suggest angina) were real, although whether they were a legitimate cause or a convenient excuse for avoiding saying mass only a year after his ordination will probably never be known. Skeptical contemporaries were doubtful of the true extent of his disability, noting his tireless energy for his own projects, including hundreds of musical compositions, his role as impresario for the Teatro Sant'Angelo, and his years of almost constant travel in Italy and the rest of Europe.

He was apparently a devout Catholic despite not having a parish assignment and was known around Venice as Il Prete Rosso, the Red Priest, because of his unusually bright red hair. Though one eyewitness said that he sometimes composed with a rosary in his hand, his religiosity did not stop him from being a shrewd and some said unscrupulous businessman, willing to sell "original" compositions in only slightly altered form to several different buyers. In truth this was a common practice among poorly paid composers pressed to satisfy demand. Vivaldi tended to be paranoid and self-pitying, but within the Inquisition-like climate of eighteenth-century Venice, with its rigid social roles and wild fluctuations in enforcement of the law, it is perhaps understandable that he would feel fearful and misused.

Vivaldi reached the peak of his success as an opera composer in Venice in roughly the same period in which he wrote *The Four Seasons*. His style, however, was already being eclipsed by that of German composers, most notably Handel and Bach. He continued to compose for patrons, and after a final attempt to revive his reputation in Venice, he left for Vienna in hopes of greener pastures at the court of Emperor Charles VI. Luck was against him when Charles died suddenly, leaving Vivaldi without prospects in a foreign city. He died penniless there in 1741 at age sixty-three, and in a tragic foreshadowing of what would happen fifty years later to Mozart in the same city, he was buried in an unmarked pauper's grave. Anna Girò, who had gone to Vienna with him, returned to Italy and married a nobleman in 1748.

The Pietà existed until the end of the century. When the Venetian Republic fell to Napoleon in 1797, many of the nunneries were disbanded, and lay institutions such as the ospedali were caught up in the same reformist fervor. The buildings of the Pietà were destroyed, and today the Hotel Metropole stands on the site of the original chapel. In the lobby several marble columns have been retained. Elsewhere in the building are a few remnants, including a spiral staircase the figlie would have used, and a stone well in the courtyard where they spent some of their recreational time. Nothing else remains of the massive building that once housed one of the great Venetian institutions. At the rebuilt chapel next door on the Riva degli Schiavoni, a plaque marks Vivaldi's involvement with the Pietà, and recently a small museum dedicated to the coro opened upstairs.

Vivaldi's work lapsed into obscurity for almost two hundred years. Not until the mid–twentieth century had anyone other than scholars of the period even heard of him. Then, in the 1930s in Turin, a large private collection of sheet music was discovered, and by the 1950s, the first recordings of *The Four Seasons* became widely available. However, even with subsequent scholarship, the disorganized and almost accidental manner in which some of the music was saved has created problems knowing for certain where, when, and for whom it was first performed. Though many of his compositions were collected and professionally published, many others are placed in context by no more than the paper they are written on, under the assumption that one supply of paper would be used up before another was purchased. Nevertheless, notes kept by the Pietà and scribbles on some of the miscellaneous sheet music that has survived verify that the compositions performed in the chapel in this book were indeed in the repertoire of the figlie di coro. So far no one has determined conclusively the early performance history of *The Four Seasons*, but the nature of the music has led many to suggest it was commissioned for a private audience. Since the figlie di coro gave many such performances, I thought it quite reasonable to conclude that they might have performed it in a setting such as the one I describe.

Today, Vivaldi has taken his place as one of the greatest composers of all time, although common knowledge of him is even now limited to a few works, such as *The Four Seasons* and the famous "Gloria." His music for female vocalists is a largely unknown treasure, and many of his other instrumental compositions, only a few of which are included here, are perhaps even more astonishing than *The Four Seasons*.

Vivaldi may have contributed to the development of the musicians and singers of the Pietà, but they also contributed greatly to the development of Vivaldi. Before he came to the Pietà as a violin teacher, he dabbled at composition but was renowned only as a superb violinist. He must have seen the discipline, dependability, and consistently high quality of the musicians of the coro as a precious resource, but the world of the Pietà had the added advantage of the serenity of a cloister, a setting where personalities and politics rarely diverted attention from the music. Indeed, despite his great interest in composing operas, not a single one of Vivaldi's operas has found its way into the repertoire of today's companies, showing clearly that Vivaldi's musical reputation depends on the kinds of music he wrote for the Pietà. Even though he wrote for other churches, courts, and individuals as well, it is his music for chamber orchestra and his generally lesser known religious works for choirs and women's voices that bear the mark of his greatness.

The Vivaldi revival has brought with it a growing interest in the figlie di coro of the four Venetian ospedali. Within their walls, women were able to flourish as musicians (and, it has recently been discovered, as composers), while Venetian society as a whole took no such interest in developing exceptional talent in their own daughters. Sadly, for all the centuries of its existence, not a single diary by a resident of the Pietà has been found, and little more than details from ledgers and other record books survive to tell of the thousands of lives spent there. Perhaps Maddalena, Chiaretta, Anna Maria, and the others in *The Four Seasons* will help speak for them.

PRONUNCIATION GUIDE

Italian pronunciations are for the most part close enough to English to be intuitive. *Coro* (KOH-roh), for example, is pronounced the way it would be if it were an English word. There are, however, a few exceptions that those who like to read aloud might want to note.

1. *Ch* and *ci* are the opposite of what they usually are in English. Thus, Chiaretta is pronounced "kee-ah-RET-tah," and *burchiello* is pronounced "bur-kee-EL-loh." On the other hand, *cimento* is pronounced "chee-MEN-toh."

2. The letter *g* is tricky. In *villegiatura* and *giubilata*, it's pronounced like the *g* in the English word *gee*. The sound of *gh*, as in *ghetto*, is pronounced as in the English word *gate*. The *g* in *figlia* and *broglio* is so nearly silent it can be ignored (FEE-lee-ah and BROH-lee-yoh). *Gn* is pronounced "nyee," as in *pugni* (POO-nyee).

3. Most multisyllable words are pronounced with the emphasis on the second to last syllable (*cadenza* is "kah-DEN-zah," and

Congregazione is "kohn-gray-gaht-zee-OH-nay"). An accent mark is used to identify stress on the last syllable, as in Pietà (pee-eh-TAH), Tomà (toh-MAH), and Girò (jee-ROH).

4. Vowels are more carefully pronounced than in English, but the reader's best guess is likely to be very close. More precise information can be found in Italian dictionaries.

5. The letter *e* on the end of a word is not silent, as in English, but pronounced like the letter *a* in *say*, as in ospedale (oh-spe-DAH-lay).

Pronunciations are included in the glossary for words that might cause difficulty or do not follow these rules.

GLOSSARY

Attiva Plural *attive*. Musician or singer in the second or later stages of training, performing as part of the choir or orchestra.

Avvogadori di Commun Group of noblemen responsible for registering patrician marriages in accordance with Venetian laws, protecting the bloodlines of the aristocracy.

Bauta Plural *baute*. Traditional combination of black hood, white mask, and black tricornered hat worn at Carnevale but also at other times to hide one's identity.

Broglio Square connecting Piazza San Marco with the Venetian Lagoon, today commonly known as the Piazzetta.

Burchiello Plural *burchielli*. Small boat common on the waterways of Venice.

Ca' Short for *casa* (house). Palatial home. The term is commonly used in Venice instead of the word *palazzo*.

Cadenza Complex and difficult solo, either written or improvised, inserted usually at the end of a piece of music to showcase a musician's skill.

Cassone A trunk used to store clothing and household items.

Castrato Plural *castrati*. Male singer castrated before puberty in hopes of retaining the purity and high range of a boy's singing voice while developing the lungs (and thus the volume) of a grown man's.

Cavaliere servente Plural *cavalieri serventi* (kah-vah-lee-AIR-ee sair-VEN-tee). Platonic male friend and confidant who accompanies and performs personal services for a woman.

Cimento Test or trial.

Commissare (kohm-mee-SAH-reh). Executor of an estate.

Concerto Plural *concerti*. Orchestral composition in three movements, featuring a solo instrument or small group of instruments.

Congregazione The governing board of the Pietà.

Continuo Simple rhythmic background played by a cello, harpsichord, or other instrument(s) to help an orchestra keep the proper tempo without a conductor.

Coro Literally choir, but referring to both orchestra and singers at the Pietà.

Council of Ten Group selected through an elaborate process by the Grand Council of Venetian nobility to serve as the main governing board of the city for a limited period of time.

Daily office The prescribed order of prayers throughout the day. Mentioned in the text are Sext, Prime, None, Vespers, Lauds, and Compline.

Doge (DOHJ). Title given to the head of the Venetian Republic.

The doge was elected by the Venetian Grand Council and served for life, with primarily ceremonial duties and little real power.

Felce (FEHL-say). Private cabin in the center of a gondola.

Ferro Silver ornament on the bow of a gondola.

Figlia Plural *figlie* (FEE-lee-eh). Literally daughter, used in the Pietà in the sense of ward.

Fondamento Plural *fondamenti*. Narrow sidewalk along smaller canals.

Frotta Territorial fight (see *pugni*).

Giubilata Plural *giubilate*. Honorary name by which a retiree of the coro was known.

Humors Four fluids (blood, phlegm, choler, and black bile) thought from ancient times to determine personality and health by their relative proportions in the body.

Impresario Manager and producer of operas.

Iniziata Plural *iniziate*. Girl in the first stage of musical training, before promotion to attiva.

Loggia (LOH-gee-ah). Covered open-air balcony.

Maestra (my-EH-stra). Plural *maestre*. Music mistress, used to delineate the highest level of female teachers, trainers, and supervisors of the figlie di coro. Sotto maestre were one step below.

Maestro (my-EH-stro). Music master, used in a variety of ways at the Pietà. The Maestro di Coro served as executive director of the coro. Under him were others, named according to their roles (Vivaldi, for example, was first maestro dal violino and later Maestro dei Concerti). To avoid confusion, I have capitalized only the highest ranking titles.

Maniera (mahn-ee-YAIR-ah). Literally manner, a music term used to describe study and practice of how one looks while performing.

Melisma Style of singing in which a number of notes are used for one syllable of a word.

Nobili Uomini Deputati (NOH-bee-lee WO-mee-nee deh-poo-TAH-tee). Group of three members of the Congregazione responsible for managing the music program of the Pietà.

Oratorio Opera-like musical composition performed without scenery, staging, or costumes.

Ospedale (oh-speh-DAHL-eh). Plural *ospedali*. Institution raising orphaned and abandoned children. The name, which means hospital, stems from these institutions' origins as wings of hospitals.

Ostinato Short musical phrase repeated again and again.

Parlatorio Visiting room in a convent or ospedale, divided by a grille.

Pasticcio (pas-TEECH-chee-yoh). Musical work pasted together from a number of sources.

Peota Plural *peote*. Small boat common on the waterways of Venice.

Pianelle Wooden platform clogs occasionally worn by the noblewomen of Venice.

Piano nobile (pee YAH-noh NOH-bee-lay). The first floor above the entry level of a Venetian casa, used primarily to receive and entertain guests.

Pizzicato Use of fingers rather than a bow to play a violin or similar instrument.

Portego Large multipurpose room stretching the entire length of a Venetian casa.

Prie-dieu (PREE-DYOO). Piece of furniture specifically for personal devotions, consisting of a place to kneel and a flat, desklike space to read from a prayer book or to rest the hands or elbows while praying.

Priora (pry-OHR-ah.) Title of the highest ranking woman at the Pietà, equivalent to headmistress or abbess.

Pugni Literally fists, but referring to the combatants in traditional territorial fights (frotte) between the Nicolotti and Castellani factions of Venice.

Putta Plural *putte*. Cherub, commonly used as a name for a figlia di coro.

Recitative (reh-sih-tah-TEEV). Vocal passage in opera and oratorio representing sung speech.

Ridotto Gambling palace.

Rio Small canal.

Ripieno Enlargement of an orchestra or choir beyond its usual size.

Riva Wide street along the Grand Canal and lagoon.

Sala Room.

Sala d'oro Room on the piano nobile used as a business office, decorated richly in gold to show the wealth of the family.

Solfeggio (sohl-FEJ-jee-oh). Italian term for the exercises used to train the voice.

Sotto maestra (SOH-toh my-EH-strah). Assistant to the maestra.

Staccato Method of playing that sounds each note separately rather than linked together.

Tavoletta Plural *tavolette*. Poster advertising a concert.

Theorbo (thee-OHR-boh). Musical instrument with a very long double neck, allowing the bass strings to connect to a separate peg box at the top of the neck and the other strings to connect farther down.

Veduta Plural *vedute*. Painting of a Venetian scene or view.

Verità (vair-ee-TAH). Truth. The title of Vivaldi's opera *La Verità in Cimento* is loosely translated as "Truth Put to the Test."

Villegiatura (vil-leh-jee-ah-TOO-rah). Long period in the summer during which the wealthy of Venice went to live at their country villas.

Zecchini Small gold coins, also known as sequins, used in the Venetian Republic.

ACKNOWLEDGMENTS

My most profound thanks go to my friends and family, who stayed interested even when the process of bringing the figlie di coro to life seemed endless, vague, and possibly fruitless. In addition to Lynn Wrench and James Fee, to whom the book is dedicated, I would like to thank my son, Ivan Corona, and Chelsea Huff, for their support and suggestions.

Among my colleagues, Stephanie Robinson gave me expert advice on the soprano voice, Elizabeth Meehan helped me understand bowing techniques, and Catherine Lopez, Judith Krumholz, Helen Elias, Farrell Foreman, and Jerry Fenwick encouraged me throughout. Other assistance on violin techniques came from professional violinist Mary Karo, and information on how untreated breast cancer might progress came from Dr. Barbara Parker.

Historical fiction requires much research, and as a result there are a number of people I never met whose works became important to the accuracy of the book. I would like to acknowledge the contributions of scholars Patrick Barbier, Jane Berdes, John Booth, Stanley Choinacki, Robert C. Davis, Robert Donnington,

Joanne M. Ferraro, Wendy Heller, H. C. Robbins Landon, Mary Laven, John Martin, Dennis Romano, and Jutta Gisela Sperling. Two others stand out. The first is Professor Michael Talbot, whose e-mail correspondence clarified several key points. The second is Philippe Monnier, whose 1910 book *Venice in the Eighteenth Century* was an inspiration.

At the Piccolo Museo della Pietà in Venice, the chief archivist, Dottore Giuseppe Ellero, gave generously of his time to help me understand life at the Pietà. *Molte grazie per tutto l'aiuto che Lei gentilmente mi ha dato.*

At Voice, Editor Sarah Landis, Editorial Director Pam Dorman, and Publisher Ellen Archer were a pleasure to work with. Editorial Assistant Kathleen Carr made sure everything went smoothly along the way. Writing is a solitary effort, but getting published takes teamwork, and I am very grateful to this wonderful group of women. And a heartfelt thank you to Laura Klynstra, Voice art director, and Jessica Shatan Heslin, the designer, responsible for the beautiful cover and interior layout of *The Four Seasons.*

Barbara Braun, my former agent, is owed sincere thanks for her work on behalf of this book.

And finally, because it's never too late to remember a teacher, a huge thank-you goes to Jane C. Bradford, now retired from The Bishop's School in La Jolla, California. She took my high school scribbles and guided me so skillfully through the process of turning them into good writing that I didn't even notice what hard work it was.

MUSIC IN THE FOUR SEASONS

In addition to *The Four Seasons,* the following music is featured in the novel.

L'Estro Armonico No. 7 in F Major (pp. 110, 116–17)
Vivaldi writes a small third violin part for Maddalena.

Nisi Dominus, RV 608 (pp. 121–22, 124)
Vivaldi does a quick rewrite so the King of Denmark will not hear only Gasparini's music.

Laudate pueri Dominum in C Minor, RV 292 (pp. 161–63)
The first piece of music Vivaldi writes for Maddalena and Chiaretta.

Salve Regina in F Major, RV 617 (pp. 164–66)
The second piece for the sisters. The figlie "dance," and Claudio Morosini hears the voice of his future bride (p. 363, Chiaretta sings this as she cradles her dying sister).

*Third Movement and Cadenza, Concerto Fatto per la Solennità
della Santa Lingua*, RV 212 (pp. 193–94)
Vivaldi's performance of the cadenza is the talk of Venice.

Juditha triumphans (pp. 195–204)
Chiaretta's farewell performance at the Pietà, where she plays the
maid, Abra, and feels upstaged.

La Verità in Cimento (pp. 269–76, 280–84)
In disguise, Chiaretta performs in Vivaldi's new opera.

"Aurea placida e serene" (Quartet) (pp. 272–73)
Overwhelmed by the beauty of the music, Chiaretta and Andrea
end up in each other's arms.

"Amato, ben tu sei la mia speranza" (Aria)
Chiaretta overcomes her inhibitions (pp. 270–72) and dazzles the
audience at the opera (p. 283).

READING GROUP GUIDE

1. Which lifestyle do you think you would prefer: the one Maddalena chooses or the one Chiaretta chooses? What about each lifestyle appeals to you?

2. At one point Chiaretta concludes that she and Maddalena were better off abandoned at the Pietà than they would have been as daughters in a noble family. Do you think that's true?

3. Does Chiaretta's infidelity have any impact on how you see her? If so, do you like or respect her less or more?

4. What do you think about the institution of the coro? Were the figlie exploited, or empowered, a little of both, or something else entirely?

5. The author decided to leave Vivaldi's relationship with Anna Girò ambiguous, since the dead cannot defend themselves. Is that a reasonable standard for a historical novelist?

6. Do you think Vivaldi loves Maddalena? Do you think she loves him? Why or why not?

7. The Pietà branded infants on the heel, or in earlier times the arm, to identify them before sending them off to foster homes. Why did they brand the children? What do you think of this practice?

8. Who would you say is the main character of the novel: Maddalena or Chiaretta? Did you follow the story of one sister more closely? Why?

AN INTERVIEW WITH
LAUREL CORONA

Q. How did you come up with the idea for *The Four Seasons*?
A. I'm a community college professor of humanities, and one of my textbooks made a reference to Vivaldi's work with female musicians in Venice. I thought that was interesting and told myself that someday I'd get around to looking into it, probably just to add a little information to my lectures.

Several years later, as I was writing my nonfiction book *Until Our Last Breath*, I discovered that I really liked the challenge and pace of writing books several hundred pages in length. I knew I wanted to write another book, so I asked myself, "What's the most interesting subject you can think of right now?" I don't know why, but the female musicians of the Pietà jumped into my head. And nonfiction never occurred to me. I knew it had to be a novel.

Q. You said the musicians jumped into your head. Why not Vivaldi himself?
A. Being female, I am always interested in the experiences of women. Vivaldi turned out to be a very intriguing character, and

the book is much richer and more complex as a result of his presence. I think I might have been able to write a compelling novel even if he were less colorful, but I certainly couldn't have if the musicians weren't sufficiently interesting in their own right. And the book would be quite different if I thought of it as being primarily about Vivaldi and his relationship with the women of the Pietà, as opposed to the other way around.

Q. Why did you choose to have sisters as main characters?
A. I realized immediately that I was going to have a problem writing about a cloistered setting because the range of experience of the girls and women was pretty narrow. And of course in this case the environment they were being protected from was one of the most dazzling cities imaginable. I knew I had to find a way to bring Venice itself into the story, and the solution I came up with was to have two main characters, one of whom lives as an adult outside the Pietà and one who remains in that rich musical environment her entire life.

I considered developing two unrelated characters of roughly the same age, but I wanted more of a bond between them, so it wouldn't feel like two stories but a single, intertwined one. I thought it would work better in the later stages of the plot to have them still be connected the way sisters are, even though I know friends can be just as loyal and just as close, and often more so.

Saying at this point that there was a moment when Maddalena and Chiaretta could have been developed differently feels a bit like murder, because they are who they are. For example, I discovered after I had created the character of Chiaretta that the soprano who sang the role of Abra in *Juditha Triumphans* was named Silvia. I did a "search and replace" in my text, and I couldn't relate to Chiaretta anymore, because she wasn't named Silvia any more than I'm named Gertrude.

Q. The stories are tightly interrelated, but did you end up seeing one sister as the main character, even if just a little?

A. Not at all. Sometimes one fades into the background for a while, but that's because writing doesn't lend itself well to being in two places at once. I think both lead interesting lives and have similar levels of complexity, and I feel very deeply connected to both of them.

Q. How did you figure out the plot? Did you know what was going to happen?
A. I thought I knew what was going to happen and then it didn't work out that way. Early on I thought the plot might revolve around discovering something momentous about their parentage, in particular who their father was. As Maddalena and Chiaretta became more full and interesting in themselves, I found I didn't care enough about who their parents were to put any effort into taking the plot in that direction. I also thought about having Maddalena leave the Pietà for a while, perhaps to teach music in a convent, because convent life in this era is very interesting to me personally. About three-quarters of the noblewomen in Venice were forced to take vows, and of course convent life was significantly affected by the fact that so many of the nuns had not chosen to be there. But eventually I had to admit that my interest in that was forcing the plot in a direction it wasn't naturally going.

And sometimes minor characters surprised me. For example, when the hooded man reaches under Chiaretta's dress to touch her thigh, I was as shocked and upset as she was. I honestly did not know he was going to do that. I went back later and made him a little creepier during the party to make the whole thing work better.

In the end, I tried to set up complex people in multifaceted and sometimes volatile situations and see what happened. Some authors say their books take on a life of their own and I understand that better now, but for me that's really only true about what I'm typing right at that moment. The overall story, character requirements, plot trajectories, subplots, backstory, and all those kinds of things take quite a bit of thought, even though sometimes the book spins off in an entirely different direction than one plans.

Q. What happens after the end of the book?
A. Sometimes when people ask that, I want to wave my hands and yell, "They don't have a future because they aren't real people!" But I don't completely believe that anymore. I suppose the best thing I can say is I don't know what happened because I lost track of them.

I'm pretty sure Chiaretta will make a spectacular success of her new role as the most powerful woman in Venice, and I bet she remains a fabulous mother. I imagine she may eventually go back to Andrea, but on her own terms. And I can't imagine what would motivate her to marry again.

Q. Are you a musician?
A. Only if the kazoo counts!

Q. Do you think this made a difference as you wrote the book?
A. I have a good background in music history and music appreciation as a result of what I teach, and I think the most that can be said is that a trained musician would have written a different but not necessarily a better fictional treatment of Vivaldi and the musicians of the Pietà. Music is at the core of the book, and it is extraordinarily difficult to capture in words. I tried to approach it poetically, because that's the way I hear it. I think there's actually some advantage to not being an expert, because I was forced to write about the music from my level of understanding, which is probably closer to that of the typical reader.

Q. If, as is often said, all fiction is autobiographical, what does _The Four Seasons_ say about you?
A. One thing it says is that I am not down on men. I have a male

friend who bemoans "sisterhood" types of books because he feels there is rarely a decent man in them. I don't want my books to fall into that kind of thinking just to create the conflict necessary to a good plot. Another thing it says is that I've had a great experience having and being a sister.

Q. Does *The Four Seasons* have a message?
A. I didn't go into it with the idea of sending a message to readers, but of course my values and general outlook influence the book. One message is that women (and men too) have the power to shape their lives even in situations that severely limit their options. Another is that we have to go out and get what we want and say what we need, and that if we don't know what that is, we can't expect other people to. And also the idea that choosing for oneself is an important part of real personhood. To me, *The Four Seasons* is about empowerment, and I hope readers who can be helped by that message find it everywhere in its pages.